THE SECRET GARDEN

作者／法蘭西絲・霍森・伯內特
（Frances Hodgson Burnett）
譯者／李桂蜜

祕密花園

原著雙語彩圖本

Contents   The Secret Garden

目錄　祕密花園

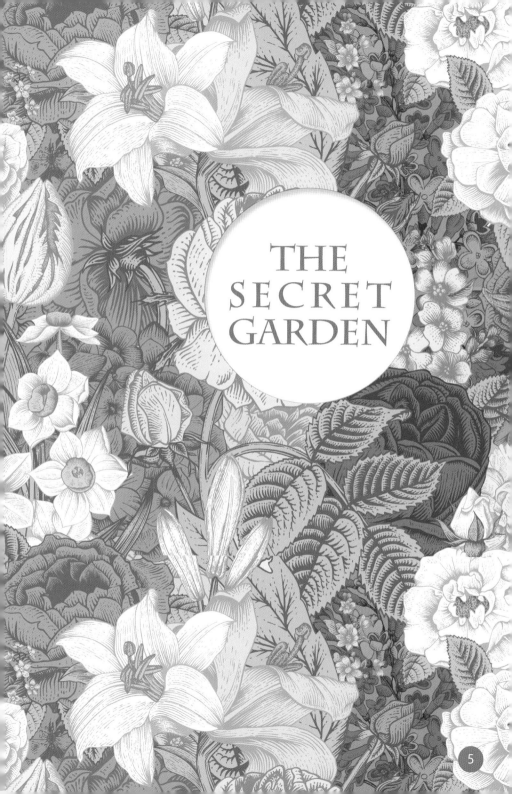

THE SECRET GARDEN

Chapter 1

There Is No One Left

When Mary Lennox was sent to Misselthwaite Manor to live with her uncle everybody said she was the most disagreeable-looking child ever seen. It was true, too. She had a little thin face and a little thin body, thin light hair and a sour expression. Her hair was yellow, and her face was yellow because she had been born in India and had always been ill in one way or another.

Her father had held a position under the English Government and had always been busy and ill himself, and her mother had been a great beauty who cared only to go to parties and amuse herself with gay people. She had not wanted a little girl at all, and when Mary was born she handed her over to the care of an Ayah, who was made to understand that if she wished to please the Mem Sahib she must keep the child out of sight as much as possible.

So when she was a sickly, fretful, ugly little baby she was kept out of the way, and when she became a sickly, fretful, toddling thing she was kept out of the way also. She never remembered seeing familiarly anything but the dark faces of her Ayah and the other native servants, and as they always obeyed her and gave her her own way in everything, because the Mem Sahib would be angry if she was disturbed by her crying, by the time she was six years old she was as tyrannical and selfish a little pig as ever lived.

The young English governess who came to teach her to read and write disliked her so much that she gave up her place in three months, and when other governesses came to try to fill it they always went away in a shorter time than the first one. So if Mary had not chosen to really want to know how to read books she would never have learned her letters at all.

One frightfully hot morning, when she was about nine years old, she awakened feeling very cross, and she became crosser still when she saw that the servant who stood by her bedside was not her Ayah.

"Why did you come?" she said to the strange woman. "I will not let you stay. Send my Ayah to me."

The woman looked frightened, but she only stammered that the Ayah could not come and when Mary threw herself into a passion and beat and kicked her, she looked only more frightened and repeated that it was not possible for the Ayah to come to Missie Sahib.

There was something mysterious in the air that morning. Nothing was done in its regular order and several of the native servants seemed missing, while those whom Mary saw slunk or hurried about with ashy and scared faces. But no one would tell her anything and her Ayah did not come.

She was actually left alone as the morning went on,

and at last she wandered out into the garden and began to play by herself under a tree near the veranda. She pretended that she was making a flowerbed, and she stuck big scarlet hibiscus blossoms into little heaps of earth, all the time growing more and more angry and muttering to herself the things she would say and the names she would call Saidie when she returned.

"Pig! Pig! Daughter of Pigs!" she said, because to call a native a pig is the worst insult of all.

She was grinding her teeth and saying this over and over again when she heard her mother come out on the veranda with some one. She was with a fair young man and they stood talking together in low strange voices. Mary knew the fair young man who looked like a boy. She had heard that he was a very young officer who had just come from England.

The child stared at him, but she stared most at her mother. She always did this when she had a chance to see her, because the Mem Sahib—Mary used to call her that oftener than anything else—was such a tall, slim, pretty person and wore such lovely clothes. Her hair was like curly silk and she had a delicate little nose which seemed to be disdaining things, and she had large laughing eyes. All her clothes were thin and floating, and Mary said they were "full of lace." They looked fuller of lace than ever this morning, but her eyes were not laughing at all. They were large and scared and lifted imploringly to the fair boy officer's face.

"Is it so very bad? Oh, is it?" Mary heard her say.

"Awfully," the young man answered in a trembling voice. "Awfully, Mrs. Lennox. You ought to have gone to the hills two weeks ago."

The Mem Sahib wrung her hands. "Oh, I know I ought!" she cried. "I only stayed to go to that silly dinner party. What a fool I was!"

At that very moment such a loud sound of wailing broke out from the servants' quarters that she clutched the young man's arm, and Mary stood shivering from head to foot. The wailing grew wilder and wilder.

"What is it? What is it?" Mrs. Lennox gasped.

"Some one has died," answered the boy officer. "You did not say it had broken out among your servants."

"I did not know!" the Mem Sahib cried. "Come with me! Come with me!" and she turned and ran into the house.

After that, appalling things happened, and the mysteriousness of the morning was explained to Mary. The cholera had broken out in its most fatal form and people were dying like flies. The Ayah had been taken ill in the night, and it was because she had just died that the servants had wailed in the huts.

Before the next day three other servants were dead and others had run away in terror. There was panic on every side, and dying people in all the bungalows.

During the confusion and bewilderment of the second day Mary hid herself in the nursery and was forgotten by everyone. Nobody thought of her, nobody wanted her, and strange things happened of which she knew nothing. Mary alternately cried and slept through the hours. She only knew that people were ill and that she heard mysterious and frightening sounds.

Once she crept into the dining-room and found it empty, though a partly finished meal was on the table and chairs and plates looked as if they had been hastily pushed back when the diners rose suddenly for some reason.

The child ate some fruit and biscuits, and being thirsty she drank a glass of wine which stood nearly filled. It was sweet, and she did not know how strong it was. Very soon it made her intensely drowsy, and she went back to her nursery and shut herself in again, frightened by cries she heard in the huts and by the hurrying sound of feet. The wine made her so sleepy that she could scarcely keep her eyes open and she lay down on her bed and knew nothing more for a long time.

Many things happened during the hours in which she slept so heavily, but she was not disturbed by the wails and the sound of things being carried in and out of the bungalow.

When she awakened she lay and stared at the wall. The house was perfectly still. She had never known it to be so silent before. She heard neither voices nor footsteps, and wondered if everybody had got well of the cholera and all the trouble was over. She wondered also who would take care of her now her Ayah was dead. There would be a new Ayah, and perhaps she would know some new stories. Mary had been rather tired of the old ones.

She did not cry because her nurse had died. She was not an affectionate child and had never cared much for anyone. The noise and hurrying about and wailing over the cholera had frightened her, and she had been angry because no one seemed to remember that she was alive. Everyone was too panic-stricken to think of a little girl no one was fond of. When people had the cholera it seemed that they remembered nothing but themselves. But if everyone had got well again, surely some one would remember and come to look for her.

But no one came, and as she lay waiting the house seemed to grow more and more silent. She heard something rustling on the matting and when she looked down she saw a little snake gliding along and watching her with eyes like jewels. She was not frightened, because he was a harmless little thing who would not hurt her and he seemed in a hurry to get out of the room. He slipped under the door as she watched him.

"How queer and quiet it is," she said. "It sounds as if there were no one in the bungalow but me and the snake."

Almost the next minute she heard footsteps in the compound, and then on the veranda. They were men's footsteps, and the men entered the bungalow and talked in low voices. No one went to meet or speak to them and they seemed to open doors and look into rooms. "What desolation!" she heard one voice say. "That pretty, pretty woman! I suppose the child, too. I heard there was a child, though no one ever saw her."

Mary was standing in the middle of the nursery when they opened the door a few minutes later. She looked an ugly, cross little thing and was frowning because she was beginning to be hungry and feel disgracefully neglected.

The first man who came in was a large officer she had once seen talking to her father. He looked tired and troubled, but when he saw her he was so startled that he almost jumped back.

"Barney!" he cried out. "There is a child here! A child alone! In a place like this! Mercy on us, who is she!"

"I am Mary Lennox," the little girl said, drawing herself up stiffly. She thought the man was very rude to call her father's bungalow "A place like this!" "I fell asleep when everyone had the cholera and I have only just wakened up. Why does nobody come?"

"It is the child no one ever saw!" exclaimed the man, turning to his companions. "She has actually been forgotten!"

"Why was I forgotten?" Mary said, stamping her foot. "Why does nobody come?"

The young man whose name was Barney looked at her very sadly. Mary even thought she saw him wink his eyes as if to wink tears away.

"Poor little kid!" he said. "There is nobody left to come."

It was in that strange and sudden way that Mary found out that she had neither father nor mother left; that they had died and been carried away in the night, and that the few native servants who had not died also had left the house as quickly as they could get out of it, none of them even remembering that there was a Missie Sahib. That was why the place was so quiet. It was true that there was no one in the bungalow but herself and the little rustling snake.

Chapter 2

Mistress Mary
Quite Contrary

Mary had liked to look at her mother from a distance and she had thought her very pretty, but as she knew very little of her, she could scarcely have been expected to love her or to miss her very much when she was gone. She did not miss her at all, in fact, and as she was a self-absorbed child she gave her entire thought to herself, as she had always done.

If she had been older she would no doubt have been very anxious at being left alone in the world, but she was very young, and as she had always been taken care of, she supposed she always would be. What she thought was that she would like to know if she was going to nice people, who would be polite to her and give her her own way as her Ayah and the other native servants had done.

She knew that she was not going to stay at the English clergyman's house where she was taken at first. She did not want to stay. The English clergyman was poor and he had five children nearly all the same age and they wore shabby clothes and were always quarreling and snatching toys from each other. Mary hated their untidy bungalow and was so disagreeable to them that after the first day or two nobody would play with her. By the second day they had given her a nickname which made her furious.

It was Basil who thought of it first. Basil was a little boy with impudent blue eyes and a turned-up nose, and Mary hated him. She was playing by herself under a tree, just as she had been playing the day the cholera broke out. She was making heaps of earth and paths for a garden and Basil came and stood near to watch her. Presently he got rather interested and suddenly made a suggestion.

"Why don't you put a heap of stones there and pretend it is a rockery?" he said. "There in the middle," and he leaned over her to point.

"Go away!" cried Mary. "I don't want boys. Go away!"

For a moment Basil looked angry, and then he began to tease. He was always teasing his sisters. He danced round and round her and made faces and sang and laughed.

"Mistress Mary, quite contrary,
How does your garden grow?
With silver bells, and cockle shells,
And marigolds all in a row."

He sang it until the other children heard and laughed, too; and the crosser Mary got, the more they sang "Mistress Mary, quite contrary"; and after that as long as she stayed with them they called her "Mistress Mary Quite Contrary" when they spoke of her to each other, and often when they spoke to her.

"You are going to be sent home," Basil said to her, "at the end of the week. And we're glad of it."

"I am glad of it, too," answered Mary. "Where is home?"

"She doesn't know where home is!" said Basil, with seven-year-old scorn. "It's England, of course. Our grandmama lives there and our sister Mabel was sent to her last year. You are not going to your grandmama. You have none. You are going to your uncle. His name is Mr. Archibald Craven."

"I don't know anything about him," snapped Mary.

"I know you don't," Basil answered. "You don't know anything. Girls never do. I heard father and mother talking about him. He lives in a great, big, desolate old house in the country and no one goes near him. He's so cross he won't let them, and they wouldn't come if he would let them. He's a hunchback, and he's horrid."

"I don't believe you," said Mary; and she turned her back and stuck her fingers in her ears, because she would not listen any more.

But she thought over it a great deal afterward; and when Mrs. Crawford told her that night that she was going to sail away to England in a few days and go to her uncle, Mr. Archibald Craven, who lived at Misselthwaite Manor, she looked so stony and stubbornly uninterested that they did not know what to think about her. They tried to be kind to her, but she only turned her face away when Mrs. Crawford attempted to kiss her, and held herself stiffly when Mr. Crawford patted her shoulder.

"She is such a plain child," Mrs. Crawford said pityingly, afterward. "And her mother was such a pretty creature. She had a very pretty manner, too, and Mary has the most unattractive ways I ever saw in a child. The children call her

'Mistress Mary Quite Contrary,' and though it's naughty of them, one can't help understanding it."

"Perhaps if her mother had carried her pretty face and her pretty manners oftener into the nursery Mary might have learned some pretty ways too. It is very sad, now the poor beautiful thing is gone, to remember that many people never even knew that she had a child at all."

"I believe she scarcely ever looked at her," sighed Mrs. Crawford. "When her Ayah was dead there was no one to give a thought to the little thing. Think of the servants running away and leaving her all alone in that deserted bungalow. Colonel McGrew said he nearly jumped out of his skin when he opened the door and found her standing by herself in the middle of the room."

Mary made the long voyage to England under the care of an officer's wife, who was taking her children to leave them in a boarding-school. She was very much absorbed in her own little boy and girl, and was rather glad to hand the child over to the woman Mr. Archibald Craven sent to meet her, in London. The woman was his housekeeper at Misselthwaite Manor, and her name was Mrs. Medlock.

She was a stout woman, with very red cheeks and sharp black eyes. She wore a very purple dress, a black silk mantle with jet fringe on it and a black bonnet with purple velvet flowers which stuck up and trembled when she moved her head.

Mary did not like her at all, but as she very seldom liked people, there was nothing remarkable in that; besides which it was very evident Mrs. Medlock did not

think much of her.

"My word! she's a plain little piece of goods!" she said. "And we'd heard that her mother was a beauty. She hasn't handed much of it down, has she, ma'am?" "Perhaps she will improve as she grows older," the officer's wife said good-naturedly. "If she were not so sallow and had a nicer expression, her features are rather good. Children alter so much."

"She'll have to alter a good deal," answered Mrs. Medlock. "And, there's nothing likely to improve children at Misselthwaite—if you ask me!"

They thought Mary was not listening because she was standing a little apart from them at the window of the private hotel they had gone to. She was watching the passing buses and cabs and people, but she heard quite well and was made very curious about her uncle and the place he lived in. What sort of a place was it, and what would he be like? What was a hunchback? She had never seen one. Perhaps there were none in India.

Since she had been living in other people's houses and had had no Ayah, she had begun to feel lonely and to think queer thoughts which were new to her. She had begun to wonder why she had never seemed to belong to anyone even when her father and mother had been alive. Other children seemed to belong to their fathers and mothers, but she had never seemed to really be anyone's little girl. She had had servants, and food and clothes, but no one had taken any notice of her. She did not know that this was because she was a disagreeable child; but then, of course, she did not know she was disagreeable. She often thought that other people were, but she did not know that she was so herself.

She thought Mrs. Medlock the most disagreeable person she had ever seen, with her common, highly colored face and her common fine bonnet. When the next day they set out on their journey to Yorkshire, she walked through the station to the railway carriage with her head up and trying to keep as far away from her as she could, because she did not want to seem to belong to her. It would have made her angry to think people imagined she was her little girl.

But Mrs. Medlock was not in the least disturbed by her and her thoughts. She was the kind of woman who would "stand no nonsense from young ones." At least, that is what she would have said if she had been asked. She had not wanted to go to London just when her sister Maria's daughter was going to be married, but she had a comfortable, well paid place as housekeeper at Misselthwaite Manor and the only way in which she could keep it was to do at once what Mr. Archibald Craven told her to do. She never dared even to ask a question.

"Captain Lennox and his wife died of the cholera," Mr. Craven had said in his short, cold way. "Captain Lennox was my wife's brother and I am their daughter's guardian. The child is to be brought here. You must go to London and bring her yourself."

So she packed her small trunk and made the journey.

Mary sat in her corner of the railway carriage and looked plain and fretful. She had nothing to read or to look at, and she had folded her thin little black-gloved hands in her lap. Her black dress made her look yellower than ever, and her limp light hair straggled from under her black crepe hat.

"A more marred-looking young one I never saw in my life," Mrs. Medlock thought. (Marred is a Yorkshire word and means spoiled and pettish.) She had never seen a child who sat so still without doing anything; and at last she got tired of watching her and began to talk in a brisk, hard voice.

"I suppose I may as well tell you something about where you are going to," she said. "Do you know anything about your uncle?"

"No," said Mary.

"Never heard your father and mother talk about him?"

"No," said Mary frowning. She frowned because she remembered that her father and mother had never talked to her about anything in particular. Certainly they had never told her things.

"Humph," muttered Mrs. Medlock, staring at her queer, unresponsive little face. She did not say any more for a few moments and then she began again.

"I suppose you might as well be told something—to prepare you. You are going to a queer place."

Mary said nothing at all, and Mrs. Medlock looked rather discomfited by her apparent indifference, but, after taking a breath, she went on.

"Not but that it's a grand big place in a gloomy way, and Mr. Craven's proud of it in his way—and that's gloomy enough, too. The house is six hundred years old and it's on the edge of the moor, and there's near a hundred rooms in it, though most of them's shut up and locked. And there's pictures and fine old furniture and things that's been there for ages, and there's a big park round it and gardens and trees with branches trailing to the ground—some of them." She paused and took another breath. "But there's nothing else," she ended suddenly.

Mary had begun to listen in spite of herself. It all sounded so unlike India, and anything new rather attracted her. But she did not intend to look as if she were interested. That was one of her unhappy, disagreeable ways. So she sat still.

"Well," said Mrs. Medlock. "What do you think of it?"

"Nothing," she answered. "I know nothing about such places."

That made Mrs. Medlock laugh a short sort of laugh.

"Eh!" she said, "but you are like an old woman. Don't you care?"

"It doesn't matter" said Mary, "whether I care or not."

"You are right enough there," said Mrs. Medlock. "It doesn't. What you're to be kept at Misselthwaite Manor for I don't know, unless because it's the easiest way. He's not going to trouble himself about you, that's sure and certain. He never troubles himself about no one."

She stopped herself as if she had just remembered something in time. "He's got a crooked back," she said. "That set him wrong. He was a sour young man and got no good of all his money and big place till he was married."

Mary's eyes turned toward her in spite of her intention not to seem to care. She had never thought of the hunchback's being married and she was a trifle surprised. Mrs. Medlock saw this, and as she was a talkative woman she continued with more interest. This was one way of passing some of the time, at any rate.

"She was a sweet, pretty thing and he'd have walked the world over to get her a blade o' grass she wanted. Nobody thought she'd marry him, but she did, and people said she married him for his money. But she didn't—she didn't," positively. "When she died—"

Mary gave a little involuntary jump.

"Oh! did she die!" she exclaimed, quite without meaning to. She had just remembered a French fairy story she had once read called "Riquet á la Houppe." It had been about a poor hunchback and a beautiful princess and it had made her suddenly sorry for Mr. Archibald Craven.

"Yes, she died," Mrs. Medlock answered. "And it made him queerer than ever. He cares about nobody. He won't see people. Most of the time he goes away, and when he is at Misselthwaite he shuts himself up in the West Wing and won't let any one but Pitcher see him. Pitcher's an old fellow, but he took care of him when he was a child and he knows his ways."

It sounded like something in a book and it did not make Mary feel cheerful. A house with a hundred rooms, nearly all shut up and with their doors locked—a house on the edge of a moor—whatsoever a moor was—sounded dreary. A man with a crooked back who shut himself up also!

She stared out of the window with her lips pinched

together, and it seemed quite natural that the rain should have begun to pour down in gray slanting lines and splash and stream down the window-panes. If the pretty wife had been alive she might have made things cheerful by being something like her own mother and by running in and out and going to parties as she had done in frocks "full of lace." But she was not there any more.

"You needn't expect to see him, because ten to one you won't," said Mrs. Medlock. "And you mustn't expect that there will be people to talk to you. You'll have to play about and look after yourself. You'll be told what rooms you can go into and what rooms you're to keep out of. There's gardens enough. But when you're in the house don't go wandering and poking about. Mr. Craven won't have it."

"I shall not want to go poking about," said sour little Mary and just as suddenly as she had begun to be rather sorry for Mr. Archibald Craven she began to cease to be sorry and to think he was unpleasant enough to deserve all that had happened to him.

And she turned her face toward the streaming panes of the window of the railway carriage and gazed out at the gray rain storm which looked as if it would go on forever and ever. She watched it so long and steadily that the grayness grew heavier and heavier before her eyes and she fell asleep.

Chapter 3

Across the Moor

She slept a long time, and when she awakened Mrs. Medlock had bought a lunch basket at one of the stations and they had some chicken and cold beef and bread and butter and some hot tea. The rain seemed to be streaming down more heavily than ever and everybody in the station wore wet and glistening waterproofs.

The guard lighted the lamps in the carriage, and Mrs. Medlock cheered up very much over her tea and chicken and beef. She ate a great deal and afterward fell asleep herself, and Mary sat and stared at her and watched her fine bonnet slip on one side until she herself fell asleep once more in the corner of the carriage, lulled by the splashing of the rain against the windows. It was quite dark when she awakened again. The train had stopped at a station and Mrs. Medlock was shaking her.

"You have had a sleep!" she said. "It's time to open your eyes! We're at Thwaite Station and we've got a long drive before us."

Mary stood up and tried to keep her eyes open while Mrs. Medlock collected her parcels. The little girl did not offer to help her, because in India native servants always picked up or carried things and it seemed quite proper that other people should wait on one.

The station was a small one and nobody but themselves seemed to be getting out of the train. The station-master spoke to Mrs. Medlock in a rough, good-natured way, pronouncing his words in a queer broad fashion which Mary found out afterward was Yorkshire.

"I see tha's got back," he said. "An' tha's browt th' young 'un with thee."

"Aye, that's her," answered Mrs. Medlock, speaking with a Yorkshire accent herself and jerking her head over her shoulder toward Mary. "How's thy Missus?"

"Well enow. Th' carriage is waitin' outside for thee."

A brougham stood on the road before the little outside platform. Mary saw that it was a smart carriage and that it was a smart footman who helped her in. His long waterproof coat and the waterproof covering of his hat were shining and dripping with rain as everything was, the burly station-master included.

When he shut the door, mounted the box with the coachman, and they drove off, the little girl found herself seated in a comfortably cushioned corner, but she was not inclined to go to sleep again. She sat and looked out of the window, curious to see something of the road over which she was being driven to the queer place Mrs. Medlock had spoken of.

She was not at all a timid child and she was not exactly frightened, but she felt that there was no knowing what might happen in a house with a hundred rooms nearly all shut up—a house standing on the edge of a moor.

"What is a moor?" she said suddenly to Mrs. Medlock.

"Look out of the window in about ten minutes and you'll see," the woman answered. "We've got to drive five miles across Missel Moor before we get to the Manor. You won't see much because it's a dark night, but you can see something."

Mary asked no more questions but waited in the darkness of her corner, keeping her eyes on the window. The carriage lamps cast rays of light a little distance ahead of them and she caught glimpses of the things they passed. After they had left the station they had driven through a tiny village and she had seen whitewashed cottages and the lights of a public house. Then they had passed a church and a vicarage and a little shop-window or so in a cottage with toys and sweets and odd things set out for sale. Then they were on the high road and she saw hedges and trees. After that there seemed nothing different for a long time—or at least it seemed a long time to her.

At last the horses began to go more slowly, as if they were climbing uphill, and presently there seemed to be no more hedges and no more trees. She could see nothing, in fact, but a dense darkness on either side. She leaned forward and pressed her face against the window just as the carriage gave a big jolt.

"Eh! We're on the moor now sure enough," said Mrs. Medlock.

The carriage lamps shed a yellow light on a rough-looking road which seemed to be cut through bushes and low-growing things which ended in the great expanse of dark apparently spread out before and around them. A wind was rising and making a singular, wild, low, rushing sound.

"It's—it's not the sea, is it?" said Mary, looking round at her companion.

"No, not it," answered Mrs. Medlock. "Nor it isn't fields nor mountains, it's just miles and miles and miles of wild land that nothing grows on but heather and gorse and broom, and nothing lives on but wild ponies and sheep."

"I feel as if it might be the sea, if there were water on it," said Mary. "It sounds like the sea just now."

"That's the wind blowing through the bushes," Mrs. Medlock said. "It's a wild, dreary enough place to my mind, though there's plenty that likes it— particularly when the heather's in bloom."

On and on they drove through the darkness, and though the rain stopped, the wind rushed by and whistled and made strange sounds. The road went up and down, and several times the carriage passed over a little bridge beneath which water rushed very fast with a great deal of noise. Mary felt as if the drive would never come to an

heather

28

end and that the wide, bleak moor was a wide expanse of black ocean through which she was passing on a strip of dry land.

"I don't like it," she said to herself. "I don't like it," and she pinched her thin lips more tightly together.

The horses were climbing up a hilly piece of road when she first caught sight of a light. Mrs. Medlock saw it as soon as she did and drew a long sigh of relief.

"Eh, I am glad to see that bit o' light twinkling," she exclaimed. "It's the light in the lodge window. We shall get a good cup of tea after a bit, at all events."

It was "after a bit," as she said, for when the carriage passed through the park gates there was still two miles of avenue to drive through and the trees (which nearly met overhead) made it seem as if they were driving through a long dark vault.

They drove out of the vault into a clear space and stopped before an immensely long but low-built house which seemed to ramble round a stone court. At first Mary thought that there were no lights at all in the windows, but as she got out of the carriage she saw that one room in a corner upstairs showed a dull glow.

The entrance door was a huge one made of massive, curiously shaped panels of oak studded with big iron nails and bound with great iron bars. It opened into an enormous hall, which was so dimly lighted that the faces in the portraits on the walls and the figures in the suits of armor made Mary feel that she did not want to look at them. As she stood on the stone floor she looked a very small, odd little black figure, and she felt as small and lost and odd as she looked.

A neat, thin old man stood near the manservant who opened the door for them.

"You are to take her to her room," he said in a husky voice. "He doesn't want to see her. He's going to London in the morning."

"Very well, Mr. Pitcher," Mrs. Medlock answered. "So long as I know what's expected of me, I can manage."

"What's expected of you, Mrs. Medlock," Mr. Pitcher said, "is that you make sure that he's not disturbed and that he doesn't see what he doesn't want to see."

And then Mary Lennox was led up a broad staircase and down a long corridor and up a short flight of steps and through another corridor and another, until a door opened in a wall and she found herself in a room with a fire in it and a supper on a table.

Mrs. Medlock said unceremoniously: "Well, here you are! This room and the next are where you'll live—and you must keep to them. Don't you forget that!"

It was in this way Mistress Mary arrived at Misselthwaite Manor and she had perhaps never felt quite so contrary in all her life.

Chapter 4

Martha

When she opened her eyes in the morning it was because a young housemaid had come into her room to light the fire and was kneeling on the hearth rug raking out the cinders noisily.

Mary lay and watched her for a few moments and then began to look about the room. She had never seen a room at all like it and thought it curious and gloomy. The walls were covered with tapestry with a forest scene embroidered on it. There were fantastically dressed people under the trees, and in the distance there was a glimpse of the turrets of a castle. There were hunters and horses and dogs and ladies. Mary felt as if she were in the forest with them. Out of a deep window she could see a great climbing stretch of land which seemed to have no trees on it, and to look rather like an endless, dull, purplish sea.

"What is that?" she said, pointing out of the window.

Martha, the young housemaid, who had just risen to her feet, looked and pointed also. "That there?" she said.

"Yes."

"That's th' moor," with a good-natured grin. "Does tha' like it?"

"No," answered Mary. "I hate it."

"That's because tha'rt not used to it," Martha said, going back to her hearth. "Tha' thinks it's too big an' bare now. But tha' will like it."

"Do you?" inquired Mary.

"Aye, that I do," answered Martha, cheerfully polishing away at the grate. "I just love it. It's none bare. It's covered wi' growin' things as smells sweet. It's fair lovely in spring an' summer when th' gorse an' broom an' heather's in flower. It smells o' honey an' there's such a lot o' fresh air—an' th' sky looks so high an' th' bees an' skylarks makes such a nice noise hummin' an' singin'. Eh! I wouldn't live away from th' moor for anythin'."

Mary listened to her with a grave, puzzled expression. The native servants she had been used to in India were not in the least like this. They were obsequious and servile and did not presume to talk to their masters as if they were their equals. They made salaams and called them "protector of the poor" and names of that sort. Indian servants were commanded to do things, not asked. It was not the custom to say "please" and "thank you" and Mary had always slapped her Ayah in the face when she was angry.

She wondered a little what this girl would do if one slapped her in the face. She was a round, rosy, good-natured-looking creature, but she had a sturdy way which made Mistress Mary wonder if she might not even slap back—if the person who slapped her was only a little girl.

"You are a strange servant," she said from her

pillows, rather haughtily.

Martha sat up on her heels, with her blacking-brush in her hand, and laughed, without seeming the least out of temper.

"Eh! I know that," she said. "If there was a grand Missus at Misselthwaite I should never have been even one of th' under house-maids. I might have been let to be scullerymaid but I'd never have been let upstairs. I'm too common an' I talk too much Yorkshire. But this is a funny house for all it's so grand. Seems like there's neither Master nor Mistress except Mr. Pitcher an' Mrs. Medlock. Mr. Craven, he won't be troubled about anythin' when he's here, an' he's nearly always away. Mrs. Medlock gave me th' place out o' kindness. She told me she could never have done it if Misselthwaite had been like other big houses."

"Are you going to be my servant?" Mary asked, still in her imperious little Indian way.

Martha began to rub her grate again.

"I'm Mrs. Medlock's servant," she said stoutly. "An' she's Mr. Craven's—but I'm to do the housemaid's work up here an' wait on you a bit. But you won't need much waitin' on."

"Who is going to dress me?" demanded Mary.

Martha sat up on her heels again and stared. She spoke in broad Yorkshire in her amazement.

"Canna' tha' dress thysen!" she said.

"What do you mean? I don't understand your language," said Mary.

"Eh! I forgot," Martha said. "Mrs. Medlock told me I'd have to be careful or you wouldn't know what I was sayin'. I mean can't you put on your own clothes?"

"No," answered Mary, quite indignantly. "I never did in my life. My Ayah dressed me, of course."

"Well," said Martha, evidently not in the least aware that she was impudent, "it's time tha' should learn. Tha' cannot begin younger. It'll do thee good to wait on thysen a bit. My mother always said she couldn't see why grand people's children didn't turn out fair fools— what with nurses an' bein' washed an' dressed an' took out to walk as if they was puppies!"

"It is different in India," said Mistress Mary disdainfully. She could scarcely stand this.

But Martha was not at all crushed.

"Eh! I can see it's different," she answered almost sympathetically. "I dare say it's because there's such a lot o' blacks there instead o' respectable white people. When I heard you was comin' from India I thought you was a black too."

Mary sat up in bed furious.

"What!" she said. "What! You thought I was a native. You—you daughter of a pig!"

Martha stared and looked hot.

"Who are you callin' names?" she said. "You needn't be so vexed. That's not th' way for a young lady to talk. I've nothin' against th' blacks. When you read about 'em in tracts they're always very religious. You always read as a black's a man an' a brother. I've never seen a black an' I was fair pleased to think I was goin' to see one close. When I come in to light your fire this mornin' I crep' up to your bed an' pulled th' cover back careful

to look at you. An' there you was," disappointedly, "no more black than me—for all you're so yeller."

Mary did not even try to control her rage and humiliation. "You thought I was a native! You dared! You don't know anything about natives! They are not people—they're servants who must salaam to you. You know nothing about India. You know nothing about anything!"

She was in such a rage and felt so helpless before the girl's simple stare, and somehow she suddenly felt so horribly lonely and far away from everything she understood and which understood her, that she threw herself face downward on the pillows and burst into passionate sobbing. She sobbed so unrestrainedly that good-natured Yorkshire Martha was a little frightened and quite sorry for her. She went to the bed and bent over her.

"Eh! you mustn't cry like that there!" she begged. "You mustn't for sure. I didn't know you'd be vexed. I don't know anythin' about anythin'—just like you said. I beg your pardon, Miss. Do stop cryin'."

There was something comforting and really friendly in her queer Yorkshire speech and sturdy way which had a good effect on Mary. She gradually ceased crying and became quiet. Martha looked relieved.

"It's time for thee to get up now," she said. "Mrs. Medlock said I was to carry tha' breakfast an' tea an' dinner into th' room next to this. It's been made into a nursery for thee. I'll help thee on with thy clothes if tha'll get out o' bed. If th' buttons are at th' back tha' cannot button them up tha'self."

When Mary at last decided to get up, the clothes Martha took from the wardrobe were not the ones she had worn when she arrived the night before with Mrs. Medlock.

"Those are not mine," she said. "Mine are black."

She looked the thick white wool coat and dress over, and added with cool approval: "Those are nicer than mine."

"These are th' ones tha' must put on," Martha answered. "Mr. Craven ordered Mrs. Medlock to get 'em in London. He said 'I won't have a child dressed in black wanderin' about like a lost soul,' he said. 'It'd make the place sadder than it is. Put color on her.' Mother she said she knew what he meant. Mother always knows what a body means. She doesn't hold with black hersel'."

"I hate black things," said Mary.

Martha

The dressing process was one which taught them both something. Martha had "buttoned up" her little sisters and brothers but she had never seen a child who stood still and waited for another person to do things for her as if she had neither hands nor feet of her own.

"Why doesn't tha' put on tha' own shoes?" she said when Mary quietly held out her foot.

"My Ayah did it," answered Mary, staring. "It was the custom."

She said that very often—"It was the custom." The native servants were always saying it. If one told them to do a thing their ancestors had not done for a thousand years they gazed at one mildly and said, "It is not the custom" and one knew that was the end of the matter.

It had not been the custom that Mistress Mary should do anything but stand and allow herself to be dressed like a doll, but before she was ready for breakfast she began to suspect that her life at Misselthwaite Manor would end by teaching her a number of things quite new to her— things such as putting on her own shoes and stockings, and picking up things she let fall.

If Martha had been a well-trained fine young lady's maid she would have been more subservient and respectful and would have known that it was her business to brush hair, and button boots, and pick things up and lay them away. She was, however, only an untrained Yorkshire rustic who had been brought up in a moorland cottage with a swarm of little brothers and sisters who had never dreamed of doing anything but waiting on themselves and on the younger ones who were either babies in arms or just learning to totter about and tumble over things.

If Mary Lennox had been a child who was ready to be amused she would perhaps have laughed at Martha's readiness to talk, but Mary only listened to her coldly and wondered at her freedom of manner. At first she was not at all interested, but gradually, as the girl rattled on in her good-tempered, homely way, Mary began to notice what she was saying.

"Eh! you should see 'em all," she said. "There's twelve of us an' my father only gets sixteen shilling a week. I can tell you my mother's put to it to get porridge for 'em all. They tumble about on th' moor an' play there all day an' mother says th' air of th' moor fattens 'em. She says she believes they eat th' grass same as th' wild ponies do. Our Dickon, he's twelve years old and he's got a young pony he calls his own."

"Where did he get it?" asked Mary.

"He found it on th' moor with its mother when it was a little one, an' he began to make friends with it an' give it bits o' bread an' pluck young grass for it. And it got to like him so it follows him about an' it lets him get on its back. Dickon's a kind lad an' animals likes him."

Mary had never possessed an animal pet of her own and had always thought she should like one. So she began to feel a slight interest in Dickon, and as she had never before been interested in any one but herself, it was the dawning of a healthy sentiment.

When she went into the room which had been made into a nursery for her, she found that it was rather like the one she had slept in. It was not a child's room, but a grown-up person's room, with gloomy old pictures on the walls and heavy old oak chairs. A table in the center was set with a good substantial breakfast. But she had always had a very small appetite, and she looked with something more than indifference at the first plate Martha set before her.

"I don't want it," she said.

"Tha' doesn't want thy porridge!" Martha exclaimed incredulously.

"No."

"Tha' doesn't know how good it is. Put a bit o' treacle on it or a bit o' sugar."

"I don't want it," repeated Mary.

"Eh!" said Martha. "I can't abide to see good victuals go to waste. If our children was at this table they'd clean it bare in five minutes."

"Why?" said Mary coldly. "Why!" echoed Martha. "Because they scarce ever had their stomachs full in their lives. They're as hungry as young hawks an' foxes."

"I don't know what it is to be hungry," said Mary, with the indifference of ignorance.

Martha looked indignant.

"Well, it would do thee good to try it. I can see that plain enough," she said outspokenly. "I've no patience with folk as sits an' just stares at good bread an' meat. My word! don't I wish Dickon and Phil an' Jane an' th' rest of 'em had what's here under their pinafores."

"Why don't you take it to them?" suggested Mary.

"It's not mine," answered Martha stoutly. "An' this

isn't my day out. I get my day out once a month same as th' rest. Then I go home an' clean up for mother an' give her a day's rest."

Mary drank some tea and ate a little toast and some marmalade.

"You wrap up warm an' run out an' play you," said Martha. "It'll do you good and give you some stomach for your meat."

Mary went to the window. There were gardens and paths and big trees, but everything looked dull and wintry.

"Out? Why should I go out on a day like this?"

"Well, if tha' doesn't go out tha'lt have to stay in, an' what has tha' got to do?"

Mary glanced about her. There was nothing to do. When Mrs. Medlock had prepared the nursery she had not thought of amusement. Perhaps it would be better to go and see what the gardens were like.

"Who will go with me?" she inquired.

Martha stared.

"You'll go by yourself," she answered. "You'll have to learn to play like other children does when they haven't got sisters and brothers. Our Dickon goes off on th' moor by himself an' plays for hours. That's how he made friends with th' pony. He's got sheep on th' moor that knows him, an' birds as comes an' eats out of his hand. However little there is to eat, he always saves a bit o' his bread to coax his pets."

It was really this mention of Dickon which made Mary decide to go out, though she was not aware of it. There would be, birds outside though there would not be ponies or sheep. They would be different from the birds in India and it might amuse her to look at them.

Martha found her coat and hat for her and a pair of stout little boots and she showed her her way downstairs.

"If tha' goes round that way tha'll come to th' gardens," she said, pointing to a gate in a wall of shrubbery. "There's lots o' flowers in summer-time, but there's nothin' bloomin' now." She seemed to hesitate a second before she added, "One of th' gardens is locked up. No one has been in it for ten years."

"Why?" asked Mary in spite of herself. Here was another locked door added to the hundred in the strange house.

"Mr. Craven had it shut when his wife died so sudden. He won't let no one go inside. It was her garden. He locked th' door an' dug a hole and buried th' key. There's Mrs. Medlock's bell ringing—I must run."

After she was gone Mary turned down the walk which led to the door in the shrubbery. She could not help thinking about the garden which no one had been into for ten years. She wondered what it would look like and whether there were any flowers still alive in it.

When she had passed through the shrubbery gate she found herself in great gardens, with wide lawns and winding walks with clipped borders. There were trees, and flowerbeds, and evergreens clipped into strange shapes, and a large pool with an old gray fountain in its midst. But the flowerbeds were bare and wintry and the fountain was not playing. This was not the garden which was shut up. How could a garden be shut up? You could always walk into a garden.

She was just thinking this when she saw that, at the end of the path she was following, there seemed to be a long wall, with ivy growing over it. She was not familiar enough with England to know that she was coming upon the kitchen-gardens where the vegetables and fruit were growing. She went toward the wall and found that there was a green door in the ivy, and that it stood open. This was not the closed garden, evidently, and she could go into it.

She went through the door and found that it was a garden with walls all round it and that it was only one of several walled gardens which seemed to open into one another. She saw another open green door, revealing bushes and pathways between beds containing winter vegetables. Fruit trees were trained flat against the wall, and over some of the beds there were glass frames. The place was bare and ugly enough, Mary thought, as she stood and stared about her. It might be nicer in summer when things were green, but there was nothing pretty about it now.

Presently an old man with a spade over his shoulder walked through the door leading from the second garden. He looked startled when he saw Mary, and then touched his cap. He had a surly old face, and did not seem at all pleased to see her—but then she was displeased with his garden and wore her "quite contrary" expression, and certainly did not seem at all pleased to see him.

"What is this place?" she asked.

"One o' th' kitchen-gardens," he answered.

"What is that?" said Mary, pointing through the other green door.

"Another of 'em," shortly. "There's another on t'other side o' th' wall an' there's th' orchard t'other side o' that."

"Can I go in them?" asked Mary.

"If tha' likes. But there's nowt to see."

Mary made no response. She went down the path and through the second green door. There, she found more walls and winter vegetables and glass frames, but in the second wall there was another green door and it was not open. Perhaps it led into the garden which no one had seen for ten years.

As she was not at all a timid child and always did what she wanted to do, Mary went to the green door and turned the handle. She hoped the door would not open because she wanted to be sure she had found the mysterious garden—but it did open quite easily and she walked through it and found herself in an orchard. There were walls all round it also and trees trained against them, and there were bare fruit trees growing in the winter-browned grass—but there was no green door to be seen anywhere.

Mary looked for it, and yet when she had entered the upper end of the garden she had noticed that the wall did not seem to end with the orchard, but to extend beyond it as if it enclosed a place at the other side. She could see the tops of trees above the wall, and when she stood still she saw a bird with a bright red breast sitting on the topmost branch of one of them, and suddenly he burst into his winter song—almost as if he had caught sight of her and was calling to her.

She stopped and listened to him and somehow his cheerful, friendly little whistle gave her a pleased feeling—even a disagreeable little girl may be lonely, and the big closed house and big bare moor and big bare gardens had made this one feel as if there was no one left in the world but herself. If she had been an affectionate child, who had been used to being loved, she would have broken her heart, but even though she was "Mistress Mary Quite Contrary" she was desolate, and the bright-breasted little bird brought a look into her sour little face which was almost a smile.

She listened to him until he flew away. He was not like an Indian bird and she liked him and wondered if she should ever see him again. Perhaps he lived in the mysterious garden and knew all about it.

Perhaps it was because she had nothing whatever to do that she thought so much of the deserted garden. She was curious about it and wanted to see what it was like. Why had Mr. Archibald Craven buried the key? If he had liked his wife so much why did he hate her garden? She wondered if she should ever see him, but she knew that if she did she should not like him, and he would not like her, and that she should only stand and stare at him and say nothing, though she should be wanting dreadfully to ask him why he had done such a queer thing.

"People never like me and I never like people," she thought. "And I never can talk as the Crawford children could. They were always talking and laughing and making noises."

She thought of the robin and of the way he seemed to sing his song at her, and as she remembered the tree-top he perched on she stopped rather suddenly on the path.

"I believe that tree was in the secret garden—I feel sure it was," she said. "There was a wall round the place and there was no door."

She walked back into the first kitchen-garden she had entered and found the old man digging there. She went and stood beside him and watched him a few moments in her cold little way. He took no notice of her and so at last she spoke to him.

"I have been into the other gardens," she said.

"There was nothin' to prevent thee," he answered crustily.

"I went into the orchard."

"There was no dog at th' door to bite thee," he answered.

"There was no door there into the other garden," said Mary.

"What garden?" he said in a rough voice, stopping his digging for a moment.

"The one on the other side of the wall," answered Mistress Mary. "There are trees there—I saw the tops of them. A bird with a red breast was sitting on one of them and he sang."

To her surprise the surly old weather-beaten face actually changed its expression. A slow smile spread over it and the gardener looked quite different. It made her think that it was curious how much nicer a person looked when he smiled. She had not thought of it before.

He turned about to the orchard side of his garden and began to whistle—a low soft whistle. She could not understand how such a surly man could make such a coaxing sound. Almost the next moment a wonderful thing happened. She heard a soft little rushing flight through the air—and it was the bird with the red breast flying to them, and he actually alighted on the big clod of earth quite near to the gardener's foot.

"Here he is," chuckled the old man, and then he spoke to the bird as if he were speaking to a child.

"Where has tha' been, tha' cheeky little beggar?" he said. "I've not seen thee before today. Has tha, begun tha' courtin' this early in th' season? Tha'rt too forrad."

The bird put his tiny head on one side and looked up at him with his soft bright eye which was like a black dewdrop. He seemed quite familiar and not the least afraid. He hopped about and pecked the earth briskly, looking for seeds and insects. It actually gave Mary a queer feeling in her heart, because he was so pretty and cheerful and seemed so like a person. He had a tiny plump body and a delicate beak, and slender delicate legs.

"Will he always come when you call him?" she asked almost in a whisper.

"Aye, that he will. I've knowed him ever since he was a fledgling. He come out of th' nest in th' other garden an' when first he flew over th' wall he was too weak to fly back for a few days an' we got friendly. When he went over th' wall again th' rest of th' brood was gone an' he was lonely an' he come back to me."

"What kind of a bird is he?" Mary asked.

"Doesn't tha' know? He's a robin redbreast an' they're th' friendliest, curiousest birds alive. They're almost as friendly as dogs—if you know how to get on with 'em. Watch him peckin' about there an' lookin' round at us now an' again. He knows we're talkin' about him."

It was the queerest thing in the world to see the old fellow. He looked at the plump little scarlet-waistcoated bird as if he were both proud and fond of him.

"He's a conceited one," he chuckled. "He likes to hear folk talk about him. An' curious—bless me, there never was his like for curiosity an' meddlin'. He's always comin' to see what I'm plantin'. He knows all th' things Mester Craven never troubles hissel' to find out. He's th' head gardener, he is."

The robin hopped about busily pecking the soil and now and then stopped and looked at them a little. Mary thought his black dewdrop eyes gazed at her with great curiosity. It really seemed as if he were finding out all about her. The queer feeling in her heart increased.

"Where did the rest of the brood fly to?" she asked.

"There's no knowin'. The old ones turn 'em out o' their nest an' make 'em fly an' they're scattered before you know it. This one was a knowin' one an' he knew he was lonely."

Mistress Mary went a step nearer to the robin and looked at him very hard.

"I'm lonely," she said.

She had not known before that this was one of the things which made her feel sour and cross. She seemed to find it out when the robin looked at her and she

looked at the robin.

The old gardener pushed his cap back on his bald head and stared at her a minute.

"Art tha' th' little wench from India?" he asked.

Mary nodded.

"Then no wonder tha'rt lonely. Tha'lt be lonlier before tha's done," he said.

He began to dig again, driving his spade deep into the rich black garden soil while the robin hopped about very busily employed.

"What is your name?" Mary inquired.

He stood up to answer her.

"Ben Weatherstaff," he answered, and then he added with a surly chuckle, "I'm lonely mysel' except when he's with me," and he jerked his thumb toward the robin. "He's th' only friend I've got."

"I have no friends at all," said Mary. "I never had. My Ayah didn't like me and I never played with any one."

It is a Yorkshire habit to say what you think with blunt frankness, and old Ben Weatherstaff was a Yorkshire moor man.

"Tha' an' me are a good bit alike," he said. "We was wove out of th' same cloth. We're neither of us good lookin' an' we're both of us as sour as we look. We've got the same nasty tempers, both of us, I'll warrant."

This was plain speaking, and Mary Lennox had never heard the truth about herself in her life. Native servants always salaamed and submitted to you, whatever you did. She had never thought much about her looks, but she wondered if she was as unattractive as Ben Weatherstaff and she also wondered if she looked as sour as he had looked before the robin came. She actually began to wonder also if she was "nasty-tempered." She felt uncomfortable.

Suddenly a clear rippling little sound broke out near her and she turned round. She was standing a few feet from a young apple-tree and the robin had flown on to one of its branches and had burst out into a scrap of a song. Ben Weatherstaff laughed outright.

"What did he do that for?" asked Mary.

"He's made up his mind to make friends with thee," replied Ben. "Dang me if he hasn't took a fancy to thee."

"To me?" said Mary, and she moved toward the little tree softly and looked up.

"Would you make friends with me?" she said to the robin just as if she was speaking to a person. "Would you?" And she did not say it either in her hard little voice or in her imperious Indian voice, but in a tone so soft and eager and coaxing that Ben Weatherstaff was as surprised as she had been when she heard him whistle.

"Why," he cried out, "tha' said that as nice an' human as if tha' was a real child instead of a sharp old woman. Tha' said it almost like Dickon talks to his wild things on th' moor."

"Do you know Dickon?" Mary asked, turning round rather in a hurry.

"Everybody knows him. Dickon's wanderin' about everywhere. Th' very blackberries an' heather-bells knows him. I warrant th' foxes shows him where their cubs lies an' th' skylarks doesn't hide their nests from him."

Mary would have liked to ask some more questions. She was almost as curious about Dickon as she was about the deserted garden. But just that moment the robin, who had ended his song, gave a little shake of his wings, spread them and flew away. He had made his visit and had other things to do.

"He has flown over the wall!" Mary cried out, watching him. "He has flown into the orchard—he has flown across the other wall—into the garden where there is no door!"

"He lives there," said old Ben. "He came out o' th' egg there. If he's courtin', he's makin' up to some young madam of a robin that lives among th' old rose trees there."

"Rose trees," said Mary. "Are there rose trees?"

Ben Weatherstaff took up his spade again and began to dig.

"There was ten year' ago," he mumbled.

"I should like to see them," said Mary. "Where is the green door? There must be a door somewhere."

Ben drove his spade deep and looked as uncompanionable as he had looked when she first saw him.

"There was ten year' ago, but there isn't now," he said.

"No door!" cried Mary. "There must be."

"None as any one can find, an' none as is any one's business. Don't you be a meddlesome wench an' poke your nose where it's no cause to go. Here, I must go on with my work. Get you gone an' play you. I've no more time."

And he actually stopped digging, threw his spade over his shoulder and walked off, without even glancing at her or saying goodbye.

Chapter 5

The Cry in the Corridor

At first each day which passed by for Mary Lennox was exactly like the others. Every morning she awoke in her tapestried room and found Martha kneeling upon the hearth building her fire; every morning she ate her breakfast in the nursery which had nothing amusing in it; and after each breakfast she gazed out of the window across to the huge moor which seemed to spread out on all sides and climb up to the sky, and after she had stared for a while she realized that if she did not go out she would have to stay in and do nothing—and so she went out.

She did not know that this was the best thing she could have done, and she did not know that, when she began to walk quickly or even run along the paths and down the avenue, she was stirring her slow blood and making herself stronger by fighting with the wind which swept down from the moor.

She ran only to make herself warm, and she hated the wind which rushed at her face and roared and held her back as if it were some giant she could not see. But the big breaths of rough fresh air blown over the heather filled her lungs with something which was good for her whole thin body and whipped some red color into her cheeks and brightened her dull eyes when she did not know anything about it.

But after a few days spent almost entirely out of doors, she wakened one morning knowing what it was to be hungry, and when she sat down to her breakfast she did not glance disdainfully at her porridge and push it away, but took up her spoon and began to eat it and went on eating it until her bowl was empty.

"Tha' got on well enough with that this mornin', didn't tha'?" said Martha.

"It tastes nice today," said Mary, feeling a little surprised herself.

"It's th' air of th' moor that's givin' thee stomach for tha' victuals," answered Martha. "It's lucky for thee that tha's got victuals as well as appetite. There's been twelve in our cottage as had th' stomach an' nothin' to put in it. You go on playin' you out o' doors every day an' you'll get some flesh on your bones an' you won't be so yeller."

"I don't play," said Mary. "I have nothing to play with."

"Nothin' to play with!" exclaimed Martha. "Our children plays with sticks and stones. They just runs about an' shouts an' looks at things."

Mary did not shout, but she looked at things. There was nothing else to do. She walked round and round the gardens and wandered about the paths in the park. Sometimes she looked for Ben Weatherstaff, but though several times she saw him at work he was too busy to look at her or was too surly. Once when she was walking toward him he picked up his spade and turned away as if he did it on purpose.

One place she went to oftener than to any other. It was the long walk outside the gardens with the walls round them. There were bare flowerbeds on either side of it and against the walls ivy grew thickly. There was one part of the wall where the creeping dark green leaves were more bushy than elsewhere. It seemed as if for a long time that part had been neglected. The rest of it had been clipped and made to look neat, but at this lower end of the walk it had not been trimmed at all.

A few days after she had talked to Ben Weatherstaff, Mary stopped to notice this and wondered why it was so. She had just paused and was looking up at a long spray of ivy swinging in the wind when she saw a gleam of scarlet and heard a brilliant chirp, and there, on the top of the wall, forward perched Ben Weatherstaff's robin redbreast, tilting forward to look at her with his small head on one side.

"Oh!" she cried out, "is it you—is it you?" And it did not seem at all queer to her that she spoke to him as if she were sure that he would understand and answer her.

He did answer. He twittered and chirped and hopped along the wall as if he were telling her all sorts of things. It seemed to Mistress Mary as if she understood him, too, though he was not speaking in words. It was as if he said:

"Good morning! Isn't the wind nice? Isn't the sun nice? Isn't everything nice? Let us both chirp and hop and twitter. Come on! Come on!"

Mary began to laugh, and as he hopped and took little

flights along the wall she ran after him. Poor little thin, sallow, ugly Mary—she actually looked almost pretty for a moment.

"I like you! I like you!" she cried out, pattering down the walk; and she chirped and tried to whistle, which last she did not know how to do in the least. But the robin seemed to be quite satisfied and chirped and whistled back at her. At last he spread his wings and made a darting flight to the top of a tree, where he perched and sang loudly.

That reminded Mary of the first time she had seen him. He had been swinging on a tree-top then and she had been standing in the orchard. Now she was on the other side of the orchard and standing in the path outside a wall—much lower down—and there was the same tree inside.

"It's in the garden no one can go into," she said to herself. "It's the garden without a door. He lives in there. How I wish I could see what it is like!"

She ran up the walk to the green door she had entered the first morning. Then she ran down the path through the other door and then into the orchard, and when she stood and looked up there was the tree on the other side of the wall, and there was the robin just finishing his song and, beginning to preen his feathers with his beak.

"It is the garden," she said. "I am sure it is."

She walked round and looked closely at that side of the orchard wall, but she only found what she had found before—that there was no door in it. Then she ran through the kitchen-gardens again and out into the walk outside the long ivy-covered wall, and she walked to the end of it and looked at it, but there was no door; and then she walked to the other end, looking again, but there was no door.

"It's very queer," she said. "Ben Weatherstaff said there was no door and there is no door. But there must have been one ten years ago, because Mr. Craven buried the key."

This gave her so much to think of that she began to be quite interested and feel that she was not sorry that she had come to Misselthwaite Manor. In India she had always felt hot and too languid to care much about anything. The fact was that the fresh wind from the moor had begun to blow the cobwebs out of her young brain and to waken her up a little.

She stayed out of doors nearly all day, and when she sat down to her supper at night she felt hungry and drowsy and comfortable. She did not feel cross when Martha chattered away. She felt as if she rather liked to hear her, and at last she thought she would ask her a question. She asked it after she had finished her supper and had sat down on the hearth rug before the fire.

"Why did Mr. Craven hate the garden?" she said.

She had made Martha stay with her and Martha had not objected at all. She was very young, and used to a crowded cottage full of brothers and sisters, and she found it dull in the great servants' hall downstairs where the footman and upper-housemaids made fun of her Yorkshire speech and looked upon her as a common little thing, and sat and whispered among themselves.

Martha liked to talk, and the strange child who had lived in India, and been waited upon by "blacks," was novelty enough to attract her.

She sat down on the hearth herself without waiting to be asked.

"Art tha' thinkin' about that garden yet?" she said. "I knew tha' would. That was just the way with me when I first heard about it."

"Why did he hate it?" Mary persisted.

Martha tucked her feet under her and made herself quite comfortable.

"Listen to th' wind wutherin' round the house," she said. "You could bare stand up on the moor if you was out on it tonight."

Mary did not know what "wutherin'" meant until she listened, and then she understood. It must mean that hollow shuddering sort of roar which rushed round and round the house as if the giant no one could see were buffeting it and beating at the walls and windows to try to break in. But one knew he could not get in, and somehow it made one feel very safe and warm inside a room with a red coal fire.

"But why did he hate it so?" she asked, after she had listened. She intended to know if Martha did.

Then Martha gave up her store of knowledge.

"Mind," she said, "Mrs. Medlock said it's not to be talked about. There's lots o' things in this place that's not to be talked over. That's Mr. Craven's orders. His troubles are none servants' business, he says. But for th' garden he wouldn't be like he is. It was Mrs. Craven's garden that she had made when first they were married an' she just loved it, an' they used to 'tend the flowers themselves. An' none o' th' gardeners was ever let to go in. Him an' her used to go in an' shut th' door an' stay there hours an' hours, readin' and talkin'. An' she was just a bit of a girl an' there was an old tree with a branch bent like a seat on it. An' she made roses grow over it an' she used to sit there. But one day when she was sittin' there th' branch broke an' she fell on th' ground an' was hurt so bad that next day she died. Th' doctors thought he'd go out o' his mind an' die, too. That's why he hates it. No one's never gone in since, an' he won't let any one talk about it."

Mary did not ask any more questions. She looked at the red fire and listened to the wind "wutherin'." It seemed to be "wutherin'" louder than ever.

At that moment a very good thing was happening to her. Four good things had happened to her, in fact, since she came to Misselthwaite Manor. She had felt as if she had understood a robin and that he had understood her; she had run in the wind until her blood had grown warm; she had been healthily hungry for the first time in her life; and she had found out what it was to be sorry for some one.

But as she was listening to the wind she began to listen to something else. She did not know what it was, because at first she could scarcely distinguish it from the wind itself. It was a curious sound—it seemed almost as if a child were crying somewhere. Sometimes the wind sounded rather like a child crying, but presently

Mistress Mary felt quite sure this sound was inside the house, not outside it. It was far away, but it was inside. She turned round and looked at Martha.

"Do you hear any one crying?" she said.

Martha suddenly looked confused.

"No," she answered. "It's th' wind. Sometimes it sounds like as if some one was lost on th' moor an' wailin'. It's got all sorts o' sounds."

"But listen," said Mary. "It's in the house—down one of those long corridors."

And at that very moment a door must have been opened somewhere downstairs; for a great rushing draft blew along the passage and the door of the room they sat in was blown open with a crash, and as they both jumped to their feet the light was blown out and the crying sound was swept down the far corridor, so that it was to be heard more plainly than ever.

"There!" said Mary. "I told you so! It is some one crying—and it isn't a grown-up person."

Martha ran and shut the door and turned the key, but before she did it they both heard the sound of a door in some far passage shutting with a bang, and then everything was quiet, for even the wind ceased "wutherin'" for a few moments.

"It was th' wind," said Martha stubbornly. "An' if it wasn't, it was little Betty Butterworth, th' scullery-maid. She's had th' toothache all day."

But something troubled and awkward in her manner made Mistress Mary stare very hard at her. She did not believe she was speaking the truth.

Chapter 6

"There Was Some One Crying—There Was!"

The next day the rain poured down in torrents again, and when Mary looked out of her window the moor was almost hidden by gray mist and cloud. There could be no going out today.

"What do you do in your cottage when it rains like this?" she asked Martha.

"Try to keep from under each other's feet mostly," Martha answered. "Eh! there does seem a lot of us then. Mother's a good-tempered woman but she gets fair moithered. The biggest ones goes out in th' cow-shed and plays there. Dickon he doesn't mind th' wet. He goes out just th' same as if th' sun was shinin'. He says he sees things on rainy days as doesn't show when it's fair weather. He once found a little fox cub half drowned in its hole and he brought it home in th' bosom of his shirt to keep it warm. Its mother had been killed nearby an' th' hole was swum out an' th' rest o' th' litter was dead. He's got it at home now. He found a half-drowned young crow another time an' he brought it home, too, an' tamed it. It's named Soot because it's so black, an' it hops an' flies about with him everywhere."

The time had come when Mary had forgotten to resent

Martha's familiar talk. She had even begun to find it interesting and to be sorry when she stopped or went away.

The stories she had been told by her Ayah when she lived in India had been quite unlike those Martha had to tell about the moorland cottage which held fourteen people who lived in four little rooms and never had quite enough to eat. The children seemed to tumble about and amuse themselves like a litter of rough, good-natured collie puppies. Mary was most attracted by the mother and Dickon. When Martha told stories of what "mother" said or did they always sounded comfortable.

"If I had a raven or a fox cub I could play with it," said Mary. "But I have nothing."

Martha looked perplexed.

"Can tha' knit?" she asked.

"No," answered Mary.

"Can tha' sew?"

"No."

"Can tha' read?"

"Yes."

"Then why doesn't tha, read somethin', or learn a bit o' spellin'? Tha'st old enough to be learnin' thy book a good bit now."

"I haven't any books," said Mary. "Those I had were left in India."

"That's a pity," said Martha. "If Mrs. Medlock'd let thee go into th' library, there's thousands o' books there."

Mary did not ask where the library was, because she was suddenly inspired by a new idea. She made up her mind to go and find it herself. She was not troubled about Mrs. Medlock. Mrs. Medlock seemed always to be in her comfortable housekeeper's sitting-room downstairs. In this queer place one scarcely ever saw any one at all.

In fact, there was no one to see but the servants, and when their master was away they lived a luxurious life below stairs, where there was a huge kitchen hung about with shining brass and pewter, and a large servants' hall where there were four or five abundant meals eaten every day, and where a great deal of lively romping went on when Mrs. Medlock was out of the way.

Mary's meals were served regularly, and Martha waited on her, but no one troubled themselves about her in the least. Mrs. Medlock came and looked at her every day or two, but no one inquired what she did or told her what to do.

She supposed that perhaps this was the English way of treating children. In India she had always been attended by her Ayah, who had followed her about and waited on her, hand and foot. She had often been tired of her company. Now she was followed by nobody and was learning to dress herself, because Martha looked as though she thought she was silly and stupid when she wanted to have things handed to her and put on.

"Hasn't tha' got good sense?" she said once, when Mary had stood waiting for her to put on her gloves for her. "Our Susan Ann is twice as sharp as thee an' she's only four year' old. Sometimes tha' looks fair soft in th' head."

Mary had worn her contrary scowl for an hour after that, but it made her think several entirely new things.

She stood at the window for about ten minutes this morning after Martha had swept up the hearth for the last time and gone downstairs. She was thinking over the new idea which had come to her when she heard of the library. She did not care very much about the library itself, because she had read very few books; but to hear of it brought back to her mind the hundred rooms with closed doors. She wondered if they were all really locked and what she would find if she could get into any of them. Were there a hundred really? Why shouldn't she go and see how many doors she could count? It would be something to do on this morning when she could not go out.

She had never been taught to ask permission to do things, and she knew nothing at all about authority, so she would not have thought it necessary to ask Mrs. Medlock if she might walk about the house, even if she had seen her.

She opened the door of the room and went into the corridor, and then she began her wanderings. It was a long corridor and it branched into other corridors and it led her up short flights of steps which mounted to others again. There were doors and doors, and there were pictures on the walls. Sometimes they were pictures of dark, curious landscapes, but oftenest they were portraits of men and women in queer, grand costumes made of satin and velvet.

She found herself in one long gallery whose walls were covered with these portraits. She had never thought there could be so many in any house. She walked slowly down this place and stared at the faces which also seemed to stare at her. She felt as if they were wondering what a little girl from India was doing in their house.

Some were pictures of children—little girls in thick satin frocks which reached to their feet and stood out about them, and boys with puffed sleeves and lace collars and long hair, or with big ruffs around their necks. She always stopped to look at the children, and wonder what their names were, and where they had gone, and why they wore such odd clothes. There was a stiff, plain little girl rather like herself. She wore a green brocade dress and held a green parrot on her finger. Her eyes had a sharp, curious look.

"Where do you live now?" said Mary aloud to her. "I wish you were here."

Surely no other little girl ever spent such a queer morning. It seemed as if there was no one in all the huge rambling house but her own small self, wandering about upstairs and down, through narrow passages and wide ones, where it seemed to her that no one but herself had ever walked. Since so many rooms had been built, people must have lived in them, but it all seemed so empty that she could not quite believe it true.

It was not until she climbed to the second floor that she thought of turning the handle of a door. All the doors were shut, as Mrs. Medlock had said they were, but at last she put her hand on the handle of one of them and turned it. She was almost frightened for a moment when she felt that it turned without difficulty and that when she pushed upon the door itself it slowly and heavily opened. It was a massive door and opened into a big bedroom. There were embroidered hangings on the wall, and inlaid furniture such as she had seen in India stood about the room. A broad window with leaded panes looked out upon the moor; and over the mantel was another portrait of the stiff, plain little girl who seemed to stare at her more curiously than ever.

"Perhaps she slept here once," said Mary. "She stares at me so that she makes me feel queer."

After that she opened more doors and more. She saw so many rooms that she became quite tired and began to think that there must be a hundred, though she had not counted them. In all of them there were old pictures or old tapestries with strange scenes worked on them. There were curious pieces of furniture and curious ornaments in nearly all of them.

In one room, which looked like a lady's sitting-room, the hangings were all embroidered velvet, and in a cabinet were about a hundred little elephants made of ivory. They were of different sizes, and some had their mahouts or palanquins on their backs. Some were much bigger than the others and some were so tiny that they seemed only babies. Mary had seen carved ivory in India and she knew all about elephants. She opened the door of the cabinet and stood on a footstool and played with these for quite a long time. When she got tired she set the elephants in order and shut the door of the cabinet.

In all her wanderings through the long corridors and the empty rooms, she had seen nothing alive; but in this room she saw something. Just after she had closed the cabinet door she heard a tiny rustling sound. It made her jump and look around at the sofa by the fireplace, from which it seemed to come. In the corner of the sofa there was a cushion, and in the velvet which covered it there was a hole, and out of the hole peeped a tiny head with a pair of frightened eyes in it.

Mary crept softly across the room to look. The bright eyes belonged to a little gray mouse, and the mouse had eaten a hole into the cushion and made a comfortable nest there. Six baby mice were cuddled up asleep near her. If there was no one else alive in the hundred rooms there were seven mice who did not look lonely at all.

"If they wouldn't be so frightened I would take them back with me," said Mary.

She had wandered about long enough to feel too tired to wander any farther, and she turned back. Two or three times she lost her way by turning down the wrong corridor and was obliged to ramble up and down until she found the right one; but at last she reached her own floor again, though she was some distance from her own room and did not know exactly where she was.

"I believe I have taken a wrong turning again," she said, standing still at what seemed the end of a short passage with tapestry on the wall. "I don't know which way to go. How still everything is!"

It was while she was standing here and just after she had said this that the stillness was broken by a sound. It was another cry, but not quite like the one she had heard last night; it was only a short one, a fretful childish whine muffled by passing through walls.

"It's nearer than it was," said Mary, her heart beating rather faster. "And it is crying."

She put her hand accidentally upon the tapestry near her, and then sprang back, feeling quite startled. The tapestry was the covering of a door which fell open and showed her that there was another part of the corridor behind it, and

Mrs. Medlock was coming up it with her bunch of keys in her hand and a very cross look on her face.

"What are you doing here?" she said, and she took Mary by the arm and pulled her away. "What did I tell you?"

"I turned round the wrong corner," explained Mary. "I didn't know which way to go and I heard some one crying." She quite hated Mrs. Medlock at the moment, but she hated her more the next.

"You didn't hear anything of the sort," said the housekeeper. "You come along back to your own nursery or I'll box your ears."

And she took her by the arm and half pushed, half pulled her up one passage and down another until she pushed her in at the door of her own room.

"Now," she said, "you stay where you're told to stay or you'll find yourself locked up. The master had better get you a governess, same as he said he would. You're one that needs some one to look sharp after you. I've got enough to do."

She went out of the room and slammed the door after her, and Mary went and sat on the hearth rug, pale with rage. She did not cry, but ground her teeth.

"There was some one crying—there was—there was!" she said to herself.

She had heard it twice now, and sometime she would find out. She had found out a great deal this morning. She felt as if she had been on a long journey, and at any rate she had had something to amuse her all the time, and she had played with the ivory elephants and had seen the gray mouse and its babies in their nest in the velvet cushion.

Chapter 7

The Key to the Garden

Two days after this, when Mary opened her eyes she sat upright in bed immediately, and called to Martha.

"Look at the moor! Look at the moor!"

The rainstorm had ended and the gray mist and clouds had been swept away in the night by the wind. The wind itself had ceased and a brilliant, deep blue sky arched high over the moorland. Never, never had Mary dreamed of a sky so blue. In India skies were hot and blazing; this was of a deep cool blue which almost seemed to sparkle like the waters of some lovely bottomless lake, and here and there, high, high in the arched blueness floated small clouds of snow-white fleece. The far-reaching world of the moor itself looked softly blue instead of gloomy purple-black or awful dreary gray.

"Aye," said Martha with a cheerful grin. "Th' storm's over for a bit. It does like this at this time o' th' year. It goes off in a night like it was pretendin' it had never been here an' never meant to come again. That's because th' springtime's on its way. It's a long way off yet, but it's comin'."

"I thought perhaps it always rained or looked dark in England," Mary said.

"Eh! no!" said Martha, sitting up on her heels among her black lead brushes. "Nowt o' th' soart!"

"What does that mean?" asked Mary seriously. In India the natives spoke different dialects which only a few people understood, so she was not surprised when Martha used words she did not know.

Martha laughed as she had done the first morning. "There now," she said. "I've talked broad Yorkshire again like Mrs. Medlock said I mustn't. 'Nowt o' th' soart' means 'nothin'-of-the-sort,'" slowly and carefully, "but it takes so long to say it. Yorkshire's th' sunniest place on earth when it is sunny. I told thee tha'd like th' moor after a bit. Just you wait till you see th' gold-colored gorse blossoms an' th' blossoms o' th' broom, an' th' heather flowerin', all purple bells, an' hundreds o' butterflies flutterin' an' bees hummin' an' skylarks soarin' up an' singin'. You'll want to get out on it as sunrise an' live out on it all day like Dickon does."

"Could I ever get there?" asked Mary wistfully, looking through her window at the far-off blue. It was so new and big and wonderful and such a heavenly color.

"I don't know," answered Martha. "Tha's never used tha' legs since tha' was born, it seems to me. Tha' couldn't walk five mile. It's five mile to our cottage."

"I should like to see your cottage."

Martha stared at her a moment curiously before she took up her polishing brush and began to rub the grate again. She was thinking that the small plain face did not look quite as sour at this moment as it had done the first morning she saw it. It looked just a trifle like little Susan Ann's when she wanted something very much.

"I'll ask my mother about it," she said. "She's one o' them that nearly always sees a way to do things. It's my day out today an' I'm goin' home. Eh! I am glad. Mrs. Medlock thinks a lot o' mother. Perhaps she could talk to her."

"I like your mother," said Mary.

"I should think tha' did," agreed Martha, polishing away.

"I've never seen her," said Mary.

"No, tha' hasn't," replied Martha.

She sat up on her heels again and rubbed the end of her nose with the back of her hand as if puzzled for a moment, but she ended quite positively. "Well, she's that sensible an' hard workin' an' goodnatured an' clean that no one could help likin' her whether they'd seen her or not. When I'm goin' home to her on my day out I just jump for joy when I'm crossin' the moor."

"I like Dickon," added Mary. "And I've never seen him."

"Well," said Martha stoutly, "I've told thee that th' very birds likes him an' th' rabbits an' wild sheep an' ponies, an' th' foxes themselves. I wonder," staring at her reflectively, "what Dickon would think of thee?"

"He wouldn't like me," said Mary in her stiff, cold little way. "No one does."

Martha looked reflective again.

"How does tha' like thysel'?" she inquired, really quite as if she were curious to know.

Mary hesitated a moment and thought it over.

"Not at all—really," she answered. "But I never thought of that before."

Martha grinned a little as if at some homely recollection. "Mother said that to me once," she said. "She was at her wash-tub an' I was in a bad temper an' talkin' ill of folk, an' she turns round on me an' says: 'Tha' young vixen, tha'! There tha' stands sayin' tha' doesn't like this one an' tha' doesn't like that one. How does tha' like thysel'?' It made me laugh an' it brought me to my senses in a minute."

She went away in high spirits as soon as she had given Mary her breakfast. She was going to walk five miles across the moor to the cottage, and she was going to help her mother with the washing and do the week's baking and enjoy herself thoroughly.

Mary felt lonelier than ever when she knew she was no longer in the house. She went out into the garden as quickly as possible, and the first thing she did was to run round and round the fountain flower garden ten times. She counted the times carefully and when she had finished she felt in better spirits.

The sunshine made the whole place look different. The high, deep, blue sky arched over Misselthwaite as well as over the moor, and she kept lifting her face and looking up into it, trying to imagine what it would be like to lie down on one of the little snow-white clouds and float about.

She went into the first kitchen-garden and found Ben Weatherstaff working there with two other gardeners. The change in the weather seemed to have done him good. He spoke to her of his own accord. "Springtime's comin,'" he said. "Cannot tha' smell it?"

Mary sniffed and thought she could.

"I smell something nice and fresh and damp," she said.

"That's th' good rich earth," he answered, digging away. "It's in a good humor makin' ready to grow things. It's glad when plantin' time comes. It's dull in th' winter when it's got nowt to do. In th' flower gardens out there things will be stirrin' down below in th' dark. Th' sun's warmin' 'em. You'll see bits o' green spikes stickin' out o' th' black earth after a bit."

"What will they be?" asked Mary.

"Crocuses an' snowdrops an' daffydowndillys. Has tha' never seen them?"

"No. Everything is hot, and wet, and green after the rains in India," said Mary. "And I think things grow up in a night."

"These won't grow up in a night," said Weatherstaff. "Tha'll have to wait for 'em. They'll poke up a bit higher here, an' push out a spike more there, an' uncurl a leaf this day an' another that. You watch 'em."

"I am going to," answered Mary.

Very soon she heard the soft rustling flight of wings again and she knew at once that the robin had come again. He was very pert and lively, and hopped about so close to her feet, and put his head on one side and looked at her so slyly that she asked Ben Weatherstaff a question.

"Do you think he remembers me?" she said.

"Remembers thee!" said Weatherstaff indignantly. "He knows every cabbage stump in th' gardens, let alone th' people. He's never seen a little wench here before, an' he's bent on findin' out all about thee. Tha's no need to try to hide anything from him."

"Are things stirring down below in the dark in that garden where he lives?" Mary inquired.

"What garden?" grunted Weatherstaff, becoming surly again.

"The one where the old rose trees are." She could not help asking, because she wanted so much to know. "Are all the flowers dead, or do some of them come again in the summer? Are there ever any roses?"

"Ask him," said Ben Weatherstaff, hunching his shoulders toward the robin. "He's the only one as knows. No one else has seen inside it for ten year'."

Ten years was a long time, Mary thought. She had been born ten years ago.

She walked away, slowly thinking. She had begun to like the garden just as she had begun to like the robin and Dickon and Martha's mother. She was beginning to like Martha, too. That seemed a good many people to like—when you were not used to liking. She thought of the robin as one of the people. She went to her walk outside the long, ivy-covered wall over which she could see the tree-tops; and the second time she walked up and down the most interesting and exciting thing happened to her, and it was all through Ben Weatherstaff's robin.

She heard a chirp and a twitter, and when she looked at the bare flowerbed at her left side there he was hopping about and pretending to peck things out of the earth to persuade her that he had not followed her. But she knew he had followed her and the surprise so filled her with delight that she almost trembled a little.

"You do remember me!" she cried out. "You do! You are prettier than anything else in the world!"

She chirped, and talked, and coaxed and he hopped, and flirted his tail and twittered. It was as if he were talking. His red waistcoat was like satin, and he puffed his tiny breast out and was so fine and so grand and so pretty that it was really as if he were showing her how important and like a human person a robin could be. Mistress Mary forgot that she had ever been contrary in her life when he allowed her to draw closer and closer to him, and bend down and talk and try to make something like robin sounds.

Oh! to think that he should actually let her come as near to him as that! He knew nothing in the world would make her put out her hand toward him or startle him in the least tiniest way. He knew it because he was a real person—only nicer than any other person in the world. She was so happy that she scarcely dared to breathe.

The flowerbed was not quite bare. It was bare of flowers because the perennial plants had been cut down for their winter rest, but there were tall shrubs and low ones which grew together at the back of the bed, and as the robin hopped about under them she saw him hop over a small pile of freshly turned up earth. He stopped on it to look for a worm. The earth had been turned up because a dog had been trying to dig up a mole and he had scratched quite a deep hole.

Mary looked at it, not really knowing why the hole was there, and as she looked she saw something almost buried in the newly-turned soil. It was something like a ring of rusty iron or brass, and when the robin flew up into a tree nearby she put out her hand and picked the ring up. It was more than a ring, however; it was an old key which looked as if it had been buried a long time.

Mistress Mary stood up and looked at it with an almost frightened face as it hung from her finger.

"Perhaps it has been buried for ten years," she said in a whisper. "Perhaps it is the key to the garden!"

Chapter 8

The Robin Who
Showed the Way

She looked at the key quite a long time. She turned it over and over, and thought about it. As I have said before, she was not a child who had been trained to ask permission or consult her elders about things. All she thought about the key was that if it was the key to the closed garden, and she could find out where the door was, she could perhaps open it and see what was inside the walls, and what had happened to the old rose trees.

It was because it had been shut up so long that she wanted to see it. It seemed as if it must be different from other places and that something strange must have happened to it during ten years. Besides that, if she liked it she could go into it every day and shut the door behind her, and she could make up some play of her own and play it quite alone, because nobody would ever know where she was, but would think the door was still locked and the key buried in the earth. The thought of that pleased her very much.

Living as it were, all by herself in a house with a hundred mysteriously closed rooms and having nothing whatever to do to amuse herself, had set her inactive

brain to working and was actually awakening her imagination. There is no doubt that the fresh, strong, pure air from the moor had a great deal to do with it. Just as it had given her an appetite, and fighting with the wind had stirred her blood, so the same things had stirred her mind.

In India she had always been too hot and languid and weak to care much about anything, but in this place she was beginning to care and to want to do new things. Already she felt less "contrary," though she did not know why.

She put the key in her pocket and walked up and down her walk. No one but herself ever seemed to come there, so she could walk slowly and look at the wall, or, rather, at the ivy growing on it. The ivy was the baffling thing. Howsoever carefully she looked, she could see nothing but thickly growing, glossy, dark green leaves. She was very much disappointed. Something of her contrariness came back to her as she paced the walk and looked over it at the tree-tops inside. It seemed so silly, she said to herself, to be near it and not be able to get in.

She took the key in her pocket when she went back to the house, and she made up her mind that she would always carry it with her when she went out, so that if she ever should find the hidden door she would be ready.

Mrs. Medlock had allowed Martha to sleep all night at the cottage, but she was back at her work in the morning with cheeks redder than ever and in the best of spirits.

"I got up at four o'clock," she said. "Eh! it was pretty on th' moor with th' birds gettin' up an' th' rabbits scamperin' about an' th' sun risin'. I didn't walk all th' way. A man gave me a ride in his cart an' I did enjoy myself."

She was full of stories of the delights of her day out. Her mother had been glad to see her, and they had got the baking and washing all out of the way. She had even made each of the children a dough cake with a bit of brown sugar in it.

"I had 'em all pipin' hot when they came in from playin' on th' moor. An' th' cottage all smelt o' nice, clean hot bakin' an' there was a good fire, an' they just shouted for joy. Our Dickon he said our cottage was good enough for a king."

In the evening they had all sat round the fire, and Martha and her mother had sewed patches on torn clothes and mended stockings, and Martha had told them about the little girl who had come from India and who had been waited on all her life by what Martha called "blacks" until she didn't know how to put on her own stockings.

"Eh! they did like to hear about you," said Martha. "They wanted to know all about th' blacks an' about th' ship you came in. I couldn't tell 'em enough."

Mary reflected a little. "I'll tell you a great deal more before your next day out," she said, "so that you will have more to talk about. I dare say they would like to hear about riding on elephants and camels, and about the officers going to hunt tigers."

"My word!" cried delighted Martha. "It would set 'em clean off their heads. Would tha' really do that, Miss? It

would be same as a wild beast show like we heard they had in York once."

"India is quite different from Yorkshire," Mary said slowly, as she thought the matter over. "I never thought of that. Did Dickon and your mother like to hear you talk about me?"

"Why, our Dickon's eyes nearly started out o' his head, they got that round," answered Martha. "But mother, she was put out about your seemin' to be all by yourself like. She said, 'Hasn't Mr. Craven got no governess for her, nor no nurse?' and I said, 'No, he hasn't, though Mrs. Medlock says he will when he thinks of it, but she says he mayn't think of it for two or three years.'"

"I don't want a governess," said Mary sharply.

"But mother says you ought to be learnin' your book by this time an' you ought to have a woman to look after you, an' she says: 'Now, Martha, you just think how you'd feel yourself, in a big place like that, wanderin' about all alone, an' no mother. You do your best to cheer her up,' she says, an' I said I would."

Mary gave her a long, steady look.

"You do cheer me up," she said. "I like to hear you talk."

Presently Martha went out of the room and came back with something held in her hands under her apron.

"What does tha' think," she said, with a cheerful grin. "I've brought thee a present."

"A present!" exclaimed Mistress Mary. How could a cottage full of fourteen hungry people give any one a present!

"A man was drivin' across the moor peddlin'," Martha explained. "An' he stopped his cart at our door. He had pots an' pans an' odds an' ends, but mother had no money to buy anythin'. Just as he was goin' away our 'Lizabeth Ellen called out, 'Mother, he's got skippin'-ropes with red an' blue handles.' An' mother she calls out quite sudden, 'Here, stop, mister! How much are they?' An' he says 'Tuppence', an' mother she began fumblin' in her pocket, an' she says to me, 'Martha, tha's brought me thy wages like a good lass, an' I've got four places to put every penny, but I'm just goin' to take tuppence out of it to buy that child a skippin'-rope,' an' she bought one an' here it is."

She brought it out from under her apron and exhibited it quite proudly. It was a strong, slender rope with a striped red and blue handle at each end, but Mary Lennox had never seen a skipping-rope before. She gazed at it with a mystified expression.

"What is it for?" she asked curiously.

"For!" cried out Martha. "Does tha' mean that they've not got skippin'-ropes in India, for all they've got elephants and tigers and camels! No wonder most of 'em's black. This is what it's for; just watch me."

And she ran into the middle of the room and, taking a handle in each hand, began to skip, and skip, and skip, while Mary turned in her chair to stare at her, and the queer faces in the old portraits seemed to stare at her, too, and wonder what on earth this common little cottager had the impudence to be doing under their very noses. But Martha did not even see them. The interest and curiosity in Mistress Mary's face delighted her, and she went on skipping and counted as she skipped until she had reached a hundred.

"I could skip longer than that," she said when she stopped. "I've skipped as much as five hundred when I was twelve, but I wasn't as fat then as I am now, an' I was in practice."

Mary got up from her chair beginning to feel excited herself.

"It looks nice," she said. "Your mother is a kind woman. Do you think I could ever skip like that?"

"You just try it," urged Martha, handing her the skipping-rope. "You can't skip a hundred at first, but if you practice you'll mount up. That's what mother said. She says, 'Nothin' will do her more good than skippin' rope. It's th' sensiblest toy a child can have. Let her play out in th' fresh air skippin' an' it'll stretch her legs an' arms an' give her some strength in 'em.'"

It was plain that there was not a great deal of strength in Mistress Mary's arms and legs when she first began to skip. She was not very clever at it, but she liked it so much that she did not want to stop.

"Put on tha' things and run an' skip out o' doors," said Martha. "Mother said I must tell you to keep out o' doors as much as you could, even when it rains a bit, so as tha' wrap up warm."

Mary put on her coat and hat and took her skipping-rope over her arm. She opened the door to go out, and then suddenly thought of something and turned back rather slowly.

"Martha," she said, "they were your wages. It was your two-pence really. Thank you." She said it stiffly because she was not used to thanking people or noticing that they did things for her. "Thank you," she said, and held out her hand because she did not know what else to do.

Martha gave her hand a clumsy little shake, as if she was not accustomed to this sort of thing either. Then she laughed. "Eh! th' art a queer, old-womanish thing," she said. "If tha'd been our 'Lizabeth Ellen tha'd have given me a kiss."

Mary looked stiffer than ever. "Do you want me to kiss you?"

Martha laughed again.

"Nay, not me," she answered. "If tha' was different, p'raps tha'd want to thysel'.But tha' isn't. Run off outside an' play with thy rope."

Mistress Mary felt a little awkward as she went out of the room. Yorkshire people seemed strange, and Martha was always rather a puzzle to her. At first she had disliked her very much, but now she did not.

The skipping-rope was a wonderful thing. She counted and skipped, and skipped and counted,

until her cheeks were quite red, and she was more interested than she had ever been since she was born. The sun was shining and a little wind was blowing—not a rough wind, but one which came in delightful little gusts and brought a fresh scent of newly turned earth with it.

She skipped round the fountain garden, and up one walk and down another. She skipped at last into the kitchen-garden and saw Ben Weatherstaff digging and talking to his robin, which was hopping about him. She skipped down the walk toward him and he lifted his head and looked at her with a curious expression. She had wondered if he would notice her. She wanted him to see her skip.

"Well!" he exclaimed. "Upon my word. P'raps tha' art a young 'un, after all, an' p'raps tha's got child's blood in thy veins instead of sour buttermilk. Tha's skipped red into thy cheeks as sure as my name's Ben Weatherstaff. I wouldn't have believed tha' could do it."

"I never skipped before," Mary said. "I'm just beginning. I can only go up to twenty."

"Tha' keep on," said Ben. "Tha' shapes well enough at it for a young 'un that's lived with heathen. Just see how he's watchin' thee," jerking his head toward the robin. "He followed after thee yesterday. He'll be at it again today. He'll be bound to find out what th' skippin'-rope is. He's never seen one. Eh!" shaking his head at the bird, "tha' curiosity will be th' death of thee sometime if tha' doesn't look sharp."

Mary skipped round all the gardens and round the orchard, resting every few minutes. At length she went to her own special walk and made up her mind to try if she could skip the whole length of it. It was a good long skip and she began slowly, but before she had gone half-way down the path she was so hot and breathless that she was obliged to stop. She did not mind much, because she had already counted up to thirty.

She stopped with a little laugh of pleasure, and there, lo and behold, was the robin swaying on a long branch of ivy. He had followed her and he greeted her with a chirp. As Mary had skipped toward him she felt something heavy in her pocket strike against her at each jump, and when she saw the robin she laughed again.

"You showed me where the key was yesterday," she said. "You ought to show me the door today; but I don't believe you know!"

The robin flew from his swinging spray of ivy on to the top of the wall and he opened his beak and sang a loud, lovely trill, merely to show off. Nothing in the world is quite as adorably lovely as a robin when he shows off—and they are nearly always doing it.

Mary Lennox had heard a great deal about Magic in her Ayah's stories, and she always said that what happened almost at that moment was Magic.

One of the nice little gusts of wind rushed down the walk, and it was a stronger one than the rest. It was strong enough to wave the branches of the trees, and it was more than strong enough to sway the trailing sprays of untrimmed ivy hanging from the wall. Mary had stepped close to the robin, and suddenly the gust of wind swung aside some loose ivy trails, and more

suddenly still she jumped toward it and caught it in her hand. This she did because she had seen something under it—a round knob which had been covered by the leaves hanging over it. It was the knob of a door.

She put her hands under the leaves and began to pull and push them aside. Thick as the ivy hung, it nearly all was a loose and swinging curtain, though some had crept over wood and iron.

Mary's heart began to thump and her hands to shake a little in her delight and excitement. The robin kept singing and twittering away and tilting his head on one side, as if he were as excited as she was. What was this under her hands which was square and made of iron and which her fingers found a hole in?

It was the lock of the door which had been closed ten years and she put her hand in her pocket, drew out the key and found it fitted the keyhole. She put the key in and turned it. It took two hands to do it, but it did turn.

And then she took a long breath and looked behind her up the long walk to see if any one was coming. No one was coming. No one ever did come, it seemed, and she took another long breath, because she could not help it, and she held back the swinging curtain of ivy and pushed back the door which opened slowly—slowly.

Then she slipped through it, and shut it behind her, and stood with her back against it, looking about her and breathing quite fast with excitement, and wonder, and delight.

She was standing inside the secret garden.

Chapter 9

The Strangest House Any One Ever Lived In

It was the sweetest, most mysterious-looking place any one could imagine. The high walls which shut it in were covered with the leafless stems of climbing roses, which were so thick that they were matted together. Mary Lennox knew they were roses because she had seen a great many roses in India. All the ground was covered with grass of a wintry brown, and out of it grew clumps of bushes which were surely rosebushes if they were alive. There were numbers of standard roses which had so spread their branches that they were like little trees.

There were other trees in the garden, and one of the things which made the place look strangest and loveliest was that climbing roses had run all over them and swung down long tendrils which made light swaying curtains, and here and there they had caught at each other or at a far-reaching branch and had crept from one tree to another and made lovely bridges of themselves.

There were neither leaves nor roses on them now and Mary did not know whether they were dead or alive, but their thin gray or brown branches and sprays looked like a sort of hazy mantle spreading over everything, walls, and trees, and even brown grass, where they had fallen from their fastenings and run along the ground. It was this hazy tangle from tree to tree which made it all look so mysterious. Mary had thought it must be different from other gardens which had not been left all by themselves so long; and indeed it was different from any other place she had ever seen in her life.

"How still it is!" she whispered. "How still!"

Then she waited a moment and listened at the stillness. The robin, who had flown to his treetop, was still as all the rest. He did not even flutter his wings; he sat without stirring, and looked at Mary.

"No wonder it is still," she whispered again. "I am the first person who has spoken in here for ten years."

She moved away from the door, stepping as softly as if she were afraid of awakening some one. She was glad that there was grass under her feet and that her steps made no sounds. She walked under one of the fairy-like gray arches between the trees and looked up at the sprays and tendrils which formed them.

"I wonder if they are all quite dead," she said. "Is it all a quite dead garden? I wish it wasn't."

If she had been Ben Weatherstaff she could have told whether the wood was alive by looking at it, but she could only see that there were only gray or brown sprays and branches and none showed any signs of even a tiny leaf-bud anywhere.

But she was inside the wonderful garden and, she could come through the door under the ivy any time, and she felt as if she had found a world all her own.

The sun was shining inside the four walls and the high arch of blue sky over this particular piece of Misselthwaite seemed even more brilliant and soft than it was over the moor. The robin flew down from his tree-top and hopped about or flew after her from one bush to another. He chirped a good deal and had a very busy air, as if he were showing her things.

Everything was strange and silent and she seemed to be hundreds of miles away from any one, but somehow she did not feel lonely at all. All that troubled her was her wish that she knew whether all the roses were dead, or if perhaps some of them had lived and might put out leaves and buds as the weather got warmer. She did not want it to be a quite dead garden. If it were a quite alive garden, how wonderful it would be, and what thousands of roses would grow on every side!

Her skipping-rope had hung over her arm when she came in and after she had walked about for a while she thought she would skip round the whole garden, stopping when she wanted to look at things. There seemed to have been grass paths here and there, and in one or two corners there were alcoves of evergreen with stone seats or tall moss-covered flower urns in them.

As she came near the second of these alcoves she stopped skipping. There had once been a flowerbed in it, and she thought she saw something sticking out of the black earth—some sharp little pale green points. She remembered what Ben Weatherstaff had said and she knelt down to look at them.

"Yes, they are tiny growing things and they might be

crocuses or snowdrops or daffodils," she whispered.

She bent very close to them and sniffed the fresh scent of the damp earth. She liked it very much.

"Perhaps there are some other ones coming up in other places," she said. "I will go all over the garden and look."

She did not skip, but walked. She went slowly and kept her eyes on the ground. She looked in the old border beds and among the grass, and after she had gone round, trying to miss nothing, she had found ever so many more sharp, pale green points, and she had become quite excited again.

"It isn't a quite dead garden," she cried out softly to herself. "Even if the roses are dead, there are other things alive."

She did not know anything about gardening, but the grass seemed so thick in some of the places where the green points were pushing their way through that she thought they did not seem to have room enough to grow. She searched about until she found a rather sharp piece of wood and knelt down and dug and weeded out the weeds and grass until she made nice little clear places around them.

"Now they look as if they could breathe," she said, after she had finished with the first ones. "I am going to do ever so many more. I'll do all I can see. If I haven't time today I can come tomorrow."

She went from place to place, and dug and weeded, and enjoyed herself so immensely that she was led on from bed to bed and into the grass under the trees. The exercise made her so warm that she first threw her coat off, and then her hat, and without knowing it she was smiling down on to the grass and the pale green points all the time.

The robin was tremendously busy. He was very much pleased to see gardening begun on his own estate. He had often wondered at Ben Weatherstaff. Where gardening is done all sorts of delightful things to eat are turned up with the soil. Now here was this new kind of creature who was not half Ben's size and yet had had the sense to come into his garden and begin at once.

Mistress Mary worked in her garden until it was time to go to her midday dinner. In fact, she was rather late in remembering, and when she put on her coat and hat, and picked up her skipping-rope, she could not believe that she had been working two or three hours. She had been actually happy all the time; and dozens and dozens of the tiny, pale green points were to be seen in cleared places, looking twice as cheerful as they had looked before when the grass and weeds had been smothering them.

"I shall come back this afternoon," she said, looking all round at her new kingdom, and speaking to the trees and the rose-bushes as if they heard her.

Then she ran lightly across the grass, pushed open the slow old door and slipped through it under the ivy.

She had such red cheeks and such bright eyes and ate such a dinner that Martha was delighted.

"Two pieces o' meat an' two helps o' rice puddin'!" she said. "Eh! Mother will be pleased when I tell her what th' skippin'-rope's done for thee."

In the course of her digging with her pointed stick

Mistress Mary had found herself digging up a sort of white root rather like an onion. She had put it back in its place and patted the earth carefully down on it, and just now she wondered if Martha could tell her what it was.

"Martha," she said, "what are those white roots that look like onions?"

"They're bulbs," answered Martha. "Lots o' spring flowers grow from 'em. Th' very little ones are snowdrops an' crocuses an' th' big ones are narcissuses an' jonquils and daffydowndillys. Th' biggest of all is  lilies an' purple flags. Eh! they are nice. Dickon's got a whole lot of 'em planted in our bit o' garden."

"Does Dickon know all about them?" asked Mary, a new idea taking possession of her.

"Our Dickon can make a flower grow out of a brick walk. Mother says he just whispers things out o' th' ground."

"Do bulbs live a long time? Would they live years and years if no one helped them?" inquired Mary anxiously.

"They're things as helps themselves," said Martha. "That's why poor folk can afford to have 'em. If you don't trouble 'em, most of 'em'll work away underground for a lifetime an' spread out an' have little 'uns. There's a place in th' park woods here where there's snowdrops by thousands. They're the prettiest sight in Yorkshire when th' spring comes. No one knows when they was first planted."

"I wish the spring was here now," said Mary. "I want

to see all the things that grow in England."

She had finished her dinner and gone to her favorite seat on the hearth rug.

"I wish—I wish I had a little spade," she said. "Whatever does tha' want a spade for?" asked Martha, laughing. "Art tha' goin' to take to diggin'? I must tell Mother that, too."

Mary looked at the fire and pondered a little. She must be careful if she meant to keep her secret kingdom. She wasn't doing any harm, but if Mr. Craven found out about the open door, he would be fearfully angry and get a new key and lock it up forevermore. She really could not bear that.

"This is such a big lonely place," she said slowly, as if she were turning matters over in her mind. "The house is lonely, and the park is lonely, and the gardens are lonely. So many places seem shut up. I never did many things in India, but there were more people to look at— natives and soldiers marching by—and sometimes bands playing, and my Ayah told me stories. There is no one to talk to here except you and Ben Weatherstaff. And you have to do your work and Ben Weatherstaff won't speak to me often. I thought if I had a little spade I could dig somewhere as he does, and I might make a little garden if he would give me some seeds."

Martha's face quite lighted up.

"There now!" she exclaimed, "if that wasn't one of th' things Mother said. She says, 'There's such a lot o' room in that big place, why don't they give her a bit for herself, even if she doesn't plant nothin' but parsley an' radishes? She'd dig an' rake away an' be right down happy over it.' Them was the very words she said."

"Were they?" said Mary. "How many things she knows, doesn't she?"

"Eh!" said Martha. "It's like she says: 'A woman as brings up twelve children learns something besides her A B C. Children's as good as 'rithmetic to set you findin' out things.'"

"How much would a spade cost—a little one?" Mary asked.

"Well," was Martha's reflective answer, "at Thwaite village there's a shop or so an' I saw little garden sets with a spade an' a rake an' a fork all tied together for two shillings. An' they was stout enough to work with, too."

"I've got more than that in my purse," said Mary. "Mrs. Morrison gave me five shillings and Mrs. Medlock gave me some money from Mr. Craven."

"Did he remember thee that much?" exclaimed Martha.

"Mrs. Medlock said I was to have a shilling a week to spend. She gives me one every Saturday. I didn't know what to spend it on."

"My word! that's riches," said Martha. "Tha' can buy anything in th' world tha' wants. Th' rent of our cottage is only one an' threepence an' it's like pullin' eye-teeth to get it. Now I've just thought of somethin'," putting her hands on her hips.

"What?" said Mary eagerly.

"In the shop at Thwaite they sell packages o' flower-seeds for a penny each, and our Dickon he knows which is th' prettiest ones an' how to make 'em grow. He walks over to Thwaite many a day just for th' fun of it. Does tha' know how to print letters?" suddenly.

"I know how to write," Mary answered.

Martha shook her head.

"Our Dickon can only read printin'. If tha' could print we could write a letter to him an' ask him to go an' buy th' garden tools an' th' seeds at th' same time."

"Oh! you're a good girl!" Mary cried. "You are, really! I didn't know you were so nice. I know I can print letters if I try. Let's ask Mrs. Medlock for a pen and ink and some paper."

"I've got some of my own," said Martha. "I bought 'em so I could print a bit of a letter to Mother of a Sunday. I'll go and get it."

She ran out of the room, and Mary stood by the fire and twisted her thin little hands together with sheer pleasure. "If I have a spade," she whispered, "I can make the earth nice and soft and dig up weeds. If I have seeds and can make flowers grow, the garden won't be dead at all—it will come alive."

She did not go out again that afternoon because when Martha returned with her pen and ink and paper she was obliged to clear the table and carry the plates and dishes downstairs and when she got into the kitchen Mrs. Medlock was there and told her to do something, so Mary waited for what seemed to her a long time before she came back.

Then it was a serious piece of work to write to Dickon. Mary had been taught very little because her governesses had disliked her too much to stay with her. She could not spell particularly well but she found that she could print letters when she tried. This was the letter Martha dictated to her:

My Dear Dicko,

This comes hoping to find you well as it leaves me at present. Miss Mary has plenty of money and will you go to Thwaite and buy her some flower seeds and a set of garden tools to make a flowerbed. Pick the prettiest ones and easy to grow because she has never done it before and lived in India which is different. Give my love to mother and every one of you. Miss Mary is going to tell me a lot more so that on my next day out you can hear about elephants and camels and gentlemen going hunting lions and tigers.

Your loving sister,
Martha Phoebe Sowerby.

"We'll put the money in th' envelope an' I'll get th' butcher boy to take it in his cart. He's a great friend o' Dickon's," said Martha.

"How shall I get the things when Dickon buys them?"

"He'll bring 'em to you himself. He'll like to walk over this way."

"Oh!" exclaimed Mary, "then I shall see him! I never thought I should see Dickon."

"Does tha' want to see him?" asked Martha suddenly, for Mary had looked so pleased.

"Yes, I do. I never saw a boy foxes and crows loved. I want to see him very much."

Martha gave a little start, as if she remembered something. "Now to think," she broke out, "to think o' me forgettin' that there; an' I thought I was goin' to tell you first thing this mornin'. I asked mother—and she said she'd ask Mrs. Medlock her own self."

"Do you mean—" Mary began.

"What I said Tuesday. Ask her if you might be driven over to our cottage some day and have a bit o' mother's hot oat cake, an' butter, an' a glass o' milk."

It seemed as if all the interesting things were happening in one day. To think of going over the moor in the daylight and when the sky was blue! To think of going into the cottage which held twelve children!

"Does she think Mrs. Medlock would let me go?" she asked, quite anxiously.

"Aye, she thinks she would. She knows what a tidy woman mother is and how clean she keeps the cottage."

"If I went I should see your mother as well as Dickon," said Mary, thinking it over and liking the idea very much. "She doesn't seem to be like the mothers in India."

Her work in the garden and the excitement of the afternoon ended by making her feel quiet and thoughtful. Martha stayed with her until tea-time, but they sat in comfortable quiet and talked very little. But just before Martha went downstairs for the tea-tray, Mary asked a question.

"Martha," she said, "has the scullery-maid had the toothache again today?"

Martha certainly started slightly. "What makes thee ask that?" she said.

"Because when I waited so long for you to come back I opened the door and walked down the corridor to see if you were coming. And I heard that far-off crying again, just as we heard it the other night. There isn't a wind today, so you see it couldn't have been the wind."

"Eh!" said Martha restlessly. "Tha' mustn't go walkin' about in corridors an' listenin'. Mr. Craven would be that there angry there's no knowin' what he'd do."

"I wasn't listening," said Mary. "I was just waiting for you—and I heard it. That's three times."

"My word! There's Mrs. Medlock's bell," said Martha, and she almost ran out of the room.

"It's the strangest house any one ever lived in," said Mary drowsily, as she dropped her head on the cushioned seat of the armchair near her. Fresh air, and digging, and skipping-rope had made her feel so comfortably tired that she fell asleep.

Chapter 10

Dickon

The sun shone down for nearly a week on the secret garden. The Secret Garden was what Mary called it when she was thinking of it. She liked the name, and she liked still more the feeling that when its beautiful old walls shut her in, no one knew where she was. It seemed almost like being shut out of the world in some fairy place.

The few books she had read and liked had been fairy-story books, and she had read of secret gardens in some of the stories. Sometimes people went to sleep in them for a hundred years, which she had thought must be rather stupid. She had no intention of going to sleep, and, in fact, she was becoming wider awake every day which passed at Misselthwaite. She was beginning to like to be out of doors; she no longer hated the wind, but enjoyed it. She could run faster, and longer, and she could skip up to a hundred.

The bulbs in the secret garden must have been much astonished. Such nice clear places were made round them that they had all the breathing space they wanted, and really, if Mistress Mary had known it, they began to cheer up under the dark earth and work tremendously.

The sun could get at them and warm them, and when the rain came down it could reach them at once, so they began to feel very much alive.

Mary was an odd, determined little person, and now she had something interesting to be determined about, she was very much absorbed, indeed. She worked and dug and pulled up weeds steadily, only becoming more pleased with her work every hour instead of tiring of it. It seemed to her like a fascinating sort of play.

She found many more of the sprouting pale green points than she had ever hoped to find. They seemed to be starting up everywhere and each day she was sure she found tiny new ones, some so tiny that they barely peeped above the earth. There were so many that she remembered what Martha had said about the "snowdrops by the thousands," and about bulbs spreading and making new ones. These had been left to themselves for ten years and perhaps they had spread, like the snowdrops, into thousands. She wondered how long it would be before they showed that they were flowers. Sometimes she stopped digging to look at the garden and try to imagine what it would be like when it was covered with thousands of lovely things in bloom.

During that week of sunshine, she became more intimate with Ben Weatherstaff. She surprised him several times by seeming to start up beside him as if she sprang out of the earth. The truth was that she was afraid that he would pick up his tools and go away if he saw her coming, so she always walked toward him as silently as possible.

But, in fact, he did not object to her as strongly as he had at first. Perhaps he was secretly rather flattered by her evident desire for his elderly company. Then, also, she was more civil than she had been. He did not know that when she first saw him she spoke to him as she would have spoken to a native, and had not known that a cross, sturdy old Yorkshire man was not accustomed to salaam to his masters, and be merely commanded by them to do things.

"Tha'rt like th' robin," he said to her one morning when he lifted his head and saw her standing by him. "I never knows when I shall see thee or which side tha'll come from."

"He's friends with me now," said Mary.

"That's like him," snapped Ben Weatherstaff. "Makin' up to th' women folk just for vanity an' flightiness. There's nothin' he wouldn't do for th' sake o' showin' off an' flirtin' his tail-feathers. He's as full o' pride as an egg's full o' meat."

He very seldom talked much and sometimes did not even answer Mary's questions except by a grunt, but this morning he said more than usual. He stood up and rested one hobnailed boot on the top of his spade while he looked her over.

"How long has tha' been here?" he jerked out.

"I think it's about a month," she answered.

"Tha's beginnin' to do Misselthwaite credit," he said. "Tha's a bit fatter than tha' was an' tha's not quite so yeller. Tha' looked like a young plucked crow when tha' first came into this garden. Thinks I to myself I never set eyes on an uglier, sourer faced young 'un."

Mary was not vain and as she had never thought much of her looks she was not greatly disturbed.

"I know I'm fatter," she said. "My stockings are getting tighter. They used to make wrinkles. There's the robin, Ben Weatherstaff."

There, indeed, was the robin, and she thought he looked nicer than ever. His red waistcoat was as glossy as satin and he flirted his wings and tail and tilted his head and hopped about with all sorts of lively graces. He seemed determined to make Ben Weatherstaff admire him. But Ben was sarcastic.

"Aye, there tha' art!" he said. "Tha' can put up with me for a bit sometimes when tha's got no one better. Tha's been reddenin' up thy waistcoat an' polishin' thy feathers this two weeks. I know what tha's up to. Tha's courtin' some bold young madam somewhere tellin' thy lies to her about bein' th' finest cock robin on Missel Moor an' ready to fight all th' rest of 'em."

"Oh! look at him!" exclaimed Mary.

The robin was evidently in a fascinating, bold mood. He hopped closer and closer and looked at Ben Weatherstaff more and more engagingly. He flew on to the nearest currant bush and tilted his head and sang a little song right at him.

"Tha' thinks tha'll get over me by doin' that," said Ben, wrinkling his face up in such a way that Mary felt sure he was trying not to look pleased. "Tha' thinks no one can stand out against thee—that's what tha' thinks."

The robin spread his wings—Mary could scarcely

believe her eyes. He flew right up to the handle of Ben Weatherstaff's spade and alighted on the top of it. Then the old man's face wrinkled itself slowly into a new expression. He stood still as if he were afraid to breathe—as if he would not have stirred for the world, lest his robin should start away.

He spoke quite in a whisper. "Well, I'm danged!" he said as softly as if he were saying something quite different. "Tha' does know how to get at a chap—tha' does! Tha's fair unearthly, tha's so knowin'."

And he stood without stirring—almost without drawing his breath—until the robin gave another flirt to his wings and flew away. Then he stood looking at the handle of the spade as if there might be Magic in it, and then he began to dig again and said nothing for several minutes.

But because he kept breaking into a slow grin now and then, Mary was not afraid to talk to him.

"Have you a garden of your own?" she asked.

"No. I'm bachelder an' lodge with Martin at th' gate."

"If you had one," said Mary, "what would you plant?"

"Cabbages an' 'taters an' onions."

"But if you wanted to make a flower garden," persisted Mary, "what would you plant?"

"Bulbs an' sweet-smellin' things—but mostly roses."

Mary's face lighted up.

"Do you like roses?" she said.

Ben Weatherstaff rooted up a weed and threw it aside before he answered. "Well, yes, I do. I was learned that by a young lady I was gardener to. She had a lot in a place she was fond of, an' she loved 'em like they was children—or robins. I've seen her bend over an' kiss 'em." He dragged out another weed and scowled at it. "That were as much as ten year' ago."

"Where is she now?" asked Mary, much interested.

"Heaven," he answered, and drove his spade deep into the soil, "'cording to what parson says."

"What happened to the roses?" Mary asked again, more interested than ever.

"They was left to themselves."

Mary was becoming quite excited. "Did they quite die? Do roses quite die when they are left to themselves?" she ventured.

"Well, I'd got to like 'em—an' I liked her—an' she liked 'em," Ben Weatherstaff admitted reluctantly. "Once or twice a year I'd go an' work at 'em a bit—prune 'em an' dig about th' roots. They run wild, but they was in rich soil, so some of 'em lived."

"When they have no leaves and look gray and brown and dry, how can you tell whether they are dead or alive?" inquired Mary.

"Wait till th' spring gets at 'em—wait till th' sun shines on th' rain and th' rain falls on th' sunshine an' then tha'll find out."

"How—how?" cried Mary, forgetting to be careful. "Look along th' twigs an' branches an' if tha' see a bit of a brown lump swelling here an' there, watch it after th' warm rain an' see what happens." He stopped suddenly and looked curiously at her eager face. "Why does tha' care so much about roses an' such, all of a sudden?" he demanded.

Mistress Mary felt her face grow red. She was almost afraid to answer. "I—I want to play that—that I have a garden of my own," she stammered. "I—there is nothing for me to do. I have nothing—and no one."

"Well," said Ben Weatherstaff slowly, as he watched her, "that's true. Tha' hasn't."

He said it in such an odd way that Mary wondered if he was actually a little sorry for her. She had never felt sorry for herself; she had only felt tired and cross, because she disliked people and things so much. But now the world seemed to be changing and getting nicer. If no one found out about the secret garden, she should enjoy herself always.

She stayed with him for ten or fifteen minutes longer and asked him as many questions as she dared. He answered every one of them in his queer grunting way and he did not seem really cross and did not pick up his spade and leave her.

He said something about roses just as she was going away and it reminded her of the ones he had said he had been fond of.

"Do you go and see those other roses now?" she asked.

"Not been this year. My rheumatics has made me too stiff in th' joints." He said it in his grumbling voice, and then quite suddenly he seemed to get angry with her, though she did not see why he should.

"Now look here!" he said sharply. "Don't tha' ask so many questions. Tha'rt th' worst wench for askin' questions I've ever come a cross. Get thee gone an' play thee. I've done talkin' for today."

And he said it so crossly that she knew there was not the least use in staying another minute. She went skipping slowly down the outside walk, thinking him over and saying to herself that, queer as it was, here was another person whom she liked in spite of his crossness. She liked old Ben Weatherstaff. Yes, she did like him. She always wanted to try to make him talk to her. Also she began to believe that he knew everything in the world about flowers.

There was a laurel-hedged walk which curved round the secret garden and ended at a gate which opened into a wood, in the park. She thought she would slip round this walk and look into the wood and see if there were any rabbits hopping about. She enjoyed the skipping very much and when she reached the little gate she opened it and went through because she heard a low, peculiar whistling sound and wanted to find out what it was.

It was a very strange thing indeed. She quite caught her breath as she stopped to look at it. A boy was sitting under a tree, with his back against it, playing on a rough wooden pipe. He was a funny looking boy about twelve. He looked very clean and his nose turned up and his cheeks were as red as poppies, and never had Mistress Mary seen such round and such blue eyes in any boy's face.

And on the trunk of the tree he leaned against, a brown squirrel was clinging and watching him, and from behind a bush nearby a cock pheasant was delicately stretching his neck to peep out, and quite near him were two rabbits sitting up and sniffing with tremulous noses—and actually it appeared as if they were all drawing near to watch him and listen to the strange low little call his pipe seemed to make.

When he saw Mary he held up his hand and spoke to her in a voice almost as low as and rather like his piping. "Don't tha' move," he said. "It'd flight 'em."

Mary remained motionless. He stopped playing his pipe and began to rise from the ground. He moved so slowly that it scarcely seemed as though he were moving at all, but at last he stood on his feet and then the squirrel scampered back up into the branches of his tree, the pheasant withdrew his head and the rabbits dropped on all fours and began to hop away, though not at all as if they were frightened.

"I'm Dickon," the boy said. "I know tha'rt Miss Mary."

Then Mary realized that somehow she had known at first that he was Dickon. Who else could have been charming rabbits and pheasants as the natives charm snakes in India? He had a wide, red, curving mouth and his smile spread all over his face.

"I got up slow," he explained, "because if tha' makes a quick move it startles 'em. A body 'as to move gentle an' speak low when wild things is about."

He did not speak to her as if they had never seen each other before, but as if he knew her quite well. Mary knew nothing about boys and she spoke to him a little stiffly because she felt rather shy.

"Did you get Martha's letter?" she asked.

He nodded his curly, rust-colored head. "That's why I come."

He stooped to pick up something which had been

lying on the ground beside him when he piped. "I've got th' garden tools. There's a little spade an' rake an' a fork an' hoe. Eh! they are good 'uns. There's a trowel, too. An' th' woman in th' shop threw in a packet o' white poppy an' one o' blue larkspur when I bought th' other seeds."

"Will you show the seeds to me?" Mary said.

She wished she could talk as he did. His speech was so quick and easy. It sounded as if he liked her and was not the least afraid she would not like him, though he was only a common moor boy, in patched clothes and with a funny face and a rough, rusty-red head.

As she came closer to him she noticed that there was a clean fresh scent of heather and grass and leaves about him, almost as if he were made of them. She liked it very much and when she looked into his funny face with the red cheeks and round blue eyes she forgot that she had felt shy.

"Let us sit down on this log and look at them," she said.

They sat down and he took a clumsy little brown paper package out of his coat pocket. He untied the string and inside there were ever so many neater and smaller packages with a picture of a flower on each one.

"There's a lot o' mignonette an' poppies," he said. "Mignonette's th' sweetest smellin' thing as grows, an' it'll grow wherever you cast it, same as poppies will. Them as'll come up an' bloom if you just whistle to 'em, them's th' nicest of all."

He stopped and turned his head quickly, his poppy-cheeked face lighting up. "Where's that robin as is callin' us?" he said.

The chirp came from a thick holly bush, bright with scarlet berries, and Mary thought she knew whose it was.

"Is it really calling us?" she asked.

"Aye," said Dickon, as if it was the most natural thing in the world, "he's callin' some one he's friends with. That's same as sayin' 'Here I am. Look at me. I wants a bit of a chat.' There he is in the bush. Whose is he?"

"He's Ben Weatherstaff's, but I think he knows me a little," answered Mary.

"Aye, he knows thee," said Dickon in his low voice again. "An' he likes thee. He's took thee on. He'll tell me all about thee in a minute."

He moved quite close to the bush with the slow movement Mary had noticed before, and then he made a sound almost like the robin's own twitter. The robin listened a few seconds, intently, and then answered quite as if he were replying to a question.

"Aye, he's a friend o' yours," chuckled Dickon.

"Do you think he is?" cried Mary eagerly. She did so want to know. "Do you think he really likes me?"

"He wouldn't come near thee if he didn't," answered Dickon. "Birds is rare choosers an' a robin can flout a body worse than a man. See, he's making up to thee now. 'Cannot tha' see a chap?' he's sayin'."

And it really seemed as if it must be true. He so sidled and twittered and tilted as he hopped on his bush.

"Do you understand everything birds say?" said Mary.

Dickon's grin spread until he seemed all wide, red, curving mouth, and he rubbed his rough head. "I think I do, and they think I do," he said. "I've lived on th' moor with 'em so long. I've watched 'em break shell an' come out an' fledge an' learn to fly an' begin to sing, till I think I'm one of 'em. Sometimes I think p'raps I'm a bird, or a fox, or a rabbit, or a squirrel, or even a beetle, an' I don't know it."

He laughed and came back to the log and began to talk about the flower seeds again. He told her what they looked like when they were flowers; he told her how to plant them, and watch them, and feed and water them.

"See here," he said suddenly, turning round to look at her. "I'll plant them for thee myself. Where is tha' garden?"

Mary's thin hands clutched each other as they lay on her lap. She did not know what to say, so for a whole minute she said nothing. She had never thought of this. She felt miserable. And she felt as if she went red and then pale.

"Tha's got a bit o' garden, hasn't tha'?" Dickon said.

It was true that she had turned red and then pale. Dickon saw her do it, and as she still said nothing, he began to be puzzled.

"Wouldn't they give thee a bit?" he asked. "Hasn't tha' got any yet?"

She held her hands tighter and turned her eyes toward him. "I don't know anything about boys," she said slowly. "Could you keep a secret, if I told you one? It's a great secret. I don't know what I should do if any one found it out. I believe I should die!" She said the last sentence quite fiercely.

Dickon looked more puzzled than ever and even rubbed his hand over his rough head again, but he answered quite good-humoredly. "I'm keepin' secrets all th' time," he said. "If I couldn't keep secrets from th' other lads, secrets about foxes' cubs, an' birds' nests, an' wild things' holes, there'd be naught safe on th' moor. Aye, I can keep secrets."

Mistress Mary did not mean to put out her hand and clutch his sleeve but she did it. "I've stolen a garden," she said very fast. "It isn't mine. It isn't anybody's. Nobody wants it, nobody cares for it, nobody ever goes into it. Perhaps everything is dead in it already. I don't know."

She began to feel hot and as contrary as she had ever felt in her life. "I don't care, I don't care! Nobody has any right to take it from me when I care about it and they don't. They're letting it die, all shut in by itself," she ended passionately, and she threw her arms over her face and burst out crying—poor little Mistress Mary.

Dickon's curious blue eyes grew rounder and rounder. "Eh-h-h!" he said, drawing his exclamation out slowly, and the way he did it meant both wonder and sympathy.

"I've nothing to do," said Mary. "Nothing belongs to me. I found it myself and I got into it myself. I was only just like the robin, and they wouldn't take it from the robin." "Where is it?" asked Dickon in a dropped voice.

Mistress Mary got up from the log at once. She knew she felt contrary again, and obstinate, and she did not care at all. She was imperious and Indian, and at the same time hot and sorrowful.

"Come with me and I'll show you," she said.

She led him round the laurel path and to the walk where the ivy grew so thickly. Dickon followed her with a queer, almost pitying, look on his face. He felt as if he were being led to look at some strange bird's nest and must move softly.

When she stepped to the wall and lifted the hanging ivy he started. There was a door and Mary pushed it slowly open and they passed in together, and then Mary stood and waved her hand round defiantly.

"It's this," she said. "It's a secret garden, and I'm the only one in the world who wants it to be alive."

Dickon looked round and round about it, and round and round again.

"Eh!" he almost whispered, "it is a queer, pretty place! It's like as if a body was in a dream."

Chapter 11

The Nest of the Missel Thrush

For two or three minutes he stood looking round him, while Mary watched him, and then he began to walk about softly, even more lightly than Mary had walked the first time she had found herself inside the four walls. His eyes seemed to be taking in everything—the gray trees with the gray creepers climbing over them and hanging from their branches, the tangle on the walls and among the grass, the evergreen alcoves with the stone seats and tall flower urns standing in them.

"I never thought I'd see this place," he said at last, in a whisper.

"Did you know about it?" asked Mary.

She had spoken aloud and he made a sign to her. "We must talk low," he said, "or some one'll hear us an' wonder what's to do in here."

"Oh! I forgot!" said Mary, feeling frightened and putting her hand quickly against her mouth. "Did you know about the garden?" she asked again when she had recovered herself.

Dickon nodded. "Martha told me there was one as no one ever went inside," he answered. "Us used to wonder what it was like."

He stopped and looked round at the lovely gray tangle about him, and his round eyes looked queerly happy.

"Eh! the nests as'll be here come springtime," he said. "It'd be th' safest nestin' place in England. No one never comin' near an' tangles o' trees an' roses to build in. I wonder all th' birds on th' moor don't build here."

Mistress Mary put her hand on his arm again without knowing it.

"Will there be roses?" she whispered. "Can you tell? I thought perhaps they were all dead."

"Eh! No! Not them—not all of 'em!" he answered. "Look here!"

He stepped over to the nearest tree—an old, old one with gray lichen all over its bark, but upholding a curtain of tangled sprays and branches. He took a thick knife out of his Pocket and opened one of its blades.

"There's lots o' dead wood as ought to be cut out," he said. "An' there's a lot o' old wood, but it made some new last year. This here's a new bit," and he touched a shoot which looked brownish green instead of hard, dry gray.

Mary touched it herself in an eager, reverent way. "That one?" she said. "Is that one quite alive quite?"

Dickon curved his wide smiling mouth. "It's as wick as you or me," he said; and Mary remembered that Martha had told her that "wick" meant "alive" or "lively."

"I'm glad it's wick!" she cried out in her whisper. "I want them all to be wick. Let us go round the garden and count how many wick ones there are."

She quite panted with eagerness, and Dickon was as eager as she was. They went from tree to tree and from bush to bush. Dickon carried his knife in his hand and showed her things which she thought wonderful.

"They've run wild," he said, "but th' strongest ones has fair thrived on it. The delicatest ones has died out, but th' others has growed an' growed, an' spread an' spread, till they's a wonder. See here!" and he pulled down a thick gray, dry-looking branch. "A body might think this was dead wood, but I don't believe it is—down to th' root. I'll cut it low down an' see."

He knelt and with his knife cut the lifeless-looking branch through, not far above the earth.

"There!" he said exultantly. "I told thee so. There's green in that wood yet. Look at it."

Mary was down on her knees before he spoke, gazing with all her might.

"When it looks a bit greenish an' juicy like that, it's wick," he explained. "When th' inside is dry an' breaks easy, like this here piece I've cut off, it's done for. There's a big root here as all this live wood sprung out of, an' if th' old wood's cut off an' it's dug round, and took care of there'll be—" he stopped and lifted his face to look up at the climbing and hanging sprays above him—"there'll be a fountain o' roses here this summer."

They went from bush to bush and from tree to tree. He was very strong and clever with his knife and knew how to cut the dry and dead wood away, and could tell when an unpromising bough or twig had still green life in it.

In the course of half an hour Mary thought she could tell too, and when he cut through a lifeless-looking branch she would cry out joyfully under her breath when she caught sight of the least shade of moist green. The spade, and hoe, and fork were very useful. He showed her how to use the fork while he dug about roots with the spade and stirred the earth and let the air in.

They were working industriously round one of the biggest standard roses when he caught sight of something which made him utter an exclamation of surprise.

"Why!" he cried, pointing to the grass a few feet away. "Who did that there?"

It was one of Mary's own little clearings round the pale green points.

"I did it," said Mary.

"Why, I thought tha' didn't know nothin' about gardenin'," he exclaimed.

"I don't," she answered, "but they were so little, and the grass was so thick and strong, and they looked as if they had no room to breathe. So I made a place for them. I don't even know what they are."

Dickon went and knelt down by them, smiling his wide smile. "Tha' was right," he said. "A gardener couldn't have told thee better. They'll grow now like Jack's bean-stalk. They're crocuses an' snowdrops, an' these here is narcissuses," turning to another patch, "an here's daffydowndillys. Eh! they will be a sight."

He ran from one clearing to another.

"Tha' has done a lot o' work for such a little wench," he said, looking her over.

"I'm growing fatter," said Mary, "and I'm growing stronger. I used always to be tired. When I dig I'm not tired at all. I like to smell the earth when it's turned up."

"It's rare good for thee," he said, nodding his head wisely. "There's naught as nice as th' smell o' good clean earth, except th' smell o' fresh growin' things when th' rain falls on 'em. I get out on th' moor many a day when it's rainin' an' I lie under a bush an' listen to th' soft swish o' drops on th' heather an' I just sniff an' sniff. My nose end fair quivers like a rabbit's, mother says."

"Do you never catch cold?" inquired Mary, gazing at him wonderingly. She had never seen such a funny boy, or such a nice one.

"Not me," he said, grinning. "I never ketched cold since I was born. I wasn't brought up nesh enough. I've chased about th' moor in all weathers same as th' rabbits does. Mother says I've sniffed up too much fresh air for twelve year' to ever get to sniffin' with cold. I'm as tough as a white-thorn knobstick."

He was working all the time he was talking and Mary was following him and helping him with her fork or the trowel.

"There's a lot of work to do here!" he said once, looking about quite exultantly.

"Will you come again and help me to do it?" Mary begged. "I'm sure I can help, too. I can dig and pull up weeds, and do whatever you tell me. Oh! do come, Dickon!"

"I'll come every day if tha' wants me, rain or shine," he answered stoutly. "It's the best fun I ever had in my life—shut in here an' wakenin' up a garden."

"If you will come," said Mary, "if you will help me to make it alive I'll—I don't know what I'll do," she ended helplessly. What could you do for a boy like that?

"I'll tell thee what tha'll do," said Dickon, with his happy grin. "Tha'll get fat an' tha'll get as hungry as a young fox an' tha'll learn how to talk to th' robin same as I do. Eh! we'll have a lot o' fun."

He began to walk about, looking up in the trees and at the walls and bushes with a thoughtful expression.

"I wouldn't want to make it look like a gardener's garden, all clipped an' spick an' span, would you?" he said. "It's nicer like this with things runnin' wild, an' swingin' an' catchin' hold of each other."

"Don't let us make it tidy," said Mary anxiously. "It wouldn't seem like a secret garden if it was tidy."

Dickon stood rubbing his rusty-red head with a rather puzzled look. "It's a secret garden sure enough," he said, "but seems like some one besides th' robin must have been in it since it was shut up ten year' ago."

"But the door was locked and the key was buried," said Mary. "No one could get in."

"That's true," he answered. "It's a queer place. Seems to me as if there'd been a bit o' prunin' done here an' there, later than ten year' ago."

"But how could it have been done?" said Mary.

He was examining a branch of a standard rose and he shook his head. "Aye! how could it!" he murmured. "With th' door locked an' th' key buried."

Mistress Mary always felt that however many years she lived she should never forget that first morning when her garden began to grow. Of course, it did seem to begin to grow for her that morning. When Dickon began to clear places to plant seeds, she remembered what Basil had sung at her when he wanted to tease her.

"Are there any flowers that look like bells?" she inquired.

"Lilies o' th' valley does," he answered, digging

away with the trowel, "an' there's Canterbury bells, an' campanulas."

"Let's plant some," said Mary. "There's lilies o' th, valley here already; I saw 'em. They'll have growed too close an' we'll have to separate 'em, but there's plenty. Th' other ones takes two years to bloom from seed, but I can bring you some bits o' plants from our cottage garden. Why does tha' want 'em?"

Then Mary told him about Basil and his brothers and sisters in India and of how she had hated them and of their calling her "Mistress Mary Quite Contrary."

"They used to dance round and sing at me. They sang—

'Mistress Mary, quite contrary,
How does your garden grow?
With silver bells, and cockle shells,
And marigolds all in a row.'

I just remembered it and it made me wonder if there were really flowers like silver bells."

She frowned a little and gave her trowel a rather spiteful dig into the earth. "I wasn't as contrary as they were."

But Dickon laughed.

"Eh!" he said, and as he crumbled the rich black soil she saw he was sniffing up the scent of it. "There doesn't seem to be no need for no one to be contrary when there's flowers an' such like, an' such lots o' friendly wild things runnin' about makin' homes for themselves, or buildin' nests an' singin' an' whistlin', does there?"

Mary, kneeling by him holding the seeds, looked at him and stopped frowning.

"Dickon," she said, "you are as nice as Martha said you were. I like you, and you make the fifth person. I never thought I should like five people."

Dickon sat up on his heels as Martha did when she was polishing the grate. He did look funny and delightful, Mary thought, with his round blue eyes and red cheeks and happy looking turned-up nose.

"Only five folk as tha' likes?" he said. "Who is th' other four?"

"Your mother and Martha," Mary checked them off on her fingers, "and the robin and Ben Weatherstaff."

Dickon laughed so that he was obliged to stifle the sound by putting his arm over his mouth. "I know tha' thinks I'm a queer lad," he said, "but I think tha' art th' queerest little lass I ever saw."

Then Mary did a strange thing. She leaned forward and asked him a question she had never dreamed of asking any one before. And she tried to ask it in Yorkshire because that was his language, and in India a native was always pleased if you knew his speech.

"Does tha' like me?" she said.

"Eh!" he answered heartily, "that I does. I likes thee wonderful, an' so does th' robin, I do believe!"

"That's two, then," said Mary. "That's two for me."

And then they began to work harder than ever and more joyfully. Mary was startled and sorry when she heard the big clock in the courtyard strike the hour of her midday dinner.

"I shall have to go," she said mournfully. "And you

will have to go too, won't you?"

Dickon grinned. "My dinner's easy to carry about with me," he said. "Mother always lets me put a bit o' somethin' in my pocket."

He picked up his coat from the grass and brought out of a pocket a lumpy little bundle tied up in a quite clean, coarse, blue and white handkerchief. It held two thick pieces of bread with a slice of something laid between them.

"It's oftenest naught but bread," he said, "but I've got a fine slice o' fat bacon with it today."

Mary thought it looked a queer dinner, but he seemed ready to enjoy it.

"Run on an' get thy victuals," he said. "I'll be done with mine first. I'll get some more work done before I start back home."

He sat down with his back against a tree.

"I'll call th' robin up," he said, "and give him th' rind o' th' bacon to peck at. They likes a bit o' fat wonderful."

Mary could scarcely bear to leave him. Suddenly it seemed as if he might be a sort of wood fairy who might be gone when she came into the garden again. He seemed too good to be true. She went slowly half-way to the door in the wall and then she stopped and went back.

"Whatever happens, you—you never would tell?" she said.

His poppy-colored cheeks were distended with his first big bite of bread and bacon, but he managed to smile encouragingly.

"If tha' was a missel thrush an' showed me where thy nest was, does tha' think I'd tell any one? Not me," he said. "Tha' art as safe as a missel thrush."

And she was quite sure she was.

Chapter 12

"Might I Have a Bit of Earth?"

Mary ran so fast that she was rather out of breath when she reached her room. Her hair was ruffled on her forehead and her cheeks were bright pink. Her dinner was waiting on the table, and Martha was waiting near it.

"Tha's a bit late," she said. "Where has tha' been?"

"I've seen Dickon!" said Mary. "I've seen Dickon!"

"I knew he'd come," said Martha exultantly. "How does tha' like him?"

"I think—I think he's beautiful!" said Mary in a determined voice.

Martha looked rather taken aback but she looked pleased, too.

"Well," she said, "he's th' best lad as ever was born, but us never thought he was handsome. His nose turns up too much."

"I like it to turn up," said Mary.

"An' his eyes is so round," said Martha, a trifle doubtful. "Though they're a nice color." "I like them round," said Mary. "And they are exactly the color of the sky over the moor."

Martha beamed with satisfaction.

"Mother says he made 'em that color with always lookin' up at th' birds an' th' clouds. But he has got a big mouth, hasn't he, now?"

"I love his big mouth," said Mary obstinately. "I wish mine were just like it."

Martha chuckled delightedly.

"It'd look rare an' funny in thy bit of a face," she said. "But I knowed it would be that way when tha' saw him. How did tha' like th' seeds an' th' garden tools?"

"How did you know he brought them?" asked Mary.

"Eh! I never thought of him not bringin' 'em. He'd be sure to bring 'em if they was in Yorkshire. He's such a trusty lad."

Mary was afraid that she might begin to ask difficult questions, but she did not. She was very much interested in the seeds and gardening tools, and there was only one moment when Mary was frightened. This was when she began to ask where the flowers were to be planted.

"Who did tha' ask about it?" she inquired.

"I haven't asked anybody yet," said Mary, hesitating. "Well, I wouldn't ask th' head gardener. He's too grand, Mr. Roach is."

"I've never seen him," said Mary. "I've only seen undergardeners and Ben Weatherstaff."

"If I was you, I'd ask Ben Weatherstaff," advised Martha. "He's not half as bad as he looks, for all he's so crabbed. Mr. Craven lets him do what he likes because he was here when Mrs. Craven was alive, an' he used to make her laugh. She liked him. Perhaps he'd find you a corner somewhere out o' the way."

"If it was out of the way and no one wanted it, no one could mind my having it, could they?" Mary said anxiously.

"There wouldn't be no reason," answered Martha. "You wouldn't do no harm."

Mary ate her dinner as quickly as she could, and when she rose from the table she was going to run to her room to put on her hat again, but Martha stopped her.

"I've got somethin' to tell you," she said. "I thought I'd let you eat your dinner first. Mr. Craven came back this mornin' and I think he wants to see you."

Mary turned quite pale.

"Oh!" she said. "Why! Why! He didn't want to see me when I came. I heard Pitcher say he didn't."

"Well," explained Martha, "Mrs. Medlock says it's because o' mother. She was walkin' to Thwaite village an' she met him. She'd never spoke to him before, but Mrs. Craven had been to our cottage two or three times. He'd forgot, but mother hadn't an' she made bold to stop him. I don't know what she said to him about you but she said somethin' as put him in th' mind to see you before he goes away again, tomorrow."

"Oh!" cried Mary, "is he going away tomorrow? I am so glad!"

"He's goin' for a long time. He mayn't come back till autumn or winter. He's goin' to travel in foreign places. He's always doin' it."

"Oh! I'm so glad—so glad!" said Mary thankfully.

If he did not come back until winter, or even autumn,

there would be time to watch the secret garden come alive. Even if he found out then and took it away from her she would have had that much at least.

"When do you think he will want to see—"

She did not finish the sentence, because the door opened, and Mrs. Medlock walked in. She had on her best black dress and cap, and her collar was fastened with a large brooch with a picture of a man's face on it. It was a colored photograph of Mr. Medlock who had died years ago, and she always wore it when she was dressed up. She looked nervous and excited.

"Your hair's rough," she said quickly. "Go and brush it. Martha, help her to slip on her best dress. Mr. Craven sent me to bring her to him in his study."

All the pink left Mary's cheeks. Her heart began to thump and she felt herself changing into a stiff, plain, silent child again. She did not even answer Mrs. Medlock, but turned and walked into her bedroom, followed by Martha.

She said nothing while her dress was changed, and her hair brushed, and after she was quite tidy she followed Mrs. Medlock down the corridors, in silence. What was there for her to say? She was obliged to go and see Mr. Craven and he would not like her, and she would not like him. She knew what he would think of her.

She was taken to a part of the house she had not been into before. At last Mrs. Medlock knocked at a door, and when some one said, "Come in," they entered the room together.

A man was sitting in an armchair before the fire, and Mrs. Medlock spoke to him.

"This is Miss Mary, sir," she said.

"You can go and leave her here. I will ring for you when I want you to take her away," said Mr. Craven.

When she went out and closed the door, Mary could only stand waiting, a plain little thing, twisting her thin hands together. She could see that the man in the chair was not so much a hunchback as a man with high, rather crooked shoulders, and he had black hair streaked with white. He turned his head over his high shoulders and spoke to her.

"Come here!" he said.

Mary went to him.

He was not ugly. His face would have been handsome if it had not been so miserable. He looked as if the sight of her worried and fretted him and as if he did not know what in the world to do with her.

"Are you well?" he asked.

"Yes," answered Mary.

"Do they take good care of you?"

"Yes."

He rubbed his forehead fretfully as he looked her over.

"You are very thin," he said.

"I am getting fatter," Mary answered in what she knew was her stiffest way.

What an unhappy face he had! His black eyes seemed as if they scarcely saw her, as if they were seeing something else, and he could hardly keep his thoughts upon her.

"I forgot you," he said. "How could I remember you? I intended to send you a governess or a nurse, or some one of that sort, but I forgot."

"Please," began Mary. "Please—" and then the lump in her throat choked her.

"What do you want to say?" he inquired.

"I am—I am too big for a nurse," said Mary. "And please—please don't make me have a governess yet."

He rubbed his forehead again and stared at her.

"That was what the Sowerby woman said," he muttered absentmindedly.

Then Mary gathered a scrap of courage.

"Is she—is she Martha's mother?" she stammered.

"Yes, I think so," he replied.

"She knows about children," said Mary. "She has twelve. She knows."

He seemed to rouse himself.

"What do you want to do?"

"I want to play out of doors," Mary answered, hoping that her voice did not tremble. "I never liked it in India. It makes me hungry here, and I am getting fatter."

He was watching her.

"Mrs. Sowerby said it would do you good. Perhaps it will," he said. "She thought you had better get stronger before you had a governess."

"It makes me feel strong when I play and the wind comes over the moor," argued Mary.

"Where do you play?" he asked next.

"Everywhere," gasped Mary. "Martha's mother sent me a skipping-rope. I skip and run—and I look about to see if things are beginning to stick up out of the earth. I don't do any harm."

"Don't look so frightened," he said in a worried voice. "You could not do any harm, a child like you! You may do what you like."

Mary put her hand up to her throat because she was afraid he might see the excited lump which she felt jump into it. She came a step nearer to him.

"May I?" she said tremulously.

Her anxious little face seemed to worry him more than ever.

"Don't look so frightened," he exclaimed. "Of course you may. I am your guardian, though I am a poor one for any child. I cannot give you time or attention. I am too ill, and wretched and distracted; but I wish you to be happy and comfortable. I don't know anything about children, but Mrs. Medlock is to see that you have all you need. I sent for you today because Mrs. Sowerby said I ought to see you. Her daughter had talked about you. She thought you needed fresh air and freedom and running about."

"She knows all about children," Mary said again in spite of herself.

"She ought to," said Mr. Craven. "I thought her rather bold to stop me on the moor, but she said—Mrs. Craven had been kind to her." It seemed hard for him to speak his dead wife's name. "She is a respectable woman. Now I have seen you I think she said sensible things. Play out of doors as much as you like. It's a big place and you may go where you like and amuse yourself as you like.

Is there anything you want?" as if a sudden thought had struck him. "Do you want toys, books, dolls?"

"Might I," quavered Mary, "might I have a bit of earth?"

In her eagerness she did not realize how queer the words would sound and that they were not the ones she had meant to say. Mr. Craven looked quite startled.

"Earth!" he repeated. "What do you mean?"

"To plant seeds in—to make things grow—to see them come alive," Mary faltered.

He gazed at her a moment and then passed his hand quickly over his eyes.

"Do you—care about gardens so much," he said slowly.

"I didn't know about them in India," said Mary. "I was always ill and tired and it was too hot. I sometimes made little beds in the sand and stuck flowers in them. But here it is different."

Mr. Craven got up and began to walk slowly across the room.

"A bit of earth," he said to himself, and Mary thought that somehow she must have reminded him of something. When he stopped and spoke to her his dark eyes looked almost soft and kind.

"You can have as much earth as you want," he said. "You remind me of some one else who loved the earth and things that grow. When you see a bit of earth you want," with something like a smile, "take it, child, and make it come alive."

"May I take it from anywhere—if it's not wanted?"

"Anywhere," he answered. "There! You must go now, I am tired." He touched the bell to call Mrs. Medlock. "Goodbye. I shall be away all summer."

Mrs. Medlock came so quickly that Mary thought she must have been waiting in the corridor.

"Mrs. Medlock," Mr. Craven said to her, "now I have seen the child I understand what Mrs. Sowerby meant. She must be less delicate before she begins lessons. Give her simple, healthy food. Let her run wild in the garden. Don't look after her too much. She needs liberty and fresh air and romping about. Mrs. Sowerby is to come and see her now and then and she may sometimes go to the cottage."

Mrs. Medlock looked pleased. She was relieved to hear that she need not "look after" Mary too much. She had felt her a tiresome charge and had indeed seen as little of her as she dared. In addition to this she was fond of Martha's mother.

"Thank you, sir," she said. "Susan Sowerby and me went to school together and she's as sensible and good-hearted a woman as you'd find in a day's walk. I never had any children myself and she's had twelve, and there never was healthier or better ones. Miss Mary can get no harm from them. I'd always take Susan Sowerby's advice about children myself. She's what you might call healthy-minded—if you understand me."

"I understand," Mr. Craven answered. "Take Miss Mary away now and send Pitcher to me."

When Mrs. Medlock left her at the end of her own corridor Mary flew back to her room. She found Martha waiting there. Martha had, in fact, hurried back after she had removed the dinner service.

"I can have my garden!" cried Mary. "I may have it where I like! I am not going to have a governess for a long time! Your mother is coming to see me and I may go to your cottage! He says a little girl like me could not do any harm and I may do what I like—anywhere!"

"Eh!" said Martha delightedly, "that was nice of him wasn't it?"

"Martha," said Mary solemnly, "he is really a nice man, only his face is so miserable and his forehead is all drawn together."

She ran as quickly as she could to the garden. She had been away so much longer than she had thought she should, and she knew Dickon would have to set out early on his five-mile walk. When she slipped through the door under the ivy, she saw he was not working where she had left him. The gardening tools were laid together under a tree. She ran to them, looking all round the place, but there was no Dickon to be seen. He had gone away and the secret garden was empty—except for the robin who had just flown across the wall and sat on a standard rose-bush watching her. "He's gone," she said woefully. "Oh! was he—was he—was he only a wood fairy?"

Something white fastened to the standard rose-bush caught her eye. It was a piece of paper, in fact, it was a piece of the letter she had printed for Martha to send to Dickon. It was fastened on the bush with a long thorn, and in a minute she knew Dickon had left it there.

There were some roughly printed letters on it and a sort of picture. At first she could not tell what it was. Then she saw it was meant for a nest with a bird sitting on it. Underneath were the printed letters and they said:

"I will cum bak."

Chapter 13

"I Am Colin"

Mary took the picture back to the house when she went to her supper and she showed it to Martha. "Eh!" said Martha with great pride. "I never knew our Dickon was as clever as that. That there's a picture of a missel thrush on her nest, as large as life an' twice as natural."

Then Mary knew Dickon had meant the picture to be a message. He had meant that she might be sure he would keep her secret. Her garden was her nest and she was like a missel thrush. Oh, how she did like that queer, common boy!

She hoped he would come back the very next day and she fell asleep looking forward to the morning.

But you never know what the weather will do in Yorkshire, particularly in the springtime. She was awakened in the night by the sound of rain beating with heavy drops against her window. It was pouring down in torrents and the wind was "wuthering" round the corners and in the chimneys of the huge old house. Mary sat up in bed and felt miserable and angry.

"The rain is as contrary as I ever was," she said. "It came because it knew I did not want it."

She threw herself back on her pillow and buried her face. She did not cry, but she lay and hated the sound of the heavily beating rain, she hated the wind and its "wuthering." She could not go to sleep again. The mournful sound kept her awake because she felt mournful herself. If she had felt happy it would probably have lulled her to sleep. How it "wuthered" and how the big raindrops poured down and beat against the pane!

"It sounds just like a person lost on the moor and wandering on and on crying," she said.

She had been lying awake turning from side to side for about an hour, when suddenly something made her sit up in bed and turn her head toward the door listening. She listened and she listened.

"It isn't the wind now," she said in a loud whisper. "That isn't the wind. It is different. It is that crying I heard before."

The door of her room was ajar and the sound came down the corridor, a far-off faint sound of fretful crying. She listened for a few minutes and each minute she became more and more sure. She felt as if she must find out what it was. It seemed even stranger than the secret garden and the buried key. Perhaps the fact that she was in a rebellious mood made her bold. She put her foot out of bed and stood on the floor.

"I am going to find out what it is," she said. "Everybody is in bed and I don't care about Mrs. Medlock—I don't care!"

There was a candle by her bedside and she took it up

and went softly out of the room. The corridor looked very long and dark, but she was too excited to mind that. She thought she remembered the corners she must turn to find the short corridor with the door covered with tapestry—the one Mrs. Medlock had come through the day she lost herself. The sound had come up that passage.

So she went on with her dim light, almost feeling her way, her heart beating so loud that she fancied she could hear it. The far-off faint crying went on and led her. Sometimes it stopped for a moment or so and then began again. Was this the right corner to turn? She stopped and thought. Yes it was. Down this passage and then to the left, and then up two broad steps, and then to the right again. Yes, there was the tapestry door.

She pushed it open very gently and closed it behind her, and she stood in the corridor and could hear the crying quite plainly, though it was not loud. It was on the other side of the wall at her left and a few yards farther on there was a door. She could see a glimmer of light coming from beneath it. The Someone was crying in that room, and it was quite a young Someone.

So she walked to the door and pushed it open, and there she was standing in the room!

It was a big room with ancient, handsome furniture in it. There was a low fire glowing faintly on the hearth and a night light burning by the side of a carved four-posted bed hung with brocade, and on the bed was lying a boy, crying fretfully.

Mary wondered if she was in a real place or if she had

fallen asleep again and was dreaming without knowing it.

The boy had a sharp, delicate face the color of ivory and he seemed to have eyes too big for it. He had also a lot of hair which tumbled over his forehead in heavy locks and made his thin face seem smaller. He looked like a boy who had been ill, but he was crying more as if he were tired and cross than as if he were in pain.

Mary stood near the door with her candle in her hand, holding her breath. Then she crept across the room, and, as she drew nearer, the light attracted the boy's attention and he turned his head on his pillow and stared at her, his gray eyes opening so wide that they seemed immense.

"Who are you?" he said at last in a half-frightened whisper. "Are you a ghost?"

"No, I am not," Mary answered, her own whisper sounding half frightened. "Are you one?"

He stared and stared and stared. Mary could not help noticing what strange eyes he had. They were agate gray and they looked too big for his face because they had black lashes all round them.

"No," he replied after waiting a moment or so. "I am Colin."

"Who is Colin?" she faltered.

"I am Colin Craven. Who are you?"

"I am Mary Lennox. Mr. Craven is my uncle."

"He is my father," said the boy.

"Your father!" gasped Mary. "No one ever told me he had a boy! Why didn't they?"

"Come here," he said, still keeping his strange eyes

fixed on her with an anxious expression.

She came close to the bed and he put out his hand and touched her.

"You are real, aren't you?" he said. "I have such real dreams very often. You might be one of them."

Mary had slipped on a woolen wrapper before she left her room and she put a piece of it between his fingers.

"Rub that and see how thick and warm it is," she said. "I will pinch you a little if you like, to show you how real I am. For a minute I thought you might be a dream, too."

"Where did you come from?" he asked.

"From my own room. The wind wuthered so I couldn't go to sleep and I heard some one crying and wanted to find out who it was. What were you crying for?"

"Because I couldn't go to sleep either and my head

ached. Tell me your name again."

"Mary Lennox. Did no one ever tell you I had come to live here?"

He was still fingering the fold of her wrapper, but he began to look a little more as if he believed in her reality.

"No," he answered. "They daren't."

"Why?" asked Mary.

"Because I should have been afraid you would see me. I won't let people see me and talk me over."

"Why?" Mary asked again, feeling more mystified every moment.

"Because I am like this always, ill and having to lie down. My father won't let people talk me over either. The servants are not allowed to speak about me. If I live I may be a hunchback, but I shan't live. My father hates to think I may be like him."

"Oh, what a queer house this is!" Mary said. "What a queer house! Everything is a kind of secret. Rooms are locked up and gardens are locked up—and you! Have you been locked up?"

"No. I stay in this room because I don't want to be moved out of it. It tires me too much."

"Does your father come and see you?" Mary ventured.

"Sometimes. Generally when I am asleep. He doesn't want to see me."

"Why?" Mary could not help asking again.

A sort of angry shadow passed over the boy's face.

"My mother died when I was born and it makes him wretched to look at me. He thinks I don't know, but I've heard people talking. He almost hates me."

"He hates the garden, because she died," said Mary half speaking to herself.

"What garden?" the boy asked.

"Oh! just—just a garden she used to like," Mary stammered. "Have you been here always?"

"Nearly always. Sometimes I have been taken to places at the seaside, but I won't stay because people stare at me. I used to wear an iron thing to keep my back straight, but a grand doctor came from London to see me and said it was stupid. He told them to take it off and keep me out in the fresh air. I hate fresh air and I don't want to go out."

"I didn't when first I came here," said Mary. "Why do you keep looking at me like that?"

"Because of the dreams that are so real," he answered rather fretfully. "Sometimes when I open my eyes I don't believe I'm awake."

"We're both awake," said Mary. She glanced round the room with its high ceiling and shadowy corners and dim fire-light. "It looks quite like a dream, and it's the middle of the night, and everybody in the house is asleep—everybody but us. We are wide awake."

"I don't want it to be a dream," the boy said restlessly.

Mary thought of something all at once.

"If you don't like people to see you," she began, "do you want me to go away?"

He still held the fold of her wrapper and he gave it a little pull.

"No," he said. "I should be sure you were a dream if you went. If you are real, sit down on that big footstool and talk. I want to hear about you."

Mary put down her candle on the table near the bed and sat down on the cushioned stool. She did not want to go away at all. She wanted to stay in the mysterious hidden-away room and talk to the mysterious boy.

"What do you want me to tell you?" she said.

He wanted to know how long she had been at Misselthwaite; he wanted to know which corridor her room was on; he wanted to know what she had been doing; if she disliked the moor as he disliked it; where she had lived before she came to Yorkshire.

She answered all these questions and many more and he lay back on his pillow and listened. He made her tell him a great deal about India and about her voyage across the ocean. She found out that because he had been an invalid he had not learned things as other children had. One of his nurses had taught him to read when he was quite little and he was always reading and looking at pictures in splendid books.

Though his father rarely saw him when he was awake, he was given all sorts of wonderful things to amuse himself with. He never seemed to have been amused, however. He could have anything he asked for and was never made to do anything he did not like to do.

"Everyone is obliged to do what pleases me," he said indifferently. "It makes me ill to be angry. No one believes I shall live to grow up."

He said it as if he was so accustomed to the idea that it had ceased to matter to him at all. He seemed to like the sound of Mary's voice. As she went on talking he listened in a drowsy, interested way. Once or twice she wondered if he were not gradually falling into a doze. But at last he asked a question which opened up a new subject.

"How old are you?" he asked.

"I am ten," answered Mary, forgetting herself for the moment, "and so are you."

"How do you know that?" he demanded in a surprised voice.

"Because when you were born the garden door was locked and the key was buried. And it has been locked for ten years."

Colin half sat up, turning toward her, leaning on his elbows.

"What garden door was locked? Who did it? Where was the key buried?" he exclaimed, as if he were suddenly very much interested.

"It—it was the garden Mr. Craven hates," said Mary nervously. "He locked the door. No one—no one knew where he buried the key." "What sort of a garden is it?" Colin persisted eagerly.

"No one has been allowed to go into it for ten years," was Mary's careful answer.

But it was too late to be careful. He was too much like herself. He too had had nothing to think about and the idea of a hidden garden attracted him as it had attracted her. He asked question after question. Where was it? Had she never looked for the door? Had she never asked the gardeners?

"They won't talk about it," said Mary. "I think they have been told not to answer questions."

"I would make them," said Colin.

"Could you?" Mary faltered, beginning to feel frightened. If he could make people answer questions, who knew what might happen!

"Everyone is obliged to please me. I told you that," he said. "If I were to live, this place would sometime belong to me. They all know that. I would make them tell me."

Mary had not known that she herself had been spoiled, but she could see quite plainly that this mysterious boy had been. He thought that the whole world belonged to him. How peculiar he was and how coolly he spoke of not living.

"Do you think you won't live?" she asked, partly because she was curious and partly in hope of making him forget the garden.

"I don't suppose I shall," he answered as indifferently as he had spoken before. "Ever since I remember anything I have heard people say I shan't. At first they thought I was too little to understand and now they think I don't hear. But I do. My doctor is my father's cousin. He is quite poor and if I die he will have all Misselthwaite when my father is dead. I should think he wouldn't want me to live."

"Do you want to live?" inquired Mary.

"No," he answered, in a cross, tired fashion. "But I don't want to die. When I feel ill I lie here and think about it until I cry and cry."

"I have heard you crying three times," Mary said, "but I did not know who it was. Were you crying about that?" She did so want him to forget the garden.

"I dare say," he answered. "Let us talk about something else. Talk about that garden. Don't you want to see it?"

"Yes," answered Mary, in quite a low voice.

"I do," he went on persistently. "I don't think I ever really wanted to see anything before, but I want to see that garden. I want the key dug up. I want the door unlocked. I would let them take me there in my chair. That would be getting fresh air. I am going to make them open the door."

He had become quite excited and his strange eyes began to shine like stars and looked more immense than ever.

"They have to please me," he said. "I will make them take me there and I will let you go, too."

Mary's hands clutched each other. Everything would be spoiled—everything! Dickon would never come back. She would never again feel like a missel thrush with a safe-hidden nest.

"Oh, don't—don't—don't—don't do that!" she cried out.

He stared as if he thought she had gone crazy!

"Why?" he exclaimed. "You said you wanted to see it."

"I do," she answered almost with a sob in her throat, "but if you make them open the door and take you in like that it will never be a secret again."

He leaned still farther forward.

"A secret," he said. "What do you mean? Tell me."

Mary's words almost tumbled over one another.

"You see—you see," she panted, "if no one knows but ourselves—if there was a door, hidden somewhere under the ivy—if there was—and we could find it; and if we could slip through it together and shut it behind us, and no one knew any one was inside and we called it our garden and pretended that—that we were missel thrushes and it was our nest, and if we played there almost every day and dug and planted seeds and made it all come alive—"

"Is it dead?" he interrupted her.

"It soon will be if no one cares for it," she went on. "The bulbs will live but the roses—"

He stopped her again as excited as she was herself.

"What are bulbs?" he put in quickly.

"They are daffodils and lilies and snowdrops. They are working in the earth now—pushing up pale green points because the spring is coming."

"Is the spring coming?" he said. "What is it like? You don't see it in rooms if you are ill."

"It is the sun shining on the rain and the rain falling on the sunshine, and things pushing up and working under the earth," said Mary. "If the garden was a secret and we could get into it we could watch the things grow bigger every day, and see how many roses are alive. Don't you see? Oh, don't you see how much nicer it would be if it was a secret?"

He dropped back on his pillow and lay there with an odd expression on his face.

"I never had a secret," he said, "except that one about not living to grow up. They don't know I know that, so it is a sort of secret. But I like this kind better."

"If you won't make them take you to the garden," pleaded Mary, "perhaps—I feel almost sure I can find out how to get in sometime. And then—if the doctor wants you to go out in your chair, and if you can always do what you want to do, perhaps—perhaps we might find some boy who would push you, and we could go alone and it would always be a secret garden."

"I should—like—that," he said very slowly, his eyes looking dreamy. "I should like that. I should not mind fresh air in a secret garden."

Mary began to recover her breath and feel safer because the idea of keeping the secret seemed to please him. She felt almost sure that if she kept on talking and could make him see the garden in his mind as she had seen it he would like it so much that he could not bear to think that everybody might tramp in to it when they chose.

"I'll tell you what I think it would be like, if we could go into it," she said. "It has been shut up so long things have grown into a tangle perhaps."

He lay quite still and listened while she went on talking about the roses which might have clambered from tree to tree and hung down—about the many birds which might have built their nests there because it was so safe. And then she told him about the robin and Ben Weatherstaff, and there was so much to tell about the robin and it was so easy and safe to talk about it that she ceased to be afraid. The robin pleased him so much that he smiled until he looked almost beautiful, and at first Mary had thought that he was even plainer than herself, with his big eyes and heavy locks of hair.

"I did not know birds could be like that," he said. "But

if you stay in a room you never see things. What a lot of things you know. I feel as if you had been inside that garden."

She did not know what to say, so she did not say anything. He evidently did not expect an answer and the next moment he gave her a surprise.

"I am going to let you look at something," he said. "Do you see that rose-colored silk curtain hanging on the wall over the mantel-piece?"

Mary had not noticed it before, but she looked up and saw it. It was a curtain of soft silk hanging over what seemed to be some picture.

"Yes," she answered.

"There is a cord hanging from it," said Colin. "Go and pull it."

Mary got up, much mystified, and found the cord. When she pulled it the silk curtain ran back on rings and when it ran back it uncovered a picture. It was the picture of a girl with a laughing face. She had bright hair tied up with a blue ribbon and her gay, lovely eyes were exactly like Colin's unhappy ones, agate gray and looking twice as big as they really were because of the black lashes all round them.

"She is my mother," said Colin complainingly. "I don't see why she died. Sometimes I hate her for doing it."

"How queer!" said Mary.

"If she had lived I believe I should not have been ill always," he grumbled. "I dare say I should have lived, too. And my father would not have hated to look at me. I dare say I should have had a strong back. Draw the curtain again."

Mary did as she was told and returned to her footstool.

"She is much prettier than you," she said, "but her eyes are just like yours—at least they are the same shape and color. Why is the curtain drawn over her?"

He moved uncomfortably.

"I made them do it," he said. "Sometimes I don't like to see her looking at me. She smiles too much when I am ill and miserable. Besides, she is mine and I don't want everyone to see her." There were a few moments of silence and then Mary spoke.

"What would Mrs. Medlock do if she found out that I had been here?" she inquired.

"She would do as I told her to do," he answered. "And I should tell her that I wanted you to come here and talk to me every day. I am glad you came."

"So am I," said Mary. "I will come as often as I can, but"—she hesitated—"I shall have to look every day for the garden door."

"Yes, you must," said Colin, "and you can tell me about it afterward."

He lay thinking a few minutes, as he had done before, and then he spoke again. "I think you shall be a secret, too," he said. "I will not tell them until they find out. I can always send the nurse out of the room and say that I want to be by myself. Do you know Martha?"

"Yes, I know her very well," said Mary. "She waits on me."

He nodded his head toward the outer corridor.

"She is the one who is asleep in the other room. The nurse went away yesterday to stay all night with her sister and she always makes Martha attend to me when she wants to go out. Martha shall tell you when to come here."

Then Mary understood Martha's troubled look when she had asked questions about the crying.

"Martha knew about you all the time?" she said.

"Yes; she often attends to me. The nurse likes to get away from me and then Martha comes."

"I have been here a long time," said Mary. "Shall I go away now? Your eyes look sleepy."

"I wish I could go to sleep before you leave me," he said rather shyly.

"Shut your eyes," said Mary, drawing her footstool closer, "and I will do what my Ayah used to do in India. I will pat your hand and stroke it and sing something quite low."

"I should like that perhaps," he said drowsily.

Somehow she was sorry for him and did not want him to lie awake, so she leaned against the bed and began to stroke and pat his hand and sing a very low little chanting song in Hindustani.

"That is nice," he said more drowsily still, and she went on chanting and stroking, but when she looked at him again his black lashes were lying close against his cheeks, for his eyes were shut and he was fast asleep.

So she got up softly, took her candle and crept away without making a sound.

Chapter 14

A Young Rajah

The moor was hidden in mist when the morning came, and the rain had not stopped pouring down. There could be no going out of doors. Martha was so busy that Mary had no opportunity of talking to her, but in the afternoon she asked her to come and sit with her in the nursery. She came bringing the stocking she was always knitting when she was doing nothing else.

"What's the matter with thee?" she asked as soon as they sat down. "Tha' looks as if tha'd somethin' to say."

"I have. I have found out what the crying was," said Mary.

Martha let her knitting drop on her knee and gazed at her with startled eyes.

"Tha' hasn't!" she exclaimed. "Never!"

"I heard it in the night," Mary went on. "And I got up and went to see where it came from. It was Colin. I found him."

Martha's face became red with fright.

"Eh! Miss Mary!" she said half crying. "Tha' shouldn't have done it—tha' shouldn't! Tha'll get me in trouble. I never told thee nothin' about him—but tha'll get me in trouble. I shall lose my place and what'll mother do!"

"You won't lose your place," said Mary. "He was glad I came. We talked and talked and he said he was glad I came."

"Was he?" cried Martha. "Art tha' sure? Tha' doesn't know what he's like when anything vexes him. He's a big lad to cry like a baby, but when he's in a passion he'll fair scream just to frighten us. He knows us daren't call our souls our own."

"He wasn't vexed," said Mary. "I asked him if I should go away and he made me stay. He asked me questions and I sat on a big footstool and talked to him about India and about the robin and gardens. He wouldn't let me go. He let me see his mother's picture. Before I left him I sang him to sleep."

Martha fairly gasped with amazement.

"I can scarcely believe thee!" she protested. "It's as if tha'd walked straight into a lion's den. If he'd been like he is most times he'd have throwed himself into one of his tantrums and roused th' house. He won't let strangers look at him."

"He let me look at him. I looked at him all the time and he looked at me. We stared!" said Mary.

"I don't know what to do!" cried agitated Martha. "If Mrs. Medlock finds out, she'll think I broke orders and told thee and I shall be packed back to mother."

"He is not going to tell Mrs. Medlock anything about it yet. It's to be a sort of secret just at first," said Mary firmly. "And he says everybody is obliged to do as he pleases."

"Aye, that's true enough—th' bad lad!" sighed Martha,

wiping her forehead with her apron.

"He says Mrs. Medlock must. And he wants me to come and talk to him every day. And you are to tell me when he wants me."

"Me!" said Martha; "I shall lose my place—I shall for sure!"

"You can't if you are doing what he wants you to do and everybody is ordered to obey him," Mary argued.

"Does tha' mean to say," cried Martha with wide open eyes, "that he was nice to thee!"

"I think he almost liked me," Mary answered.

"Then tha' must have bewitched him!" decided Martha, drawing a long breath.

"Do you mean Magic?" inquired Mary. "I've heard about Magic in India, but I can't make it. I just went into his room and I was so surprised to see him I stood and stared. And then he turned round and stared at me. And he thought I was a ghost or a dream and I thought perhaps he was. And it was so queer being there alone together in the middle of the night and not knowing about each other. And we began to ask each other questions. And when I asked him if I must go away he said I must not."

"Th' world's comin' to a end!" gasped Martha.

"What is the matter with him?" asked Mary.

"Nobody knows for sure and certain," said Martha. "Mr. Craven went off his head like when he was born. Th' doctors thought he'd have to be put in a 'sylum. It was because Mrs. Craven died like I told you. He wouldn't set eyes on th' baby. He just raved and said it'd be another hunchback like him and it'd better die."

"Is Colin a hunchback?" Mary asked. "He didn't look like one."

"He isn't yet," said Martha. "But he began all wrong. Mother said that there was enough trouble and raging in th' house to set any child wrong. They was afraid his back was weak an' they've always been takin' care of it—keepin' him lyin' down and not lettin' him walk. Once they made him wear a brace but he fretted so he was downright ill. Then a big doctor came to see him an' made them take it off. He talked to th' other doctor quite rough—in a polite way. He said there'd been too much medicine and too much lettin' him have his own way."

"I think he's a very spoiled boy," said Mary.

"He's th' worst young nowt as ever was!" said Martha. "I won't say as he hasn't been ill a good bit. He's had coughs an' colds that's nearly killed him two or three times. Once he had rheumatic fever an' once he had typhoid. Eh! Mrs. Medlock did get a fright then. He'd been out of his head an' she was talkin' to th' nurse, thinkin' he didn't know nothin', an' she said, 'He'll die this time sure enough, an' best thing for him an' for everybody.' An' she looked at him an' there he was with his big eyes open, starin' at her as sensible as she was herself. She didn't know wha'd happen but he just stared at her an' says, 'You give me some water an' stop talkin'.'"

"Do you think he will die?" asked Mary.

"Mother says there's no reason why any child should live that gets no fresh air an' doesn't do nothin' but lie on his back an' read picture-books an' take medicine.

He's weak and hates th' trouble o' bein' taken out o' doors, an' he gets cold so easy he says it makes him ill."

Mary sat and looked at the fire. "I wonder," she said slowly, "if it would not do him good to go out into a garden and watch things growing. It did me good."

"One of th' worst fits he ever had," said Martha, "was one time they took him out where the roses is by the fountain. He'd been readin' in a paper about people gettin' somethin' he called 'rose cold' an' he began to sneeze an' said he'd got it an' then a new gardener as didn't know th' rules passed by an' looked at him curious. He threw himself into a passion an' he said he'd looked at him because he was going to be a hunchback. He cried himself into a fever an' was ill all night."

"If he ever gets angry at me, I'll never go and see him again," said Mary.

"He'll have thee if he wants thee," said Martha. "Tha' may as well know that at th' start."

Very soon afterward a bell rang and she rolled up her knitting.

"I dare say th' nurse wants me to stay with him a bit," she said. "I hope he's in a good temper."

She was out of the room about ten minutes and then she came back with a puzzled expression.

"Well, tha' has bewitched him," she said. "He's up on his sofa with his picture-books. He's told the nurse to stay away until six o'clock. I'm to wait in the next room. Th' minute she was gone he called me to him an' says, 'I want Mary Lennox to come and talk to me, and remember you're not to tell any one.' You'd better go as quick as you can."

Mary was quite willing to go quickly. She did not want to see Colin as much as she wanted to see Dickon; but she wanted to see him very much.

There was a bright fire on the hearth when she entered his room, and in the daylight she saw it was a very beautiful room indeed. There were rich colors in the rugs and hangings and pictures and books on the walls which made it look glowing and comfortable even in spite of the gray sky and falling rain. Colin looked rather like a picture himself. He was wrapped in a velvet dressing-gown and sat against a big brocaded cushion. He had a red spot on each cheek.

"Come in," he said. "I've been thinking about you all morning."

"I've been thinking about you, too," answered Mary. "You don't know how frightened Martha is. She says Mrs. Medlock will think she told me about you and then she will be sent away."

He frowned.

"Go and tell her to come here," he said. "She is in the next room."

Mary went and brought her back. Poor Martha was shaking in her shoes. Colin was still frowning.

"Have you to do what I please or have you not?" he demanded.

"I have to do what you please, sir," Martha faltered, turning quite red.

"Has Medlock to do what I please?"

"Everybody has, sir," said Martha.

"Well, then, if I order you to bring Miss Mary to me, how can Medlock send you away if she finds it out?"

"Please don't let her, sir," pleaded Martha.

"I'll send her away if she dares to say a word about such a thing," said Master Craven grandly. "She wouldn't like that, I can tell you."

"Thank you, sir," bobbing a curtsy, "I want to do my duty, sir."

"What I want is your duty" said Colin more grandly still. "I'll take care of you. Now go away."

When the door closed behind Martha, Colin found Mistress Mary gazing at him as if he had set her wondering.

"Why do you look at me like that?" he asked her. "What are you thinking about?"

"I am thinking about two things."

"What are they? Sit down and tell me."

"This is the first one," said Mary, seating herself on the big stool. "Once in India I saw a boy who was a Rajah. He had rubies and emeralds and diamonds stuck all over him. He spoke to his people just as you spoke to Martha. Everybody had to do everything he told them—in a minute. I think they would have been killed if they hadn't."

"I shall make you tell me about Rajahs presently," he said, "but first tell me what the second thing was."

"I was thinking," said Mary, "how different you are from Dickon."

"Who is Dickon?" he said. "What a queer name!"

She might as well tell him, she thought she could talk about Dickon without mentioning the secret garden. She had liked to hear Martha talk about him. Besides, she longed to talk about him. It would seem to bring him nearer.

"He is Martha's brother. He is twelve years old," she explained. "He is not like any one else in the world. He can charm foxes and squirrels and birds just as the natives in India charm snakes. He plays a very soft tune on a pipe and they come and listen."

There were some big books on a table at his side and he dragged one suddenly toward him. "There is a picture of a snake-charmer in this," he exclaimed. "Come and look at it."

The book was a beautiful one with superb colored illustrations and he turned to one of them.

"Can he do that?" he asked eagerly.

"He played on his pipe and they listened," Mary explained. "But he doesn't call it Magic. He says it's because he lives on the moor so much and he knows their ways. He says he feels sometimes as if he was a bird or a rabbit himself, he likes them so. I think he asked the robin questions. It seemed as if they talked to each other in soft chirps."

Colin lay back on his cushion and his eyes grew larger and larger and the spots on his cheeks burned.

"Tell me some more about him," he said.

"He knows all about eggs and nests," Mary went on. "And he knows where foxes and badgers and otters live. He keeps them secret so that other boys won't find their holes and frighten them. He knows about everything that grows or lives on the moor."

"Does he like the moor?" said Colin. "How can he

when it's such a great, bare, dreary place?"

"It's the most beautiful place," protested Mary. "Thousands of lovely things grow on it and there are thousands of little creatures all busy building nests and making holes and burrows and chippering or singing or squeaking to each other. They are so busy and having such fun under the earth or in the trees or heather. It's their world."

"How do you know all that?" said Colin, turning on his elbow to look at her.

"I have never been there once, really," said Mary suddenly remembering. "I only drove over it in the dark. I thought it was hideous. Martha told me about it first and then Dickon. When Dickon talks about it you feel as if you saw things and heard them and as if you were standing in the heather with the sun shining and the gorse smelling like honey—and all full of bees and butterflies."

"You never see anything if you are ill," said Colin restlessly. He looked like a person listening to a new sound in the distance and wondering what it was.

"You can't if you stay in a room," said Mary.

"I couldn't go on the moor," he said in a resentful tone.

Mary was silent for a minute and then she said something bold.

"You might—sometime."

He moved as if he were startled.

"Go on the moor! How could I? I am going to die."

"How do you know?" said Mary unsympathetically. She didn't like the way he had of talking about dying. She did not feel very sympathetic. She felt rather as if he almost boasted about it.

"Oh, I've heard it ever since I remember," he answered crossly. "They are always whispering about it and thinking I don't notice. They wish I would, too."

Mistress Mary felt quite contrary. She pinched her lips together.

"If they wished I would," she said, "I wouldn't. Who wishes you would?"

"The servants—and of course Dr. Craven because he would get Misselthwaite and be rich instead of poor. He daren't say so, but he always looks cheerful when I am worse. When I had typhoid fever his face got quite fat. I think my father wishes it, too."

"I don't believe he does," said Mary quite obstinately.

That made Colin turn and look at her again.

"Don't you?" he said.

And then he lay back on his cushion and was still, as if he were thinking. And there was quite a long silence. Perhaps they were both of them thinking strange things children do not usually think.

"I like the grand doctor from London, because he made them take the iron thing off," said Mary at last "Did he say you were going to die?"

"No.".

"What did he say?"

"He didn't whisper," Colin answered. "Perhaps he knew I hated whispering. I heard him say one thing quite aloud. He said, 'The lad might live if he would make up his mind to it. Put him in the humor.' It sounded as if he was in a temper."

"I'll tell you who would put you in the humor, perhaps," said Mary reflecting. She felt as if she would like this thing to be settled one way or the other. "I believe Dickon would. He's always talking about live things. He never talks about dead things or things that are ill. He's always looking up in the sky to watch birds flying—or looking down at the earth to see something growing. He has such round blue eyes and they are so wide open with looking about. And he laughs such a big laugh with his wide mouth—and his cheeks are as red—as red as cherries." She pulled her stool nearer to the sofa and her expression quite changed at the remembrance of the wide curving mouth and wide open eyes.

"See here," she said. "Don't let us talk about dying; I don't like it. Let us talk about living. Let us talk and talk about Dickon. And then we will look at your pictures."

It was the best thing she could have said. To talk about Dickon meant to talk about the moor and about the cottage and the fourteen people who lived in it on sixteen shillings a week—and the children who got fat on the moor grass like the wild ponies. And about Dickon's mother—and the skipping-rope—and the moor with the sun on it—and about pale green points sticking up out of the black sod.

And it was all so alive that Mary talked more than she had ever talked before—and Colin both talked and listened as he had never done either before. And they both began to laugh over nothings as children will when they are happy together. And they laughed so that in the end they were making as much noise as if they had been two ordinary healthy natural ten-year-old creatures— instead of a hard, little, unloving girl and a sickly boy who believed that he was going to die.

They enjoyed themselves so much that they forgot the pictures and they forgot about the time. They had been laughing quite loudly over Ben Weatherstaff and his robin, and Colin was actually sitting up as if he had forgotten about his weak back, when he suddenly remembered something.

"Do you know there is one thing we have never once thought of," he said. "We are cousins."

It seemed so queer that they had talked so much and never remembered this simple thing that they laughed more than ever, because they had got into the humor to laugh at anything. And in the midst of the fun the door opened and in walked Dr. Craven and Mrs. Medlock.

Dr. Craven started in actual alarm and Mrs. Medlock almost fell back because he had accidentally bumped against her.

"Good Lord!" exclaimed poor Mrs. Medlock with her eyes almost starting out of her head. "Good Lord!"

"What is this?" said Dr. Craven, coming forward. "What does it mean?"

Then Mary was reminded of the boy Rajah again. Colin answered as if neither the doctor's alarm nor Mrs. Medlock's terror were of the slightest consequence. He was as little disturbed or frightened as if an elderly cat and dog had walked into the room.

"This is my cousin, Mary Lennox," he said. "I asked her to come and talk to me. I like her. She must come

and talk to me whenever I send for her."

Dr. Craven turned reproachfully to Mrs. Medlock. "Oh, sir" she panted. "I don't know how it's happened. There's not a servant on the place tha'd dare to talk— they all have their orders."

"Nobody told her anything," said Colin. "She heard me crying and found me herself. I am glad she came. Don't be silly, Medlock."

Mary saw that Dr. Craven did not look pleased, but it was quite plain that he dare not oppose his patient. He sat down by Colin and felt his pulse.

"I am afraid there has been too much excitement. Excitement is not good for you, my boy," he said.

"I should be excited if she kept away," answered Colin, his eyes beginning to look dangerously sparkling. "I am better. She makes me better. The nurse must bring up her tea with mine. We will have tea together."

Mrs. Medlock and Dr. Craven looked at each other in a troubled way, but there was evidently nothing to be done.

"He does look rather better, sir," ventured Mrs. Medlock. "But"—thinking the matter over—"he looked better this morning before she came into the room."

"She came into the room last night. She stayed with me a long time. She sang a Hindustani song to me and it made me go to sleep," said Colin. "I was better when I wakened up. I wanted my breakfast. I want my tea now. Tell nurse, Medlock."

Dr. Craven did not stay very long. He talked to the nurse for a few minutes when she came into the room and said a few words of warning to Colin. He must not talk too much; he must not forget that he was ill; he must not forget that he was very easily tired. Mary thought that there seemed to be a number of uncomfortable things he was not to forget.

Colin looked fretful and kept his strange black-lashed eyes fixed on Dr. Craven's face.

"I want to forget it," he said at last. "She makes me forget it. That is why I want her."

Dr. Craven did not look happy when he left the room. He gave a puzzled glance at the little girl sitting on the large stool. She had become a stiff, silent child again as soon as he entered and he could not see what the attraction was. The boy actually did look brighter, however—and he sighed rather heavily as he went down the corridor.

"They are always wanting me to eat things when I don't want to," said Colin, as the nurse brought in the tea and put it on the table by the sofa. "Now, if you'll eat I will. Those muffins look so nice and hot. Tell me about Rajahs."

Chapter 15

Nest Building

After another week of rain the high arch of blue sky appeared again and the sun which poured down was quite hot. Though there had been no chance to see either the secret garden or Dickon, Mistress Mary had enjoyed herself very much. The week had not seemed long. She had spent hours of every day with Colin in his room, talking about Rajahs or gardens or Dickon and the cottage on the moor.

They had looked at the splendid books and pictures and sometimes Mary had read things to Colin, and sometimes he had read a little to her. When he was amused and interested she thought he scarcely looked like an invalid at all, except that his face was so colorless and he was always on the sofa.

"You are a sly young one to listen and get out of your bed to go following things up like you did that night," Mrs. Medlock said once. "But there's no saying it's not been a sort of blessing to the lot of us. He's not had a tantrum or a whining fit since you made friends. The nurse was just going to give up the case because she was so sick of him, but she says she doesn't mind staying now you've gone on duty with her," laughing a little.

In her talks with Colin, Mary had tried to be very cautious about the secret garden. There were certain things she wanted to find out from him, but she felt that she must find them out without asking him direct questions. In the first place, as she began to like to be with him, she wanted to discover whether he was the kind of boy you could tell a secret to. He was not in the least like Dickon, but he was evidently so pleased with the idea of a garden no one knew anything about that she thought perhaps he could be trusted. But she had not known him long enough to be sure.

The second thing she wanted to find out was this: If he could be trusted—if he really could—wouldn't it be possible to take him to the garden without having any one find it out? The grand doctor had said that he must have fresh air and Colin had said that he would not mind fresh air in a secret garden. Perhaps if he had a great deal of fresh air and knew Dickon and the robin and saw things growing he might not think so much about dying.

Mary had seen herself in the glass sometimes lately when she had realized that she looked quite a different creature from the child she had seen when she arrived from India. This child looked nicer. Even Martha had seen a change in her.

"Th' air from th' moor has done thee good already," she had said. "Tha'rt not nigh so yeller and tha'rt not nigh so scrawny. Even tha' hair doesn't slamp down on tha' head so flat. It's got some life in it so as it sticks out a bit."

"It's like me," said Mary. "It's growing stronger and

fatter. I'm sure there's more of it."

"It looks it, for sure," said Martha, ruffling it up a little round her face. "Tha'rt not half so ugly when it's that way an' there's a bit o' red in tha' cheeks."

If gardens and fresh air had been good for her perhaps they would be good for Colin. But then, if he hated people to look at him, perhaps he would not like to see Dickon.

"Why does it make you angry when you are looked at?" she inquired one day.

"I always hated it," he answered, "even when I was very little. Then when they took me to the seaside and I used to lie in my carriage everybody used to stare and ladies would stop and talk to my nurse and then they would begin to whisper and I knew then they were saying I shouldn't live to grow up. Then sometimes the ladies would pat my cheeks and say 'Poor child!' Once when a lady did that I screamed out loud and bit her hand. She was so frightened she ran away."

"She thought you had gone mad like a dog," said Mary, not at all admiringly.

"I don't care what she thought," said Colin, frowning.

"I wonder why you didn't scream and bite me when I came into your room?" said Mary. Then she began to smile slowly.

"I thought you were a ghost or a dream," he said. "You can't bite a ghost or a dream, and if you scream they don't care."

"Would you hate it if—if a boy looked at you?" Mary asked uncertainly.

He lay back on his cushion and paused thoughtfully.

"There's one boy," he said quite slowly, as if he were thinking over every word, "there's one boy I believe I shouldn't mind. It's that boy who knows where the foxes live—Dickon."

"I'm sure you wouldn't mind him," said Mary.

"The birds don't and other animals," he said, still thinking it over, "perhaps that's why I shouldn't. He's a sort of animal charmer and I am a boy animal."

Then he laughed and she laughed too; in fact it ended in their both laughing a great deal and finding the idea of a boy animal hiding in his hole very funny indeed.

What Mary felt afterward was that she need not fear about Dickon.

On that first morning when the sky was blue again Mary wakened very early. The sun was pouring in slanting rays through the blinds and there was something so joyous in the sight of it that she jumped out of bed and ran to the window. She drew up the blinds and opened the window itself and a great waft of fresh, scented air blew in upon her. The moor was blue and the whole world looked as if something Magic had happened to it. There were tender little fluting sounds here and there and everywhere, as if scores of birds were beginning to tune up for a concert. Mary put her hand out of the window and held it in the sun.

"It's warm—warm!" she said. "It will make the green points push up and up and up, and it will make the bulbs and roots work and struggle with all their might under the earth."

She kneeled down and leaned out of the window as far as she could, breathing big breaths and sniffing the air until she laughed because she remembered what Dickon's mother had said about the end of his nose quivering like a rabbit's.

"It must be very early," she said. "The little clouds are all pink and I've never seen the sky look like this. No one is up. I don't even hear the stable boys."

A sudden thought made her scramble to her feet.

"I can't wait! I am going to see the garden!"

She had learned to dress herself by this time and she put on her clothes in five minutes. She knew a small side door which she could unbolt herself and she flew downstairs in her stocking feet and put on her shoes in the hall.

She unchained and unbolted and unlocked and when the door was open she sprang across the step with one bound, and there she was standing on the grass, which seemed to have turned green, and with the sun pouring down on her and warm sweet wafts about her and the fluting and twittering and singing coming from every bush and tree.

She clasped her hands for pure joy and looked up in the sky and it was so blue and pink and pearly and white and flooded with springtime light that she felt as if she must flute and sing aloud herself and knew that thrushes and robins and skylarks could not possibly help it. She ran around the shrubs and paths towards the secret garden.

"It is all different already," she said. "The grass is greener and things are sticking up everywhere and

things are uncurling and green buds of leaves are showing. This afternoon I am sure Dickon will come."

The long warm rain had done strange things to the herbaceous beds which bordered the walk by the lower wall. There were things sprouting and pushing out from the roots of clumps of plants and there were actually here and there glimpses of royal purple and yellow unfurling among the stems of crocuses. Six months before Mistress Mary would not have seen how the world was waking up, but now she missed nothing.

When she had reached the place where the door hid itself under the ivy, she was startled by a curious loud sound. It was the caw—caw of a crow and it came from the top of the wall, and when she looked up, there sat a big glossy-plumaged blue-black bird, looking down at her very wisely indeed. She had never seen a crow so close before and he made her a little nervous, but the next moment he spread his wings and flapped away across the garden.

She hoped he was not going to stay inside and she pushed the door open wondering if he would. When she got fairly into the garden she saw that he probably did intend to stay because he had alighted on a dwarf apple-tree and under the apple-tree was lying a little reddish animal with a Bushy tail, and both of them were watching the stooping body and rust-red head of Dickon, who was kneeling on the grass working hard.

Mary flew across the grass to him.

"Oh, Dickon! Dickon!" she cried out. "How could you get here so early! How could you! The sun has only just got up!"

He got up himself, laughing and glowing, and tousled; his eyes like a bit of the sky.

"Eh!" he said. "I was up long before him. How could I have stayed abed! Th' world's all fair begun again this mornin', it has. An' it's workin' an' hummin' an' scratchin' an' pipin' an' nest-buildin' an' breathin' out scents, till you've got to be out on it 'stead o' lyin' on your back. When th' sun did jump up, th' moor went mad for joy, an' I was in the midst of th' heather, an' I run like mad myself, shoutin' an' singin'. An' I come straight here. I couldn't have stayed away. Why, th' garden was lyin' here waitin'!"

Mary put her hands on her chest, panting, as if she had been running herself.

"Oh, Dickon! Dickon!" she said. "I'm so happy I can scarcely breathe!"

Seeing him talking to a stranger, the little bushy-tailed animal rose from its place under the tree and came to him, and the rook, cawing once, flew down from its branch and settled quietly on his shoulder.

"This is th' little fox cub," he said, rubbing the little reddish animal's head. "It's named Captain. An' this here's Soot. Soot he flew across th' moor with me an' Captain he run same as if th' hounds had been after him. They both felt same as I did."

Neither of the creatures looked as if he were the least afraid of Mary. When Dickon began to walk about, Soot stayed on his shoulder and Captain trotted quietly close to his side.

"See here!" said Dickon. "See how these has pushed up, an' these an' these! An' Eh! Look at these here!"

He threw himself upon his knees and Mary went down beside him. They had come upon a whole clump of crocuses burst into purple and orange and gold. Mary bent her face down and kissed and kissed them.

"You never kiss a person in that way," she said when she lifted her head. "Flowers are so different."

He looked puzzled but smiled.

"Eh!" he said, "I've kissed mother many a time that way when I come in from th' moor after a day's roamin' an' she stood there at th' door in th' sun, lookin' so glad an' comfortable."

They ran from one part of the garden to another and found so many wonders that they were obliged to remind themselves that they must whisper or speak low. He showed her swelling leafbuds on rose branches which had seemed dead.

He showed her ten thousand new green points pushing through the mould. They put their eager young noses close to the earth and sniffed its warmed springtime breathing; they dug and pulled and laughed low with rapture until Mistress Mary's hair was as tumbled as Dickon's and her cheeks were almost as poppy red as his.

There was every joy on earth in the secret garden that morning, and in the midst of them came a delight more delightful than all, because it was more wonderful.

Swiftly something flew across the wall and darted through the trees to a close grown corner, a little flare of red-breasted bird with something hanging from its beak. Dickon stood quite still and put his hand on Mary almost as if they had suddenly found themselves laughing in a church.

"We munnot stir," he whispered in broad Yorkshire. "We munnot scarce breathe. I knowed he was mate-huntin' when I seed him last. It's Ben Weatherstaff's robin. He's buildin' his nest. He'll stay here if us don't fight him." They settled down softly upon the grass and sat there without moving.

"Us mustn't seem as if us was watchin' him too close," said Dickon. "He'd be out with us for good if he got th' notion us was interferin' now. He'll be a good bit different till all this is over. He's settin' up housekeepin'. He'll be shyer an' readier to take things ill. He's got no time for visitin' an' gossipin'. Us must keep still a bit an' try to look as if us was grass an' trees an' bushes. Then when he's got used to seein' us I'll chirp a bit an' he'll know us'll not be in his way."

Mistress Mary was not at all sure that she knew, as Dickon seemed to, how to try to look like grass and trees and bushes. But he had said the queer thing as if it were the simplest and most natural thing in the world, and she felt it must be quite easy to him, and indeed she watched him for a few minutes carefully, wondering if it was possible for him to quietly turn green and put out branches and leaves. But he only sat wonderfully still, and when he spoke dropped his voice to such a softness that it was curious that she could hear him, but she could.

"It's part o' th' springtime, this nest-buildin' is," he said. "I warrant it's been goin' on in th' same way every year since th' world was begun. They've got their way o' thinkin' and doin' things an' a body had better not meddle. You can lose a friend in springtime easier than any other season if you're too curious."

"If we talk about him I can't help looking at him," Mary said as softly as possible. "We must talk of something else. There is something I want to tell you."

"He'll like it better if us talks o' somethin' else," said Dickon. "What is it tha's got to tell me?"

"Well—do you know about Colin?" she whispered.

He turned his head to look at her.

"What does tha' know about him?" he asked.

"I've seen him. I have been to talk to him every day this week. He wants me to come. He says I'm making him forget about being ill and dying," answered Mary.

Dickon looked actually relieved as soon as the surprise died away from his round face.

"I am glad o' that," he exclaimed. "I'm right down glad. It makes me easier. I knowed I must say nothin' about him an' I don't like havin' to hide things."

"Don't you like hiding the garden?" said Mary.

"I'll never tell about it," he answered. "But I says to mother, 'Mother,' I says, 'I got a secret to keep. It's not a bad 'un, tha' knows that. It's no worse than hidin' where a bird's nest is. Tha' doesn't mind it, does tha'?'"

Mary always wanted to hear about mother.

"What did she say?" she asked, not at all afraid to hear.

Dickon grinned sweet-temperedly.

"It was just like her, what she said," he answered. "She give my head a bit of a rub an' laughed an' she says, 'Eh, lad, tha' can have all th' secrets tha' likes. I've knowed thee twelve year'.'"

"How did you know about Colin?" asked Mary.

"Everybody as knowed about Mester Craven knowed there was a little lad as was like to be a cripple, an' they knowed Mester Craven didn't like him to be talked about. Folks is sorry for Mester Craven because Mrs. Craven was such a pretty young lady an' they was so fond of each other. Mrs. Medlock stops in our cottage whenever she goes to Thwaite an' she doesn't mind talkin' to mother before us children, because she knows us has been brought up to be trusty. How did tha' find out about him? Martha was in fine trouble th' last time she came home. She said tha'd heard him frettin' an' tha' was askin' questions an' she didn't know what to say."

Mary told him her story about the midnight wuthering of the wind which had wakened her and about the faint far-off sounds of the complaining voice which had led her down the dark corridors with her candle and had ended with her opening of the door of the dimly lighted room with the carven four-posted bed in the corner. When she described the small ivory-white face and the strange black-rimmed eyes Dickon shook his head.

"Them's just like his mother's eyes, only hers was always laughin', they say," he said. "They say as Mr. Craven can't bear to see him when he's awake an' it's because his eyes is so like his mother's an' yet looks so different in his miserable bit of a face."

"Do you think he wants to die?" whispered Mary.

"No, but he wishes he'd never been born. Mother she says that's th' worst thing on earth for a child. Them as is not wanted scarce ever thrives. Mester Craven he'd buy anythin' as money could buy for th' poor lad but he'd like to forget as he's on earth. For one thing, he's afraid he'll look at him some day and find he's growed hunchback."

"Colin's so afraid of it himself that he won't sit up," said Mary. "He says he's always thinking that if he should feel a lump coming he should go crazy and scream himself to death."

"Eh! he oughtn't to lie there thinkin' things like that," said Dickon. "No lad could get well as thought them sort o' things."

The fox was lying on the grass close by him, looking up to ask for a pat now and then, and Dickon bent down and rubbed his neck softly and thought a few minutes in silence. Presently he lifted his head and looked round the garden.

"When first we got in here," he said, "it seemed like everything was gray. Look round now and tell me if tha' doesn't see a difference."

Mary looked and caught her breath a little.

"Why!" she cried, "the gray wall is changing. It is as if a green mist were creeping over it. It's almost like a green gauze veil."

"Aye," said Dickon. "An' it'll be greener and greener till th' gray's all gone. Can tha' guess what I was thinkin'?"

"I know it was something nice," said Mary eagerly. "I

believe it was something about Colin."

"I was thinkin' that if he was out here he wouldn't be watchin' for lumps to grow on his back; he'd be watchin' for buds to break on th' rose-bushes, an' he'd likely be healthier," explained Dickon. "I was wonderin' if us could ever get him in th' humor to come out here an' lie under th' trees in his carriage."

"I've been wondering that myself. I've thought of it almost every time I've talked to him," said Mary. "I've wondered if he could keep a secret and I've wondered if we could bring him here without any one seeing us. I thought perhaps you could push his carriage. The doctor said he must have fresh air and if he wants us to take him out no one dare disobey him. He won't go out for other people and perhaps they will be glad if he will go out with us. He could order the gardeners to keep away so they wouldn't find out."

Dickon was thinking very hard as he scratched Captain's back.

"It'd be good for him, I'll warrant," he said. "Us'd not be thinkin' he'd better never been born. Us'd be just two children watchin' a garden grow, an' he'd be another. Two lads an' a little lass just lookin' on at th' springtime. I warrant it'd be better than doctor's stuff."

"He's been lying in his room so long and he's always been so afraid of his back that it has made him queer," said Mary. "He knows a good many things out of books but he doesn't know anything else. He says he has been too ill to notice things and he hates going out of doors and hates gardens and gardeners. But he likes to hear about this garden because it is a secret. I daren't tell him much but he said he wanted to see it."

"Us'll have him out here sometime for sure," said Dickon. "I could push his carriage well enough. Has tha' noticed how th' robin an' his mate has been workin' while we've been sittin' here? Look at him perched on that branch wonderin' where it'd be best to put that twig he's got in his beak."

He made one of his low whistling calls and the robin turned his head and looked at him inquiringly, still holding his twig. Dickon spoke to him as Ben Weatherstaff did, but Dickon's tone was one of friendly advice.

"Wheres'ever tha' puts it," he said, "it'll be all right. Tha' knew how to build tha' nest before tha' came out o' th' egg. Get on with thee, lad. Tha'st got no time to lose."

"Oh, I do like to hear you talk to him!" Mary said, laughing delightedly. "Ben Weatherstaff scolds him and makes fun of him, and he hops about and looks as if he understood every word, and I know he likes it. Ben Weatherstaff says he is so conceited he would rather have stones thrown at him than not be noticed."

Dickon laughed too and went on talking.

"Tha' knows us won't trouble thee," he said to the robin. "Us is near bein' wild things ourselves. Us is nest-buildin' too, bless thee. Look out tha' doesn't tell on us."

And though the robin did not answer, because his beak was occupied, Mary knew that when he flew away with his twig to his own corner of the garden the darkness of his dew-bright eye meant that he would not tell their secret for the world.

Chapter 16

"I Won't!"
Said Mary

They found a great deal to do that morning and Mary was late in returning to the house and was also in such a hurry to get back to her work that she quite forgot Colin until the last moment.

"Tell Colin that I can't come and see him yet," she said to Martha. "I'm very busy in the garden."

Martha looked rather frightened.

"Eh! Miss Mary," she said, "it may put him all out of humor when I tell him that."

But Mary was not as afraid of him as other people were and she was not a self-sacrificing person.

"I can't stay," she answered. "Dickon's waiting for me;" and she ran away.

The afternoon was even lovelier and busier than the morning had been. Already nearly all the weeds were cleared out of the garden and most of the roses and trees had been pruned or dug about. Dickon had brought a spade of his own and he had taught Mary to use all her tools, so that by this time it was plain that though the lovely wild place was not likely to become a "gardener's garden" it would be a wilderness of growing things before the springtime was over.

"There'll be apple blossoms an' cherry blossoms overhead," Dickon said, working away with all his might. "An' there'll be peach an' plum trees in bloom against th' walls, an' th' grass'll be a carpet o' flowers."

The little fox and the rook were as happy and busy as they were, and the robin and his mate flew backward and forward like tiny streaks of lightning. Sometimes the rook flapped his black wings and soared away over the tree-tops in the park. Each time he came back and perched near Dickon and cawed several times as if he were relating his adventures, and Dickon talked to him just as he had talked to the robin. Once when Dickon was so busy that he did not answer him at first, Soot flew on to his shoulders and gently tweaked his ear with his large beak.

When Mary wanted to rest a little Dickon sat down with her under a tree and once he took his pipe out of his pocket and played the soft strange little notes and two squirrels appeared on the wall and looked and listened.

"Tha's a good bit stronger than tha' was," Dickon said, looking at her as she was digging. "Tha's beginning to look different, for sure."

Mary was glowing with exercise and good spirits.

"I'm getting fatter and fatter every day," she said quite exultantly. "Mrs. Medlock will have to get me some bigger dresses. Martha says my hair is growing thicker. It isn't so flat and stringy."

The sun was beginning to set and sending deep gold-colored rays slanting under the trees when they parted.

"It'll be fine tomorrow," said Dickon. "I'll be at work by sunrise."

"So will I," said Mary.

She ran back to the house as quickly as her feet would carry her. She wanted to tell Colin about Dickon's fox cub and the rook and about what the springtime had been doing. She felt sure he would like to hear. So it was not very pleasant when she opened the door of her room, to see Martha standing waiting for her with a doleful face.

"What is the matter?" she asked. "What did Colin say when you told him I couldn't come?"

"Eh!" said Martha, "I wish tha'd gone. He was nigh goin' into one o' his tantrums. There's been a nice to do all afternoon to keep him quiet. He would watch the clock all th' time."

Mary's lips pinched themselves together. She was no more used to considering other people than Colin was and she saw no reason why an ill-tempered boy should interfere with the thing she liked best. She knew nothing about the pitifulness of people who had been ill and nervous and who did not know that they could control their tempers and need not make other people ill and nervous, too. When she had had a headache in India she had done her best to see that everybody else also had a headache or something quite as bad. And she felt she was quite right; but of course now she felt that Colin was quite wrong.

He was not on his sofa when she went into his room. He was lying flat on his back in bed and he did not turn his head toward her as she came in. This was a bad beginning and Mary marched up to him with her stiff manner.

"Why didn't you get up?" she said.

"I did get up this morning when I thought you were coming," he answered, without looking at her. "I made them put me back in bed this afternoon. My back ached and my head ached and I was tired. Why didn't you come?" "I was working in the garden with Dickon," said Mary.

Colin frowned and condescended to look at her.

"I won't let that boy come here if you go and stay with him instead of coming to talk to me," he said.

Mary flew into a fine passion. She could fly into a passion without making a noise. She just grew sour and obstinate and did not care what happened.

"If you send Dickon away, I'll never come into this room again!" she retorted.

"You'll have to if I want you," said Colin.

"I won't!" said Mary.

"I'll make you," said Colin. "They shall drag you in."

"Shall they, Mr. Rajah!" said Mary fiercely. "They may drag me in but they can't make me talk when they get me here. I'll sit and clench my teeth and never tell you one thing. I won't even look at you. I'll stare at the floor!"

They were a nice agreeable pair as they glared at each other. If they had been two little street boys they would have sprung at each other and had a rough-and-tumble fight. As it was, they did the next thing to it.

"You are a selfish thing!" cried Colin.

"What are you?" said Mary. "Selfish people always say that. Any one is selfish who doesn't do what they want. You're more selfish than I am. You're the most selfish boy I ever saw."

"I'm not!" snapped Colin. "I'm not as selfish as your fine Dickon is! He keeps you playing in the dirt when he knows I am all by myself. He's selfish, if you like!"

Mary's eyes flashed fire.

"He's nicer than any other boy that ever lived!" she said. "He's—he's like an angel!" It might sound rather silly to say that but she did not care.

"A nice angel!" Colin sneered ferociously. "He's a common cottage boy off the moor!"

"He's better than a common Rajah!" retorted Mary. "He's a thousand times better!"

Because she was the stronger of the two she was beginning to get the better of him. The truth was that he had never had a fight with any one like himself in his life and, upon the whole, it was rather good for him, though neither he nor Mary knew anything about that.

He turned his head on his pillow and shut his eyes and a big tear was squeezed out and ran down his

cheek. He was beginning to feel pathetic and sorry for himself—not for any one else.

"I'm not as selfish as you, because I'm always ill, and I'm sure there is a lump coming on my back," he said. "And I am going to die besides."

"You're not!" contradicted Mary unsympathetically.

He opened his eyes quite wide with indignation. He had never heard such a thing said before. He was at once furious and slightly pleased, if a person could be both at one time.

"I'm not?" he cried. "I am! You know I am! Everybody says so."

"I don't believe it!" said Mary sourly. "You just say that to make people sorry. I believe you're proud of it. I don't believe it! If you were a nice boy it might be true—but you're too nasty!"

In spite of his invalid back Colin sat up in bed in quite a healthy rage.

"Get out of the room!" he shouted and he caught hold of his pillow and threw it at her. He was not strong enough to throw it far and it only fell at her feet, but Mary's face looked as pinched as a nutcracker.

"I'm going," she said. "And I won't come back!" She walked to the door and when she reached it she turned round and spoke again.

"I was going to tell you all sorts of nice things," she said. "Dickon brought his fox and his rook and I was going to tell you all about them. Now I won't tell you a single thing!"

She marched out of the door and closed it behind her, and there to her great astonishment she found the trained nurse standing as if she had been listening and, more amazing still—she was laughing.

She was a big handsome young woman who ought not to have been a trained nurse at all, as she could not bear invalids, and she was always making excuses to leave Colin to Martha or any one else who would take her place. Mary had never liked her, and she simply stood and gazed up at her as she stood giggling into her handkerchief.

"What are you laughing at?" she asked her.

"At you two young ones," said the nurse. "It's the best thing that could happen to the sickly pampered thing to have some one to stand up to him that's as spoiled as himself;" and she laughed into her handkerchief again. "If he'd had a young vixen of a sister to fight with it would have been the saving of him."

"Is he going to die?"

"I don't know and I don't care," said the nurse. "Hysterics and temper are half what ails him."

"What are hysterics?" asked Mary.

"You'll find out if you work him into a tantrum after this—but at any rate you've given him something to have hysterics about, and I'm glad of it."

Mary went back to her room not feeling at all as she had felt when she had come in from the garden. She was cross and disappointed but not at all sorry for Colin. She had looked forward to telling him a great many things and she had meant to try to make up her mind whether it would be safe to trust him with the great secret. She had been beginning to think it would be, but now she had changed her mind entirely. She would never tell him and he could stay in his room and never get any fresh air and die if he liked! It would serve him right!

She felt so sour and unrelenting that for a few minutes she almost forgot about Dickon and the green veil creeping over the world and the soft wind blowing down from the moor.

Martha was waiting for her and the trouble in her face had been temporarily replaced by interest and curiosity. There was a wooden box on the table and its cover had been removed and revealed that it was full of neat packages.

"Mr. Craven sent it to you," said Martha. "It looks as if it had picture-books in it."

Mary remembered what he had asked her the day she had gone to his room. "Do you want anything—dolls—toys—books?" She opened the package wondering if he had sent a doll, and also wondering what she should do with it if he had. But he had not sent one.

There were several beautiful books such as Colin had, and two of them were about gardens and were full of pictures. There were two or three games and there was a beautiful little writing-case with a gold monogram on it and a gold pen and inkstand.

Everything was so nice that her pleasure began to crowd her anger out of her mind. She had not expected him to remember her at all and her hard little heart grew quite warm.

"I can write better than I can print," she said, "and the first thing I shall write with that pen will be a letter to tell him I am much obliged."

If she had been friends with Colin she would have run

to show him her presents at once, and they would have looked at the pictures and read some of the gardening books and perhaps tried playing the games, and he would have enjoyed himself so much he would never once have thought he was going to die or have put his hand on his spine to see if there was a lump coming. He had a way of doing that which she could not bear. It gave her an uncomfortable frightened feeling because he always looked so frightened himself. He said that if he felt even quite a little lump some day he should know his hunch had begun to grow.

Something he had heard Mrs. Medlock whispering to the nurse had given him the idea and he had thought over it in secret until it was quite firmly fixed in his mind. Mrs. Medlock had said his father's back had begun to show its crookedness in that way when he was a child. He had never told any one but Mary that most of his "tantrums," as they called them grew out of his hysterical hidden fear. Mary had been sorry for him when he had told her.

"He always began to think about it when he was cross or tired," she said to herself. "And he has been cross today. Perhaps—perhaps he has been thinking about it all afternoon."

She stood still, looking down at the carpet and thinking.

"I said I would never go back again—" she hesitated, knitting her brows—"but perhaps, just perhaps, I will go and see—if he wants me—in the morning. Perhaps he'll try to throw his pillow at me again, but—I think—I'll go."

Chapter 17

A Tantrum

She had got up very early in the morning and had worked hard in the garden and she was tired and sleepy, so as soon as Martha had brought her supper and she had eaten it, she was glad to go to bed. As she laid her head on the pillow she murmured to herself:

"I'll go out before breakfast and work with Dickon and then afterward—I believe—I'll go to see him."

She thought it was the middle of the night when she was awakened by such dreadful sounds that she jumped out of bed in an instant. What was it—what was it? The next minute she felt quite sure she knew. Doors were opened and shut and there were hurrying feet in the corridors and some one was crying and screaming at the same time, screaming and crying in a horrible way.

"It's Colin," she said. "He's having one of those tantrums the nurse called hysterics. How awful it sounds."

As she listened to the sobbing screams she did not wonder that people were so frightened that they gave him his own way in everything rather than hear them. She put her hands over her ears and felt sick and shivering.

"I don't know what to do. I don't know what to do," she kept saying. "I can't bear it."

Once she wondered if he would stop if she dared go to him and then she remembered how he had driven her out of the room and thought that perhaps the sight of her might make him worse.

Even when she pressed her hands more tightly over her ears she could not keep the awful sounds out. She hated them so and was so terrified by them that suddenly they began to make her angry and she felt as if she should like to fly into a tantrum herself and frighten him as he was frightening her. She was not used to any one's tempers but her own. She took her hands from her ears and sprang up and stamped her foot.

"He ought to be stopped! Somebody ought to make him stop! Somebody ought to beat him!" she cried out.

Just then she heard feet almost running down the corridor and her door opened and the nurse came in. She was not laughing now by any means. She even looked rather pale.

"He's worked himself into hysterics," she said in a great hurry. "He'll do himself harm. No one can do anything with him. You come and try, like a good child. He likes you."

"He turned me out of the room this morning," said Mary, stamping her foot with excitement.

The stamp rather pleased the nurse. The truth was that she had been afraid she might find Mary crying and hiding her head under the bed-clothes.

"That's right," she said. "You're in the right humor. You go and scold him. Give him something new to think of. Do go, child, as quick as ever you can."

It was not until afterward that Mary realized that the

thing had been funny as well as dreadful—that it was funny that all the grown-up people were so frightened that they came to a little girl just because they guessed she was almost as bad as Colin himself.

She flew along the corridor and the nearer she got to the screams the higher her temper mounted. She felt quite wicked by the time she reached the door. She slapped it open with her hand and ran across the room to the four-posted bed.

"You stop!" she almost shouted. "You stop! I hate you! Everybody hates you! I wish everybody would run out of the house and let you scream yourself to death! You will scream yourself to death in a minute, and I wish you would!" A nice sympathetic child could neither have thought nor said such things, but it just happened that the shock of hearing them was the best possible thing for this hysterical boy whom no one had ever dared to restrain or contradict.

He had been lying on his face beating his pillow with his hands and he actually almost jumped around, he turned so quickly at the sound of the furious little voice. His face looked dreadful, white and red and swollen, and he was gasping and choking; but savage little Mary did not care an atom.

"If you scream another scream," she said, "I'll scream too—and I can scream louder than you can and I'll frighten you, I'll frighten you!"

He actually had stopped screaming because she had startled him so. The scream which had been coming almost choked him. The tears were streaming down his face and he shook all over.

"I can't stop!" he gasped and sobbed. "I can't—I can't!"

"You can!" shouted Mary. "Half that ails you is hysterics and temper—just hysterics—hysterics—hysterics!" and she stamped each time she said it.

"I felt the lump—I felt it," choked out Colin. "I knew I should. I shall have a hunch on my back and then I shall die," and he began to writhe again and turned on his face and sobbed and wailed but he didn't scream.

"You didn't feel a lump!" contradicted Mary fiercely. "If you did it was only a hysterical lump. Hysterics makes lumps. There's nothing the matter with your horrid back—nothing but hysterics! Turn over and let me look at it!"

She liked the word "hysterics" and felt somehow as if it had an effect on him. He was probably like herself and had never heard it before.

"Nurse," she commanded, "come here and show me his back this minute!"

The nurse, Mrs. Medlock and Martha had been standing huddled together near the door staring at her, their mouths half open. All three had gasped with fright more than once. The nurse came forward as if she were half afraid. Colin was heaving with great breathless sobs.

"Perhaps he—he won't let me," she hesitated in a low voice.

Colin heard her, however, and he gasped out between two sobs: "Sh-show her! She-she'll see then!"

It was a poor thin back to look at when it was bared. Every rib could be counted and every joint of the spine, though Mistress Mary did not count them as she bent over and examined them with a solemn savage little face. She looked so sour and old-fashioned that the nurse turned her head aside to hide the twitching of her mouth.

There was just a minute's silence, for even Colin tried to hold his breath while Mary looked up and down his spine, and down and up, as intently as if she had been the great doctor from London.

"There's not a single lump there!" she said at last. "There's not a lump as big as a pin—except backbone lumps, and you can only feel them because you're thin. I've got backbone lumps myself, and they used to stick out as much as yours do, until I began to get fatter, and I am not fat enough yet to hide them. There's not a lump as big as a pin! If you ever say there is again, I shall laugh!"

No one but Colin himself knew what effect those crossly spoken childish words had on him. If he had ever had any one to talk to about his secret terrors—if he had ever dared to let himself ask questions—if he had had childish companions and had not lain on his back in the huge closed house, breathing an atmosphere heavy with the fears of people who were most of them ignorant and tired of him, he would have found out that most of his fright and illness was created by himself.

But he had lain and thought of himself and his aches and weariness for hours and days and months and years. And now that an angry unsympathetic little girl insisted obstinately that he was not as ill as he thought he was he actually felt as if she might be speaking the truth.

"I didn't know," ventured the nurse, "that he thought he had a lump on his spine. His back is weak because he won't try to sit up. I could have told him there was no lump there."

Colin gulped and turned his face a little to look at her.

"C-could you?" he said pathetically.

"Yes, sir."

"There!" said Mary, and she gulped too.

Colin turned on his face again and but for his long-drawn broken breaths, which were the dying down of his storm of sobbing, he lay still for a minute, though great tears streamed down his face and wet the pillow. Actually the tears meant that a curious great relief had come to him. Presently he turned and looked at the nurse again and strangely enough he was not like a Rajah at all as he spoke to her.

"Do you think—I could—live to grow up?" he said.

The nurse was neither clever nor soft-hearted but she could repeat some of the London doctor's words.

"You probably will if you will do what you are told to do and not give way to your temper, and stay out a great deal in the fresh air."

Colin's tantrum had passed and he was weak and worn out with crying and this perhaps made him feel gentle. He put out his hand a little toward Mary, and I am glad to say that, her own tantum having passed, she was softened too and met him half-way with her hand, so that it was a sort of making up.

"I'll—I'll go out with you, Mary," he said. "I shan't hate fresh air if we can find—" He remembered just in time to stop himself from saying "if we can find the secret garden" and he ended, "I shall like to go out with you if Dickon will come and push my chair. I do so want to see Dickon and the fox and the crow."

The nurse remade the tumbled bed and shook and straightened the pillows. Then she made Colin a cup of beef tea and gave a cup to Mary, who really was very glad to get it after her excitement. Mrs. Medlock and Martha gladly slipped away, and after everything was neat and calm and in order the nurse looked as if she would very gladly slip away also. She was a healthy young woman who resented being robbed of her sleep and she yawned quite openly as she looked at Mary, who had pushed her big footstool close to the four-posted bed and was holding Colin's hand.

"You must go back and get your sleep out," she said. "He'll drop off after a while—if he's not too upset. Then I'll lie down myself in the next room."

"Would you like me to sing you that song I learned from my Ayah?" Mary whispered to Colin.

His hand pulled hers gently and he turned his tired eyes on her appealingly.

"Oh, yes!" he answered. "It's such a soft song. I shall go to sleep in a minute."

"I will put him to sleep," Mary said to the yawning nurse. "You can go if you like."

"Well," said the nurse, with an attempt at reluctance. "If he doesn't go to sleep in half an hour you must call me."

"Very well," answered Mary.

The nurse was out of the room in a minute and as soon as she was gone Colin pulled Mary's hand again.

"I almost told," he said; "but I stopped myself in time. I won't talk and I'll go to sleep, but you said you had a whole lot of nice things to tell me. Have you—do you think you have found out anything at all about the way into the secret garden?"

Mary looked at his poor little tired face and swollen eyes and her heart relented.

"Ye-es," she answered, "I think I have. And if you

will go to sleep I will tell you tomorrow." His hand quite trembled.

"Oh, Mary!" he said. "Oh, Mary! If I could get into it I think I should live to grow up! Do you suppose that instead of singing the Ayah song—you could just tell me softly as you did that first day what you imagine it looks like inside? I am sure it will make me go to sleep."

"Yes," answered Mary. "Shut your eyes."

He closed his eyes and lay quite still and she held his hand and began to speak very slowly and in a very low voice.

"I think it has been left alone so long—that it has grown all into a lovely tangle. I think the roses have climbed and climbed and climbed until they hang from the branches and walls and creep over the ground— almost like a strange gray mist. Some of them have died but many—are alive and when the summer comes there will be curtains and fountains of roses. I think the ground is full of daffodils and snowdrops and lilies and iris working their way out of the dark. Now the spring has begun—perhaps—perhaps—"

The soft drone of her voice was making him stiller and stiller and she saw it and went on.

"Perhaps they are coming up through the grass— perhaps there are clusters of purple crocuses and gold ones—even now. Perhaps the leaves are beginning to break out and uncurl—and perhaps—the gray is changing and a green gauze veil is creeping—and creeping over— everything. And the birds are coming to look at it—because it is—so safe and still. And perhaps—perhaps—perhaps—" very softly and slowly indeed, "the robin has found a mate—and is building a nest."

And Colin was asleep.

Chapter 18

"Tha' Munnot Waste No Time"

Of course Mary did not waken early the next morning. She slept late because she was tired, and when Martha brought her breakfast she told her that though. Colin was quite quiet he was ill and feverish as he always was after he had worn himself out with a fit of crying. Mary ate her breakfast slowly as she listened.

"He says he wishes tha' would please go and see him as soon as tha' can," Martha said. "It's queer what a fancy he's took to thee. Tha' did give it him last night for sure—didn't tha? Nobody else would have dared to do it. Eh! poor lad! He's been spoiled till salt won't save him. Mother says as th' two worst things as can happen to a child is never to have his own way—or always to have it. She doesn't know which is th' worst. Tha' was in a fine temper tha'self, too. But he says to me when I went into his room, 'Please ask Miss Mary if she'll please come an' talk to me?' Think o' him saying please! Will you go, Miss?"

"I'll run and see Dickon first," said Mary. "No, I'll go and see Colin first and tell him—I know what I'll tell him," with a sudden inspiration.

She had her hat on when she appeared in Colin's room and for a second he looked disappointed. He was in bed. His face was pitifully white and there were dark circles round his eyes.

"I'm glad you came," he said. "My head aches and I ache all over because I'm so tired. Are you going somewhere?"

Mary went and leaned against his bed.

"I won't be long," she said. "I'm going to Dickon, but I'll come back. Colin, it's—it's something about the garden."

His whole face brightened and a little color came into it.

"Oh! is it?" he cried out. "I dreamed about it all night I heard you say something about gray changing into green, and I dreamed I was standing in a place all filled with trembling little green leaves—and there were birds on nests everywhere and they looked so soft and still. I'll lie and think about it until you come back."

In five minutes Mary was with Dickon in their garden. The fox and the crow were with him again and this time he had brought two tame squirrels. "I came over on the pony this mornin'," he said. "Eh! he is a good little chap— Jump is! I brought these two in my pockets. This here one he's called Nut an' this here other one's called Shell."

When he said "Nut" one squirrel leaped on to his right shoulder and when he said "Shell" the other one leaped on to his left shoulder.

When they sat down on the grass with Captain curled at their feet, Soot solemnly listening on a tree and Nut and Shell nosing about close to them, it seemed to

Mary that it would be scarcely bearable to leave such delightfulness, but when she began to tell her story somehow the look in Dickon's funny face gradually changed her mind. She could see he felt sorrier for Colin than she did. He looked up at the sky and all about him.

"Just listen to them birds—th' world seems full of 'em—all whistlin' an' pipin'," he said. "Look at 'em dartin' about, an' hearken at 'em callin' to each other. Come springtime seems like as if all th' world's callin'. The leaves is uncurlin' so you can see 'em—an', my word, th' nice smells there is about!" sniffing with his happy turned-up nose. "An' that poor lad lyin' shut up an' seein' so little that he gets to thinkin' o' things as sets him screamin'. Eh! my! we mun get him out here— we mun get him watchin' an listenin' an' sniffin' up th' air an' get him just soaked through wi' sunshine. An' we munnot lose no time about it."

When he was very much interested he often spoke quite broad Yorkshire though at other times he tried to modify his dialect so that Mary could better understand. But she loved his broad Yorkshire and had in fact been trying to learn to speak it herself. So she spoke a little now.

"Aye, that we mun," she said (which meant "Yes, indeed, we must"). "I'll tell thee what us'll do first," she proceeded, and Dickon grinned, because when the little wench tried to twist her tongue into speaking Yorkshire it amused him very much.

"He's took a graidely fancy to thee. He wants to see thee and he wants to see Soot an' Captain. When I go back to the house to talk to him I'll ax him if tha' canna' come an' see him tomorrow mornin'—an'. bring tha' creatures wi' thee—an' then—in a bit, when there's more leaves out, an' happen a bud or two, we'll get him to come out an' tha' shall push him in his chair an' we'll bring him here an' show him everything."

When she stopped she was quite proud of herself. She had never made a long speech in Yorkshire before and she had remembered very well.

"Tha' mun talk a bit o' Yorkshire like that to Mester Colin," Dickon chuckled. "Tha'll make him laugh an' there's nowt as good for ill folk as laughin' is. Mother says she believes as half a hour's good laugh every mornin' 'ud cure a chap as was makin' ready for typhus fever."

"I'm going to talk Yorkshire to him this very day," said Mary, chuckling herself.

The garden had reached the time when every day and every night it seemed as if Magicians were passing through it drawing loveliness out of the earth and the boughs with wands. It was hard to go away and leave it all, particularly as Nut had actually crept on to her dress and Shell had scrambled down the trunk of the apple-tree they sat under and stayed there looking at her with inquiring eyes. But she went back to the house and when she sat down close to Colin's bed he began to sniff as Dickon did though not in such an experienced way.

"You smell like flowers and—and fresh things," he cried out quite joyously. "What is it you smell of? It's cool and warm and sweet all at the same time."

"It's th' wind from th' moor," said Mary. "It comes o' sittin' on th' grass under a tree wi' Dickon an' wi' Captain an' Soot an' Nut an' Shell. It's th' springtime an' out o' doors an' sunshine as smells so graidely."

She said it as broadly as she could, and you do not know how broadly Yorkshire sounds until you have heard some one speak it. Colin began to laugh.

"What are you doing?" he said. "I never heard you talk like that before. How funny it sounds."

"I'm givin' thee a bit o' Yorkshire," answered Mary triumphantly. "I canna' talk as graidely as Dickon an' Martha can but tha' sees I can shape a bit. Doesn't tha' understand a bit o' Yorkshire when tha' hears it? An' tha' a Yorkshire lad thysel' bred an' born! Eh! I wonder tha'rt not ashamed o' thy face."

And then she began to laugh too and they both laughed until they could not stop themselves and they laughed until the room echoed and Mrs. Medlock opening the door to come in drew back into the corridor and stood listening amazed.

"Well, upon my word!" she said, speaking rather broad Yorkshire herself because there was no one to hear her and she was so astonished. "Whoever heard th' like! Whoever on earth would ha' thought it!"

There was so much to talk about. It seemed as if Colin could never hear enough of Dickon and Captain and Soot and Nut and Shell and the pony whose name was Jump.

Mary had run round into the wood with Dickon to see Jump. He was a tiny little shaggy moor pony with thick

locks hanging over his eyes and with a pretty face and a nuzzling velvet nose. He was rather thin with living on moor grass but he was as tough and wiry as if the muscle in his little legs had been made of steel springs. He had lifted his head and whinnied softly the moment he saw Dickon, and he had trotted up to him and put his head across his shoulder, and then Dickon had talked into his ear and Jump had talked back in odd little whinnies and puffs and snorts. Dickon had made him give Mary his small front hoof and kiss her on her cheek with his velvet muzzle.

"Does he really understand everything Dickon says?" Colin asked.

"It seems as if he does," answered Mary. "Dickon says anything will understand if you're friends with it for sure, but you have to be friends for sure."

Colin lay quiet a little while and his strange gray eyes seemed to be staring at the wall, but Mary saw he was thinking.

"I wish I was friends with things," he said at last, "but I'm not. I never had anything to be friends with, and I can't bear people."

"Can't you bear me?" asked Mary.

"Yes, I can," he answered. "It's funny but I even like you."

"Ben Weatherstaff said I was like him," said Mary. "He said he'd warrant we'd both got the same nasty tempers. I think you are like him too. We are all three alike—you and I and Ben Weatherstaff. He said we were neither of us much to look at and we were as sour as we looked. But I don't feel as sour as I used to before I knew the robin and Dickon."

"Did you feel as if you hated people?"

"Yes," answered Mary without any affectation. "I should have detested you if I had seen you before I saw the robin and Dickon."

Colin put out his thin hand and touched her.

"Mary," he said, "I wish I hadn't said what I did about sending Dickon away. I hated you when you said he was like an angel and I laughed at you but—but perhaps he is."

"Well, it was rather funny to say it," she admitted

frankly, "because his nose does turn up and he has a big mouth and his clothes have patches all over them and he talks broad Yorkshire, but—but if an angel did come to Yorkshire and live on the moor—if there was a Yorkshire angel—I believe he'd understand the green things and know how to make them grow and he would know how to talk to the wild creatures as Dickon does and they'd know he was friends for sure."

"I shouldn't mind Dickon looking at me," said Colin; "I want to see him."

"I'm glad you said that," answered Mary, "because— because—"

Quite suddenly it came into her mind that this was the minute to tell him.

Colin knew something new was coming.

"Because what?" he cried eagerly.

Mary was so anxious that she got up from her stool and came to him and caught hold of both his hands.

"Can I trust you? I trusted Dickon because birds trusted him. Can I trust you—for sure—for sure?" she implored.

Her face was so solemn that he almost whispered his answer.

"Yes—yes!"

"Well, Dickon will come to see you tomorrow morning, and he'll bring his creatures with him."

"Oh! Oh!" Colin cried out in delight.

"But that's not all," Mary went on, almost pale with solemn excitement. "The rest is better. There is a door into the garden. I found it. It is under the ivy on the wall."

If he had been a strong healthy boy Colin would probably have shouted "Hooray! Hooray! Hooray!" but he was weak and rather hysterical; his eyes grew bigger and bigger and he gasped for breath.

"Oh! Mary!" he cried out with a half sob. "Shall I see it? Shall I get into it? Shall I live to get into it?" and he clutched her hands and dragged her toward him.

"Of course you'll see it!" snapped Mary indignantly. "Of course you'll live to get into it! Don't be silly!"

And she was so un-hysterical and natural and childish that she brought him to his senses and he began to laugh at himself, and a few minutes afterward she was sitting on her stool again telling him not what she imagined the secret garden to be like, but what it really was, and Colin's aches and tiredness were forgotten and he was listening enraptured.

"It is just what you thought it would be," he said at last. "It sounds just as if you had really seen it. You know I said that when you told me first."

Mary hesitated about two minutes and then boldly spoke the truth.

"I had seen it—and I had been in," she said. "I found the key and got in weeks ago. But I daren't tell you—I daren't because I was so afraid I couldn't trust you—for sure!"

Chapter 19

"It Has Come!"

Of course Dr. Craven had been sent for the morning after Colin had had his tantrum. He was always sent for at once when such a thing occurred and he always found, when he arrived, a white shaken boy lying on his bed, sulky and still so hysterical that he was ready to break into fresh sobbing at the least word. In fact, Dr. Craven dreaded and detested the difficulties of these visits. On this occasion he was away from Misselthwaite Manor until afternoon.

"How is he?" he asked Mrs. Medlock rather irritably when he arrived. "He will break a blood-vessel in one of those fits some day. The boy is half insane with hysteria and self-indulgence."

"Well, sir," answered Mrs. Medlock, "you'll scarcely believe your eyes when you see him. That plain sour-faced child that's almost as bad as himself has just bewitched him. How she's done it there's no telling. The Lord knows she's nothing to look at and you scarcely ever hear her speak, but she did what none of us dare do. She just flew at him like a little cat last night, and stamped her feet and ordered him to stop screaming, and somehow she startled him so that he actually did stop, and this afternoon—well just come up and see, sir. It's past crediting."

The scene which Dr. Craven beheld when he entered his patient's room was indeed rather astonishing to him. As Mrs. Medlock opened the door he heard laughing and chattering. Colin was on his sofa in his dressing-gown and he was sitting up quite straight looking at a picture in one of the garden books and talking to the plain child who at that moment could scarcely be called plain at all because her face was so glowing with enjoyment.

"Those long spires of blue ones— we'll have a lot of those," Colin was announcing. "They're called Del-phin-iums."

"Dickon says they're larkspurs made big and grand," cried Mistress Mary. "There are clumps there already."

Then they saw Dr. Craven and stopped. Mary became quite still and Colin looked fretful.

"I am sorry to hear you were ill last night, my boy," Dr. Craven said a trifle nervously. He was rather a nervous man.

"I'm better now—much better," Colin answered, rather like a Rajah. "I'm going out in my chair in a day or two if it is fine. I want some fresh air."

Dr. Craven sat down by him and felt his pulse and looked at him curiously.

"It must be a very fine day," he said, "and you must be very careful not to tire yourself."

"Fresh air won't tire me," said the young Rajah.

As there had been occasions when this same young gentleman had shrieked aloud with rage and had insisted that fresh air would give him cold and kill him, it is not to be wondered at that his doctor felt somewhat startled.

"I thought you did not like fresh air," he said.

"I don't when I am by myself," replied the Rajah; "but my cousin is going out with me."

"And the nurse, of course?" suggested Dr. Craven.

"No, I will not have the nurse," so magnificently that Mary could not help remembering how the young native Prince had looked with his diamonds and emeralds and pearls stuck all over him and the great rubies on the small dark hand he had waved to command his servants to approach with salaams and receive his orders.

"My cousin knows how to take care of me. I am always better when she is with me. She made me better last night. A very strong boy I know will push my carriage."

Dr. Craven felt rather alarmed. If this tiresome hysterical boy should chance to get well he himself would lose all chance of inheriting Misselthwaite; but he was not an unscrupulous man, though he was a weak one, and he did not intend to let him run into actual danger.

"He must be a strong boy and a steady boy," he said. "And I must know something about him. Who is he? What is his name?"

"It's Dickon," Mary spoke up suddenly.

She felt somehow that everybody who knew the moor must know Dickon. And she was right, too. She saw that in a moment Dr. Craven's serious face relaxed into a relieved smile.

"Oh, Dickon," he said. "If it is Dickon you will be safe enough. He's as strong as a moor pony, is Dickon."

"And he's trusty," said Mary. "He's th' trustiest lad i' Yorkshire." She had been talking Yorkshire to Colin and she forgot herself.

"Did Dickon teach you that?" asked Dr. Craven, laughing outright.

"I'm learning it as if it was French," said Mary rather coldly. "It's like a native dialect in India. Very clever people try to learn them. I like it and so does Colin."

"Well, well," he said. "If it amuses you perhaps it won't do you any harm. Did you take your bromide last night, Colin?"

"No," Colin answered. "I wouldn't take it at first and after Mary made me quiet she talked me to sleep—in a low voice—about the spring creeping into a garden."

"That sounds soothing," said Dr. Craven, more perplexed than ever and glancing sideways at Mistress Mary sitting on her stool and looking down silently at the carpet. "You are evidently better, but you must remember—"

"I don't want to remember," interrupted the Rajah, appearing again. "When I lie by myself and remember I begin to have pains everywhere and I think of things that make me begin to scream because I hate them so. If there was a doctor anywhere who could make you forget you were ill instead of remembering it I would have him brought here." And he waved a thin hand which ought really to have been covered with royal signet rings made of rubies. "It is because my cousin makes me forget that she makes me better."

Dr. Craven had never made such a short stay after a "tantrum"; usually he was obliged to remain a very long time and do a great many things. This afternoon he did not give any medicine or leave any new orders and he was spared any disagreeable scenes. When he went downstairs he looked very thoughtful and when he talked to Mrs. Medlock in the library she felt that he was a much puzzled man.

"Well, sir," she ventured, "could you have believed it?"

"It is certainly a new state of affairs," said the doctor. "And there's no denying it is better than the old one."

"I believe Susan Sowerby's right—I do that," said Mrs. Medlock. "I stopped in her cottage on my way to Thwaite yesterday and had a bit of talk with her. And she says to me, 'Well, Sarah Ann, she mayn't be a good child, an' she mayn't be a pretty one, but she's a child, an' children needs children.' We went to school together, Susan Sowerby and me."

"She's the best sick nurse I know," said Dr. Craven. "When I find her in a cottage I know the chances are that I shall save my patient."

Mrs. Medlock smiled. She was fond of Susan Sowerby.

"She's got a way with her, has Susan," she went on quite volubly. "I've been thinking all morning of one thing she said yesterday. She says, 'Once when I was givin' th' children a bit of a preach after they'd been fightin' I ses to 'em all, "When I was at school my jography told as th' world was shaped like a orange an' I found out before I was ten that th' whole orange doesn't belong to nobody. No one owns more than his bit of a quarter an' there's times it seems like there's not enow quarters to go round. But don't you—none o' you—think as you own th' whole orange or you'll find out you're mistaken, an' you won't find it out without hard knocks." 'What children learns from children,' she says, 'is that there's no sense in grabbin' at th' whole orange—peel an' all. If you do you'll likely not get even th' pips, an' them's too bitter to eat.'"

"She's a shrewd woman," said Dr. Craven, putting on his coat.

"Well, she's got a way of saying things," ended Mrs. Medlock, much pleased. "Sometimes I've said to her, 'Eh! Susan, if you was a different woman an' didn't talk such broad Yorkshire I've seen the times when I should have said you was clever.'"

That night Colin slept without once awakening and when he opened his eyes in the morning he lay still and smiled without knowing it—smiled because he felt so curiously comfortable. It was actually nice to be awake, and he turned over and stretched his limbs luxuriously. He felt as if tight strings which had held him had loosened themselves and let him go. He did not know that Dr. Craven would have said that his nerves had relaxed and rested themselves.

Instead of lying and staring at the wall and wishing he had not awakened, his mind was full of the plans he and Mary had made yesterday, of pictures of the garden and of Dickon and his wild creatures. It was so nice to have things to think about.

And he had not been awake more than ten minutes when he heard feet running along the corridor and Mary was at the door. The next minute she was in the room and had run across to his bed, bringing with her a waft of fresh air full of the scent of the morning.

"You've been out! You've been out! There's that nice smell of leaves!" he cried.

She had been running and her hair was loose and blown and she was bright with the air and pink-cheeked, though he could not see it.

"It's so beautiful!" she said, a little breathless with her speed. "You never saw anything so beautiful! It has come! I thought it had come that other morning, but it was only coming. It is here now! It has come, the Spring! Dickon says so!"

"Has it?" cried Colin, and though he really knew nothing about it he felt his heart beat. He actually sat up in bed.

"Open the window!" he added, laughing half with joyful excitement and half at his own fancy. "Perhaps we may hear golden trumpets!"

And though he laughed, Mary was at the window in a moment and in a moment more it was opened wide and freshness and softness and scents and birds' songs were pouring through.

"That's fresh air," she said. "Lie on your back and draw in long breaths of it. That's what Dickon does when he's lying on the moor. He says he feels it in his veins and it makes him strong and he feels as if he could live forever and ever. Breathe it and breathe it."

She was only repeating what Dickon had told her, but

she caught Colin's fancy.

"'Forever and ever'! Does it make him feel like that?" he said, and he did as she told him, drawing in long deep breaths over and over again until he felt that something quite new and delightful was happening to him.

Mary was at his bedside again.

"Things are crowding up out of the earth," she ran on in a hurry. "And there are flowers uncurling and buds on everything and the green veil has covered nearly all the gray and the birds are in such a hurry about their nests for fear they may be too late that some of them are even fighting for places in the secret garden. And the rose-bushes look as wick as wick can be, and there are primroses in the lanes and woods, and the seeds we planted are up, and Dickon has brought the fox and the crow and the squirrels and a newborn lamb."

And then she paused for breath. The newborn lamb Dickon had found three days before lying by its dead mother among the gorse bushes on the moor. It was not the first motherless lamb he had found and he knew what to do with it. He had taken it to the cottage wrapped in his jacket and he had let it lie near the fire and had fed it with warm milk. It was a soft thing with a darling silly baby face and legs rather long for its body.

Dickon had carried it over the moor in his arms and its feeding bottle was in his pocket with a squirrel, and when Mary had sat under a tree with its limp warmth huddled on her lap she had felt as if she were too full of strange joy to speak. A lamb—a lamb! A living lamb who lay on your lap like a baby!

She was describing it with great joy and Colin was listening and drawing in long breaths of air when the nurse entered. She started a little at the sight of the open window. She had sat stifling in the room many a warm day because her patient was sure that open windows gave people cold.

"Are you sure you are not chilly, Master Colin?" she inquired.

"No," was the answer. "I am breathing long breaths of fresh air. It makes you strong. I am going to get up to the sofa for breakfast. My cousin will have breakfast with me."

The nurse went away, concealing a smile, to give the order for two breakfasts. She found the servants' hall a more amusing place than the invalid's chamber and just now everybody wanted to hear the news from upstairs. There was a great deal of joking about the unpopular young recluse who, as the cook said, "had found his master, and good for him." The servants' hall had been very tired of the tantrums, and the butler, who was a man with a family, had more than once expressed his opinion that the invalid would be all the better "for a good hiding."

When Colin was on his sofa and the breakfast for two was put upon the table he made an announcement to the nurse in his most Rajah-like manner.

"A boy, and a fox, and a crow, and two squirrels, and a newborn lamb, are coming to see me this morning. I want them brought upstairs as soon as they come," he said. "You are not to begin playing with the animals in the servants' hall and keep them there. I want them here." The nurse gave a slight gasp and tried to conceal it with a cough.

"Yes, sir," she answered.

"I'll tell you what you can do," added Colin, waving his hand. "You can tell Martha to bring them here. The boy is Martha's brother. His name is Dickon and he is an animal charmer."

"I hope the animals won't bite, Master Colin," said the nurse.

"I told you he was a charmer," said Colin austerely. "Charmers' animals never bite."

"There are snake-charmers in India," said Mary. "And they can put their snakes' heads in their mouths."

"Goodness!" shuddered the nurse.

They ate their breakfast with the morning air pouring in upon them. Colin's breakfast was a very good one and Mary watched him with serious interest.

"You will begin to get fatter just as I did," she said. "I never wanted my breakfast when I was in India and now I always want it."

"I wanted mine this morning," said Colin. "Perhaps it was the fresh air. When do you think Dickon will come?"

He was not long in coming.

In about ten minutes Mary held up her hand.

"Listen!" she said. "Did you hear a caw?"

Colin listened and heard it, the oddest sound in the world to hear inside a house, a hoarse "caw-caw."

"Yes," he answered.

"That's Soot," said Mary. "Listen again. Do you hear a

bleat—a tiny one?"

"Oh, yes!" cried Colin, quite flushing.

"That's the newborn lamb," said Mary. "He's coming."

Dickon's moorland boots were thick and clumsy and though he tried to walk quietly they made a clumping sound as he walked through the long corridors. Mary and Colin heard him marching—marching, until he passed through the tapestry door on to the soft carpet of Colin's own passage.

"If you please, sir," announced Martha, opening the door, "if you please, sir, here's Dickon an' his creatures."

Dickon came in smiling his nicest wide smile. The newborn lamb was in his arms and the little red fox trotted by his side. Nut sat on his left shoulder and Soot on his right and Shell's head and paws peeped out of his coat pocket.

Colin slowly sat up and stared and stared—as he had stared when he first saw Mary; but this was a stare of wonder and delight. The truth was that in spite of all he had heard he had not in the least understood what this boy would be like and that his fox and his crow and his squirrels and his lamb were so near to him and his friendliness that they seemed almost to be part of himself. Colin had never talked to a boy in his life and he was so overwhelmed by his own pleasure and curiosity that he did not even think of speaking.

But Dickon did not feel the least shy or awkward. He had not felt embarrassed because the crow had not known his language and had only stared and had not spoken to him the first time they met. Creatures were always like that until they found out about you. He walked over to Colin's sofa and put the newborn lamb quietly on his lap, and immediately the little creature turned to the warm velvet dressing-gown and began to nuzzle and nuzzle into its folds and butt its tight-curled head with soft impatience against his side. Of course no boy could have helped speaking then.

"What is it doing?" cried Colin. "What does it want?"

"It wants its mother," said Dickon, smiling more and more. "I brought it to thee a bit hungry because I knowed tha'd like to see it feed."

He knelt down by the sofa and took a feeding-bottle from his pocket.

"Come on, little 'un," he said, turning the small woolly white head with a gentle brown hand. "This is what tha's after. Tha'll get more out o' this than tha' will out o' silk velvet coats. There now," and he pushed the rubber tip of the bottle into the nuzzling mouth and the lamb began to suck it with ravenous ecstasy.

After that there was no wondering what to say. By the time the lamb fell asleep questions poured forth and Dickon answered them all. He told them how he had found the lamb just as the sun was rising three mornings ago. He had been standing on the moor listening to a skylark and watching him swing higher and higher into the sky until he was only a speck in the heights of blue.

"I'd almost lost him but for his song an' I was wonderin' how a chap could hear it when it seemed as if he'd get out o' th' world in a minute—an' just then

I heard somethin' else far off among th' gorse bushes. It was a weak bleatin' an' I knowed it was a new lamb as was hungry an' I knowed it wouldn't be hungry if it hadn't lost its mother somehow, so I set off searchin'. Eh! I did have a look for it. I went in an' out among th' gorse bushes an' round an' round an' I always seemed to take th' wrong turnin'. But at last I seed a bit o' white by a rock on top o' th' moor an' I climbed up an' found th' little 'un half dead wi' cold an' clemmin'."

While he talked, Soot flew solemnly in and out of the open window and cawed remarks about the scenery while Nut and Shell made excursions into the big trees outside and ran up and down trunks and explored branches. Captain curled up near Dickon, who sat on the hearth rug from preference.

They looked at the pictures in the gardening books and Dickon knew all the flowers by their country names and knew exactly which ones were already growing in the secret garden.

"I couldna' say that there name," he said, pointing to one under which was written "Aquilegia," "but us calls that a columbine, an' that there one it's a snapdragon and they both grow wild in hedges, but these is garden ones an' they're bigger an' grander. There's some big clumps o' columbine in th' garden. They'll look like a bed o' blue an' white butterflies flutterin' when they're out."

"I'm going to see them," cried Colin. "I am going to see them!"

"Aye, that tha' mun," said Mary quite seriously. "An' tha' munnot lose no time about it."

Chapter 20

"I Shall Live Forever— and Ever—and Ever!"

But they were obliged to wait more than a week because first there came some very windy days and then Colin was threatened with a cold, which two things happening one after the other would no doubt have thrown him into a rage but that there was so much careful and mysterious planning to do and almost every day Dickon came in, if only for a few minutes, to talk about what was happening on the moor and in the lanes and hedges and on the borders of streams.

The things he had to tell about otters' and badgers' and water-rats' houses, not to mention birds' nests and field-mice and their burrows, were enough to make you almost tremble with excitement when you heard all the intimate details from an animal charmer and realized with what thrilling eagerness and anxiety the whole busy underworld was working.

"They're same as us," said Dickon, "only they have to build their homes every year. An' it keeps 'em so busy they fair scuffle to get 'em done."

The most absorbing thing, however, was the preparations to be made before Colin could be transported with sufficient secrecy to the garden. No one must see the chair-carriage and Dickon and Mary after they turned a certain corner of the shrubbery and entered upon the walk outside the ivied walls.

As each day passed, Colin had become more and more fixed in his feeling that the mystery surrounding the garden was one of its greatest charms. Nothing must spoil that. No one must ever suspect that they had a secret. People must think that he was simply going out with Mary and Dickon because he liked them and did not object to their looking at him.

They had long and quite delightful talks about their route. They would go up this path and down that one and cross the other and go round among the fountain flowerbeds as if they were looking at the "bedding-out plants" the head gardener, Mr. Roach, had been having arranged. That would seem such a rational thing to do that no one would think it at all mysterious. They would turn into the shrubbery walks and lose themselves until they came to the long walls. It was almost as serious and elaborately thought out as the plans of march made by great generals in time of war.

Rumors of the new and curious things which were occurring in the invalid's apartments had of course filtered through the servants' hall into the stable yards and out among the gardeners, but notwithstanding this, Mr. Roach was startled one day when he received orders from Master Colin's room to the effect that he must report himself in the apartment no outsider had ever seen, as the invalid himself desired to speak to him.

"Well, well," he said to himself as he hurriedly

changed his coat, "what's to do now? His Royal Highness that wasn't to be looked at calling up a man he's never set eyes on."

Mr. Roach was not without curiosity. He had never caught even a glimpse of the boy and had heard a dozen exaggerated stories about his uncanny looks and ways and his insane tempers. The thing he had heard oftenest was that he might die at any moment and there had been numerous fanciful descriptions of a humped back and helpless limbs, given by people who had never seen him.

"Things are changing in this house, Mr. Roach," said Mrs. Medlock, as she led him up the back staircase to the corridor on to which opened the hitherto mysterious chamber.

"Let's hope they're changing for the better, Mrs. Medlock," he answered.

"They couldn't well change for the worse," she continued; "and queer as it all is there's them as finds their duties made a lot easier to stand up under. Don't you be surprised, Mr. Roach, if you find yourself in the middle of a menagerie and Martha Sowerby's Dickon more at home than you or me could ever be."

There really was a sort of Magic about Dickon, as Mary always privately believed. When Mr. Roach heard his name he smiled quite leniently.

"He'd be at home in Buckingham Palace or at the bottom of a coal mine," he said. "And yet it's not impudence, either. He's just fine, is that lad."

It was perhaps well he had been prepared or he might have been startled. When the bedroom door was opened a large crow, which seemed quite at home perched on the high back of a carven chair, announced the entrance of a visitor by saying "Caw—Caw" quite loudly. In spite of Mrs. Medlock's warning, Mr. Roach only just escaped being sufficiently undignified to jump backward.

The young Rajah was neither in bed nor on his sofa. He was sitting in an armchair and a young lamb was standing by him shaking its tail in feeding-lamb fashion as Dickon knelt giving it milk from its bottle. A squirrel was perched on Dickon's bent back attentively nibbling a nut. The little girl from India was sitting on a big footstool looking on.

"Here is Mr. Roach, Master Colin," said Mrs. Medlock.

The young Rajah turned and looked his servitor over— at least that was what the head gardener felt happened.

"Oh, you are Roach, are you?" he said. "I sent for you to give you some very important orders."

"Very good, sir," answered Roach, wondering if he was to receive instructions to fell all the oaks in the park or to transform the orchards into water-gardens.

"I am going out in my chair this afternoon," said Colin. "If the fresh air agrees with me I may go out every day. When I go, none of the gardeners are to be anywhere near the Long Walk by the garden walls. No one is to be there. I shall go out about two o'clock and everyone must keep away until I send word that they may go back to their work."

"Very good, sir," replied Mr. Roach, much relieved to hear that the oaks might remain and that the orchards were safe. "Mary," said Colin, turning to her, "what is that thing you say in India when you have finished talking and want people to go?"

"You say, 'You have my permission to go,'" answered Mary.

The Rajah waved his hand.

"You have my permission to go, Roach," he said. "But, remember, this is very important."

"Caw—Caw!" remarked the crow hoarsely but not impolitely.

"Very good, sir. Thank you, sir," said Mr. Roach, and Mrs. Medlock took him out of the room.

Outside in the corridor, being a rather good-natured man, he smiled until he almost laughed.

"My word!" he said, "he's got a fine lordly way with him, hasn't he? You'd think he was a whole Royal Family rolled into one—Prince Consort and all.".

"Eh!" protested Mrs. Medlock, "we've had to let him trample all over every one of us ever since he had feet and he thinks that's what folks was born for."

"Perhaps he'll grow out of it, if he lives," suggested Mr. Roach.

"Well, there's one thing pretty sure," said Mrs. Medlock. "If he does live and that Indian child stays here I'll warrant she teaches him that the whole orange does not belong to him, as Susan Sowerby says. And he'll be likely to find out the size of his own quarter."

Inside the room Colin was leaning back on his cushions.

"It's all safe now," he said. "And this afternoon I shall see it—this afternoon I shall be in it!"

Dickon went back to the garden with his creatures and Mary stayed with Colin. She did not think he looked tired but he was very quiet before their lunch came and he was quiet while they were eating it. She wondered why and asked him about it.

"What big eyes you've got, Colin," she said. "When you are thinking they get as big as saucers. What are you thinking about now?"

"I can't help thinking about what it will look like," he answered.

"The garden?" asked Mary.

"The springtime," he said. "I was thinking that I've really never seen it before. I scarcely ever went out and when I did go I never looked at it. I didn't even think about it."

"I never saw it in India because there wasn't any," said Mary.

Shut in and morbid as his life had been, Colin had more imagination than she had and at least he had spent a good deal of time looking at wonderful books and pictures.

"That morning when you ran in and said 'It's come! It's come!', you made me feel quite queer. It sounded as if things were coming with a great procession and big bursts and wafts of music. I've a picture like it in one of my books—crowds of lovely people and children with garlands and branches with blossoms on them, everyone laughing and dancing and crowding and playing on pipes. That was why I said, 'Perhaps we shall hear golden trumpets' and told you to throw open the window."

"How funny!" said Mary. "That's really just what it feels like. And if all the flowers and leaves and green things and birds and wild creatures danced past at once, what a crowd it would be! I'm sure they'd dance and sing

and flute and that would be the wafts of music."

They both laughed but it was not because the idea was laughable but because they both so liked it.

A little later the nurse made Colin ready. She noticed that instead of lying like a log while his clothes were put on he sat up and made some efforts to help himself, and he talked and laughed with Mary all the time.

"This is one of his good days, sir," she said to Dr. Craven, who dropped in to inspect him. "He's in such good spirits that it makes him stronger."

"I'll call in again later in the afternoon, after he has come in," said Dr. Craven. "I must see how the going out agrees with him. I wish," in a very low voice, "that he would let you go with him."

"I'd rather give up the case this moment, sir, than even stay here while it's suggested," answered the nurse. With sudden firmness.

"I hadn't really decided to suggest it," said the doctor, with his slight nervousness. "We'll try the experiment. Dickon's a lad I'd trust with a newborn child."

The strongest footman in the house carried Colin down stairs and put him in his wheeled chair near which Dickon waited outside. After the manservant had arranged his rugs and cushions the Rajah waved his hand to him and to the nurse.

"You have my permission to go," he said, and they both disappeared quickly and it must be confessed giggled when they were safely inside the house.

Dickon began to push the wheeled chair slowly and steadily. Mistress Mary walked beside it and Colin leaned back and lifted his face to the sky. The arch of it looked very high and the small snowy clouds seemed like white birds floating on outspread wings below its crystal blueness. The wind swept in soft big breaths down from the moor and was strange with a wild clear scented sweetness. Colin kept lifting his thin chest to draw it in, and his big eyes looked as if it were they which were listening—listening, instead of his ears.

"There are so many sounds of singing and humming and calling out," he said. "What is that scent the puffs of wind bring?"

"It's gorse on th' moor that's openin' out," answered Dickon. "Eh! th' bees are at it wonderful today."

Not a human creature was to be caught sight of in the paths they took. In fact every gardener or gardener's lad had been witched away. But they wound in and out among the shrubbery and out and round the fountain beds, following their carefully planned route for the mere mysterious pleasure of it. But when at last they turned into the Long Walk by the ivied walls the excited sense of an approaching thrill made them, for some curious reason they could not have explained, begin to speak in whispers.

"This is it," breathed Mary. "This is where I used to walk up and down and wonder and wonder."

"Is it?" cried Colin, and his eyes began to search the ivy with eager curiousness. "But I can see nothing," he whispered. "There is no door."

"That's what I thought," said Mary.

Then there was a lovely breathless silence and the chair wheeled on.

"That is the garden where Ben Weatherstaff works,"

said Mary.

"Is it?" said Colin.

A few yards more and Mary whispered again.

"This is where the robin flew over the wall," she said.

"Is it?" cried Colin. "Oh! I wish he'd come again!"

"And that," said Mary with solemn delight, pointing under a big lilac bush, "is where he perched on the little heap of earth and showed me the key."

Then Colin sat up.

"Where? Where? There?" he cried, and his eyes were as big as the wolf's in Red Riding-Hood, when Red Riding-Hood felt called upon to remark on them.

Dickon stood still and the wheeled chair stopped.

"And this," said Mary, stepping on to the bed close to the ivy, "is where I went to talk to him when he chirped at me from the top of the wall. And this is the ivy the wind blew back," and she took hold of the hanging green curtain.

"Oh! is it—is it!" gasped Colin.

"And here is the handle, and here is the door. Dickon push him in—push him in quickly!"

And Dickon did it with one strong, steady, splendid push.

But Colin had actually dropped back against his cushions, even though he gasped with delight, and he had covered his eyes with his hands and held them there shutting out everything until they were inside and the chair stopped as if by magic and the door was closed.

Not till then did he take them away and look round and round and round as Dickon and Mary had done. And over walls and earth and trees and swinging sprays and tendrils the fair green veil of tender little leaves had crept, and in the grass under the trees and the gray urns in the alcoves and here and there everywhere were touches or splashes of gold and purple and white and the trees were showing pink and snow above his head and there were fluttering of wings and faint sweet pipes and humming and scents and scents.

And the sun fell warm upon his face like a hand with a lovely touch. And in wonder Mary and Dickon stood and stared at him. He looked so strange and different because a pink glow of color had actually crept all over him—ivory face and neck and hands and all.

"I shall get well! I shall get well!" he cried out. "Mary! Dickon! I shall get well! And I shall live forever and ever and ever!"

Chapter 21

Ben Weatherstaff

One of the strange things about living in the world is that it is only now and then one is quite sure one is going to live forever and ever and ever. One knows it sometimes when one gets up at the tender solemn dawn-time and goes out and stands alone and throws one's head far back and looks up and up and watches the pale sky slowly changing and flushing and marvelous unknown things happening until the East almost makes one cry out and one's heart stands still at the strange unchanging majesty of the rising of the sun—which has been happening every morning for thousands and thousands and thousands of years. One knows it then for a moment or so.

And one knows it sometimes when one stands by oneself in a wood at sunset and the mysterious deep gold stillness slanting through and under the branches seems to be saying slowly again and again something one cannot quite hear, however much one tries.

Then sometimes the immense quiet of the dark blue at night with millions of stars waiting and watching makes one sure; and sometimes a sound of far-off music makes it true; and sometimes a look in some one's eyes.

And it was like that with Colin when he first saw and heard and felt the Springtime inside the four high walls of a hidden garden.

That afternoon the whole world seemed to devote itself to being perfect and radiantly beautiful and kind to one boy. Perhaps out of pure heavenly goodness the spring came and crowned everything it possibly could into that one place. More than once Dickon paused in what he was doing and stood still with a sort of growing wonder in his eyes, shaking his head softly.

"Eh! it is graidely," he said. "I'm twelve goin' on thirteen an' there's a lot o' afternoons in thirteen years, but seems to me like I never seed one as graidely as this 'ere."

"Aye, it is a graidely one," said Mary, and she sighed for mere joy. "I'll warrant it's the graidelest one as ever was in this world."

"Does tha' think," said Colin with dreamy carefulness, "as happen it was made loike this 'ere all o' purpose for me?"

"My word!" cried Mary admiringly, "that there is a bit o' good Yorkshire. Tha'rt shapin' first-rate—that tha' art."

And delight reigned. They drew the chair under the plum-tree, which was snow-white with blossoms and musical with bees. It was like a king's canopy, a fairy king's. There were flowering cherry-trees near and apple-trees whose buds were pink and white, and here and there one had burst open wide. Between the blossoming branches of the canopy bits of blue sky looked down like wonderful eyes.

Mary and Dickon worked a little here and there and Colin watched them. They brought him things to look at—buds which were opening, buds which were tight closed, bits of twig whose leaves were just showing green, the feather of a woodpecker which had dropped on the grass, the empty shell of some bird early hatched.

Dickon pushed the chair slowly round and round the garden, stopping every other moment to let him look at wonders springing out of the earth or trailing down from trees. It was like being taken in state round the country of a magic king and queen and shown all the mysterious riches it contained.

"I wonder if we shall see the robin?" said Colin.

"Tha'll see him often enow after a bit," answered Dickon. "When th' eggs hatches out th' little chap he'll be kep' so busy it'll make his head swim. Tha'll see him flyin' backward an' for'ard carryin' worms nigh as big as himsel' an' that much noise goin' on in th' nest when he gets there as fair flusters him so as he scarce knows which big mouth to drop th' first piece in. An' gapin' beaks an' squawks on every side. Mother says as when she sees th' work a robin has to keep them gapin' beaks filled, she feels like she was a lady with nothin' to do. She says she's seen th' little chaps when it seemed like th' sweat must be droppin' off 'em, though folk can't see it."

This made them giggle so delightedly that they were obliged to cover their mouths with their hands, remembering that they must not be heard. Colin had been instructed as to the law of whispers and low voices several days before. He liked the mysteriousness of it and did his best, but in the midst of excited enjoyment it is rather difficult never to laugh above a whisper.

Every moment of the afternoon was full of new things and every hour the sunshine grew more golden. The wheeled chair had been drawn back under the canopy and Dickon had sat down on the grass and had just drawn out his pipe when Colin saw something he had not had time to notice before.

"That's a very old tree over there, isn't it?" he said. Dickon looked across the grass at the tree and Mary looked and there was a brief moment of stillness.

"Yes," answered Dickon, after it, and his low voice had a very gentle sound.

Mary gazed at the tree and thought.

"The branches are quite gray and there's not a single leaf anywhere," Colin went on. "It's quite dead, isn't it?"

"Aye," admitted Dickon. "But them roses as has climbed all over it will near hide every bit o' th' dead wood when they're full o' leaves an' flowers. It won't look dead then. It'll be th' prettiest of all."

Mary still gazed at the tree and thought.

"It looks as if a big branch had been broken off," said Colin. "I wonder how it was done."

"It's been done many a year," answered Dickon. "Eh!" with a sudden relieved start and laying his hand on Colin. "Look at that robin! There he is! He's been foragin' for his mate."

Colin was almost too late but he just caught sight of him, the flash of red-breasted bird with something in his beak. He darted through the greenness and into the close-grown corner and was out of sight. Colin leaned back on his cushion again, laughing a little. "He's taking her tea to her. Perhaps it's five o'clock. I think I'd like some tea myself."

And so they were safe.

"It was Magic which sent the robin," said Mary secretly to Dickon afterward. "I know it was Magic."

For both she and Dickon had been afraid Colin might ask something about the tree whose branch had broken off ten years ago and they had talked it over together and Dickon had stood and rubbed his head in a troubled way.

"We mun look as if it wasn't no different from th' other trees," he had said. "We couldn't never tell him how it broke, poor lad. If he says anything about it we mun—we mun try to look cheerful."

"Aye, that we mun," had answered Mary.

But she had not felt as if she looked cheerful when she gazed at the tree. She wondered and wondered in those few moments if there was any reality in that other thing Dickon had said.

He had gone on rubbing his rust-red hair in a puzzled way, but a nice comforted look had begun to grow in his blue eyes. "Mrs. Craven was a very lovely young lady," he had gone on rather hesitatingly. "An' mother she thinks maybe she's about Misselthwaite many a time lookin' after Mester Colin, same as all mothers do when they're took out o' th' world. They have to come back, tha' sees. Happen she's been in the garden an' happen it was her set us to work, an' told us to bring him here."

Mary had thought he meant something about Magic. She was a great believer in Magic. Secretly she quite believed that Dickon worked Magic, of course good Magic, on everything near him and that was why people liked him so much and wild creatures knew he was their friend.

She wondered, indeed, if it were not possible that his gift had brought the robin just at the right moment when Colin asked that dangerous question. She felt that his Magic was working all the afternoon and making Colin look like an entirely different boy. It did not seem possible that he could be the crazy creature who had screamed and beaten and bitten his pillow. Even his ivory whiteness seemed to change. The faint glow of color which had shown on his face and neck and hands when he first got inside the garden really never quite died away. He looked as if he were made of flesh instead of ivory or wax.

They saw the robin carry food to his mate two or three times, and it was so suggestive of afternoon tea that Colin felt they must have some.

"Go and make one of the men servants bring some in a basket to the rhododendron walk," he said. "And then you and Dickon can bring it here."

It was an agreeable idea, easily carried out, and when the white cloth was spread upon the grass, with hot tea and buttered toast and crumpets, a delightfully hungry meal was eaten, and several birds on domestic errands paused to inquire what was going on and were led into investigating crumbs with great activity.

Nut and Shell whisked up trees with pieces of cake and Soot took the entire half of a buttered crumpet into a corner and pecked at and examined and turned it over and made hoarse remarks about it until he decided to swallow it all joyfully in one gulp.

The afternoon was dragging towards its mellow hour. The sun was deepening the gold of its lances, the bees were going home and the birds were flying past less often. Dickon and Mary were sitting on the grass, the tea-basket was repacked ready to be taken back to the house, and Colin was lying against his cushions with his heavy locks pushed back from his forehead and his face looking quite a natural color.

"I don't want this afternoon to go," he said; "but I shall come back tomorrow, and the day after, and the day after, and the day after."

"You'll get plenty of fresh air, won't you?" said Mary. "I'm going to get nothing else," he answered. "I've seen the spring now and I'm going to see the summer. I'm going to see everything grow here. I'm going to grow here myself."

"That tha' will," said Dickon. "Us'll have thee walkin' about here an' diggin' same as other folk afore long."

Colin flushed tremendously.

"Walk!" he said. "Dig! Shall I?"

Dickon's glance at him was delicately cautious. Neither he nor Mary had ever asked if anything was the matter with his legs.

"For sure tha' will," he said stoutly. "Tha—tha's got

legs o' thine own, same as other folks!"

Mary was rather frightened until she heard Colin's answer.

"Nothing really ails them," he said, "but they are so thin and weak. They shake so that I'm afraid to try to stand on them."

Both Mary and Dickon drew a relieved breath.

"When tha' stops bein' afraid tha'lt stand on 'em," Dickon said with renewed cheer. "An' tha'lt stop bein' afraid in a bit."

"I shall?" said Colin, and he lay still as if he were wondering about things.

They were really very quiet for a little while. The sun was dropping lower. It was that hour when everything stills itself, and they really had had a busy and exciting afternoon. Colin looked as if he were resting luxuriously. Even the creatures had ceased moving about and had drawn together and were resting near them. Soot had perched on a low branch and drawn up one leg and dropped the gray film drowsily over his eyes. Mary privately thought he looked as if he might snore in a minute.

In the midst of this stillness it was rather startling when Colin half lifted his head and exclaimed in a loud suddenly alarmed whisper:

"Who is that man?" Dickon and Mary scrambled to their feet.

"Man!" they both cried in low quick voices.

Colin pointed to the high wall. "Look!" he whispered excitedly. "Just look!"

Mary and Dickon wheeled about and looked. There was Ben Weatherstaff's indignant face glaring at them over the wall from the top of a ladder! He actually shook his fist at Mary.

"If I wasn't a bachelder, an' tha' was a wench o' mine," he cried, "I'd give thee a hidin'!"

He mounted another step threateningly as if it were his energetic intention to jump down and deal with her; but as she came toward him he evidently thought better of it and stood on the top step of his ladder shaking his fist down at her.

"I never thowt much o' thee!" he harangued. "I couldna' abide thee th' first time I set eyes on thee. A scrawny buttermilk-faced young besom, allus askin' questions an' pokin' tha' nose where it wasna, wanted. I never knowed how tha' got so thick wi' me. If it hadna' been for th' robin— Drat him—"

"Ben Weatherstaff," called out Mary, finding her breath. She stood below him and called up to him with a sort of gasp. "Ben Weatherstaff, it was the robin who showed me the way!"

Then it did seem as if Ben really would scramble down on her side of the wall, he was so outraged.

"Tha' young bad 'un!" he called down at her. "Layin' tha' badness on a robin—not but what he's impidint enow for anythin'. Him showin' thee th' way! Him! Eh! tha' young nowt"—she could see his next words burst out because he was overpowered by curiosity—"however i' this world did tha' get in?"

"It was the robin who showed me the way," she

protested obstinately. "He didn't know he was doing it but he did. And I can't tell you from here while you're shaking your fist at me."

He stopped shaking his fist very suddenly at that very moment and his jaw actually dropped as he stared over her head at something he saw coming over the grass toward him.

At the first sound of his torrent of words Colin had been so surprised that he had only sat up and listened as if he were spellbound. But in the midst of it he had recovered himself and beckoned imperiously to Dickon.

"Wheel me over there!" he commanded. "Wheel me quite close and stop right in front of him!"

And this, if you please, this is what Ben Weatherstaff beheld and which made his jaw drop. A wheeled chair with luxurious cushions and robes which came toward him looking rather like some sort of State Coach because a young Rajah leaned back in it with royal command in his great black-rimmed eyes and a thin white hand extended haughtily toward him. And it stopped right under Ben Weatherstaff's nose. It was really no wonder his mouth dropped open.

"Do you know who I am?" demanded the Rajah.

How Ben Weatherstaff stared! His red old eyes fixed themselves on what was before him as if he were seeing a ghost. He gazed and gazed and gulped a lump down his throat and did not say a word. "Do you know who I am?" demanded Colin still more imperiously. "Answer!"

Ben Weatherstaff put his gnarled hand up and passed it over his eyes and over his forehead and then he did answer in a queer shaky voice.

"Who tha' art?" he said. "Aye, that I do—wi' tha' mother's eyes starin' at me out o' tha' face. Lord knows how tha' come here. But tha'rt th' poor cripple."

Colin forgot that he had ever had a back. His face flushed scarlet and he sat bolt upright.

"I'm not a cripple!" he cried out furiously. "I'm not!"

"He's not!" cried Mary, almost shouting up the wall in her fierce indignation. "He's not got a lump as big as a pin! I looked and there was none there—not one!"

Ben Weatherstaff passed his hand over his forehead again and gazed as if he could never gaze enough. His hand shook and his mouth shook and his voice shook. He was an ignorant old man and a tactless old man and he could only remember the things he had heard.

"Tha'—tha' hasn't got a crooked back?" he said hoarsely.

"No!" shouted Colin.

"Tha'—tha' hasn't got crooked legs?" quavered Ben more hoarsely yet.

It was too much. The strength which Colin usually threw into his tantrums rushed through him now in a new way. Never yet had he been accused of crooked legs—even in whispers—and the perfectly simple belief in their existence which was revealed by Ben Weatherstaff's voice was more than Rajah flesh and blood could endure. His anger and insulted pride made him forget everything but this one moment and filled him with a power he had never known before, an almost unnatural strength.

"Come here!" he shouted to Dickon, and he actually began to tear the coverings off his lower limbs and disentangle himself. "Come here! Come here! This minute!"

Dickon was by his side in a second. Mary caught her breath in a short gasp and felt herself turn pale.

"He can do it! He can do it! He can do it! He can!" she gabbled over to herself under her breath as fast as ever she could.

There was a brief fierce scramble, the rugs were tossed on the ground, Dickon held Colin's arm, the thin legs were out, the thin feet were on the grass. Colin was standing upright—upright—as straight as an arrow and looking strangely tall—his head thrown back and his strange eyes flashing lightning. "Look at me!" he flung up at Ben Weatherstaff. "Just look at me—you! Just look at me!"

"He's as straight as I am!" cried Dickon. "He's as straight as any lad i' Yorkshire!"

What Ben Weatherstaff did Mary thought queer beyond measure. He choked and gulped and suddenly tears ran down his weather-wrinkled cheeks as he struck his old hands together.

"Eh!" he burst forth, "th' lies folk tells! Tha'rt as thin as a lath an' as white as a wraith, but there's not a knob on thee. Tha'lt make a mon yet. God bless thee!"

Dickon held Colin's arm strongly but the boy had not begun to falter. He stood straighter and straighter and looked Ben Weatherstaff in the face.

"I'm your master," he said, "when my father is away.

And you are to obey me. This is my garden. Don't dare to say a word about it! You get down from that ladder and go out to the Long Walk and Miss Mary will meet you and bring you here. I want to talk to you. We did not want you, but now you will have to be in the secret. Be quick!"

Ben Weatherstaff's crabbed old face was still wet with that one queer rush of tears. It seemed as if he could not take his eyes from thin straight Colin standing on his feet with his head thrown back.

"Eh! lad," he almost whispered. "Eh! my lad!" And then remembering himself he suddenly touched his hat gardener fashion and said, "Yes, sir! Yes, sir!" and obediently disappeared as he descended the ladder.

Chapter 22

When the Sun Went Down

When his head was out of sight Colin turned to Mary. "Go and meet him," he said; and Mary flew across the grass to the door under the ivy.

Dickon was watching him with sharp eyes. There were scarlet spots on his cheeks and he looked amazing, but he showed no signs of falling.

"I can stand," he said, and his head was still held up and he said it quite grandly.

"I told thee tha' could as soon as tha' stopped bein' afraid," answered Dickon. "An' tha's stopped."

"Yes, I've stopped," said Colin.

Then suddenly he remembered something Mary had said.

"Are you making Magic?" he asked sharply.

Dickon's curly mouth spread in a cheerful grin.

"Tha's doin' Magic thysel'," he said. "It's same Magic as made these 'ere work out o' th' earth," and he touched with his thick boot a clump of crocuses in the grass. Colin looked down at them.

"Aye," he said slowly, "there couldna' be bigger Magic than that there—there couldna' be."

He drew himself up straighter than ever.

"I'm going to walk to that tree," he said, pointing to one a few feet away from him. "I'm going to be standing when Weatherstaff comes here. I can rest against the tree if I like. When I want to sit down I will sit down, but not before. Bring a rug from the chair."

He walked to the tree and though Dickon held his arm he was wonderfully steady. When he stood against the tree trunk it was not too plain that he supported himself against it, and he still held himself so straight that he looked tall.

When Ben Weatherstaff came through the door in the wall he saw him standing there and he heard Mary muttering something under her breath.

"What art sayin'?" he asked rather testily because he did not want his attention distracted from the long thin straight boy figure and proud face.

But she did not tell him. What she was saying was this: "You can do it! You can do it! I told you you could! You can do it! You can do it! You can!"

She was saying it to Colin because she wanted to make Magic and keep him on his feet looking like that. She could not bear that he should give in before Ben Weatherstaff. He did not give in. She was uplifted by a sudden feeling that he looked quite beautiful in spite of his thinness. He fixed his eyes on Ben Weatherstaff in his funny imperious way.

"Look at me!" he commanded. "Look at me all over! Am I a hunchback? Have I got crooked legs?"

Ben Weatherstaff had not quite got over his emotion, but he had recovered a little and answered almost in his usual way.

"Not tha'," he said. "Nowt o' th' sort. What's tha' been doin' with thysel'—hidin' out o' sight an' lettin' folk think tha' was cripple an' half-witted?"

"Half-witted!" said Colin angrily. "Who thought that?"

"Lots o' fools," said Ben. "Th' world's full o' jackasses brayin' an' they never bray nowt but lies. What did tha' shut thysel' up for?"

"Everyone thought I was going to die," said Colin shortly. "I'm not!"

And he said it with such decision Ben Weatherstaff looked him over, up and down, down and up.

"Tha' die!" he said with dry exultation. "Nowt o' th'

sort! Tha's got too much pluck in thee. When I seed thee put tha' legs on th' ground in such a hurry I knowed tha' was all right. Sit thee down on th' rug a bit young Mester an' give me thy orders."

There was a queer mixture of crabbed tenderness and shrewd understanding in his manner. Mary had poured out speech as rapidly as she could as they had come down the Long Walk. The chief thing to be remembered, she had told him, was that Colin was getting well— getting well. The garden was doing it. No one must let him remember about having humps and dying.

The Rajah condescended to seat himself on a rug under the tree.

"What work do you do in the gardens, Weatherstaff?" he inquired.

"Anythin' I'm told to do," answered old Ben. "I'm kep' on by favor—because she liked me."

"She?" said Colin.

"Tha' mother," answered Ben Weatherstaff.

"My mother?" said Colin, and he looked about him quietly. "This was her garden, wasn't it?"

"Aye, it was that!" and Ben Weatherstaff looked about him too. "She were main fond of it."

"It is my garden now. I am fond of it. I shall come here every day," announced Colin. "But it is to be a secret. My orders are that no one is to know that we come here. Dickon and my cousin have worked and made it come alive. I shall send for you sometimes to help—but you must come when no one can see you."

Ben Weatherstaff's face twisted itself in a dry old

smile.

"I've come here before when no one saw me," he said.

"What!" exclaimed Colin.

"When?"

"Th' last time I was here," rubbing his chin and looking round, "was about two year' ago."

"But no one has been in it for ten years!" cried Colin.

"There was no door!"

"I'm no one," said old Ben dryly. "An' I didn't come through th' door. I come over th' wall. Th' rheumatics held me back th' last two year'."

"Tha' come an' did a bit o' prunin'!" cried Dickon. "I couldn't make out how it had been done."

"She was so fond of it—she was!" said Ben Weatherstaff slowly. "An' she was such a pretty young thing. She says to me once, 'Ben,' says she laughin', 'if ever I'm ill or if I go away you must take care of my roses.' When she did go away th' orders was no one was ever to come nigh. But I come," with grumpy obstinacy. "Over th' wall I come—until th' rheumatics stopped me—an' I did a bit o' work once a year. She'd gave her order first."

"It wouldn't have been as wick as it is if tha' hadn't done it," said Dickon. "I did wonder."

"I'm glad you did it, Weatherstaff," said Colin. "You'll know how to keep the secret."

"Aye, I'll know, sir," answered Ben. "An' it'll be easier for a man wi' rheumatics to come in at th' door."

On the grass near the tree Mary had dropped her trowel. Colin stretched out his hand and took it up. An odd expression came into his face and he began to scratch at the earth. His thin hand was weak enough but presently as they watched him—Mary with quite breathless interest—he drove the end of the trowel into the soil and turned some over.

"You can do it! You can do it!" said Mary to herself. "I tell you, you can!"

Dickon's round eyes were full of eager curiousness but he said not a word. Ben Weatherstaff looked on with interested face.

Colin persevered. After he had turned a few trowelfuls of soil he spoke exultantly to Dickon in his best Yorkshire.

"Tha' said as tha'd have me walkin' about here same as other folk—an' tha' said tha'd have me diggin'. I thowt tha' was just leein' to please me. This is only th' first day an' I've walked—an' here I am diggin'."

Ben Weatherstaff's mouth fell open again when he heard him, but he ended by chuckling.

"Eh!" he said, "that sounds as if tha'd got wits enow. Tha'rt a Yorkshire lad for sure. An' tha'rt diggin', too. How'd tha' like to plant a bit o' somethin'? I can get thee a rose in a pot."

"Go and get it!" said Colin, digging excitedly. "Quick! Quick!"

It was done quickly enough indeed. Ben Weatherstaff went his way forgetting rheumatics. Dickon took his spade and dug the hole deeper and wider than a new digger with thin white hands could make it. Mary slipped out to run and bring back a watering-can. When Dickon had deepened the hole Colin went on turning the soft earth over and over. He looked up at the sky, flushed and glowing with the strangely new exercise, slight as it was.

"I want to do it before the sun goes quite—quite down," he said.

Mary thought that perhaps the sun held back a few minutes just on purpose. Ben Weatherstaff brought the rose in its pot from the greenhouse. He hobbled over the grass as fast as he could. He had begun to be excited, too. He knelt down by the hole and broke the pot from the mould.

"Here, lad," he said, handing the plant to Colin. "Set it in the earth thysel' same as th' king does when he goes to a new place."

The thin white hands shook a little and Colin's flush grew deeper as he set the rose in the mould and held it while old Ben made firm the earth. It was filled in and pressed down and made steady. Mary was leaning forward on her hands and knees. Soot had flown down and marched forward to see what was being done. Nut and Shell chattered about it from a cherry-tree.

"It's planted!" said Colin at last. "And the sun is only slipping over the edge. Help me up, Dickon. I want to be standing when it goes. That's part of the Magic."

And Dickon helped him, and the Magic—or whatever it was—so gave him strength that when the sun did slip over the edge and end the strange lovely afternoon for them there he actually stood on his two feet—laughing.

Chapter 23

Magic

D r. Craven had been waiting some time at the house when they returned to it. He had indeed begun to wonder if it might not be wise to send some one out to explore the garden paths. When Colin was brought back to his room the poor man looked him over seriously.

"You should not have stayed so long," he said. "You must not overexert yourself."

"I am not tired at all," said Colin. "It has made me well. Tomorrow I am going out in the morning as well as in the afternoon."

"I am not sure that I can allow it," answered Dr. Craven. "I am afraid it would not be wise."

"It would not be wise to try to stop me," said Colin quite seriously. "I am going."

Even Mary had found out that one of Colin's chief peculiarities was that he did not know in the least what a rude little brute he was with his way of ordering people about. He had lived on a sort of desert island all his life and as he had been the king of it he had made his own manners and had had no one to compare himself with.

Mary had indeed been rather like him herself and since

she had been at Misselthwaite had gradually discovered that her own manners had not been of the kind which is usual or popular. Having made this discovery she naturally thought it of enough interest to communicate to Colin. So she sat and looked at him curiously for a few minutes after Dr. Craven had gone. She wanted to make him ask her why she was doing it and of course she did.

"What are you looking at me for?" he said.

"I'm thinking that I am rather sorry for Dr. Craven."

"So am I," said Colin calmly, but not without an air of some satisfaction. "He won't get Misselthwaite at all now I'm not going to die."

"I'm sorry for him because of that, of course," said Mary, "but I was thinking just then that it must have been very horrid to have had to be polite for ten years to a boy who was always rude. I would never have done it."

"Am I rude?" Colin inquired undisturbedly.

"If you had been his own boy and he had been a slapping sort of man," said Mary, "he would have slapped you."

"But he daren't," said Colin.

"No, he daren't," answered Mistress Mary, thinking the thing out quite without prejudice. "Nobody ever dared to do anything you didn't like—because you were going to die and things like that. You were such a poor thing."

"But," announced Colin stubbornly, "I am not going to be a poor thing. I won't let people think I'm one. I stood on my feet this afternoon."

"It is always having your own way that has made you so queer," Mary went on, thinking aloud.

Colin turned his head, frowning.

"Am I queer?" he demanded.

"Yes," answered Mary, "very. But you needn't be cross," she added impartially, "because so am I queer—and so is Ben Weatherstaff. But I am not as queer as I was before I began to like people and before I found the garden."

"I don't want to be queer," said Colin. "I am not going to be," and he frowned again with determination.

He was a very proud boy. He lay thinking for a while and then Mary saw his beautiful smile begin and gradually change his whole face.

"I shall stop being queer," he said, "if I go every day to the garden. There is Magic in there—good Magic, you know, Mary. I am sure there is." "So am I," said Mary.

"Even if it isn't real Magic," Colin said, "we can pretend it is. Something is there—something!"

"It's Magic," said Mary, "but not black. It's as white as snow."

They always called it Magic and indeed it seemed like it in the months that followed—the wonderful months— the radiant months—the amazing ones. Oh! the things which happened in that garden! If you have never had a garden you cannot understand, and if you have had a garden you will know that it would take a whole book to describe all that came to pass there.

At first it seemed that green things would never cease pushing their way through the earth, in the grass, in the beds, even in the crevices of the walls. Then the green things began to show buds and the buds began to unfurl and show color, every shade of blue, every shade of purple, every tint and hue of crimson. In its happy days flowers had been tucked away into every inch and hole and corner.

Ben Weatherstaff had seen it done and had himself scraped out mortar from between the bricks of the wall and made pockets of earth for lovely clinging things to grow on. Iris and white lilies rose out of the grass in sheaves, and the green alcoves filled themselves with amazing armies of the blue and white flower lances of tall delphiniums or columbines or campanulas.

"She was main fond o' them—she was," Ben Weatherstaff said. "She liked them things as was allus pointin' up to th' blue sky, she used to tell. Not as she was one o' them as looked down on th' earth—not her. She just loved it but she said as th' blue sky allus looked so joyful."

The seeds Dickon and Mary had planted grew as if fairies had tended them. Satiny poppies of all tints danced in the breeze by the score, gaily defying flowers which had lived in the garden for years and which it might be confessed seemed rather to wonder how such new people had got there.

And the roses—the roses! Rising out of the grass, tangled

round the sun-dial, wreathing the tree trunks and hanging from their branches, climbing up the walls and spreading over them with long garlands falling in cascades—they came alive day by day, hour by hour. Fair fresh leaves, and buds—and buds—tiny at first but swelling and working Magic until they burst and uncurled into cups of scent delicately spilling themselves over their brims and filling the garden air.

Colin saw it all, watching each change as it took place. Every morning he was brought out and every hour of each day when it didn't rain he spent in the garden. Even gray days pleased him.

He would lie on the grass "watching things growing," he said. If you watched long enough, he declared, you could see buds unsheath themselves. Also you could make the acquaintance of strange busy insect things running about on various unknown but evidently serious errands, sometimes carrying tiny scraps of straw or feather or food, or climbing blades of grass as if they were trees from whose tops one could look out to explore the country.

A mole throwing up its mound at the end of its burrow and making its way out at last with the long-nailed paws which looked so like elfish hands, had absorbed him one whole morning. Ants' ways, beetles' ways, bees' ways, frogs' ways, birds' ways, plants' ways, gave him a new world to explore and when Dickon revealed them all and added foxes' ways, otters' ways, ferrets' ways, squirrels' ways, and trout' and water-rats' and badgers' ways, there was no end to the things to talk about and think over.

And this was not the half of the Magic. The fact that he had really once stood on his feet had set Colin thinking tremendously and when Mary told him of the spell she had worked he was excited and approved of it greatly. He talked of it constantly.

"Of course there must be lots of Magic in the world," he said wisely one day, "but people don't know what it is like or how to make it. Perhaps the beginning is just to say nice things are going to happen until you make them happen. I am going to try and experiment."

The next morning when they went to the secret garden he sent at once for Ben Weatherstaff. Ben came as quickly as he could and found the Rajah standing on his feet under a tree and looking very grand but also very beautifully smiling.

"Good morning, Ben Weatherstaff," he said. "I want you and Dickon and Miss Mary to stand in a row and listen to me because I am going to tell you something very important."

"Aye, aye, sir!" answered Ben Weatherstaff, touching his forehead. (One of the long concealed charms of Ben Weatherstaff was that in his boyhood he had once run away to sea and had made voyages. So he could reply like a sailor.)

"I am going to try a scientific experiment," explained the Rajah. "When I grow up I am going to make great scientific discoveries and I am going to begin now with this experiment."

"Aye, aye, sir!" said Ben Weatherstaff promptly, though this was the first time he had heard of great scientific discoveries.

It was the first time Mary had heard of them, either, but even at this stage she had begun to realize that, queer as he was, Colin had read about a great many singular things and was somehow a very convincing sort of boy. When he held up his head and fixed his strange eyes on you it seemed as if you believed him almost in spite of yourself though he was only ten years old—going on eleven. At this moment he was especially convincing because he suddenly felt the fascination of actually making a sort of speech like a grown-up person.

"The great scientific discoveries I am going to make," he went on, "will be about Magic. Magic is a great thing and scarcely any one knows anything about it except a few people in old books—and Mary a little, because she was born in India where there are fakirs. I believe Dickon knows some Magic, but perhaps he doesn't know he knows it. He charms animals and people. I would never have let him come to see me if he had not been an animal charmer—which is a boy charmer, too, because a boy is an animal. I am sure there is Magic in everything, only we have not sense enough to get hold of it and make it do things for us—like electricity and horses and steam."

This sounded so imposing that Ben Weatherstaff became quite excited and really could not keep still. "Aye, aye, sir," he said and he began to stand up quite straight.

"When Mary found this garden it looked quite dead," the orator proceeded. "Then something began pushing things up out of the soil and making things out of nothing. One day things weren't there and another they were. I had never watched things before and it made me feel very curious. Scientific people are always curious and I am going to be scientific. I keep saying to myself, 'What is it? What is it?' It's something. It can't be nothing! I don't know its name so I call it Magic. I have never seen the sun rise but Mary and Dickon have and from what they tell me I am sure that is Magic too. Something pushes it up and draws it. Sometimes since I've been in the garden I've looked up through the trees at the sky and I have had a strange feeling of being happy as if something were pushing and drawing in my chest and making me breathe fast. Magic is always pushing and drawing and making things out of nothing. Everything is made out of Magic, leaves and trees, flowers and birds, badgers and foxes and squirrels and people. So it must be all around us. In this garden—in all the places. The Magic in this garden has made me stand up and know I am going to live to be a man. I am going to make the scientific experiment of trying to get some and put it in myself and make it push and draw me and make me strong. I don't know how to do it but I think that if you keep thinking about it and calling it perhaps it will come. Perhaps that is the first baby way to get it. When I was going to try to stand that first time Mary kept saying to herself as fast as she could, 'You can do it! You can do it!' and I did. I had to try myself at the same time, of course, but her Magic helped me—and so did Dickon's. Every morning and evening and as often in the daytime as I can remember I am going to say, 'Magic is in me! Magic is making me well! I am going to be as strong as Dickon, as strong as Dickon!' And you must all do it, too. That is my experiment Will you help, Ben Weatherstaff?"

"Aye, aye, sir!" said Ben Weatherstaff. "Aye, aye!"

"If you keep doing it every day as regularly as soldiers go through drill we shall see what will happen and find out if the experiment succeeds. You learn things by saying them over and over and thinking about them until they stay in your mind forever and I think it will be the same with Magic. If you keep calling it to come to you and help you it will get to be part of you and it will stay and do things." "I once heard an officer in India tell my mother that there were fakirs who said words over and over thousands of times," said Mary.

"I've heard Jem Fettleworth's wife say th' same thing over thousands o' times—callin' Jem a drunken brute," said Ben Weatherstaff dryly. "Summat allus come o' that, sure enough. He gave her a good hidin' an' went to th' Blue Lion an' got as drunk as a lord."

Colin drew his brows together and thought a few minutes. Then he cheered up.

"Well," he said, "you see something did come of it. She used the wrong Magic until she made him beat her. If she'd used the right Magic and had said something nice perhaps he wouldn't have got as drunk as a lord and perhaps—perhaps he might have bought her a new bonnet."

Ben Weatherstaff chuckled and there was shrewd admiration in his little old eyes.

"Tha'rt a clever lad as well as a straight-legged one, Mester Colin," he said. "Next time I see Bess Fettleworth

I'll give her a bit of a hint o' what Magic will do for her. She'd be rare an' pleased if th' sinetifik 'speriment worked—an' so 'ud Jem."

Dickon had stood listening to the lecture, his round eyes shining with curious delight. Nut and Shell were on his shoulders and he held a long-eared white rabbit in his arm and stroked and stroked it softly while it laid its ears along its back and enjoyed itself.

"Do you think the experiment will work?" Colin asked him, wondering what he was thinking. He so often wondered what Dickon was thinking when he saw him looking at him or at one of his "creatures" with his happy wide smile.

He smiled now and his smile was wider than usual.

"Aye," he answered, "that I do. It'll work same as th' seeds do when th' sun shines on 'em. It'll work for sure. Shall us begin it now?"

Colin was delighted and so was Mary. Fired by recollections of fakirs and devotees in illustrations Colin suggested that they should all sit cross-legged under the tree which made a canopy.

"It will be like sitting in a sort of temple," said Colin. "I'm rather tired and I want to sit down."

"Eh!" said Dickon, "tha' mustn't begin by sayin' tha'rt tired. Tha' might spoil th' Magic."

Colin turned and looked at him—into his innocent round eyes.

"That's true," he said slowly. "I must only think of the Magic."

It all seemed most majestic and mysterious when

they sat down in their circle. Ben Weatherstaff felt as if he had somehow been led into appearing at a prayer-meeting. Ordinarily he was very fixed in being what he called "agen' prayer-meetin's" but this being the Rajah's affair he did not resent it and was indeed inclined to be gratified at being called upon to assist. Mistress Mary felt solemnly enraptured. Dickon held his rabbit in his arm, and perhaps he made some charmer's signal no one heard, for when he sat down, cross-legged like the rest, the crow, the fox, the squirrels and the lamb slowly drew near and made part of the circle, settling each into a place of rest as if of their own desire.

"The 'creatures' have come," said Colin gravely. "They want to help us."

Colin really looked quite beautiful, Mary thought. He held his head high as if he felt like a sort of priest and his strange eyes had a wonderful look in them. The light shone on him through the tree canopy.

"Now we will begin," he said. "Shall we sway backward and forward, Mary, as if we were dervishes?"

"I canna' do no swayin' back'ard and for'ard," said Ben Weatherstaff. "I've got th' rheumatics."

"The Magic will take them away," said Colin in a High Priest tone, "but we won't sway until it has done it. We will only chant."

"I canna' do no chantin'" said Ben Weatherstaff a trifle testily. "They turned me out o' th' church choir th' only time I ever tried it."

No one smiled. They were all too much in earnest. Colin's face was not even crossed by a shadow. He was thinking only of the Magic.

"Then I will chant," he said. And he began, looking like a strange boy spirit. "The sun is shining—the sun is shining. That is the Magic. The flowers are growing—the roots are stirring. That is the Magic. Being alive is the Magic—being strong is the Magic. The Magic is in me— the Magic is in me. It is in me—it is in me. It's in every one of us. It's in Ben Weatherstaff's back. Magic! Magic! Come and help!"

He said it a great many times—not a thousand times but quite a goodly number. Mary listened entranced. She felt as if it were at once queer and beautiful and she wanted him to go on and on. Ben Weatherstaff began to feel soothed into a sort of dream which was quite agreeable.

The humming of the bees in the blossoms mingled with the chanting voice and drowsily melted into a doze. Dickon sat cross-legged with his rabbit asleep on his arm and a hand resting on the lamb's back. Soot had pushed away a squirrel and huddled close to him on his shoulder, the gray film dropped over his eyes. At last Colin stopped.

"Now I am going to walk round the garden," he announced.

Ben Weatherstaff's head had just dropped forward and he lifted it with a jerk.

"You have been asleep," said Colin.

"Nowt o' th' sort," mumbled Ben. "Th' sermon was good enow—but I'm bound to get out afore th' collection."

He was not quite awake yet.

"You're not in church," said Colin.

"Not me," said Ben, straightening himself. "Who said I were? I heard every bit of it. You said th' Magic was in my back. Th' doctor calls it rheumatics."

The Rajah waved his hand.

"That was the wrong Magic," he said. "You will get better. You have my permission to go to your work. But come back tomorrow."

"I'd like to see thee walk round the garden," grunted Ben.

It was not an unfriendly grunt, but it was a grunt. In fact, being a stubborn old party and not having entire faith in Magic he had made up his mind that if he were sent away he would climb his ladder and look over the wall so that he might be ready to hobble back if there were any stumbling.

The Rajah did not object to his staying and so the procession was formed. It really did look like a procession. Colin was at its head with Dickon on one side and Mary on the other. Ben Weatherstaff walked behind, and the "creatures" trailed after them, the lamb and the fox cub keeping close to Dickon, the white rabbit hopping along or stopping to nibble and Soot following with the solemnity of a person who felt himself in charge.

It was a procession which moved slowly but with dignity. Every few yards it stopped to rest. Colin leaned on Dickon's arm and privately Ben Weatherstaff kept a sharp lookout, but now and then Colin took his hand from its support and walked a few steps alone. His head was held up all the time and he looked very grand.

"The Magic is in me!" he kept saying. "The Magic is making me strong! I can feel it! I can feel it!"

It seemed very certain that something was upholding and uplifting him. He sat on the seats in the alcoves, and once or twice he sat down on the grass and several times he paused in the path and leaned on Dickon, but he would not give up until he had gone all round the garden. When he returned to the canopy tree his cheeks were flushed and he looked triumphant.

"I did it! The Magic worked!" he cried. "That is my first scientific discovery.".

"What will Dr. Craven say?" broke out Mary.

"He won't say anything," Colin answered, "because he will not be told. This is to be the biggest secret of all. No one is to know anything about it until I have grown so strong that I can walk and run like any other boy. I shall come here every day in my chair and I shall be taken back in it. I won't have people whispering and asking questions and I won't let my father hear about it until the experiment has quite succeeded. Then sometime when he comes back to Misselthwaite I shall just walk into his study and say 'Here I am; I am like any other boy. I am quite well and I shall live to be a man. It has been done by a scientific experiment.'"

"He will think he is in a dream," cried Mary. "He won't believe his eyes."

Colin flushed triumphantly. He had made himself believe that he was going to get well, which was really more than half the battle, if he had been aware of it. And the thought which stimulated him more than any other was this imagining what his father would look like when he saw that he had a son who was as straight and strong as other fathers' sons. One of his darkest miseries in the unhealthy morbid past days had been his hatred of being a sickly weak-backed boy whose father was afraid to look at him.

"He'll be obliged to believe them," he said. "One of the things I am going to do, after the Magic works and before I begin to make scientific discovercies, is to be an athlete."

"We shall have thee takin' to boxin' in a week or so," said Ben Weatherstaff. "Tha'lt end wi' winnin' th' Belt an' bein' champion prize-fighter of all England."

Colin fixed his eyes on him sternly.

"Weatherstaff," he said, "that is disrespectful. You must not take liberties because you are in the secret. However much the Magic works I shall not be a prize-fighter. I shall be a Scientific Discoverer."

"Ax pardon—ax pardon, sir" answered Ben, touching his forehead in salute. "I ought to have seed it wasn't a jokin' matter," but his eyes twinkled and secretly he was immensely pleased. He really did not mind being snubbed since the snubbing meant that the lad was gaining strength and spirit.

Chapter 24

"Let Them Laugh"

The secret garden was not the only one Dickon worked in. Round the cottage on the moor there was a piece of ground enclosed by a low wall of rough stones. Early in the morning and late in the fading twilight and on all the days Colin and Mary did not see him, Dickon worked there planting or tending potatoes and cabbages, turnips and carrots and herbs for his mother.

In the company of his "creatures" he did wonders there and was never tired of doing them, it seemed. While he dug or weeded he whistled or sang bits of Yorkshire moor songs or talked to Soot or Captain or the brothers and sisters he had taught to help him.

"We'd never get on as comfortable as we do," Mrs. Sowerby said, "if it wasn't for Dickon's garden. Anything'll grow for him. His 'taters and cabbages is twice th' size of any one else's an' they've got a flavor with 'em as nobody's has."

When she found a moment to spare she liked to go out and talk to him. After supper there was still a long clear twilight to work in and that was her quiet time. She could sit upon the low rough wall and look on and hear stories of the day. She loved this time.

There were not only vegetables in this garden. Dickon had bought penny packages of flower seeds now and then and sown bright sweet-scented things among gooseberry bushes and even cabbages and he grew borders of mignonette and pinks and pansies  and things whose seeds he could save year after year or whose roots would bloom each spring and spread in time into fine clumps.

 The low wall was one of the prettiest things in Yorkshire because he had tucked moorland foxglove and ferns and rock-cress and hedgerow flowers into every crevice until only here and there glimpses of the stones were to be seen.

"All a chap's got to do to make 'em thrive, mother," he would say, "is to be friends with 'em for sure. They're just like th' 'creatures.' If they're thirsty give 'em drink and if they're hungry give 'em a bit o' food. They want to live same as we do. If they died I should feel as if I'd been a bad lad and somehow treated them heartless."

It was in these twilight hours that Mrs. Sowerby heard of all that happened at Misselthwaite Manor. At first she was only told that "Mester Colin" had taken a fancy to going out into the grounds with Miss Mary and that it was doing him good. But it was not long before it was agreed between the two children that Dickon's mother might "come into the secret." Somehow it was not doubted that she was "safe for sure."

So one beautiful still evening Dickon told the whole story, with all the thrilling details of the buried key and the robin and the gray haze which had seemed like deadness and the secret Mistress Mary had planned never to reveal. The coming of Dickon and how it had been told to him, the doubt of Mester Colin and the final drama of his introduction to the hidden domain, combined with the incident of Ben Weatherstaff's angry face peering over the wall and Mester Colin's sudden indignant strength, made Mrs. Sowerby's nice-looking face quite change color several times.

"My word!" she said. "It was a good thing that little lass came to th' Manor. It's been th' makin' o' her an' th' savin, o' him. Standin' on his feet! An' us all thinkin' he was a poor half-witted lad with not a straight bone in him."

She asked a great many questions and her blue eyes were full of deep thinking.

"What do they make of it at th' Manor—him being so well an' cheerful an' never complainin'?" she inquired.

"They don't know what to make of it," answered Dickon. "Every day as comes round his face looks different. It's fillin' out and doesn't look so sharp an' th' waxy color is goin'. But he has to do his bit o' complainin'," with a highly entertained grin.

"What for, i' Mercy's name?" asked Mrs. Sowerby.

Dickon chuckled.

"He does it to keep them from guessin' what's happened. If the doctor knew he'd found out he could stand on his feet he'd likely write and tell Mester Craven.

Mester Colin's savin' th' secret to tell himself. He's goin' to practise his Magic on his legs every day till his father comes back an' then he's goin' to march into his room an' show him he's as straight as other lads. But him an' Miss Mary thinks it's best plan to do a bit o' groanin' an' frettin' now an' then to throw folk off th' scent."

Mrs. Sowerby was laughing a low comfortable laugh long before he had finished his last sentence.

"Eh!" she said, "that pair's enjoyin' their-selves I'll warrant. They'll get a good bit o' actin' out of it an' there's nothin' children likes as much as play actin'. Let's hear what they do, Dickon lad." Dickon stopped weeding and sat up on his heels to tell her. His eyes were twinkling with fun.

"Mester Colin is carried down to his chair every time he goes out," he explained. "An' he flies out at John, th' footman, for not carryin' him careful enough. He makes himself as helpless lookin' as he can an' never lifts his head until we're out o' sight o' th' house. An' he grunts an' frets a good bit when he's bein' settled into his chair. Him an' Miss Mary's both got to enjoyin' it an' when he groans an' complains she'll say, 'Poor Colin! Does it hurt you so much? Are you so weak as that, poor Colin?'— but th' trouble is that sometimes they can scarce keep from burstin' out laughin'. When we get safe into the garden they laugh till they've no breath left to laugh with. An' they have to stuff their faces into Mester Colin's cushions to keep the gardeners from hearin', if any of, 'em's about."

"Th' more they laugh th' better for 'em!" said Mrs. Sowerby, still laughing herself. "Good healthy child laughin's better than pills any day o' th' year. That pair'll plump up for sure."

"They are plumpin' up," said Dickon. "They're that hungry they don't know how to get enough to eat without makin' talk. Mester Colin says if he keeps sendin' for more food they won't believe he's an invalid at all. Miss Mary says she'll let him eat her share, but he says that if she goes hungry she'll get thin an' they mun both get fat at once."

Mrs. Sowerby laughed so heartily at the revelation of this difficulty that she quite rocked backward and forward in her blue cloak, and Dickon laughed with her.

"I'll tell thee what, lad," Mrs. Sowerby said when she could speak. "I've thought of a way to help 'em. When tha' goes to 'em in th' mornin's tha' shall take a pail o' good new milk an' I'll bake 'em a crusty cottage loaf or some buns wi' currants in 'em, same as you children like. Nothin's so good as fresh milk an' bread. Then they could take off th' edge o' their hunger while they were in their garden an' th, fine food they get indoors 'ud polish off th' corners."

"Eh! mother!" said Dickon admiringly, "what a wonder tha' art! Tha' always sees a way out o' things. They was quite in a pother yesterday. They didn't see how they was to manage without orderin' up more food—they felt that empty inside."

"They're two young 'uns growin' fast, an' health's comin' back to both of 'em. Children like that feels like young wolves an' food's flesh an' blood to 'em," said Mrs. Sowerby. Then she smiled Dickon's own curving smile. "Eh! but they're enjoyin' theirselves for sure," she said.

She was quite right, the comfortable wonderful mother creature—and she had never been more so than when she said their "play actin'" would be their joy. Colin and Mary found it one of their most thrilling sources of entertainment. The idea of protecting themselves from suspicion had been unconsciously suggested to them first by the puzzled nurse and then by Dr. Craven himself.

"Your appetite. Is improving very much, Master Colin," the nurse had said one day. "You used to eat nothing, and so many things disagreed with you."

"Nothing disagrees with me now" replied Colin, and then seeing the nurse looking at him curiously he suddenly remembered that perhaps he ought not to appear too well just yet. "At least things don't so often disagree with me. It's the fresh air."

"Perhaps it is," said the nurse, still looking at him with a mystified expression. "But I must talk to Dr. Craven about it."

"How she stared at you!" said Mary when she went away. "As if she thought there must be something to find out."

"I won't have her finding out things," said Colin. "No one must begin to find out yet."

When Dr. Craven came that morning he seemed puzzled, also. He asked a number of questions, to Colin's great annoyance.

"You stay out in the garden a great deal," he suggested. "Where do you go?"

Colin put on his favorite air of dignified indifference to opinion.

"I will not let any one know where I go," he answered. "I go to a place I like. Every one has orders to keep out of the way. I won't be watched and stared at. You know that!"

"You seem to be out all day but I do not think it has done you harm—I do not think so. The nurse says that you eat much more than you have ever done before."

"Perhaps," said Colin, prompted by a sudden inspiration, "perhaps it is an unnatural appetite."

"I do not think so, as your food seems to agree with you," said Dr. Craven. "You are gaining flesh rapidly and your color is better."

"Perhaps—perhaps I am bloated and feverish," said Colin, assuming a discouraging air of gloom. "People who are not going to live are often—different." Dr. Craven shook his head. He was holding Colin's wrist and he pushed up his sleeve and felt his arm.

"You are not feverish," he said thoughtfully, "and such flesh as you have gained is healthy. If you can keep this up, my boy, we need not talk of dying. Your father will be happy to hear of this remarkable improvement."

"I won't have him told!" Colin broke forth fiercely. "It will only disappoint him if I get worse again—and I may get worse this very night. I might have a raging fever. I feel as if I might be beginning to have one now. I won't have letters written to my father—I won't—I won't! You are making me angry and you know that is bad for me. I feel hot already. I hate being written about and being talked over as much as I hate being stared at!"

"Hush-h! my boy," Dr. Craven soothed him. "Nothing shall be written without your permission. You are too sensitive about things. You must not undo the good which has been done."

He said no more about writing to Mr. Craven and when he saw the nurse he privately warned her that such a possibility must not be mentioned to the patient.

"The boy is extraordinarily better," he said. "His advance seems almost abnormal. But of course he is doing now of his own free will what we could not make him do before. Still, he excites himself very easily and nothing must be said to irritate him." Mary and Colin were much alarmed and talked together anxiously. From this time dated their plan of "play actin'."

"I may be obliged to have a tantrum," said Colin regretfully. "I don't want to have one and I'm not miserable enough now to work myself into a big one. Perhaps I couldn't have one at all. That lump doesn't come in my throat now and I keep thinking of nice things instead of horrible ones. But if they talk about writing to my father I shall have to do something."

He made up his mind to eat less, but unfortunately it was not possible to carry out this brilliant idea when he wakened each morning with an amazing appetite and the table near his sofa was set with a breakfast of home-made bread and fresh butter, snow-white eggs, raspberry jam and clotted cream. Mary always breakfasted with him and when they found themselves at the table—particularly if there were delicate slices of sizzling ham sending forth tempting odors from under a hot silver cover—they would look into each other's eyes in desperation.

"I think we shall have to eat it all this morning, Mary," Colin always ended by saying. "We can send away some of the lunch and a great deal of the dinner."

But they never found they could send away anything and the highly polished condition of the empty plates returned to the pantry awakened much comment.

"I do wish," Colin would say also, "I do wish the slices of ham were thicker, and one muffin each is not enough for any one."

"It's enough for a person who is going to die," answered Mary when first she heard this, "but it's not enough for a person who is going to live. I sometimes feel as if I could eat three when those nice fresh heather and gorse smells from the moor come pouring in at the open window."

The morning that Dickon—after they had been enjoying themselves in the garden for about two hours—went behind a big rosebush and brought forth two tin pails and revealed that one was full of rich new milk with cream on the top of it, and that the other held cottage-made currant buns folded in a clean blue and white napkin, buns so carefully tucked in that they were still hot, there was a riot of surprised joyfulness. What a wonderful thing for Mrs. Sowerby to think of! What a kind, clever woman she must be! How good the buns were! And what delicious fresh milk!

"Magic is in her just as it is in Dickon," said Colin. "It makes her think of ways to do things—nice things. She is a Magic person. Tell her we are grateful, Dickon—extremely grateful." He was given to using rather grown-up phrases at times. He enjoyed them. He liked this so much that he improved upon it.

"Tell her she has been most bounteous and our

gratitude is extreme."

And then forgetting his grandeur he fell to and stuffed himself with buns and drank milk out of the pail in copious draughts in the manner of any hungry little boy who had been taking unusual exercise and breathing in moorland air and whose breakfast was more than two hours behind him.

This was the beginning of many agreeable incidents of the same kind. They actually awoke to the fact that as Mrs. Sowerby had fourteen people to provide food for she might not have enough to satisfy two extra appetites every day. So they asked her to let them send some of their shillings to buy things.

Dickon made the stimulating discovery that in the wood in the park outside the garden where Mary had first found him piping to the wild creatures there was a deep little hollow where you could build a sort of tiny oven with stones and roast potatoes and eggs in it. Roasted eggs were a previously unknown luxury and very hot potatoes with salt and fresh butter in them were fit for a woodland king—besides being deliciously satisfying. You could buy both potatoes and eggs and eat as many as you liked without feeling as if you were taking food out of the mouths of fourteen people.

Every beautiful morning the Magic was worked by the mystic circle under the plum-tree which provided a canopy of thickening green leaves after its brief blossom-time was ended. After the ceremony Colin always took his walking exercise and throughout the day he exercised his newly found power at intervals. Each day he grew stronger and could walk more steadily and cover more ground. And each day his belief in the Magic grew stronger—as well it might. He tried one experiment after another as he felt himself gaining strength and it was Dickon who showed him the best things of all.

"Yesterday," he said one morning after an absence, "I went to Thwaite for mother an' near th' Blue Cow Inn I seed Bob Haworth. He's the strongest chap on th' moor. He's the champion wrestler an' he can jump higher than any other chap an' throw th' hammer farther. He's gone all th' way to Scotland for th' sports some years. He's knowed me ever since I was a little 'un an' he's a friendly sort an' I axed him some questions. Th' gentry calls him a athlete and I thought o' thee, Mester Colin, and I says, 'How did tha' make tha' muscles stick out that way, Bob? Did tha' do anythin' extra to make thysel' so strong?' An' he says 'Well, yes, lad, I did. A strong man in a show that came to Thwaite once showed me how to exercise my arms an' legs an' every muscle in my body. An' I says, 'Could a delicate chap make himself stronger with 'em, Bob?' an' he laughed an' says, 'Art tha' th' delicate chap?' an' I says, 'No, but I knows a young gentleman that's gettin' well of a long illness an' I wish I knowed some o' them tricks to tell him about.' I didn't say no names an' he didn't ask none. He's friendly same as I said an' he stood up an' showed me good-natured like, an' I imitated what he did till I knowed it by heart."

Colin had been listening excitedly.

"Can you show me?" he cried. "Will you?"

"Aye, to be sure," Dickon answered, getting up. "But he says tha' mun do 'em gentle at first an' be careful not to tire thysel'. Rest in between times an' take deep breaths an' don't overdo."

"I'll be careful," said Colin. "Show me! Show me! Dickon, you are the most Magic boy in the world!"

Dickon stood up on the grass and slowly went through a carefully practical but simple series of muscle exercises. Colin watched them with widening eyes. He could do a few while he was sitting down. Presently he did a few gently while he stood upon his already steadied feet. Mary began to do them also. Soot, who was watching the performance, became much disturbed and left his branch and hopped about restlessly because he could not do them too.

From that time the exercises were part of the day's duties as much as the Magic was. It became possible for both Colin and Mary to do more of them each time they tried, and such appetites were the results that but for the basket Dickon put down behind the bush each morning when he arrived they would have been lost. But the little oven in the hollow and Mrs. Sowerby's bounties were so satisfying that Mrs. Medlock and the nurse and Dr. Craven became mystified again. You can trifle with your breakfast and seem to disdain your dinner if you are full to the brim with roasted eggs and potatoes and richly frothed new milk and oatcakes and buns and heather honey and clotted cream.

"They are eating next to nothing," said the nurse. "They'll die of starvation if they can't be persuaded to take some nourishment. And yet see how they look."

"Look!" exclaimed Mrs. Medlock indignantly. "Eh! I'm moithered to death with them. They're a pair of young Satans. Bursting their jackets one day and the next turning up their noses at the best meals Cook can tempt them with. Not a mouthful of that lovely young fowl and bread sauce did they set a fork into yesterday—and the poor woman fair invented a pudding for them—and back it's sent. She almost cried. She's afraid she'll be blamed if they starve themselves into their graves."

Dr. Craven came and looked at Colin long and carefully, He wore an extremely worried expression when the nurse talked with him and showed him the almost untouched tray of breakfast she had saved for him to look at—but it was even more worried when he sat down by Colin's sofa and examined him.

He had been called to London on business and had not seen the boy for nearly two weeks. When young things begin to gain health they gain it rapidly. The waxen tinge had left, Colins skin and a warm rose showed through it; his beautiful eyes were clear and the hollows under them and in his cheeks and temples had filled out. His once dark, heavy locks had begun to look as if they sprang healthily from his forehead and were soft and warm with life. His lips were fuller and of a normal color. In fact as an imitation of a boy who was a confirmed invalid he was a disgraceful sight. Dr. Craven held his chin in his hand and thought him over.

"I am sorry to hear that you do not eat anything," he said. "That will not do. You will lose all you have gained—and you have gained amazingly. You ate so well a short time ago."

"I told you it was an unnatural appetite," answered Colin.

Mary was sitting on her stool nearby and she

suddenly made a very queer sound which she tried so violently to repress that she ended by almost choking.

"What is the matter?" said Dr. Craven, turning to look at her.

Mary became quite severe in her manner.

"It was something between a sneeze and a cough," she replied with reproachful dignity, "and it got into my throat."

"But," she said afterward to Colin, "I couldn't stop myself. It just burst out because all at once I couldn't help remembering that last big potato you ate and the way your mouth stretched when you bit through that thick lovely crust with jam and clotted cream on it."

"Is there any way in which those children can get food secretly?" Dr. Craven inquired of Mrs. Medlock.

"There's no way unless they dig it out of the earth or pick it off the trees," Mrs. Medlock answered. "They stay out in the grounds all day and see no one but each other. And if they want anything different to eat from what's sent up to them they need only ask for it."

"Well," said Dr. Craven, "so long as going without food agrees with them we need not disturb ourselves. The boy is a new creature."

"So is the girl," said Mrs. Medlock. "She's begun to be downright pretty since she's filled out and lost her ugly little sour look. Her hair's grown thick and healthy looking and she's got a bright color. The glummest, ill-natured little thing she used to be and now her and Master Colin laugh together like a pair of crazy young ones. Perhaps they're growing fat on that."

"Perhaps they are," said Dr. Craven. "Let them laugh."

Chapter 25

The Curtain

And the secret garden bloomed and bloomed and every morning revealed new miracles. In the robin's nest there were Eggs and the robin's mate sat upon them keeping them warm with her feathery little breast and careful wings.

At first she was very nervous and the robin himself was indignantly watchful. Even Dickon did not go near the close-grown corner in those days, but waited until by the quiet working of some mysterious spell he seemed to have conveyed to the soul of the little pair that in the garden there was nothing which was not quite like themselves—nothing which did not understand the wonderfulness of what was happening to them—the immense, tender, terrible, heart-breaking beauty and solemnity of Eggs.

If there had been one person in that garden who had not known through all his or her innermost being that if an Egg were taken away or hurt the whole world would whirl round and crash through space and come to an end—if there had been even one who did not feel it and act accordingly there could have been no happiness even in that golden springtime air. But they all knew it and felt it and the robin and his mate knew they knew it.

At first the robin watched Mary and Colin with sharp anxiety. For some mysterious reason he knew he need not watch Dickon. The first moment he set his dew-bright black eye on Dickon he knew he was not a stranger but a sort of robin without beak or feathers. He could speak robin (which is a quite distinct language not to be mistaken for any other). To speak robin to a robin is like speaking French to a Frenchman.

Dickon always spoke it to the robin himself, so the queer gibberish he used when he spoke to humans did not matter in the least. The robin thought he spoke this gibberish to them because they were not intelligent enough to understand feathered speech. His movements also were robin. They never startled one by being sudden enough to seem dangerous or threatening. Any robin could understand Dickon, so his presence was not even disturbing.

But at the outset it seemed necessary to be on guard against the other two. In the first place the boy creature did not come into the garden on his legs. He was pushed in on a thing with wheels and the skins of wild animals were thrown over him. That in itself was doubtful. Then when he began to stand up and move about he did it in a queer unaccustomed way and the others seemed to have to help him.

The robin used to secrete himself in a bush and watch this anxiously, his head tilted first on one side and then on the other. He thought that the slow movements might mean that he was preparing to pounce, as cats do. When cats are preparing to pounce they creep over the ground very slowly. The robin talked this over with his mate a great deal for a few days but after that he decided not to speak of the subject because her terror was so great that he was afraid it might be injurious to the Eggs.

When the boy began to walk by himself and even to move more quickly it was an immense relief. But for a long time—or it seemed a long time to the robin—he was a source of some anxiety. He did not act as the other humans did. He seemed very fond of walking but he had a way of sitting or lying down for a while and then getting up in a disconcerting manner to begin again.

One day the robin remembered that when he himself had been made to learn to fly by his parents he had done much the same sort of thing. He had taken short flights of a few yards and then had been obliged to rest. So it occurred to him that this boy was learning to fly— or rather to walk.

He mentioned this to his mate and when he told her that the Eggs would probably conduct themselves in the same way after they were fledged she was quite comforted and even became eagerly interested and derived great pleasure from watching the boy over the edge of her nest—though she always thought that the Eggs would be much cleverer and learn more quickly. But then she said indulgently that humans were always more clumsy and slow than Eggs and most of them never seemed really to learn to fly at all. You never met them in the air or on tree-tops.

After a while the boy began to move about as the others did, but all three of the children at times did unusual things. They would stand under the trees and move their arms and legs and heads about in a way which was neither walking nor running nor sitting down. They went through these movements at intervals every day and the robin was never able to explain to his mate what they were doing or tying to do. He could only say that he was sure that the Eggs would never flap about in such a manner; but as the boy who could speak robin so fluently was doing the thing with them, birds could be quite sure that the actions were not of a dangerous nature.

Of course neither the robin nor his mate had ever heard of the champion wrestler, Bob Haworth, and his exercises for making the muscles stand out like lumps. Robins are not like human beings; their muscles are always exercised from the first and so they develop themselves in a natural manner. If you have to fly about to find every meal you eat, your muscles do not become atrophied (atrophied means wasted away through want of use).

When the boy was walking and running about and digging and weeding like the others, the nest in the corner was brooded over by a great peace and content. Fears for the Eggs became things of the past. Knowing that your Eggs were as safe as if they were locked in a bank vault and the fact that you could watch so many curious things going on made setting a most entertaining occupation. On wet days the Eggs' mother sometimes felt even a little dull because the children did not come into the garden.

But even on wet days it could not be said that Mary and Colin were dull. One morning when the rain streamed down unceasingly and Colin was beginning to feel a little restive, as he was obliged to remain on his sofa because it was not safe to get up and walk about, Mary had an inspiration.

"Now that I am a real boy," Colin had said, "my legs and arms and all my body are so full of Magic that I can't keep them still. They want to be doing things all the time. Do you know that when I waken in the morning, Mary, when it's quite early and the birds are just shouting outside and everything seems just shouting for joy—even the trees and things we can't really hear— I feel as if I must jump out of bed and shout myself. If I did it, just think what would happen!"

Mary giggled inordinately.

"The nurse would come running and Mrs. Medlock would come running and they would be sure you had gone crazy and they'd send for the doctor," she said.

Colin giggled himself. He could see how they would all look—how horrified by his outbreak and how amazed to see him standing upright.

"I wish my father would come home," he said. "I want to tell him myself. I'm always thinking about it—but we couldn't go on like this much longer. I can't stand lying still and pretending, and besides I look too different. I wish it wasn't raining today."

It was then Mistress Mary had her inspiration.

"Colin," she began mysteriously, "do you know how many rooms there are in this house?"

"About a thousand, I suppose," he answered.

"There's about a hundred no one ever goes into," said Mary. "And one rainy day I went and looked into ever so many of them. No one ever knew, though Mrs. Medlock nearly found me out. I lost my way when I was coming back and I stopped at the end of your corridor. That was the second time I heard you crying."

Colin started up on his sofa.

"A hundred rooms no one goes into," he said. "It sounds almost like a secret garden. Suppose we go and look at them. Wheel me in my chair and nobody would know we went."

"That's what I was thinking," said Mary. "No one would dare to follow us. There are galleries where you could run. We could do our exercises. There is a little Indian room where there is a cabinet full of ivory elephants. There are all sorts of rooms."

"Ring the bell," said Colin.

When the nurse came in he gave his orders.

"I want my chair," he said. "Miss Mary and I are going to look at the part of the house which is not used. John can push me as far as the picture-gallery because there are some stairs. Then he must go away and leave us alone until I send for him again."

Rainy days lost their terrors that morning. When the footman had wheeled the chair into the picture-gallery and left the two together in obedience to orders, Colin and Mary looked at each other delighted. As soon as

Mary had made sure that John was really on his way back to his own quarters below stairs, Colin got out of his chair.

"I am going to run from one end of the gallery to the other," he said, "and then I am going to jump and then we will do Bob Haworth's exercises."

And they did all these things and many others. They looked at the portraits and found the plain little girl dressed in green brocade and holding the parrot on her finger.

"All these," said Colin, "must be my relations. They lived a long time ago. That parrot one, I believe, is one of my great, great, great, great aunts. She looks rather like you, Mary—not as you look now but as you looked when you came here. Now you are a great deal fatter and better looking."

"So are you," said Mary, and they both laughed.

They went to the Indian room and amused themselves with the ivory elephants. They found the rose-colored brocade boudoir and the hole in the cushion the mouse had left, but the mice had grown up and run away and the hole was empty. They saw more rooms and made more discoveries than Mary had made on her first pilgrimage. They found new corridors and corners and flights of steps and new old pictures they liked and weird old things they did not know the use of.

It was a curiously entertaining morning and the feeling of wandering about in the same house with other people but at the same time feeling as if one were miles away from them was a fascinating thing.

"I'm glad we came," Colin said. "I never knew I lived in such a big queer old place. I like it. We will ramble about every rainy day. We shall always be finding new queer corners and things."

That morning they had found among other things such good appetites that when they returned to Colin's room it was not possible to send the luncheon away untouched.

When the nurse carried the tray down-stairs she slapped it down on the kitchen dresser so that Mrs. Loomis, the cook, could see the highly polished dishes and plates.

"Look at that!" she said. "This is a house of mystery, and those two children are the greatest mysteries in it."

"If they keep that up every day," said the strong young footman John, "there'd be small wonder that he weighs twice as much today as he did a month ago. I should have to give up my place in time, for fear of doing my muscles an injury."

That afternoon Mary noticed that something new had happened in Colin's room. She had noticed it the day before but had said nothing because she thought the change might have been made by chance. She said nothing today but she sat and looked fixedly at the picture over the mantel. She could look at it because the curtain had been drawn aside. That was the change she noticed.

"I know what you want me to tell you," said Colin, after she had stared a few minutes. "I always know when you want me to tell you something. You are wondering why the curtain is drawn back. I am going to keep it like that."

"Why?" asked Mary.

"Because it doesn't make me angry any more to see her laughing. I wakened when it was bright moonlight two nights ago and felt as if the Magic was filling the room and making everything so splendid that I couldn't lie still. I got up and looked out of the window. The room was quite light and there was a patch of moonlight on the curtain and somehow that made me go and pull the cord. She looked right down at me as if she were laughing because she was glad I was standing there. It made me like to look at her. I want to see her laughing like that all the time. I think she must have been a sort of Magic person perhaps."

"You are so like her now," said Mary, "that sometimes I think perhaps you are her ghost made into a boy."

That idea seemed to impress Colin. He thought it over and then answered her slowly.

"If I were her ghost—my father would be fond of me."

"Do you want him to be fond of you?" inquired Mary.

"I used to hate it because he was not fond of me. If he grew fond of me I think I should tell him about the Magic. It might make him more cheerful."

Chapter 26

It's Mother!"

Their belief in the Magic was an abiding thing. After the morning's incantations Colin sometimes gave them Magic lectures.

"I like to do it," he explained, "because when I grow up and make great scientific discoveries I shall be obliged to lecture about them and so this is practise. I can only give short lectures now because I am very young, and besides Ben Weatherstaff would feel as if he were in church and he would go to sleep."

"Th' best thing about lecturin'," said Ben, "is that a chap can get up an' say aught he pleases an' no other chap can answer him back. I wouldn't be agen' lecturin' a bit mysel' sometimes."

But when Colin held forth under his tree old Ben fixed devouring eyes on him and kept them there. He looked him over with critical affection. It was not so much the lecture which interested him as the legs which looked straighter and stronger each day, the boyish head which held itself up so well, the once sharp chin and hollow cheeks which had filled and rounded out and the eyes which had begun to hold the light he remembered in another pair.

Sometimes when Colin felt Ben's earnest gaze meant that he was much impressed he wondered what he was reflecting on and once when he had seemed quite entranced he questioned him.

"What are you thinking about, Ben Weatherstaff?" he asked.

"I was thinkin'" answered Ben, "as I'd warrant tha's, gone up three or four pound this week. I was lookin' at tha' calves an' tha' shoulders. I'd like to get thee on a pair o' scales."

"It's the Magic and—and Mrs. Sowerby's buns and milk and things," said Colin. "You see the scientific experiment has succeeded."

That morning Dickon was too late to hear the lecture. When he came he was ruddy with running and his funny face looked more twinkling than usual.

As they had a good deal of weeding to do after the rains they fell to work. They always had plenty to do after a warm deep sinking rain. The moisture which was good for the flowers was also good for the weeds which thrust up tiny blades of grass and points of leaves which must be pulled up before their roots took too firm hold. Colin was as good at weeding as any one in these days and he could lecture while he was doing it.

"The Magic works best when you work, yourself," he said this morning. "You can feel it in your bones and muscles. I am going to read books about bones and muscles, but I am going to write a book about Magic. I am making it up now. I keep finding out things."

It was not very long after he had said this that he laid down his trowel and stood up on his feet. He had been silent for several minutes and they had seen that he was thinking out lectures, as he often did. When he dropped his trowel and stood upright it seemed to Mary and Dickon as if a sudden strong thought had made him do it.

He stretched himself out to his tallest height and he threw out his arms exultantly. Color glowed in his face and his strange eyes widened with joyfulness. All at once he had realized something to the full.

"Mary! Dickon!" he cried. "Just look at me!"

They stopped their weeding and looked at him.

"Do you remember that first morning you brought me in here?" he demanded.

Dickon was looking at him very hard. Being an animal charmer he could see more things than most people could and many of them were things he never talked about. He saw some of them now in this boy. "Aye, that we do," he answered.

Mary looked hard too, but she said nothing.

"Just this minute," said Colin, "all at once I remembered it myself—when I looked at my hand digging with the trowel—and I had to stand up on my feet to see if it was real. And it is real! I'm well—I'm well!"

"Aye, that th' art!" said Dickon.

"I'm well! I'm well!" said Colin again, and his face went quite red all over.

He had known it before in a way, he had hoped

it and felt it and thought about it, but just at that minute something had rushed all through him—a sort of rapturous belief and realization and it had been so strong that he could not help calling out.

"I shall live forever and ever and ever!" he cried grandly. "I shall find out thousands and thousands of things. I shall find out about people and creatures and everything that grows—like Dickon—and I shall never stop making Magic. I'm well! I'm well! I feel—I feel as if I want to shout out something—something thankful, joyful!"

Ben Weatherstaff, who had been working near a rose-bush, glanced round at him.

"Tha' might sing th' Doxology," he suggested in his dryest grunt. He had no opinion of the Doxology and he did not make the suggestion with any particular reverence.

But Colin was of an exploring mind and he knew nothing about the Doxology.

"What is that?" he inquired.

"Dickon can sing it for thee, I'll warrant," replied Ben Weatherstaff.

Dickon answered with his all-perceiving animal charmer's smile.

"They sing it i' church," he said. "Mother says she believes th' skylarks sings it when they gets up i' th' mornin'."

"If she says that, it must be a nice song," Colin answered. "I've never been in a church myself. I was always too ill. Sing it, Dickon. I want to hear it."

Dickon was quite simple and unaffected about it. He understood what Colin felt better than Colin did himself. He understood by a sort of instinct so natural that he did not know it was understanding. He pulled off his cap and looked round still smiling.

"Tha' must take off tha' cap," he said to Colin, "an' so mun tha', Ben—an' tha' mun stand up, tha' knows."

Colin took off his cap and the sun shone on and warmed his thick hair as he watched Dickon intently. Ben Weatherstaff scrambled up from his knees and bared his head too with a sort of puzzled half-resentful look on his old face as if he didn't know exactly why he was doing this remarkable thing.

Dickon stood out among the trees and rose-bushes and began to sing in quite a simple matter-of-fact way and in a nice strong boy voice:

"Praise God from whom all blessings flow,
Praise Him all creatures here below,
Praise Him above ye Heavenly Host,
Praise Father, Son, and Holy Ghost.
Amen."

When he had finished, Ben Weatherstaff was standing quite still with his jaws set obstinately but with a disturbed look in his eyes fixed on Colin. Colin's face was thoughtful and appreciative.

"It is a very nice song," he said. "I like it. Perhaps it means just what I mean when I want to shout out that

I am thankful to the Magic." He stopped and thought in a puzzled way. "Perhaps they are both the same thing. How can we know the exact names of everything? Sing it again, Dickon. Let us try, Mary. I want to sing it, too. It's my song. How does it begin? 'Praise God from whom all blessings flow'?"

And they sang it again, and Mary and Colin lifted their voices as musically as they could and Dickon's swelled quite loud and beautiful—and at the second line Ben Weatherstaff raspingly cleared his throat and at the third line he joined in with such vigor that it seemed almost savage and when the "Amen" came to an end Mary observed that the very same thing had happened to him which had happened when he found out that Colin was not a cripple—his chin was twitching and he was staring and winking and his leathery old cheeks were wet.

"I never seed no sense in th' Doxology afore," he said hoarsely, "but I may change my mind i' time. I should say tha'd gone up five pound this week Mester Colin— five on 'em!"

Colin was looking across the garden at something attracting his attention and his expression had become a startled one.

"Who is coming in here?" he said quickly. "Who is it?"

The door in the ivied wall had been pushed gently open and a woman had entered. She had come in with the last line of their song and she had stood still listening and looking at them. With the ivy behind her, the sunlight drifting through the trees and dappling her long blue cloak, and her nice fresh face smiling across the greenery she was rather like a softly colored illustration in one of Colin's books. She had wonderful affectionate eyes which seemed to take everything in— all of them, even Ben Weatherstaff and the "creatures" and every flower that was in bloom. Unexpectedly as she had appeared, not one of them felt that she was an intruder at all. Dickon's eyes lighted like lamps.

"It's mother—that's who it is!" he cried and went across the grass at a run.

Colin began to move toward her, too, and Mary went with him. They both felt their pulses beat faster.

"It's mother!" Dickon said again when they met halfway. "I knowed tha' wanted to see her an' I told her where th' door was hid."

Colin held out his hand with a sort of flushed royal shyness but his eyes quite devoured her face.

"Even when I was ill I wanted to see you," he said, "you and Dickon and the secret garden. I'd never wanted to see any one or anything before."

The sight of his uplifted face brought about a sudden change in her own. She flushed and the corners of her mouth shook and a mist seemed to sweep over her eyes.

"Eh! dear lad!" she broke out tremulously. "Eh! dear lad!" as if she had not known she were going to say it. She did not say, "Mester Colin," but just "dear lad" quite suddenly. She might have said it to Dickon in the same way if she had seen something in his face which touched her. Colin liked it.

"Are you surprised because I am so well?" he asked. She put her hand on his shoulder and smiled the mist out of her eyes. "Aye, that I am!" she said; "but tha'rt so like thy mother tha' made my heart jump."

"Do you think," said Colin a little awkwardly, "that will make my father like me?"

"Aye, for sure, dear lad," she answered and she gave his shoulder a soft quick pat. "He mun come home—he mun come home."

"Susan Sowerby," said Ben Weatherstaff, getting close to her. "Look at th' lad's legs, wilt tha'? They was like drumsticks i' stockin' two month' ago—an' I heard folk tell as they was bandy an' knock-kneed both at th' same time. Look at 'em now!"

Susan Sowerby laughed a comfortable laugh.

"They're goin' to be fine strong lad's legs in a bit," she said. "Let him go on playin' an' workin' in the garden an' eatin' hearty an' drinkin' plenty o' good sweet milk an' there'll not be a finer pair i' Yorkshire, thank God for it."

She put both hands on Mistress Mary's shoulders and looked her little face over in a motherly fashion.

"An' thee, too!" she said. "Tha'rt grown near as hearty as our 'Lisabeth Ellen. I'll warrant tha'rt like thy mother too. Our Martha told me as Mrs. Medlock heard she was a pretty woman. Tha'lt be like a blush rose when tha' grows up, my little lass, bless thee."

She did not mention that when Martha came home on her "day out" and described the plain sallow child she had said that she had no confidence whatever in what Mrs. Medlock had heard. "It doesn't stand to reason that a pretty woman could be th' mother o' such a fou' little lass," she had added obstinately.

Mary had not had time to pay much attention to her changing face. She had only known that she looked "different" and seemed to have a great deal more hair and that it was growing very fast. But remembering her pleasure in looking at the Mem Sahib in the past she was glad to hear that she might some day look like her.

Susan Sowerby went round their garden with them and was told the whole story of it and shown every bush and tree which had come alive. Colin walked on one side of her and Mary on the other. Each of them kept looking up at her comfortable rosy face, secretly curious about the delightful feeling she gave them—a sort of warm, supported feeling.

It seemed as if she understood them as Dickon understood his "creatures." She stooped over the flowers and talked about them as if they were children. Soot followed her and once or twice cawed at her and flew upon her shoulder as if it were Dickon's. When they told her about the robin and the first flight of the young ones she laughed a motherly little mellow laugh in her throat.

"I suppose learnin' 'em to fly is like learnin' children to walk, but I'm feared I should be all in a worrit if mine had wings instead o' legs," she said.

It was because she seemed such a wonderful woman in her nice moorland cottage way that at last she was told about the Magic.

"Do you believe in Magic?" asked Colin after he had explained about Indian fakirs. "I do hope you do."

"That I do, lad," she answered. "I never knowed it by

that name but what does th' name matter? I warrant they call it a different name i' France an' a different one i' Germany. Th' same thing as set th' seeds swellin' an' th' sun shinin' made thee a well lad an' it's th' Good Thing. It isn't like us poor fools as think it matters if us is called out of our names. Th' Big Good Thing doesn't stop to worrit, bless thee. It goes on makin' worlds by th' million—worlds like us. Never thee stop believin' in th' Big Good Thing an' knowin' th' world's full of it—an' call it what tha' likes. Tha' wert singin' to it when I come into th' garden."

"I felt so joyful," said Colin, opening his beautiful strange eyes at her. "Suddenly I felt how different I was—how strong my arms and legs were, you know—and how I could dig and stand—and I jumped up and wanted to shout out something to anything that would listen."

"Th' Magic listened when tha' sung th' Doxology. It would ha' listened to anything tha'd sung. It was th' joy that mattered. Eh! lad, lad—what's names to th' Joy Maker," and she gave his shoulders a quick soft pat again.

She had packed a basket which held a regular feast this morning, and when the hungry hour came and Dickon brought it out from its hiding place, she sat down with them under their tree and watched them devour their food, laughing and quite gloating over their appetites. She was full of fun and made them laugh at all sorts of odd things. She told them stories in broad Yorkshire and taught them new words. She laughed as if she could not help it when they told her of the increasing difficulty there was in pretending that Colin was still a fretful invalid.

"You see we can't help laughing nearly all the time when we are together," explained Colin. "And it doesn't sound ill at all. We try to choke it back but it will burst out and that sounds worse than ever."

"There's one thing that comes into my mind so often," said Mary, "and I can scarcely ever hold in when I think of it suddenly. I keep thinking suppose Colin's face should get to look like a full moon. It isn't like one yet but he gets a tiny bit fatter every day—and suppose some morning it should look like one—what should we do!"

"Bless us all, I can see tha' has a good bit o' play actin' to do," said Susan Sowerby. "But tha' won't have to keep it up much longer. Mester Craven'll come home."

"Do you think he will?" asked Colin. "Why?"

Susan Sowerby chuckled softly.

"I suppose it 'ud nigh break thy heart if he found out before tha' told him in tha' own way," she said. "Tha's laid awake nights plannin' it."

"I couldn't bear any one else to tell him," said Colin. "I think about different ways every day, I think now I just want to run into his room." "That'd be a fine start for him," said Susan Sowerby. "I'd like to see his face, lad. I would that! He mun come back—that he mun."

One of the things they talked of was the visit they were to make to her cottage. They planned it all. They were to drive over the moor and lunch out of doors among the heather. They would see all the twelve children and Dickon's garden and would not come back until they were tired.

Susan Sowerby got up at last to return to the house and Mrs. Medlock. It was time for Colin to be wheeled back also. But before he got into his chair he stood quite close to Susan and fixed his eyes on her with a kind of bewildered adoration and he suddenly caught hold of the fold of her blue cloak and held it fast.

"You are just what I—what I wanted," he said. "I wish you were my mother—as well as Dickon's!"

All at once Susan Sowerby bent down and drew him with her warm arms close against the bosom under the blue cloak—as if he had been Dickon's brother. The quick mist swept over her eyes.

"Eh! dear lad!" she said. "Thy own mother's in this 'ere very garden, I do believe. She couldna' keep out of it. Thy father mun come back to thee—he mun!"

Chapter 27

In the Garden

In each century since the beginning of the world wonderful things have been discovered. In the last century more amazing things were found out than in any century before. In this new century hundreds of things still more astounding will be brought to light. At first people refuse to believe that a strange new thing can be done, then they begin to hope it can be done, then they see it can be done—then it is done and all the world wonders why it was not done centuries ago.

One of the new things people began to find out in the last century was that thoughts—just mere thoughts—are as powerful as electric batteries—as good for one as sunlight is, or as bad for one as poison. To let a sad thought or a bad one get into your mind is as dangerous as letting a scarlet fever germ get into your body. If you let it stay there after it has got in you may never get over it as long as you live.

So long as Mistress Mary's mind was full of dis-agreeable thoughts about her dislikes and sour opinions of people and her determination not to be pleased by or interested in anything, she was a yellow-faced, sickly, bored and wretched child. Circumstances, however, were very kind to her, though she was not at all aware of it.

They began to push her about for her own good. When her mind gradually filled itself with robins, and moorland cottages crowded with children, with queer crabbed old gardeners and common little Yorkshire housemaids, with springtime and with secret gardens coming alive day by day, and also with a moor boy and his "creatures," there was no room left for the disagreeable thoughts which affected her liver and her digestion and made her yellow and tired.

So long as Colin shut himself up in his room and thought only of his fears and weakness and his detestation of people who looked at him and reflected hourly on humps and early death, he was a hysterical half-crazy little hypochondriac who knew nothing of the sunshine and the spring and also did not know that he could get well and could stand upon his feet if he tried to do it.

When new beautiful thoughts began to push out the old hideous ones, life began to come back to him, his blood ran healthily through his veins and strength poured into him like a flood. His scientific experiment was quite practical and simple and there was nothing weird about it at all. Much more surprising things can happen to any one who, when a disagreeable or discouraged thought comes into his mind, just has the sense to remember in time and push it out by putting in an agreeable determinedly courageous one. Two things cannot be in one place.

"Where, you tend a rose, my lad,
A thistle cannot grow."

While the secret garden was coming alive and two children were coming alive with it, there was a man wandering about certain far-away beautiful places in the Norwegian fiords and the valleys and mountains of Switzerland and he was a man who for ten years had kept his mind filled with dark and heart-broken thinking. He had not been courageous; he had never tried to put any other thoughts in the place of the dark ones.

He had wandered by blue lakes and thought them; he had lain on mountain-sides with sheets of deep blue gentians blooming all about him and flower breaths filling all the air and he had thought them. A terrible sorrow had fallen upon him when he had been happy and he had let his soul fill itself with blackness and had refused obstinately to allow any rift of light to pierce through. He had forgotten and deserted his home and his duties.

When he traveled about, darkness so brooded over him that the sight of him was a wrong done to other people because it was as if he poisoned the air about him with gloom. Most strangers thought he must be either half mad or a man with some hidden crime on his soul. He, was a tall man with a drawn face and crooked shoulders and the name he always entered on hotel registers was, "Archibald Craven, Misselthwaite Manor, Yorkshire, England."

He had traveled far and wide since the day he saw Mistress Mary in his study and told her she might have her "bit of earth." He had been in the most beautiful places in Europe, though he had remained nowhere more than a few days. He had chosen the quietest and remotest spots. He had been on the tops of mountains whose heads were in the clouds and had looked down on other mountains when the sun rose and touched them with such light as made it seem as if the world were just being born.

But the light had never seemed to touch himself until one day when he realized that for the first time in ten years a strange thing had happened. He was in a wonderful valley in the Austrian Tyrol and he had been walking alone through such beauty as might have lifted, any man's soul out of shadow. He had walked a long way and it had not lifted his. But at last he had felt tired and had thrown himself down to rest on a carpet of moss by a stream.

It was a clear little stream which ran quite merrily along on its narrow way through the luscious damp greenness. Sometimes it made a sound rather like very low laughter as it bubbled over and round stones. He saw birds come and dip their heads to drink in it and then flick their wings and fly away. It seemed like a thing alive and yet its tiny voice made the stillness seem deeper. The valley was very, very still.

As he sat gazing into the clear running of the water, Archibald Craven gradually felt his mind and body both grow quiet, as quiet as the valley itself. He wondered if he were going to sleep, but he was not.

He sat and gazed at the sunlit water and his eyes began to see things growing at its edge. There was one lovely mass of blue forget-me-nots growing so close to the stream that its leaves were wet and at these he found himself looking as he remembered he had looked at such things years ago. He was actually thinking tenderly how lovely it was and what wonders of blue its hundreds of little blossoms were. He did not know that just that simple thought was slowly filling his mind— filling and filling it until other things were softly pushed aside. It was as if a sweet clear spring had begun to rise in a stagnant pool and had risen and risen until at last it swept the dark water away.

But of course he did not think of this himself. He only knew that the valley seemed to grow quieter and quieter as he sat and stared at the bright delicate blueness. He did not know how long he sat there or what was happening to him, but at last he moved as if he were awakening and he got up slowly and stood on the moss carpet, drawing a long, deep, soft breath and wondering at himself. Something seemed to have been unbound and released in him, very quietly.

"What is it?" he said, almost in a whisper, and he passed his hand over his forehead. "I almost feel as if—I were alive!"

I do not know enough about the wonderfulness of undiscovered things to be able to explain how this had happened to him. Neither does any one else yet. He did not understand at all himself—but he remembered this strange hour months afterward when he was at Misselthwaite again and he found out quite by accident that on this very day Colin had cried out as he went into the secret garden:

"I am going to live forever and ever and ever!"

The singular calmness remained with him the rest of the evening and he slept a new reposeful sleep; but it was not with him very long. He did not know that it could be kept.

By the next night he had opened the doors wide to his dark thoughts and they had come trooping and rushing back. He left the valley and went on his wandering way again. But, strange as it seemed to him, there were minutes—sometimes half-hours—when, without his knowing why, the black burden seemed to lift itself again and he knew he was a living man and not a dead one. Slowly—slowly—for no reason that he knew of—he was "coming alive" with the garden.

As the golden summer changed into the deep golden autumn he went to the Lake of Como. There he found the loveliness of a dream. He spent his days upon the crystal blueness of the lake or he walked back into the soft thick verdure of the hills and tramped until he was tired so that he might sleep. But by this time he had begun to sleep better, he knew, and his dreams had ceased to be a terror to him.

"Perhaps," he thought, "my body is growing stronger."

It was growing stronger but—because of the rare peaceful hours when his thoughts were changed—his soul was slowly growing stronger, too. He began to think of Misselthwaite and wonder if he should not go home. Now and then he wondered vaguely about his boy and asked himself what he should feel when he went and stood by the carved four-posted bed again and looked down at the sharply chiseled ivory-white face while it slept and, the black lashes rimmed so startlingly the close-shut eyes. He shrank from it.

One marvel of a day he had walked so far that when he returned the moon was high and full and all the world was purple shadow and silver. The stillness of lake and shore and wood was so wonderful that he did not go into the villa he lived in. He walked down to a little bowered terrace at the water's edge and sat upon a seat and breathed in all the heavenly scents of the night. He felt the strange calmness stealing over him and it grew deeper and deeper until he fell asleep.

He did not know when he fell asleep and when he began to dream; his dream was so real that he did not feel as if he were dreaming. He remembered afterward how intensely wide awake and alert he had thought he was. He thought that as he sat and breathed in the scent of the late roses and listened to the lapping of the water at his feet he heard a voice calling. It was sweet and clear and happy and far away. It seemed very far, but he heard it as distinctly as if it had been at his very side.

"Archie! Archie! Archie!" it said, and then again, sweeter and clearer than before, "Archie! Archie!"

He thought he sprang to his feet not even startled. It was such a real voice and it seemed so natural that he should hear it.

"Lilias! Lilias!" he answered. "Lilias! where are you?"

"In the garden," it came back like a sound from a golden flute. "In the garden!"

And then the dream ended. But he did not awaken. He slept soundly and sweetly all through the lovely night. When he did awake at last it was brilliant morning and a servant was standing staring at him. He was an Italian servant and was accustomed, as all the servants of the villa were, to accepting without question any strange thing his foreign master might do. No one ever knew when he would go out or come in or where he would choose to sleep or if he would roam about the garden or lie in the boat on the lake all night.

The man held a salver with some letters on it and he waited quietly until Mr. Craven took them. When he had gone away Mr. Craven sat a few moments holding them in his hand and looking at the lake. His strange calm was still upon him and something more—a lightness as if the cruel thing which had been done had not happened as he thought—as if something had changed. He was remembering the dream—the real—real dream.

"In the garden!" he said, wondering at himself. "In the garden! But the door is locked and the key is buried deep."

When he glanced at the letters a few minutes later he saw that the one lying at the top of the rest was an English letter and came from Yorkshire. It was directed in a plain woman's hand but it was not a hand he knew. He opened it, scarcely thinking of the writer, but the first words attracted his attention at once.

Dear Sir:

I am Susan Sowerby that made bold to speak to you once on the moor. It was about Miss Mary I spoke. I will make bold to speak again. Please, sir, I would come home if I was you. I think you would be glad to come and—if you will excuse me, sir—I think your lady would ask you to come if she was here.

Your obedient servant,
Susan Sowerby.

Mr. Craven read the letter twice before he put it back in its envelope. He kept thinking about the dream.

"I will go back to Misselthwaite," he said. "Yes, I'll go at once."

And he went through the garden to the villa and ordered Pitcher to prepare for his return to England.

In a few days he was in Yorkshire again, and on his long railroad journey he found himself thinking of his boy as he had never thought in all the ten years past. During those years he had only wished to forget him. Now, though he did not intend to think about him, memories of him constantly drifted into his mind.

He remembered the black days when he had raved like a madman because the child was alive and the mother was dead. He had refused to see it, and when he had gone to look at it at last it had been, such a weak wretched thing that everyone had been sure it would die in a few days. But to the surprise of those who took care of it the days passed and it lived and then everyone believed it would be a deformed and crippled creature.

He had not meant to be a bad father, but he had not felt like a father at all. He had supplied doctors and nurses and luxuries, but he had shrunk from the mere thought of the boy and had buried himself in his own misery. The first time after a year's absence he returned to Misselthwaite and the small miserable looking thing languidly and indifferently lifted to his face the great gray eyes with black lashes round them, so like and yet so horribly unlike the happy eyes he had adored, he could not bear the sight of them and turned away pale as death.

After that he scarcely ever saw him except when he was asleep, and all he knew of him was that he was a confirmed invalid, with a vicious, hysterical, half-insane temper. He could only be kept from furies dangerous to himself by being given his own way in every detail.

All this was not an uplifting thing to recall, but as the train whirled him through mountain passes and golden plains the man who was "coming alive" began to think in a new way and he thought long and steadily and deeply.

"Perhaps I have been all wrong for ten years," he said to himself. "Ten years is a long time. It may be too late to do anything—quite too late. What have I been thinking of!"

Of course this was the wrong Magic—to begin by saying "too late." Even Colin could have told him that. But he knew nothing of Magic—either black or white. This he had yet to learn. He wondered if Susan Sowerby had taken courage and written to him only because the motherly creature had realized that the boy was much worse—was fatally ill.

If he had not been under the spell of the curious calmness which had taken possession of him he would have been more wretched than ever. But the calm had brought a sort of courage and hope with it. Instead of giving way to thoughts of the worst he actually found he was trying to believe in better things.

"Could it be possible that she sees that I may be able to do him good and control him?" he thought. "I will go and see her on my way to Misselthwaite."

But when on his way across the moor he stopped the

carriage at the cottage, seven or eight children who were playing about gathered in a group and bobbing seven or eight friendly and polite curtsies told him that their mother had gone to the other side of the moor early in the morning to help a woman who had a new baby. "Our Dickon," they volunteered, was over at the Manor working in one of the gardens where he went several days each week.

Mr. Craven looked over the collection of sturdy little bodies and round red-cheeked faces, each one grinning in its own particular way, and he awoke to the fact that they were a healthy likable lot. He smiled at their friendly grins and took a golden sovereign from his pocket and gave it to "our 'Lizabeth Ellen" who was the oldest.

"If you divide that into eight parts there will be half a crown for each of, you," he said.

Then amid grins and chuckles and bobbing of curtsies he drove away, leaving ecstasy and nudging elbows and little jumps of joy behind.

The drive across the wonderfulness of the moor was a soothing thing. Why did it seem to give him a sense of homecoming which he had been sure he could never feel again—that sense of the beauty of land and sky and purple bloom of distance and a warming of the heart at drawing, nearer to the great old house which had held those of his blood for six hundred years?

How he had driven away from it the last time, shuddering to think of its closed rooms and the boy lying in the four-posted bed with the brocaded hangings. Was it possible that perhaps he might find him changed a little for the better and that he might overcome his shrinking from him? How real that dream had been—how wonderful and clear the voice which called back to him, "In the garden—In the garden!"

"I will try to find the key," he said. "I will try to open the door. I must—though I don't know why."

When he arrived at the Manor the servants who received him with the usual ceremony noticed that he looked better and that he did not go to the remote rooms where he usually lived attended by Pitcher. He went into the library and sent for Mrs. Medlock. She came to him somewhat excited and curious and flustered.

"How is Master Colin, Medlock?" he inquired. "Well, sir," Mrs. Medlock answered, "he's—he's different, in a manner of speaking."

"Worse?" he suggested.

Mrs. Medlock really was flushed.

"Well, you see, sir," she tried to explain, "neither Dr. Craven, nor the nurse, nor me can exactly make him out."

"Why is that?"

"To tell the truth, sir, Master Colin might be better and he might be changing for the worse. His appetite, sir, is past understanding—and his ways—"

"Has he become more—more peculiar?" her master, asked, knitting his brows anxiously.

"That's it, sir. He's growing very peculiar—when you compare him with what he used to be. He used to eat nothing and then suddenly he began to eat something enormous—and then he stopped again all at once and the meals were sent back just as they used to be. You never knew, sir, perhaps, that out of doors he never would let himself be taken. The things we've gone through to get him to go out in his chair would leave a body trembling like a leaf. He'd throw himself into such a state that Dr. Craven said he couldn't be responsible for forcing him. Well, sir, just without warning—not long after one of his worst tantrums he suddenly insisted on being taken out every day by Miss Mary and Susan Sowerby's boy Dickon that could push his chair. He took a fancy to both Miss Mary and Dickon, and Dickon brought his tame animals, and, if you'll credit it, sir, out of doors he will stay from morning until night."

"How does he look?" was the next question.

"If he took his food natural, sir, you'd think he was putting on flesh—but we're afraid it may be a sort of bloat. He laughs sometimes in a queer way when he's alone with Miss Mary. He never used to laugh at all. Dr. Craven is coming to see you at once, if you'll allow him. He never was as puzzled in his life."

"Where is Master Colin now?" Mr. Craven asked.

"In the garden, sir. He's always in the garden—though not a human creature is allowed to go near for fear they'll look at him."

Mr. Craven scarcely heard her last words.

"In the garden," he said, and after he had sent Mrs. Medlock away he stood and repeated it again and again. "In the garden!"

He had to make an effort to bring himself back to the place he was standing in and when he felt he was on earth again he turned and went out of the room. He took his way, as Mary had done, through the door in the shrubbery and among the laurels and the fountain beds. The fountain was playing now and was encircled by beds of brilliant autumn flowers. He crossed the lawn and turned into the Long Walk by the ivied walls.

He did not walk quickly, but slowly, and his eyes were on the path. He felt as if he were being drawn back to the place he had so long forsaken, and he did not know why. As he drew near to it his step became still more slow. He knew where the door was even though the ivy hung thick over it—but he did not know exactly where it lay—that buried key.

So he stopped and stood still, looking about him, and almost the moment after he had paused he started and listened—asking himself if he were walking in a dream.

The ivy hung thick over the door, the key was buried under the shrubs, no human being had passed that portal for ten lonely years—and yet inside the garden there were sounds. They were the sounds of running scuffling feet seeming to chase round and round under the trees, they were strange sounds of lowered suppressed voices—exclamations and smothered joyous cries. It seemed actually like the laughter of young things, the uncontrollable laughter of children who were trying not to be heard but who in a moment or so—as their excitement mounted—would burst forth.

What in heaven's name was he dreaming of—what in heaven's name did he hear? Was he losing his reason and thinking he heard things which were not for human ears? Was it that the far clear voice had meant?

And then the moment came, the uncontrollable moment when the sounds forgot to hush themselves. The feet ran faster and faster—they were nearing the garden door—there was quick strong young breathing and a wild outbreak of laughing shows which could not be contained—and the door in the wall was flung wide open, the sheet of ivy swinging back, and a boy burst through it at full speed and, without seeing the outsider, dashed almost into his arms.

Mr. Craven had extended them just in time to save him from falling as a result of his unseeing dash against him, and when he held him away to look at him in amazement at his being there he truly gasped for breath.

He was a tall boy and a handsome one. He was glowing with life and his running had sent splendid color leaping to his face. He threw the thick hair back from his forehead and lifted a pair of strange gray eyes—eyes full of boyish laughter and rimmed with black lashes like a fringe. It was the eyes which made Mr. Craven gasp for breath. "Who—What? Who!" he stammered.

This was not what Colin had expected—this was not what he had planned. He had never thought of such a meeting. And yet to come dashing out—winning a race—perhaps it was even better. He drew himself up to his very tallest. Mary, who had been running with him and had dashed through the door too, believed that he managed to make himself look taller than he had ever looked before—inches taller.

"Father," he said, "I'm Colin. You can't believe it. I scarcely can myself. I'm Colin."

Like Mrs. Medlock, he did not understand what his father meant when he said hurriedly:

"In the garden! In the garden!"

"Yes," hurried on Colin. "It was the garden that did it—and Mary and Dickon and the creatures—and the Magic. No one knows. We kept it to tell you when you came. I'm well, I can beat Mary in a race. I'm going to be an athlete."

He said it all so like a healthy boy—his face flushed, his words tumbling over each other in his eagerness—that Mr. Craven's soul shook with unbelieving joy.

Colin put out his hand and laid it on his father's arm.

"Aren't you glad, Father?" he ended. "Aren't you glad? I'm going to live forever and ever and ever!"

Mr. Craven put his hands on both the boy's shoulders and held him still. He knew he dared not even try to speak for a moment.

"Take me into the garden, my boy," he said at last. "And tell me all about it."

And so they led him in.

The place was a wilderness of autumn gold and purple and violet blue and flaming scarlet and on every side were sheaves of late lilies standing together—lilies which were white or white and ruby. He remembered well when the first of them had been planted that just at this season of the year their late glories should reveal themselves. Late roses climbed and hung and clustered and the sunshine deepening the hue of the yellowing trees made one feel that one, stood in an embowered temple of gold.

The newcomer stood silent just as the children had

done when they came into its grayness. He looked round and round.

"I thought it would be dead," he said.

"Mary thought so at first," said Colin. "But it came alive."

Then they sat down under their tree—all but Colin, who wanted to stand while he told the story.

It was the strangest thing he had ever heard, Archibald Craven thought, as it was poured forth in headlong boy fashion. Mystery and Magic and wild creatures, the weird midnight meeting—the coming of the spring—the passion of insulted pride which had dragged the young Rajah to his feet to defy old Ben Weatherstaff to his face. The odd companionship, the play acting, the great secret so carefully kept.

The listener laughed until tears came into his eyes and sometimes tears came into his eyes when he was not laughing. The Athlete, the Lecturer, the Scientific Discoverer was a laughable, lovable, healthy young human thing.

"Now," he said at the end of the story, "it need not be a secret any more. I dare say it will frighten them nearly into fits when they see me—but I am never going to get into the chair again. I shall walk back with you, Father—to the house."

Ben Weatherstaff's duties rarely took him away from the gardens, but on this occasion he made an excuse to carry some vegetables to the kitchen and being invited into the servants' hall by Mrs. Medlock to drink a glass of beer he was on the spot—as he had hoped to be—when the most dramatic event Misselthwaite Manor had seen during the present generation actually took place. One of the windows looking upon the courtyard gave also a glimpse of the lawn. Mrs. Medlock, knowing Ben had come from the gardens, hoped that he might have caught sight of his master and even by chance of his meeting with Master Colin.

"Did you see either of them, Weatherstaff?" she asked.

Ben took his beer-mug from his mouth and wiped his lips with the back of his hand.

"Aye, that I did," he answered with a shrewdly significant air.

"Both of them?" suggested Mrs. Medlock.

"Both of 'em," returned Ben Weatherstaff. "Thank ye kindly, ma'am, I could sup up another mug of it."

"Together?" said Mrs. Medlock, hastily overfilling his beer-mug in her excitement.

"Together, ma'am," and Ben gulped down half of his new mug at one gulp.

"Where was Master Colin? How did he look? What did they say to each other?"

"I didna' hear that," said Ben, "along o' only bein' on th' stepladder lookin, over th' wall. But I'll tell thee this. There's been things goin' on outside as you house people knows nowt about. An' what tha'll find out tha'll find out soon."

And it was not two minutes before he swallowed the last of his beer and waved his mug solemnly toward the window which took in through the shrubbery a piece of the lawn.

"Look there," he said, "if tha's curious. Look what's comin' across th' grass."

When Mrs. Medlock looked she threw up her hands and gave a little shriek and every man and woman servant within hearing bolted across the servants' hall and stood looking through the window with their eyes almost starting out of their heads.

Across the lawn came the Master of Misselthwaite and he looked as many of them had never seen him. And by his, side with his head up in the air and his eyes full of laughter walked as strongly and steadily as any boy in Yorkshire—Master Colin.

祕密花園

第一章

沒有人留下來

瑪莉‧雷諾克斯被送到密朔兌莊園去投靠姑丈時，大家都說沒見過這麼不得人緣的小孩。這倒也是事實，瑪莉的臉蛋和身材瘦瘦小小的，淺色的頭髮稀稀疏疏的，老擺著一張臭臉。她在印度出生，體弱多病，所以髮色和臉色都偏黃。她的父親是英國政府的官員，公務繁重，自己也常常掛病號。她的母親是位大美人，只熱衷於參加宴會，和大夥人一起尋歡作樂。她壓根兒就不想要有小孩，所以瑪莉一出生就丟給印度保母去照顧。母親還讓保母明白到一點，想要討好她這位白人太太，就要盡量讓瑪莉遠離她的視線。

所以當瑪莉還是個病弱、吵鬧、長得不起眼的小嬰兒時，母親就不曾陪在身邊。等到她長成了一個多病、吵鬧、蹣跚學步的小孩子時，母親還是不在身邊。所以除了印度保母和其他土著僕人黝黑的面孔之外，瑪莉不太記得什麼。僕人們會任由瑪莉為所欲為，因為瑪莉的哭聲要是吵到白人太太，白人太太就會發火。等到瑪莉六歲時，已變成了一隻霸道自私的小豬，無人能比。

來教瑪莉讀書寫字的英國年輕女家庭教師不喜歡瑪莉，教了三個月就辭職。之後請來的家庭教師，待的時間都更短。所以要不是瑪莉自己想要讀書識字，她根本就永遠學不會字母。

P1-1

在瑪莉約莫九歲的一個炎熱早晨，她醒來時就是一陣暴怒，當她看到旁邊站的不是保母時，就更火大了。

「妳來幹嘛？」她對陌生的婦人說：「不准待在這裡，叫我的保母來。」

女人一臉驚恐，結結巴巴地說保母不能來了。瑪莉聽了氣得跳腳，對她拳打腳踢。婦人顯得更加驚慌失措，重複地說保母再也不可能來見英國小姐了。

那天早晨，空氣中瀰漫著一股神祕的氣氛，一切都不照常規進行，有好幾個印度僕人都不見了，瑪莉眼前只看到幾個僕人臉色慘白，驚慌失措地急忙溜走，沒有人來跟瑪莉說是怎麼一回事，也不見保母身影。

這整個早晨都沒有人理會瑪莉，最後她遊蕩到花園，在樓下廊外附近的樹下獨自玩耍。她將大朵鮮紅的扶桑花插進小土堆裡，假裝是在鋪花床。但她愈想愈生氣，嘴裡唸著等一下回去之後要對姍蒂開罵的話。

「豬！豬！妳這豬生的！」她罵道。叫印度人豬是最侮辱人的字眼了。

她咬牙切齒地重複這些罵人的話。這時，她聽到媽媽和別人走到廊下的聲音。她身邊站著一個俊秀青年，兩人壓低聲音用奇怪的音調交談著。瑪莉認得這個貌似男孩的俊秀男子，聽說是剛從英國調過來的年輕軍官。

小女孩盯著他看，不過目光主要還是盯著媽媽。瑪莉一有機會看到媽媽，就會這樣盯著她看，因為「夫人」（瑪莉最常這樣稱呼媽媽）瘦瘦高高的，長得很美，而且穿的衣服也都很漂亮。她有一頭絲綢般的波浪秀髮，細緻小巧的鼻子彷彿傲視一切，還有一雙含笑的大眼眸。她的衣服都是輕薄飄逸的，瑪莉說那種衣服「滿滿都是蕾絲」。今天早上，夫人衣服上的蕾絲比以往還要多，不過她的眼眸卻失去了笑容。一雙受到驚嚇的大眼睛，懇懇哀求地望著軍官男孩般英俊的臉龐。

「真的很嚴重嗎？」瑪莉聽到媽媽這麼說。

「很慘，」年輕男子聲音顫抖地回：「很慘啊，雷諾克斯太太，你們兩個星期前就該去山上的。」

夫人搓揉著雙手。

「哦！我知道該去的！」她哭著：「就為了參加那個愚

蠢的宴會留下來，我真是笨啊！」

這時候僕人室突然傳來很大一聲哀號，她不由得揪住年輕人的手臂。瑪莉也嚇得全身發抖。哀號聲愈來愈淒厲。

「怎麼了？怎麼了？」雷諾克斯太太喘著氣問。

「有人死了。」年輕軍官回答：「您並沒有說府上的僕人也被傳染了。」

「我也不知道啊！」夫人叫道：「跟我來！跟我來！」說完便轉身跑進屋裡去。

發生了這些駭人的事情，終於有人跟瑪莉說了今天早上的神祕氛圍是怎麼一回事了。爆發了嚴重致命的霍亂，人們像蒼蠅般大量地死亡。印度保母前一晚病倒，剛剛才斷氣，所以傭人房才傳來那些哀號聲。

就在當天又有三位僕人死去，其他僕人都嚇得逃跑了。到處一片恐慌，家家戶戶都有人染病在等死。

隔天，在一片慌張混亂中，瑪莉躲進了兒童房，大家都忘了她，沒有人想到她，沒有人來找她。怪異之事正在發生，但她卻一無所知。瑪莉哭了又睡，睡了又哭，這樣過了幾小時，她只知道人們生病了，而且傳來了神祕的駭人聲音。

她曾偷溜進餐廳，看到裡面空蕩蕩的。桌上的飯菜沒吃完，從椅子和餐盤看來，用餐的人好像因為什麼事突然起身，把菜餚慌張地推開。

小女孩吃了些水果和餅乾，又因為口渴把快一滿杯的酒都喝光了。酒甜甜的，她不知道酒有多烈。很快地，她感到昏昏欲睡，便回到兒童房再把自己關在裡面。傭人房的哀號聲和匆忙的腳步聲嚇壞了她，但紅酒讓她很想睡覺，眼皮都快撐不開了。她躺回床上，睡了好長一段時間，不醒人事。

在她沉睡的這幾個小時裡發生了許多事情，不過她並沒有被哀號聲或是物品搬進搬出的聲音給吵醒。

她醒來後，躺在床上盯著牆壁看。房子裡一片死寂，從來沒有這麼安靜過，沒有說話聲，沒有腳步聲，她心想，大家的霍亂是不是都好了？事情是不是都平息了？保母死了，會換誰來照顧她？會有新的保母來，保母可能會講一些新的故事，那些老調牙的故事，瑪莉都聽膩了。

保母死了，她並沒有哭，她不是那種感情豐富的小孩，從來就不在乎別人。霍亂所引起的喧嘩、慌亂和哀號把她嚇壞了。她也感到憤怒，因為似乎沒有人想到她還活著。人人都太過驚慌失措，壓根沒人想到這不討人喜愛的小女孩。人們遇到霍亂時只會想到自己，但等到大家的身體都康復了，一定會有人想到她，會回來找她。

不過，並沒有人回來找她。她躺下來靜待著，整個屋子愈來愈安靜。她聽到草蓆上有東西在窸窣作響，往下一看，有一隻小蛇在攀爬，用寶石般的眼睛看著她。她並不感到害怕，因為這隻無害的小東西並不會傷害她，而且牠似乎急著要爬出屋外。瑪莉就看著蛇從門縫下溜了出去。

「好奇怪，又好安靜，整棟屋子裡好像就只剩下我和這隻蛇了。」她說。

才下一刻瑪莉就聽到院子裡傳來腳步聲，接著來到廊下。這是人的腳步聲，這些人進到屋子裡低聲交談。屋內沒有人去迎接或是和他們說話，他們似乎自己打開門檢查房間。

「真是悽慘！」她聽到一個聲音這麼說：「那個大美人！我猜她的小孩應該也很漂亮吧。聽說她有一個小孩，只是沒人見過。」

　　不久，他們打開兒童房的門，看到瑪莉就站在房間正中央。她看起來就是個壞脾氣的醜小孩，因為開始感到肚子餓，也感覺被忽略了而皺起了眉頭。

　　先走進來的是一個魁梧的軍官，瑪莉看過他和爸爸在講話。軍官一臉疲憊與不安，不過一看到瑪莉便驚訝得差一點往後跳。

　　「班尼！這裡有個小孩！」他大聲喊道：「她居然自己一個人在這種地方！謝天謝地！她是誰？」

　　「我是瑪莉・雷諾克斯。」小女孩說。她全身僵硬，站得直挺挺的。她覺得這個人把爸爸的房子說成是「這種地方」真是沒禮貌。「大家得霍亂的時候，我睡著了，剛剛才醒來，怎麼沒有人來？」

　　「這就是那個沒有人見過的小孩！」男人轉向同伴喊道：「大家真的是把她給忘了！」

　　「為什麼大家把我給忘了？」瑪莉跺著腳說道：「為什麼沒有人來？」

　　名叫班尼的年輕人於心不忍地看著瑪莉，瑪莉看到他在眨眼睛，感覺好像是在眨眼淚。

　　「可憐的孩子！沒有人能來找妳了。」他說。

　　就是在這種猝及不防的怪異情況下，瑪莉得知爸爸媽媽都走了。他們都過世了，夜裡就被移走了。少數幾個倖存的印度僕人連忙逃走，沒有人記得屋子裡還有一個白人小姐，所以屋子裡才鴉雀無聲。除了她和那隻窸窣作響的小蛇，屋內確實空無一人了。

第二章

執拗的瑪莉小姐

瑪莉喜歡遠遠地看著母親，她覺得媽媽很漂亮，不過她並不熟悉媽媽，所以對媽媽也就沒有什麼感情，媽媽走了，她也不會太想念媽媽。的確，瑪莉一點也不懷念媽媽，而且她這個孩子又只關心自己，只會想著自己的事。

如果她年紀稍微大一點，一定會很難過自己現在孤苦無依了。不過她還太小，而且被照顧習慣了，以為還會有人來照顧她。她關心的是自己會不會遇到好人家，會對她很客氣，什麼事都順著她，就像保母和其他的僕人那樣。

瑪莉先是被帶到一位英國牧師家裡。她知道自己不會一直待在那裡，她也不想留在那裡。英國牧師很窮，有五個年紀差不多的小孩，他們衣服破舊，一天到晚吵吵鬧鬧、搶奪玩具。瑪莉很討厭他們雜亂的小房子，對他們很不客氣，所以過了一、兩天就沒有人要跟她玩了。第二天，他們給她取了個綽號，讓她氣壞了。

是巴佐先想到這個綽號的。巴佐是個小男孩，有一雙目中無人的藍眼睛，長了個朝天鼻，瑪莉討厭死他了。當時瑪莉自己一個人在樹下玩，就像霍亂爆發那天一樣，她堆了土堆當花圃，也做了花園步道。巴佐走過來看著她，他一個興起，突然給了她一個建議。

「妳幹嘛不放一堆石頭在那邊當作假山？就在中間這裡。」他傾身靠向瑪莉，指給她看。

「走開！」瑪莉叫道：「我不要男生來。走開！」

巴佐一時之間也很火大，不過接著他開始捉弄起瑪莉，他平常就喜歡捉弄姊妹。他繞著瑪莉跳舞，扮鬼臉、唱歌、哈哈大笑。

「執拗的瑪莉小姐喲，
你的花園長得如何？
銀色的鈴鐺海扇殼，
金盞花長成一直排。」

他唱著這首歌，其他的孩子聽到了，也都笑了起來。瑪莉愈生氣，《執拗的瑪莉小姐》（譯註：一首啟蒙兒歌）這首歌他們就唱得愈起勁。從此以後，當他們講到瑪莉或是和瑪莉說話的時候，都會叫她「執拗的瑪莉小姐」。

「他們這個週末就要把妳送回家了，我們都很高興。」巴佐對她說。

「我也很高興。」瑪莉回答：「家在哪裡？」

「她居然不知道家在哪裡！」巴佐用七歲小孩的嘲弄語氣說：「當然是在英國囉！我們奶奶就住在那裡，我妹妹美寶去年就是被送去那裡。不過妳不會被送去妳奶奶家，因為妳沒有奶奶。妳會被送到妳姑丈家，他叫做亞契柏・柯萊文。」

「我又就不認識他。」瑪莉生氣地說。

「我知道妳不認識他，」巴佐回答：「因為妳什麼都不知道。女生什麼也不知道。我聽到我爸媽講到他，他住在鄉下一棟很漂亮、很大但是很荒涼的古宅裡。沒有人會去找他，他脾氣很大，不讓別人靠近他，別人也不會接近他。他是個駝子，很可怕。」

「我才不信。」瑪莉轉過身，用手指堵住耳朵，不想再聽下去。

不過這件事一直懸在她心上，那天晚上，克羅福太太告訴她，幾天以後她就要坐船去英國投靠她的姑丈亞契柏・柯萊文先生，他住在密朔兌莊園。瑪莉聽了之後面無表情，表現得無動於衷，大家不知道她是怎麼想的。他們想安撫她，可是當克羅福太太想要親吻她時，她把臉轉開。克羅福先生拍拍她的肩膀，她只是全身僵硬地站著。

「她長得真不起眼，」克羅福太太後來憐憫地說：「她媽媽那麼漂亮，舉止也很優雅，但是瑪莉卻是我見過最不得人緣的小孩了。孩子們叫她『執拗的瑪莉小姐』，雖然他們這樣做很頑皮，但是很可以理解。」

「如果她媽媽經常將她美麗的臉蛋和優雅的舉止帶進兒童室，瑪莉也許會學到一些優雅的舉止。不幸地，這個可憐的美人已經走了，很多人都還不知道她有個小孩。」

「我想她一定很少去看這個孩子，」克羅福太太嘆息道：「瑪莉的印度保母死了，就沒有人會想到這個可憐的孩子。你想想看，僕人都跑光了，她一個人被留在平屋裡。麥克魯上校說他打開門時，看到瑪莉自己一個人站在房間的中央，他嚇得差點跳了起來。」

瑪莉在一位軍官太太的照顧之下，長途跋涉來到了英

國。這位太太要帶自己的兒子和女兒去寄宿學校，她只關心自己的小孩，所以很高興把瑪莉交給梅德洛太太，她是密朔兌莊園的管家，柯萊文先生派她去倫敦接瑪莉。

管家長得胖胖壯壯的，臉頰紅潤，有一雙銳利的黑眼睛。她一身大紫色洋裝，披著無袖的黑色絲質外套，上面還有黑色流蘇。她的頭上戴了頂黑色的圓形小軟帽，上面有紫色的天鵝絨花，她一轉頭，那些小花就會直直地顫動。

瑪莉一點也不喜歡她，不過這也沒什麼好奇怪的，她一向很少喜歡誰，再說梅德洛太太顯然也不怎麼在乎她。

「哎呀，她長得真是不起眼！」梅德洛太太說：「聽說她媽媽是個美人，看來是沒有遺傳給小孩，不是嗎？太太？」

「女大十八變啦。」軍官太太溫厚地說：「她要是氣色好一點、表情可愛一點，五官都還不錯，小孩子變得很快。」

「那可有得變了，」梅德洛太太說：「而且依我看啊，密朔兌莊園沒有什麼東西能夠讓小孩改變喲！」

她們以為瑪莉沒有在聽她們講話，因為她站在離她們有點遠的旅館窗前，看著馬路上來來往往的公車、計程車和行人。其實她們的談話瑪莉聽得一清二楚，她也因此對姑丈和密朔兌莊園產生了好奇心，那會是一個什麼樣的地方呢？姑丈又是一個什麼樣的人呢？駝子是長什麼樣子的？她沒見過駝子，印度可能沒有駝子。

自從瑪莉開始寄人籬下，又沒有了保母的照顧之後，她開始感覺到孤單，甚至有了一些從來沒有過的怪念頭。她開始想，為什麼即使爸爸媽媽都還活著的時候，她也好像從來不屬於任何人？別的小孩好像都屬於他們的爸爸媽媽，而她似乎從來不屬於任何人。她以前有僕人服侍，也有得吃、有得穿，可是卻沒有人會對她用心。她不知道這是因為她是個討人厭的小孩，當然啦，她並不知道自己討人厭。她常常覺得別人很討厭，卻不知道自己也一樣討人厭。

她覺得梅德洛太太是她所見過最討厭的人，她討厭梅德洛太太那張紅通通而平凡的臉，還她那頂俗氣的圓帽。第二天，她們要出發前往約克郡，瑪莉將頭抬得高高地穿越車站，走到火車的客車廂，盡可能地離梅德洛太太遠一點，她可不希望別人誤以為她是梅德洛太太的孩子。想到別人可能會這樣誤解，她就很生氣。

不過，瑪莉和瑪莉的那些怪念頭一點也不會礙著梅德洛太太。她是那種「不接受小孩子無理取鬧」的人，起碼她自己是這麼說的，要是有人問起的話。她妹妹瑪麗亞的女兒就要結婚了，她不想這個時候還跑來倫敦，不過為了保住在密朔兌莊園這分愜意又高薪的管家工作，柯萊文先生交待的事就得趕緊照辦，不敢過問。

「雷諾克斯上尉和夫人都得了霍亂去世了，」柯萊文先生用他簡短冷漠的方式說：「雷諾克斯上尉是我妻子的哥哥，我現在是他們女兒的監護人。那個小孩會送到這裡來，妳去倫敦接她。」

梅德洛太太於是簡單收拾了行李，啟程來到倫敦。

瑪莉坐在車廂的一角，看起來既不起眼又煩躁不安。她沒有東西可以讀、可以看，就將戴著黑手套的細瘦小手交叉放在大腿上。黑色洋裝讓她的膚色看起來更黃，黑色縐紗帽下，散亂著一頭柔軟淺色的頭髮。

「真沒見過這麼驕兒的小孩。」梅德洛太太心想（驕兒是約克郡口音，指被寵壞了，很驕縱）。她也沒見過小孩這樣一動不動地坐著。等她看膩了瑪莉，便開始用急促而冷淡的語氣說起話來。

她說：「我可以跟你講一下妳現在要去的地方，妳聽過妳姑丈的事嗎？」

「沒聽過。」瑪莉說。

「沒聽過爸爸媽媽講過他？」

「沒有。」瑪莉皺著眉頭。她皺眉頭是因為她想到爸媽從來不會特別跟她說什麼，他們是不跟她講什麼事的。

「哼。」梅德洛太太應了一聲，看著瑪莉怪異的表情、毫無反應的小臉蛋。她停頓了好一會兒後才又開口。

「我想還是跟妳交代一下吧，讓妳有心理準備。妳現在要去的是一個很奇怪的地方。」

瑪莉沒有任何反應，她無動於衷的樣子讓梅德洛太太感到不舒服，不過她吸了一口氣，又繼續說下去。

「那地方又大又陰暗，這很合柯萊文先生的意，跟他一樣陰陽怪氣。房子有六百年的歷史，面對著高沼地，有快一百個房間，大部分的房間都被關起來上了鎖。屋子裡有很多畫像、精緻的古董家具和古董物品。房子周圍有大庭園，有很多花園和樹木，有些樹的樹枝都垂到了地上。」她停了一下，又吸了一口氣，「就這樣了。」她話就打住了。

瑪莉不由自主地聽她說話，梅德洛太太所說的一切都和印度截然不同，新鮮的事物總是能吸引她。不過她不想讓別人看出來她感興趣，這是她討人厭的地方。所以她仍然動也不動地只是坐著。

梅德洛太太說：「妳聽了覺得如何？」

「沒有想法」，瑪莉回答：「我對那種地方一無所知。」

梅德洛太太不禁笑了出來。

「唉！妳可真像個老太婆。」她說：「妳都無所謂？」

「有沒有所謂都無關緊要。」瑪莉說。

「這一點妳倒是說對了，的確是無關緊要。」梅德洛太太說：「不知道他們為什麼要讓妳來密朔兌莊園，除非這是最省事的方法。他是不會去管妳的，這一點無庸置疑。他從來不會為別人費心。」

說著，梅德洛太太好像突然想到了什麼，停頓了一會兒後說道：「他是個駝子，所以脾氣很古怪。財富和地產沒給他帶來什麼好處，他在結婚以前是個苛刻的年輕人。」

瑪莉想佯裝不在意，可是還是將目光轉向了梅德洛太太。沒想到駝子居然可以結婚，她有點吃驚。梅德洛太太很愛閒嗑牙，一看到瑪莉有反應，就講得更起勁了，好歹也可以消磨時間。

「她個性好，人又漂亮，他願意為了她走遍全世界去找一株她想要的草。沒有人想到她會嫁給他，不過他們真的結婚了。人家說她是為了錢才嫁給他，不過這不是真的。」梅德洛太太很肯定地說：「她過世的時候──」

瑪莉不由自主地跳了一下。

「哦！她死了？」她不禁地叫出聲來。她想到她讀過的法國童話故事《捲髮里克》，裡面講到一個可憐的駝子和一位美麗的公主，這讓她一時之間對柯萊文先生同情了起來。

「是啊，她死了，然後他就變得更古怪了。他不關心任何人，也不想見到任何人。他大部分的時間都不在密朔兌莊園，就算在，也只是把自己關在西廂房，不見任何人，除了皮丘。皮丘是個老先生，從小看著柯萊文先生長大，很清楚柯萊文先生的脾性。」梅德洛太太回答。

　　這聽起來就像書裡面所寫的故事一樣，但是瑪莉並沒有因此感到興奮。有一百間房間的屋子，房間幾乎都被關起來上了鎖，一座高沼地旁邊的屋子，高沼地究竟是什麼樣子的？聽起來就好淒涼，還有一個駝背的男人把自己關在房間裡！

　　瑪莉抿著雙唇，望著窗外，傾盆而下的雨水形成斜斜的銀色線條，雨滴噴濺在窗子上，沿著玻璃滑下來，看起來很平常。那個漂亮的妻子如果還活著，她也許會像媽媽那樣穿著綴滿蕾絲的洋裝，跑進跑出地參加宴會，生氣勃勃的。不過她已經不在人世了。

　　「妳不要期待會見到柯萊文先生，妳十之八九是見不到他的。」梅德洛太太說：「妳也千萬不要期待會有人和妳講話，妳得自己一個人玩，自己照顧自己。有人會告訴妳哪些房間可以進去、哪些不可以。那裡有很多花園，妳可以在花園裡玩，就是不要在屋子裡四處閒逛，這是柯萊文先生不允許的事。」

　　「我不會四處閒逛。」個性乖戾的小瑪莉說。她突然間為柯萊文先生感到難過，轉眼又無所謂了，她覺得柯萊文先生就是因為太討人厭，才會遭到那些報應。

　　她轉過頭，看著車窗滑下的雨水，望著窗外灰濛濛的大雨，雨好像永遠下不完似的。她看了好一會兒，眼前灰暗的天色愈來愈濃，然後她便睡著了。

第三章

橫越高沼地

瑪莉睡了很久，等她醒來的時候，梅德洛太太已經從剛才經過的一個車站買來了午餐盒。她們吃了雞肉、冷牛肉、奶油麵包，喝了熱茶。雨勢更大了，車站裡的人都穿著發亮的溼雨衣。

火車管理員點亮車廂裡的燈。梅德洛太太喝了茶，吃了雞肉和牛肉，心情很好。她吃了不少東西，之後就睡著了。瑪莉坐在那裡盯著她看，看到梅德洛太太俗麗的圓帽滑到一邊。她又看著潑濺在車窗上的雨水，最後自己也睡著了。當她再度醒來時，天色已經很暗了。火車靠站了，梅德洛太太正在搖醒她。

「妳睡著了！」她說：「快睜開眼，我們已經到兌特村車站了，我們還要去搭馬車，還有很長的一段路要走。」

瑪莉站起身，睜著惺忪的睡眼，梅德洛太太在一旁收拾行李，她並沒有伸手幫忙。在印度，拿東西這種事情都是土著僕人在張羅的，由幾個人來伺候一個人是很正常的事。

這是個小站，似乎只有她們兩個在這裡下車。站長率直而親切地和梅德洛太太打招呼，他的口音很重，瑪莉後來才知道那是約克郡的口音。

「汝回來啦，還帶了囝兒。」他說。

「是啊，就是這個团兒。」梅德洛太太一邊操著約克郡口音回答，一邊把頭轉向瑪莉的方向。「汝太太好嗎？」

「很好。馬車在外頭等汝們。」

一輛單馬四輪廂型的馬車停在外面的小月台前。瑪莉看到馬車很漂亮，還有一位服裝整齊的男僕幫她登上馬車。男僕的長雨衣和雨帽閃閃發光，和其他東西一樣都在滴著水，魁梧的站長身上也不斷滴著水。

男僕將車門關上，和車夫一起爬上駕駛座，將馬車駛離車站。瑪莉發現自己坐的位子有座墊，很舒適，不過她沒有睡意了。她望著窗外，這條路將要帶她到梅德洛太太口中那個奇怪的地方，她好奇這一路上會是什麼樣子的。

瑪莉不是個膽小的小孩，所以她並不害怕，她只是感到未知──臨著高沼地的府邸，有著一百間房間，房門幾乎都上了鎖，不知將會發生什麼事。

「高沼地是什麼？」她忽然問梅德洛太太。

「妳十分鐘後看看窗外就知道了。」梅德洛太太回答：「我們會先穿越五哩長的密朔高沼地，才會抵達莊園。天色很暗，大概看不到什麼，不過好歹可以看一看。」

瑪莉沒再多問，她在漆黑的角落靜待著，眼睛緊盯著窗戶。馬車燈的光線投射在前方，瑪莉可以稍微瞥見一路所經過的地方。他們離開車站以後，已經穿越了一座小村莊，她看到了石灰牆砌成的村舍，也看到酒館裡流瀉出來的燈光。接著他們經過教堂、教區牧師的住宅，還有一間小商店的櫥窗，屋子賣著玩具、甜食，還有一些擺在外面賣的奇異物品。接著他們駛上大道，瑪莉看到了籬笆和樹木。之後好長的一段時間景色都沒有變化──至少她覺得是很長的時間。

之後，馬匹開始放慢速度，像是在爬坡，外面沒看到籬笆和樹木，事實上馬車的兩旁一片漆黑，什麼也看不見。馬車劇烈地搖晃，瑪莉的身體往前傾，臉貼上了窗戶。

「啊！我們現在一定是在高沼地了。」梅德洛太太說。

馬車燈在崎嶇不平的路上投射出黃色光芒，這條路好像是從灌木叢和低矮植物之中開闢出來的。那些低矮的植物一直延伸到四周茫茫一片的廣大黑暗之中，一陣風吹來，傳來了猛烈的聲音，低沉而急促，聲音很特別。

「那不是海吧？」瑪莉看著梅德洛太太說。

「不是。也不是田野、不是山，那是綿延好幾英哩的荒涼土地，這裡只生長帚石楠、荊豆和金雀花，只有小野馬和綿羊在這生活。」梅德洛太太回答。

「這裡要是有水的話，就會變成海了，它現在聽起來就像海一樣。」瑪莉說。

「那是風吹過灌木叢所發出的聲音。我覺得這個地方又荒蕪又淒涼，不過還是有人喜歡這裡，尤其是在帚石楠開花的季節。」梅德洛太太說。

他們在黑暗中一路行駛，雨已經停了，但是猛烈的風還是颼颼地吹著，發出奇怪的聲響。道路上下起伏著，馬車駛過好幾座小橋，橋下的湍急水流嘩嘩作響。瑪莉覺得這趟路途好像永無止境，荒涼陰沉的高沼地，猶如一望無際的黑色海洋，她正在穿越這片海洋上的一片狹長土地。

「我不喜歡這裡，」她自言自語道：「我不喜歡這裡。」然後將她的薄唇抿得更緊。

馬車爬上一段陡峭的路，這時終於看到了燈火。梅德洛太太也看到了，便放心地長嘆了一口氣。

她叫道：「啊！真高興看到那點閃爍的燈光，那是門房的燈。等我們待會到了，說什麼都要先來杯好茶。」

她所說的「待會」實際上還有兩英哩的路，因為馬車進入密朔兌莊園的大門之後，還得行駛兩英哩的林蔭大道。兩旁的樹木在空中交會，就像在通過又長又暗的山洞一樣。

　　駛出洞穴後，是一片廣闊的地方。他們在一棟蓋得很長的低層樓府邸前面停了下來，府邸似乎是繞著鋪石地板的院子蜿蜒過去。瑪莉起初以為窗戶裡面都沒有燈光，不過當她走出馬車時，看到樓上一角的房間裡透出暗淡的光線。

　　府邸的大門由又大又硬、奇形怪狀的橡樹鑲板所做成，上面鑲嵌著大鐵釘，而且閂著很大的鐵條。打開大門，裡面是一個很大的門廳，燈光很暗淡，瑪莉索性也就不想看牆上那些肖像畫的臉和牆邊的鎧甲。她站在石地板上，看過去就像個奇怪的黑色小人像，她自己也感到渺小、茫然而古怪。

　　幫忙開門的男僕旁邊站著一位服裝端正、身材削瘦的老人。

　　「帶她去她的房間，」老人用沙啞的聲音說：「他不想見她，他明天早上要去倫敦。」

　　「好的，皮丘先生。」梅德洛太太回答：「只要有吩咐，我就會去處理。」

　　皮丘先生說：「梅德洛太太，要吩咐您的，就是確保不會吵到他，不要讓他看到他不想看的東西。」

　　瑪莉被帶領著走上寬闊的樓梯，經過一條長廊，又爬了一小段樓梯，再穿越走廊，來到牆上一扇敞開的房門前。她走進去，房間裡生了爐火，桌上擺放著晚餐。

　　梅德洛太太不拘禮地說：「喏，這就是妳的房間了！這個房間和隔壁那一間是妳以後起居的地方，妳只能待在這兩個房間裡。千萬要記住！」

　　這就是瑪莉小姐抵達密朔兌莊園的經過，她一輩子都沒有覺得這麼彆扭過。

第四章

瑪莎

第二天早上，一位年輕的女僕走進房間裡生火，她跪在火爐前的地毯上把灰燼耙出來，發出很大的聲響，吵醒了瑪莉。

瑪莉躺在床上看了她一會兒，接著開始環顧房間。她沒見過像這樣的房間，古怪又陰暗。牆壁上裝飾著掛毯，上面繡著森林，站在樹下的人們一身奇裝異服，遠方可見城堡的小塔，還有獵人、馬、小狗和貴婦，瑪莉覺得自己也和他們一樣置身在森林裡。瑪莉又從一個縱深的窗戶看出去，那裡是一大片土地，地勢隆起，沒有什麼樹木，看起來就像一片暗淡而略帶紫色的無盡海洋。

「那是什麼？」她指著窗外問。

年輕的女傭瑪莎站起身來，看了看，也指向窗外。

「那邊嗎？」她說。

「對。」

「那是高沼地，妳喜歡嗎？」她親切地露出微笑。

瑪莉回答：「不喜歡，我討厭。」

「那是因為汝還不習慣，」瑪莎回到壁爐前，「汝現在覺得那裡又大又禿，不過汝以後會喜歡的。」

「妳喜歡那裡嗎？」瑪莉問道。

「是啊，我喜歡。」瑪莎精神奕奕地擦著壁爐，回答道：「我喜歡，那裡才不是光禿禿的，上面長了很多東西，聞起來很香。荊豆、金雀花、帚石楠在春夏開花的時候，景色就會變得很漂亮，而且聞起來就像蜂蜜，空氣很清新，天高氣爽，還有蜜蜂和雲雀嗡嗡歌唱的聲音，很悅耳。啊！說什麼我都不會離開高沼地。」

瑪莉在一旁聽著，露出嚴肅又困惑的表情。在印度，僕人不是這個樣子的，他們都卑躬屈膝的，和主人講話時不敢這樣平起平坐的。他們會行額手鞠躬禮，稱呼主人為「窮人的保護者」之類的。印度的僕人只能被使喚，不能問問題，主人也沒有習慣對他們說「請」或「謝謝」，瑪莉生氣的時候還會打印度保母的耳光。

瑪莉在想，如果有人打這個女孩耳光，她不知道會有什麼反應。瑪莎長得有點肉肉的，看起來很樂觀，性情很好，態度堅定。瑪莉想，要是有小女孩打她耳光，她會打回來嗎？

「妳真是個奇怪的傭人。」瑪莉躺在枕頭上，傲慢地說。

瑪莎這時坐在腳跟上，手上拿著黑蠟刷子，噗嗤笑了出來，一點也沒有生氣的樣子。

「是啊！我知道。如果密朔兒莊園有個威嚴十足的女主人，那我就沒有當女傭的分了，大概只能幫忙洗碗盤，不能上樓來。我太普通了，約克郡的口音又很重。不過這個豪華的府邸可有趣了，沒有男主人、女主人似的，只有皮丘先生和梅德洛太太。柯萊文先生在的時候，啥都不管，而且他幾乎都不住在這裡。梅德洛太太好心給了我這份工作。她告訴我，這個莊園要是跟其他的大戶人家一個樣的話，她就不會找我來了。」她說。

「妳會是我的僕人嗎？」瑪莉用她在印度時那種傲慢的說話態度問道。

瑪莎又擦起了壁爐。

「我是梅德洛太太的女傭，而她是柯萊文先生的女傭。」瑪莎堅定地說：「我會上樓做傭人的工作，也稍微服侍妳一下，不過妳並不需要太多的伺候。」

「那誰來幫我穿衣服？」瑪莉問道。

瑪莎又坐在腳跟上，瞪著瑪莉，吃驚得約克郡口音都跑了出來。

「汝難道不會自個兒著衣嗎？」

「妳在說什麼？我聽不懂。」瑪莉說。

瑪莎說：「對喔！我忘了，梅德洛太太告訴過我要注意，不然妳會聽不懂我說的話。我的意思是說，妳難道不會自己穿衣服嗎？」

「不會，我沒有自己穿過衣服。不用說，以前都是印度保母幫我穿的。」瑪莉生氣地說。

「好吧！」瑪莎顯然一點也沒有意識到她的目中無人，「那妳現在應該學著自個兒穿衣服了。妳已經夠大了，自個兒稍微動動手，對妳有好處的。我媽老是說，真搞不懂大人物的小孩怎麼不會變成呆子，保母幫他們洗澡、穿衣服，帶他們出去散步，好像在帶小狗一樣。」

「印度跟這裡不一樣。」瑪莉輕蔑地說。她快受不了了。

不過瑪莎一點也沒有被擊倒。

「是啊！我看得出來是不一樣的。」她頗有同感地說：「我敢說那是因為那裡黑人很多，沒有可敬的白人。當我聽說妳是從印度來的，我還以為妳也是黑人呢。」

341

瑪莉氣呼呼地從床上坐起來。

　　「什麼！什麼！妳以為我是印度土著？妳──妳這個豬生的！」她說。

　　瑪莎睜大了眼睛，激動地看著瑪莉。

　　「妳罵誰是豬生的？」她說：「妳用不著生氣，年輕小姐不應該這麼說話。我對黑人並不反感，妳要是讀過一些宗教小冊子，就會發現他們都是很虔誠的信徒。書上寫說，黑人是我們的弟兄。我沒見過黑人，所以當我以為可以近距離看到黑人的時候，真是很高興。今天早上我進來給妳生火的時候，我爬到妳的床上，小心翼翼地把被單掀起來，想看看妳長什麼樣子，結果妳卻是這副模樣，」她失望地說：「沒有比我黑，只是比較黃而已。」

　　瑪莉完全不去壓抑自己的憤怒和被羞辱的感覺。「妳居然以為我是印度土著！妳真是大膽！妳一點也不瞭解土著！他們不是人，他們只是下人，要向我們行額手禮。妳根本就不瞭解印度，妳什麼都不知道！」

　　瑪莎沒心眼地盯著她看，瑪莉又生氣又無奈。她忽然一陣強烈的孤單感，覺得熟悉的一切都離她而去了。她把臉埋進枕頭裡，激動地啜泣起來。她恣意地哭著，連好性情的約克郡女孩瑪莎都有點被嚇到了。瑪莎也為瑪莉感到難過，她走到床邊，彎腰靠向瑪莉。

　　「呃，好啦，妳不要這樣哭了！」她乞求著：「千萬別哭了，我不知道妳會為了這個生氣。就像妳說的，我什麼都不知道。我求求妳原諒我，小姐，請不要再哭了。」

　　瑪莎奇怪的約克郡口音和堅定的態度，聽起來既能撫慰人心又友善，這才讓瑪莉慢慢停止哭泣，安靜了下來。瑪莎

總算鬆了一口氣。

「汝該起床了，梅德洛太太說，我接下來還得把汝的早餐、茶和晚餐送到隔壁房間去，那裡是妳的兒童室。汝要是下床了，我會幫汝穿衣服。鈕扣如果在背後，汝是無法自己扣扣子的。」她說。

瑪莉終於決定起床了。瑪莎從衣櫥拿出來的衣服，並不是前一天晚上她和梅德洛太太抵達這裡時所穿的那一套。

她說：「這不是我的衣服，我的衣服是黑色的。」

瑪莉看了看白色的厚羊毛外套和洋裝，表示認可地冷冷說道：「這比我的衣服好。」

「汝要穿這些衣服，」瑪莎回答：「這是柯萊文先生交待梅德洛太太從倫敦買回來的。他說：『我不想看到一個穿黑衣服的小孩到處亂跑，像個迷路的亡魂一樣，那會讓這個地方顯得更淒涼。讓她穿上有顏色的衣服。」我媽說她知道柯萊文先生的意思，我媽很善解人意，她自己也不贊成穿黑色的衣服。」

「我討厭黑色的東西。」瑪莉說。

穿衣服的過程讓她們兩個都長了見識。瑪莎幫過弟弟妹妹扣扣子，不過她沒見過哪個小孩像瑪莉這樣，只是一動也不動地站著，等著別人伺候，好像自己沒手沒腳一樣。

「汝為什麼不自己穿鞋子？」當瑪莉安靜地伸出腳時，她這麼問。

「印度保母會幫我穿。」瑪莉睜大了眼睛回答：「習慣上就是這麼做。」

她常會說這句話，「習慣上就是這麼做」，印度僕人都是這麼說的。假如有人叫他們去做一件祖先幾千年來都沒做過的事，他們就會和善地看著那個人，然後說：「習慣上不這麼做。」這樣一來，對方就知道要作罷了。

習慣上瑪莉小姐什麼都不需要做，她只需要站著，然後像個洋娃娃一樣讓別人幫她穿衣服。不過在準備吃早餐之前，她已經開始發現莊園的生活會讓她學到許多新的事物，例如要自己穿鞋子、穿襪子，東西掉下去要自己撿起來。

瑪莎如果是個訓練有素、專門服侍千金小姐的侍女，她就會更卑屈恭敬，她會知道幫小姐梳頭、扣鞋扣、把東西撿起來放好，都是份內的工作。可她是個沒受過訓練的約克郡鄉下人，和一群年幼的弟妹住在高沼地的農舍裡，而且這群弟妹很明白自己得照顧自己，甚至還要照顧更小的弟妹，這些小小弟妹不是還在襁褓中，就是才剛蹣跚學步。

瑪莉如果是個好逗弄的小孩，瑪莎的健談就會逗得她呵呵笑，不過瑪莉只是冷冷地聽她說話，對瑪莎不羈的舉止感到納悶。瑪莉一開始毫無興致，不過慢慢地，當這位脾氣溫和的女孩喋喋不休地話家常時，瑪莉開始注意聽她說話了。

她說：「啊！他們每個人妳都應該瞧瞧，我家有十二個囝兒，而我爸爸一個星期只賺十六先令，我媽媽很勉強才能幫他們買上麥片粥。他們在高沼地打滾，玩上一整天，媽媽說高沼地的空氣讓他們都長胖了。她說她相信他們跟野生小馬一樣在吃草。我家迪肯今年十二歲，他馴服了一匹小馬，說那是他的馬。」

「他是在哪裡找到小馬的？」瑪莉問。

「在高沼地，小馬當時還跟著牠媽媽。迪肯開始跟小馬做朋友，他會給牠一點新鮮的麵包吃，也會拔新鮮的草餵牠。小馬就開始喜歡迪肯，尾隨他到處逛，還讓迪肯騎在牠的背上。迪肯是個好心的囝兒，動物都很喜歡他。」

瑪莉沒有養過寵物，她一直覺得自己也會想養隻寵物，所以就對迪肯有點感興趣了。她一向只關注自己，所以這樣也算是健康心靈的開端。

她走進為她布置好的兒童室，發現兒童室和臥室很像。那是大人的房間，並不是小孩的房間，牆上掛著陰鬱的陳舊肖像，還有笨重的老舊橡木椅子。房間中央的桌子上擺著豐盛美味的早餐，不過瑪莉的胃口很小。瑪莎把第一道菜端到她的面前時，她的態度豈止是冷淡而已。

「我不想吃。」她說。

「妳不想吃麥片粥！」瑪莎難以置信地叫道。

「不想。」

「汝不知道這有多好吃！汝可以加糖漿或是砂糖。」

「我不想吃。」瑪莉重複道。

「呃！我不能忍受人家糟蹋好食物，要是換成我家的囡兒，他們五分鐘之內就會全部吃光光。」瑪莎說。

「為什麼？」瑪莉冷冷地問。

「為什麼？」瑪莎重複她的話：「因為他們都沒有吃飽過，餓得像小老鷹或是小狐狸一樣。」

「我不知道肌餓是什麼感覺。」瑪莉用無知冷漠的語氣說。

瑪莎看起來很生氣。

「汝最好嚐嚐看挨餓的滋味，那種結果我可清楚了。」她大聲地說：「看著美味的麵包和肉卻不動手，我無法忍受這種人。哎呀！我真希望迪肯、菲爾、珍還有其他的囡兒，在他們的圍兜下方也有這些食物。」

「妳何不把這些食物帶回去給他們吃？」瑪莉建議道。

「這不是我的東西，」瑪莎堅定地回答：「而且今天不是我的休假日。我跟其他人一樣，一個月休息一天。休假的時候，我會回家幫媽媽打掃家裡，好讓她休息一天。」

瑪莉喝了點茶，吃了點塗上果醬的烤麵包。

「妳穿暖和些，出去跑一跑、玩一玩，這樣對妳會有好處的，也會讓妳的胃口好一些。」瑪莎說。

瑪莉走到窗邊，外面有花園、步道、大樹，看起來又沉悶又寒冷。

「出去？我幹嘛在這種天氣出去？」

「妳不出去，就得待在屋子裡，那妳要做啥呢？」

瑪莉環顧了一下四周，的確是沒有事情可做。梅德洛太太為她布置兒童室的時候，並沒有想到遊戲的問題。也許出

去看看花園長什麼樣子會比較好。

「誰會陪我出去？」她問道。

瑪莎睜大了眼睛。

她回答：「妳得自個兒出去，妳得學會自己玩，跟沒有兄弟姐妹的囝兒一樣。我家迪肯都是自己一個人跑到高沼地，可以玩上好幾個鐘頭，他就是這樣才跟小野馬交上朋友。高沼地有幾隻羊都認識他了，小鳥也會飛來吃他手上的東西。他自己的食物再少，也會留一點來哄他的寵物們。」

就是因為聽到了迪肯的事，瑪莉才決定出去，但她自己並沒有意識到這一點。外面雖然不會有小馬或羊，可是有小鳥。這些小鳥應該和印度的鳥不一樣，看看小鳥，也許不賴。

瑪莎幫她拿來了外套、帽子，還有一雙牢固的小靴子，並且告訴她下樓以後要怎麼走。

「汝繞著那邊走，就會走到花園，」她指著灌木牆上的一扇門，說道：「夏天的時候，那裡會有很多花，不過現在沒有花。」她猶豫了一下，繼續說道：「其中有一個花園被鎖了起來，已經有十年沒有人進去過了。」

「為什麼？」瑪莉不禁問道。這個怪怪的屋子有一百個門都鎖著，現在又多了一個。

「柯萊文夫人突然去世之後，柯萊文先生就把花園的門鎖上了，不讓任何人進去。那是柯萊文夫人的花園。柯萊文先生把門鎖上，就挖了洞把鑰匙埋起來。梅德洛太太在搖鈴了，我得趕快過去。」

瑪莎離開後，瑪莉便往灌木叢中的門走去。她無法不去想那個已經十年沒有人進去過的花園。她想知道花園是長什麼樣子的，裡面的花是否還活著。

她穿過灌木叢的大門，來到一個偌大的花園裡，裡面有雜草叢生的草地、蜿蜒的步道、修剪過的狹長花床、樹木、花壇、修剪成奇形怪狀的常綠樹，還有一個大水池，池子中央有個灰色的古老噴泉。不過花壇光禿荒涼，噴泉也沒有在噴水。這不是被鎖起來的那個花園，花園怎麼可能被鎖起來呢？總是有辦法可以進到花園裡的。

　　瑪莉思索著，這時她看到走道盡頭有一道長牆，上面攀滿了常春藤。她對英格蘭還不熟，所以不知道自己走到了種植蔬菜水果的菜園。她朝著牆的方向走過去，發現常春藤裡有一扇綠色的門，而且門是開著的。顯然，這也不是那個被鎖起來的花園，她還可以走進去。

　　她穿過門，發現花園四周都圍著牆，看起來像是幾個相通的圍牆花園中的一個。接著，她看到另一道綠色的門，門敞開著，裡面有灌木叢和步道，步道兩旁的苗圃長著冬天的蔬菜。牆邊的果樹修剪得很整齊，一些苗圃的上方覆蓋著禦寒用的玻璃罩。瑪莉佇足，環顧四周，覺得這裡光禿醜陋，或許夏天長出綠色植物時會好看些，現在沒有什麼好看的。

　　就在這時候，一個老人肩上扛了把鏟子，從第二道門走了進來。他一看到瑪莉，露出驚訝的神情，摸了摸帽子。他的臉看起來很蒼老，看到瑪莉也沒有一點欣喜的神情。瑪莉也不喜歡他這個花園，一副「真是拗」的表情，一點也不情願看到他。

　　「這是什麼地方？」她問。

　　「菜園。」老人回答。

　　「那邊又是什麼？」瑪莉指著另一道綠色的門。

　　「也是菜園，」老人簡短地回答：「牆的那邊還有一個菜園，再過去是果園。」

　　「我可以進去嗎？」瑪莉問。

　　「汝想進去就進去，不過裡面沒啥好看的。」

　　瑪莉沒有應聲。她沿著步道走，穿過第二扇綠色的門，看到了更多的牆，還有更多的冬季蔬菜和玻璃罩。不過在第二道牆上有一道緊閉的綠色門，搞不好那個十年沒有人進去過的花園，就是從這道門進去的。

　　瑪莉不是個膽小的小孩，她一直是為所欲為的。她走到綠色門的前面，轉動門把，她倒是希望門是打不開的，這樣就可以確定自己找到了那個神祕的花園。不過，門很輕易就打開了，瑪莉走進去，看到裡面是一座果園。果園也蓋了牆圍，牆邊同樣長著修剪過的樹木，黃褐色的草地上長著果樹，樹的葉子都掉光了，四處都不見綠色的門。

　　瑪莉一路尋找著門，她走到花園的北側，發現牆並沒有在果園的另一頭就終止，而是延伸到果園之外，好像在牆的另一邊圍住了另一個地方。她可以看到牆上方露出的樹梢，樹梢的頂端站著一隻有著鮮紅色胸部的小鳥。小鳥突然唱起冬之頌，彷彿是因為看到了瑪莉在召喚著牠。

　　瑪莉駐足聆聽鳥鳴，小鳥愉快親切的細聲鳴囀，給瑪莉帶來了好心情。沒人緣的小女孩也是會覺得孤單的，封閉的大宅院、光禿禿的廣大高沼地和大花園，讓瑪莉覺得世界上好像只剩下她孤伶伶一個人。瑪莉如果是個感情豐富、受人疼愛的小女孩，她會很難受。不過就算她是「執拗的瑪莉小姐」，她也會感到孤單，而這隻胸部鮮艷的小鳥，讓她那張小小的臭臉隱約露出了笑容。

她聽著小鳥唱歌，直到小鳥飛走。這隻鳥和印度的鳥長得很不一樣，瑪莉很喜歡牠，她想知道何時會再見到這隻小鳥，搞不好牠就住在那個神祕的花園裡，對花園瞭如指掌。

瑪莉大概是因為無事可做，所以心裡一直掛念著那個荒廢的花園。她對那個花園充滿了好奇心，很想知道它長什麼樣子。為什麼柯萊文先生要將鑰匙埋起來？他要是那麼深愛著妻子，為什麼又會討厭她的花園？瑪莉不知道自己會不會見到柯萊文先生本人，不過她知道，就算兩人碰面了，彼此也是不對盤，自己只會呆呆站在那裡看著他，一句話都吐不出來，儘管她很想問他幹嘛做這麼奇怪的事。

「沒有人喜歡我，我也不喜歡別人。」她想，「我不會像克羅福家的小孩那樣子講話，他們不是講話就是哈哈大笑，很吵。」

瑪莉想起那隻知更鳥，還有牠像是在對著她唱歌的模樣。她想到小鳥所棲息的樹梢，便在步道上突然停下腳步。

「我想那棵樹是長在祕密花園裡面的，一定錯不了，那裡被牆圍住，卻看不到門。」她說。

她回到剛才經過的第一個菜園，看到老人正在挖土。瑪莉走過去，來到他的身邊，冷冷地看了他一會兒。老人沒有理睬她，瑪莉只好主動攀談。

「我去了其他的花園。」她說。

「我又不能攔汝。」老人沒好氣地回答。

「我也去了果園。」

「門口又沒有狗會咬汝。」老人回答。

「那裡沒有門可以進去另一個花園。」瑪莉說。

「哪個花園？」老人停下挖土，用粗啞的聲音說。

「牆那邊的花園，那裡有樹，我看到樹梢上有隻紅色胸脯的小鳥停在那裡唱歌。」瑪莉回答。

沒想到的是，這個滿臉風霜、沒好脾氣的老人突然換了表情，緩緩露出笑容，彷彿變了個人。瑪莉很驚訝，原來人笑起來會變得這麼親切，她以前都沒有發現過這一點。

老人轉身望向花園的果樹林那一邊，吹起了低緩的口哨聲。瑪莉想不透這一個沒好脾氣的人，也能發出這麼柔和的聲音。就在這時候，不可思議的事情發生了，空中傳來輕柔的穿梭聲音，那隻紅色胸脯的小鳥朝著他們飛過來，然後停在園丁腳邊的大土堆上。

「就是牠。」老人低聲輕笑，對著小鳥說話，就像在對小孩說話那樣。

「汝去哪兒啦？汝這個羞羞臉的傢伙！」他說：「我昨天沒有看到汝，汝這麼早就開始去找伴兒了？汝還真是急。」

小鳥把小小的頭側向一邊，用溫柔明亮、黑色露珠般的眼睛仰望老人，好像很熟悉這一切，一點也不害怕。牠四處亂跳，敏捷地啄起泥土，找尋種子和昆蟲。瑪莉的心中生起一種很特別的感覺，小鳥那麼漂亮，精神奕奕的，就像人類一樣。牠的身體嬌小豐腴，嘴巴很細緻，一雙細腳很精巧。

「你每次叫牠，牠都會飛過來？」瑪莉悄聲地問。

「是啊，都會飛過來。牠剛學會飛的時候，我就認識牠了。牠從另一個花園的鳥巢裡飛出來，越過了牆，不過牠那時候還太弱小，飛不回去。沒幾天我們就成了好朋友了。等到牠能夠飛回牆的那邊時，其他的雛鳥都飛走了，只留下牠一個，所以牠又飛回來找我了。」

「牠是什麼鳥？」瑪莉問道。

「汝不知道？牠是紅胸知更鳥，牠們是最友善、最好奇的鳥了。牠們簡直和狗一樣友善，不過汝要知道怎麼跟牠們相處。汝看，牠在那邊啄土，卻不時地往我們這邊看，牠知道我們在講牠呢！」

老人看起來真是古怪極了，他看著豐腴的紅胸小鳥，一副很疼愛牠、以牠為榮的樣子。

「牠可自負了，」老人低聲笑道：「牠喜歡聽人家談論牠，好奇心很重，哎呀，沒有人像牠這麼好奇又愛管閒事，老是來看我在種啥。柯萊文先生不想花心思知道的事，牠都知道。牠是園丁的領班，沒錯。」

知更鳥四處亂跳忙著啄土，還不時停下來看看他們。小鳥用黑色露珠般的眼睛好奇地盯著瑪莉看，瑪莉覺得牠好像把自己都看穿了，心中那種特別的感覺更強烈了。

「其他的雛鳥飛去哪裡了？」她問。

「不知道。老鳥把牠們趕出鳥巢，要牠們去飛，牠們一下子就各自分飛了。這隻鳥知道只留下牠自己孤單一隻了。」

瑪莉朝知更鳥走近一步，目不轉睛地盯著牠看。

「我很孤單。」她說。

在這之前，瑪莉並不知道原來這就是讓她煩躁和生氣的原因。當她和知更鳥互相注視的時候，才隱約察覺到這一點。

老園丁將頭上的帽子往後推，看了瑪莉一會兒。

「汝是從印度來的那個囡兒？」他問。

瑪莉點點頭。

「難怪汝會覺得孤單，汝以後還會更孤單喲！」他說。

他又把鏟子插進肥沃的黑土裡，開始挖掘，知更鳥則忙著四處亂跳。

「你叫什麼名字？」瑪莉問。

園丁站起身來回答。

「班‧威特斯戴夫。我自個兒也很孤單，只有牠跟我作伴。」他用姆指指著知更鳥的方向，「牠是我唯一的朋友。」

瑪莉說：「我一個朋友也沒有，沒有過朋友。我的印度保母不喜歡我，我也沒有什麼玩伴。」

約克郡人講話很直，想什麼就講什麼，老班就是典型的約克郡高沼地人。

他說：「我倆有點像，同一個樣子，長得都不好看，臉都很臭，我敢說我們的脾氣也一樣壞。」

他講得真坦白，瑪莉這輩子還沒有聽過有人把她這樣講出來。印度僕人都會向她行額手禮，對她百依百順。她沒怎麼想過自己的長相，不過她想知道自己是不是和班一樣不得人緣，在知更鳥飛過來之前，自己的臉也是不是一樣臭。她也開始想自己是不是真的脾氣很壞。她心裡覺得不是滋味。

突然，旁邊傳來一陣清脆的細細聲音，瑪莉轉過身。她站在離一棵小蘋果樹幾步遠的地方，知更鳥這時飛到了枝頭上唱起小曲。班率直地笑了起來。

「牠這是在做什麼？」瑪莉問。

班回答：「牠決定跟汝做朋友了，牠鐵定是喜歡上汝。」

「喜歡上我？」瑪莉輕輕地走向小樹，抬頭往上看。

「你會和我做朋友嗎？」她對著知更鳥說，像是在和人說話那樣，「可以嗎？」她說話的方式，不是用她慣有的刺耳小聲音，也不是用她在印度時那種傲慢的方式，而是輕聲細語、耐心地哄著。班看了很驚訝，一如瑪莉剛才看到班在吹口哨一樣。

他大聲叫道：「怎麼的，汝這麼說話才像樣嘛，才像個真正的小孩，而不是刻薄的老太婆。汝說話的樣子，就像迪肯在高沼地和野生動物說話一樣。」

「你認識迪肯嗎？」瑪莉急忙轉身問道。

「大家都認識他，迪肯喜歡到處閒晃。黑莓和歐石南花都認識他。我敢說狐狸們會向他指出小狐狸睡覺的地方，雲雀也會讓他知道牠們的鳥巢在哪裡。」

瑪莉很想再多問幾個問題，她對迪肯和荒廢的花園一樣好奇。但這時候知更鳥唱完歌，輕輕拍動翅膀，展開雙翼飛走了。牠已經登門拜訪過了，現在要去辦其他的事情。

「牠飛過牆去了！」瑪莉看著牠，一邊大叫著：「牠飛進果園，又越過別的牆，飛進那個沒有門的花園裡了！」

老班說：「牠住在那裡，在那裡破殼出生的。如果牠是趕著要去求偶，那一定是要去找玫瑰老樹上的知更鳥小姐。」

「玫瑰樹，那裡有玫瑰樹？」瑪莉說。

班重又拿起鏟子挖土。

「十年前有。」他喃喃地說。

瑪莉說：「我真想看看那些樹，綠色的門在哪裡？一定在某個地方。」

班將鏟子深深插進土裡，換回初見時那張不友善的臉。

「十年前有，現在已經沒有了。」他說。

「沒有門！」瑪莉叫了起來，「一定有的。」

「沒有人找得到，而且這不干別人的事。不要像個愛管閒事的姑娘一樣，到處打探別人的事。好了，我要繼續幹活，妳去別的地方玩！我沒空了。」

班不再掘土，他將鏟子扛在肩上，看也不看瑪莉一眼，連聲再見也沒說就走開了。

第五章

走廊裡的哭聲

　　一開始，瑪莉每天重複著同樣的生活。每天早上，她在掛著壁毯的房間裡醒來時，都會看到瑪莎跪在火爐前生火。瑪莉每天在兒童室裡吃早餐，那裡沒有什麼有趣的東西。吃過早餐之後，她會看著窗外一望無際的高沼地蜿蜒到天邊。這樣看了一會兒後，她知道如果不出門，就只能待在屋子裡無所事事，於是便出了門。

　　她並不知道走出屋外對她來說是最好的事了。她不知道當她開始快步走路，或是沿著步道或林蔭大道跑步時，血液循環開始活絡起來，而且去抵抗高沼地吹來的風，也讓她變得更強壯。

　　不過她跑步只是為了取暖。她討厭風颳在臉上，風就像個隱形的巨人在吼叫著，阻擋她前進。但是吹過帚石楠的大風，往她的肺裡裝滿了對她瘦小身子有益的東西，讓她臉色變得紅潤，原本黯淡的雙眼也明亮了起來。她自己對這一切渾然不知。

　　過了幾天這樣的戶外生活之後，這一天早上醒來時，她總算嚐到了飢餓的滋味。當她坐下來吃早餐時，她非但沒有輕蔑地瞅一下麥片粥就把粥推開，反而是拿起湯匙，吃個碗底朝天。

「看來，汝很滿意今天的早餐？」瑪莎問道。

「今天的麥片粥很好吃。」瑪莉說，她自己也有點意外。

「是高沼地的空氣讓汝胃口大開。」瑪莎回答：「汝真是好命，有得吃，又有胃口。我家農舍裡的十二個囝兒只有胃口，卻沒有東西可以塞到胃裡面去。妳要是繼續每天這樣去外面玩，骨頭上就會多長出一點肉，臉色也不會那麼黃。」

「我沒得玩，我又沒有東西可以玩。」瑪莉說。

「沒有東西可以玩？」瑪莎驚叫道：「我家的小孩會拿棍子和石頭玩，他們會到處跑、大聲叫，東看看西看看的。」

瑪莉不會大聲叫，但是她會東看看西看看的，不然無事可做。她一圈又一圈地繞著花園逛，在庭園的步道上閒晃。她有時候會去找班，但是有好幾次班都在忙著工作，看都不看她一眼，要不然就是沒好臉色。有一次瑪莉朝他走過去，他居然拿起鏟子掉頭就走，擺明著的態度。

瑪莉最常去的地方是花園圍牆外的長走道，走道兩旁的花壇光禿禿的，牆上的常春藤卻長得很茂盛。其中有一段牆上的常春藤特別茂密，葉子的顏色特別深，好像很久沒人整理了。牆上的常春藤都修剪得整整齊齊的，就只有步道盡頭那裡沒有修剪。

瑪莉和班說過話的幾天後，才注意到這個情況，她很好奇。她停下腳步，抬頭望著一根長長的常春藤小枝在風中搖曳，這時候她看到一閃而過的鮮紅色光線，傳來了清脆的啁啾聲，班的紅胸知更鳥就停在牆上。牠的身子向前傾斜，側著頭看著瑪莉。

「哦！」瑪莉大叫：「是你嗎？是你嗎？」她一點也不覺得和小鳥說話是什麼奇怪的事，彷彿她很確定小鳥會明白她在說什麼，而且會回答她。

小鳥並沒有回答，牠一會兒鳴囀，一會兒啁啾，一會兒沿著牆蹦蹦跳跳，像是在向瑪莉訴說許多事情。小鳥雖然沒有講話，但是瑪莉小姐好像都聽得懂。

牠彷彿在說：「早安！風很柔和，對吧？太陽很暖和，是不是啊？一切都很好，可不是嗎？我們一起來唱歌、跳躍吧！來啊！來啊！」

瑪莉笑了起來。小鳥在牆上蹦蹦跳跳，沿著牆小段小段地飛，瑪莉跟在後面跑。那一刻，瘦小而蒼白、醜陋又可憐的瑪莉，看起來簡直可以說是漂亮了。

「我喜歡你！我喜歡你！」她大聲喊叫，啪噠啪噠地沿著步道跑。她一會啁啾叫，一會吹口哨，雖然她根本不會吹。不過知更鳥似乎很滿意，也對瑪莉啁啾叫、吹口哨，回應著她。最後牠展開翅膀，沖天飛向樹梢，停在那裡大聲唱歌。

瑪莉想起第一次見到小鳥的景況，那時候牠在樹梢上晃悠，瑪莉站在果園裡。現在，她在果園的另一邊，站在圍牆外面的步道上，這道牆的位置比較低，牆裡面同樣是那棵樹。

「這棵樹長在沒有人可以進去的花園裡，」她自言自語道：「就是那個沒有門的花園，知更鳥就住在裡面，真想看看裡面是長什麼樣子的！」

瑪莉跑到她第一天早上去過的那道綠色門的走道上，一路跑進另一道門，進到果園裡。她停下腳步，抬頭往上看，這就是牆裡面的那棵樹，知更鳥就停在上面，牠剛唱完歌，開始用鳥喙整理羽毛。

她說：「就是這個花園，我確定就是這個花園。」

她繞過去仔細看了看果園的牆，不過和先前她所看的一樣，牆上並沒有門。接著，她又穿越過菜園，來到爬滿常春藤的長牆旁的步道上。她走到步道盡頭，還是沒有看到門。她又走到步道的另一端，還是沒有門。

她說：「太奇怪了，班說沒有門，就真的沒有門。不過柯萊文先生把門的鑰匙埋起來了，那就表示十年前還有門。」

這件事占據了瑪莉的整個心思，她開始覺得有趣了，也不再後悔來到莊園。在印度時，天氣很熱，整個人懶洋洋的，對什麼事都提不起勁來。從高沼地吹來的清新的風，拂走了她小腦袋裡的蜘蛛網，讓她甦醒了些。

她幾乎整天都待在戶外，晚上坐下來吃飯時，已經又餓又睏，覺得很舒暢。瑪莎喋喋不休時，她也不會生氣，覺得自己好像還滿喜歡聽瑪莎說話，她很想問瑪莎一個問題。晚餐過後，坐在火爐前的地毯上時，她問了出來。

「為什麼柯萊文先生討厭那個花園？」瑪莉說。

瑪莉要瑪莎留下來陪她，瑪莎沒意見。瑪莎很年輕，而且習慣和滿屋子的弟弟妹妹在一起。她覺得樓下的僕人大廳很沉悶，而且男僕和女僕領班會坐在一起竊竊私語，取笑她的約克鎮口音，不太瞧得上她。

瑪莎喜歡講話，而這個住過印度、一向被「黑人」服侍的奇怪小孩，對她來講真是新奇又有趣。她不等瑪莉叫她坐下，她就自己坐到壁爐前的毯子上了。

「汝還在想那個花園嗎？」瑪莎說：「我就知道，我剛聽說這件事情的時候也是這樣。」

「他為什麼討厭那個花園？」瑪莉又問了一次。

瑪莎蜷著腿舒服地坐著。

她說：「妳聽，風繞著房子呼嘯，晚上出去的話，在高沼地連站都站不穩的。」

瑪莉原本不知道「呼嘯」是什麼意思，她聽著聲音，這才懂了。那一定是指什麼轟轟的吼聲，在屋子四周圍竄來竄去，彷彿有個隱形的巨人在捶打牆壁和窗戶，想闖進來。不過人們知道它是進不來的，坐在燒著紅炭火的房間裡，讓人覺得很安全、很溫暖。

「他為什麼討厭那個花園？」聽過風聲以後，瑪莉問道。她很想跟瑪莎打聽出來。

瑪莎便將她所知道的事都說了出來。

「要記住，梅德洛太太說這件事不能講出去的。」她說：「這個地方有很多事情都是不可以討論的，這是柯萊文先生的命令，他說他自己的問題和佣人無關。不過要不是因為那個花園，他也不會變成現在這個樣子。那是柯萊文夫人的花園，他們剛結婚的時候，柯萊文夫人就布置了這個花園，她很喜歡那裡，他們也會一起去花園裡，自己動手照顧花朵。所有的園丁都不可以進到裡面去。他們進去花園以後，會把門關起來，在裡頭待上好幾個小時，看看書、聊聊天。柯萊文夫人很嬌小，花園裡有棵老樹的樹枝彎下來像個椅子，樹上開滿了玫瑰花，柯萊文夫人會坐在那個樹枝椅子上。然而，有一天，她坐在上面時，樹枝突然斷了，她摔到地上，傷得很嚴重，隔天就過世了。醫生們認為柯萊文先生瘋掉了，彷彿也跟著死去一樣。這就是為什麼柯萊文先生討厭那個花園的原因了。從那個時候起，就再也沒有人進去過那個花園，他也不讓任何人去講花園的事。」

瑪莉沒有再問下去。她看著爐火，聽著「呼嘯」的風聲，「呼嘯」聲彷彿變得特別大聲。

這一刻，有一件美好的事情發生在她身上。事實上，打從她來到莊園以後，已經有四件好事發生在她的身上了。首先，她覺得自己和知更鳥心靈相通。再來，她在風中奔跑，血液都暖和起來了。還有，她生平第一次能感覺到肚子餓。現在她察覺自己懂得什麼是感同身受了。

在聽著風聲之際，她也開始聽到了另外一種聲音。她不知道那是什麼聲音，一開始是和風聲混在一起，很難分辨，是很奇怪的聲音，好像是哪裡有小孩在哭一樣。有時候風聲聽起來也像小孩的哭聲，不過瑪莉很確定聲音不是從外面傳進來，而是從屋子裡面傳出來的。她轉過身，看著瑪莎。

「妳有聽到哭聲嗎？」她說。

瑪莎突然一陣惶恐。

「沒有，那是風聲。」她回答：「風聲有時候聽起來就像有人在高沼地裡迷路哀號一樣，什麼樣的聲音都有。」

「可是妳聽，聲音在屋子裡面，從哪個走廊傳過來的。」瑪莉說。

就在這時候，一定是樓下的哪扇門被打開了，很大的一陣風吹進走廊，把瑪莉房間的門都吹開了，房間裡的燈火也被吹熄，她們兩個都跳了起來。哭聲從長廊的一端傳送過來，聽起來格外清楚。

「妳聽，我就說嘛，有人在哭，而且不是大人的哭聲。」瑪莉說。

瑪莎跑過去把門關起來，並用鑰匙鎖上，不過在門關上之前，她們都聽到了在哪個遠遠的走廊上，有扇門砰地一聲被關上了，接著一片寂靜，甚至有一會兒連風也停止了呼嘯。

「那是風。」瑪莎不改口地說：「如果不是風，那就是洗碗的小女傭貝蒂，她一整天都在鬧牙疼。」

瑪莎的舉止顯得侷促不安，瑪莉直直盯著她看。她不認為瑪莎說出了實情。

第六章

「有人在哭，真的！」

隔天，又是滂沱大雨。瑪莉看著窗外，整片高沼地都被淹沒在雲霧裡。今天是別想出去了。

「像這樣的下雨天，你們在農舍裡都在做什麼？」她問瑪莎。

「差不多都在留意不要被人踩到。」瑪莎回答：「沒辦法，我家人口眾多。媽媽的脾氣很好，但是常常要為我們擔心。比較大的囡兒會去牛棚玩。迪肯不在乎被淋濕，照樣跑出去，就好像外面出大太陽一樣，他說下雨天可以看到晴天時看不到的東西。有一次，他看到一隻小狐狸差點淹死在洞穴裡，他把牠抱在胸口幫牠取暖，然後把牠帶回家裡來。小狐狸的媽媽在附近被射死了，牠們的洞穴淹了水，其他的小狐狸都死了。他現在把這隻小狐狸養在家裡。還有一次，他發現一隻快要淹死的小烏鴉，他也把牠帶回家馴養。小烏鴉很黑，所以叫『煤灰』，牠喜歡跟著迪肯到處跳、到處飛。」

瑪莉不再討厭瑪莎那種有點隨便的說話方式，甚至開始覺得瑪莎這樣說話很好玩，當瑪莎閉嘴不說話或是走開時，瑪莉甚至還會感到失落。

瑪莎說她一家十四口人住在高沼地上的農舍裡，大家

擠在四間小房間裡，食物永遠不夠吃，這跟以前在印度時，保母跟她講的故事完全不一樣。瑪莎家的孩子們到處跌跌撞撞，像一窩粗野而溫馴的小牧羊犬在玩耍一樣。其中最吸引瑪莉的是「媽媽」和迪肯。只要瑪莎講到「媽媽」所說的話、所做的事，瑪莉就覺得特別舒服。

「我要是有隻烏鴉或是小狐狸，那我就可以跟牠們玩。」瑪莉說：「可是我什麼都沒有。」

瑪莎露出困惑的表情。

「汝不會打毛線嗎？」

「不會。」瑪莉回答。

「縫紉呢？」

「也不會。」

「那汝會看書吧？」

「會。」

「那汝為什麼不看看書或是學寫字？汝已經夠大了，可以學著看些書了。」

「我沒有書」，瑪莉說：「我的書都在印度。」

瑪莎說：「真可惜，梅德洛太太要是同意讓汝進去書房，那就可以看到好幾千本的書呢！」

瑪莉沒有追問書房在哪裡，因為她靈機一動，決定自己去找書房。她不擔心梅德洛太太，因為梅德洛太太似乎都是待在樓下那間舒適的管家客廳裡。在這個奇怪的地方幾乎看不到任何人。

事實上，除了佣人以外，瑪莉沒有見過其他人。主人不在這裡的時候，佣人們就在樓下過著奢華的生活。那裡有一間很大的廚房，裡面掛著發亮的黃銅器皿和白鑞製品，還有一間很大的佣人廳，每天有四、五頓的豐盛餐點。梅德洛太太不在時，他們就在裡面快活地嬉鬧著。

　　瑪莉的餐點每天準時送上來，瑪莎伺候她用餐，除此之外，沒有人會費心來管她。梅德洛太太每隔一、兩天會來看看她，但是沒有人會問她在做什麼，也不告訴她應該做什麼。

　　瑪莉心想，這大概就是英國人對待小孩的方式吧。在印度，保母會照料她，緊緊跟在旁邊，無微不至地照顧她，讓她常常覺得很煩。現在，沒有人會跟著她了，她也要學著自己穿衣服，因為她要瑪莎拿衣服給她穿時，瑪莎的神情好像在說她又蠢又笨。

　　「妳這樣可真不懂事。」瑪莎有一次這麼說，那時瑪莉正站著等她幫自己戴手套，「我家的蘇珊安才四歲，她可比汝伶俐多了。汝有時候看起來還真有點傻。」

　　這話讓瑪莉皺了一個小時的眉頭，也讓她因此想了一些從沒想過的事情。

　　這天早上，瑪莎最後一次清完火爐下樓去之後，瑪莉在窗邊站了十分鐘左右，反覆想著當她聽到書房時，腦海裡閃過的新點子。不過她想的倒不是書房，畢竟她讀過的書還很少，是書房讓她想起那一百間被關上的房間，她想知道房間是不是真的都鎖起來了？要是有房間可以進去，裡面會有什麼東西？真的有一百個房間嗎？她為什麼不去數數看到底有幾個門？既然今天早上不能出去，就不妨找這件事來做。

　　沒有人教導她在做事情之前要先徵求別人的同意，她對權力這種事一點概念也沒有，所以就算她看到梅德洛太太了，她也不會想到要詢問能否在屋子裡四處蹓躂。

　　瑪莉打開房門來到走廊上，開始四處閒逛。走廊很長，而且岔出其他的走廊，她沿著走廊上了一小段樓梯，轉進另一個走廊。到處都有門，牆上掛著許多畫，有的是陰暗奇怪的風景，不過更多的是男女肖像，他們穿著絲綢或是天鵝絨做成的華麗衣服，看起來很奇怪。

瑪莉走進一個掛滿肖像的長廊，真沒想到屋子裡可以掛這麼多肖像畫。她慢慢地走過長廊，注視著那些臉，畫中的人物彷彿也在注視著她。瑪莉覺得他們大概是在想，一個從印度來的小女孩在他們的屋子裡做什麼。

還有一些是兒童的肖像畫，小女孩們穿著厚厚的緞子連衣裙，衣服長到腳邊，衣服比人還搶眼。男孩子們穿的衣服有蓬鬆的袖子和蕾絲衣領，留著長頭髮，或是在脖子上戴著很大的縐領。瑪莉都會停下來看看這些小孩，她想知道他們叫什麼名字，去了哪裡，還有為什麼要穿著一身奇裝異服。其中，有一個全身僵硬、長相普通的小女孩，長得很像瑪莉。她穿著綠色的織錦洋裝，手指上停著一隻鸚鵡，眼神很銳利，充滿好奇。

瑪莉大聲地對她說：「妳現在住在哪裡？真希望妳就在這裡。」

沒有小女孩會經歷這麼一個古怪的上午。整棟大府邸裡好像就只有她這麼一個小人兒，她樓上樓下四處閒逛，在大大小小的走道上穿梭，彷彿這些地方就只有她來過。屋子裡既然有這麼多房間，就表示有人住過，不過現在空空蕩蕩的，很難相信曾經住過人。

她來到二樓之後，才想到要轉動房間的把手看看。梅德洛太太說所有的門都被關起來了，不過瑪莉最後還是用手轉動了一間房間的門把。門把很輕易地就轉開，瑪莉嚇了一跳。

她推著門，門自己重重地緩緩打開。這扇門很大，裡面是一間大寢室。牆上掛著許多刺繡，還有一些她在印度看過的鑲嵌家具。有一扇鉛框大窗子面向高沼地，壁爐架上方掛著那個全身僵硬、長相普通的小女孩的另外一張肖像，小女孩看起來好像更加好奇地注視著瑪莉。

「她以前可能睡過這個房間，她這樣盯著我看，感覺好怪。」瑪莉說。

之後，瑪莉又打開了更多的房門。看了這麼多房間，都覺得累了，她開始相信這裡真的有一百間房間，雖然她並沒有真的一個個去數。所有的房間都掛著舊畫像或是舊掛氈，掛氈上面織著奇怪的景物，也都擺著奇怪的家具和裝飾品。

有一個房間看起來像是夫人的起居室，掛氈都是天鵝絨織成的，還有一個櫥櫃，裡面大約有一百隻用象牙做成的大象，大小不一，有的大象的背上還有馭象夫或是轎子。有些象比較大，有些象很小，像是剛出生的小象。瑪莉在印度時看過象牙雕刻，她很熟悉大象。她打開櫥櫃的門，站在一個腳凳上玩了好一會兒。等玩膩了，再把它們放回去，關上櫥櫃的門。

瑪莉在長廊和空房間閒逛時，沒有看到任何活的東西，不過她在這個房間裡倒是看到了活的東西。她關上櫥櫃的門時，聽到了微弱的窸窣聲。她跳了起來，看了看火爐旁邊的沙發，聲音像是從那裡傳來的。沙發的一角有個座墊，座墊上的天鵝絨有個洞，一個小腦袋從洞裡頭探出來，露出一對驚慌的眼睛。

瑪莉悄悄地繞到房間的另一邊，原來是小灰鼠閃亮亮的眼睛。老鼠在座墊上咬出一個洞，在裡面做了窩，有六隻老鼠寶寶依偎在牠的身邊睡覺。如果其他一百間房間裡都沒有活生生的東西，最起碼這裡有七隻小老鼠互相作伴，一點也不孤單。

「牠們要是沒有這麼驚恐，我就把牠們帶回去。」瑪莉說。

她已經閒逛很久了，累得不想再逛，便轉身往回走。她迷路了兩、三回，走錯走廊，上上下下好幾遍才找到路，最後終於回到她住的樓層，只是離自己的房間還有一段距離，她搞不清楚方向。

「我剛剛一定又轉錯彎了。」她停在一個走廊底，走廊短短的，兩邊的牆上掛著掛氈。「不知道要走哪一條，這裡好安靜啊！」

她站在那裡，話才一說完，一個聲音打破了寂靜，那是哭泣的聲音，不過和昨晚聽到的不太一樣，這個哭聲很短，是小孩在鬧脾氣的啜泣聲，哭聲透過牆傳過來，聲音很微弱。

「這一次聽起來比較近，有人在哭。」瑪莉心跳加快。

瑪莉不經意地將手擱在旁邊的掛氈上，接著吃驚地往後跳了一下，因為掛氈後面有扇門打開了。她看到門後面還有走廊，這時梅德洛太太手上拿著一串鑰匙，正從走廊的另一頭走過來，臉色很難看。

「妳在這裡做什麼？」她拉著瑪莉的手臂把她拖走，一邊說道：「我是怎麼跟妳說的？」

「我剛剛轉錯彎了，不知道要走哪個走廊，然後我聽到有人在哭。」瑪莉解釋。瑪莉這時討厭死梅德洛太太了，沒想到接下來她更氣了。

「妳什麼哭聲也沒聽到，回到妳的兒童室去，不然我就賞妳耳光。」管家說。

　　她拉著瑪莉的手臂，半推半拉帶著她穿上穿下走廊，直到最後將瑪莉推進她的房裡。

　　她說：「從現在開始，妳得乖乖地待在妳要待的地方，不然就把妳鎖起來。主人最好是照他說的那樣幫妳找個家庭教師，妳這個小孩得讓人盯緊一些。我自己都夠忙的了。」

　　說完，梅德洛太太走出房門，將門砰一聲地關上。瑪莉走到火爐前的地毯上坐下，她氣得臉色發白、咬牙切齒，但是沒有哭。

　　「有人在哭，真的，真的！」她自言自語道。

　　到目前為止，她已經聽過兩次哭聲了，總有一天她會查出真相。今天早上，她發現的東西可不少，覺得自己好像是遊歷了一段漫長的旅程。不管怎麼說，剛剛整個過程中都有好玩的東西，她還玩了象牙大象，還看到了天鵝絨墊下的灰老鼠和老鼠寶寶。

第七章

花園的鑰匙

兩天後，瑪莉一睜開眼睛就立刻從床上坐起來，呼喚瑪莎。

「妳看高沼地！妳看高沼地！」

暴風雨過去了，夜風吹走了黑色雲霧，連風也停了，蔚藍的明亮天空高高地掛在高沼地上方。瑪莉做夢也沒想到天空可以這麼藍，印度的天空又熱又刺眼，這裡天空很涼爽，一片湛藍，很像深不見底的美麗湖泊在閃閃發光。高高的藍色穹蒼到處飄浮著羊毛似的白色小雲朵，綿延無際的高沼地也透出微藍，不再有黯淡的紫黑色或是陰沉的灰色。

「是啊！」瑪莎愉快地笑著說：「暴風雨暫時停了，每年這個時候都像這樣，暴風雨可以在一夜之間就消失無蹤，好像根本沒有來過或是不會再來了一樣。這是因為春天快到了，雖然還要等一陣子，不過就快了。」

「我還以為英國不是下雨就是陰天。」瑪莉說。

「才不是呢！」瑪莎在壁爐刷堆裡坐直了起來，說道：「不素皆樣的！」

「妳說什麼？」瑪莉認真地問。在印度，當地有好幾種只有少數人才聽得懂的方言，所以當瑪莎講一些讓人聽不懂的話時，瑪莉並不感到驚訝。

瑪莎像第一天早晨那樣笑了起來，說道：「我又來了，又說約克郡方言了，梅德洛太太叫我不要這樣說話。我的意思是『根本就不是這樣的』。」瑪莎慢慢地把話說清楚：「不過這樣說太慢了。天氣好的時候，約克郡就是全世界最晴朗的地方。我說過，汝不久就會喜歡上高沼地，等妳看到金色的荊豆花和金雀花，還有開花的帚 石楠，到時候到處都會看到紫色的鐘形花，成群蝴蝶飛來飛去，蜜蜂四處嗡嗡叫，雲雀也在高空翱翔唱歌。太陽一出來，妳就會想去高沼地，想在那裡待上一整天，就像迪肯一樣。」

　　「我真的可以去高沼地嗎？」瑪莉看著窗外遠處的藍色大地，滿心期待地問道。高沼地很遼闊，清新又美麗，帶著天堂般的色彩。

　　「這我不知道，我覺得汝好像打從出娘胎就不習慣走路，不可能走五哩路。去我家農舍，要走五哩路。」瑪莎說。

　　「我很想看看你們家的農舍。」

　　瑪莎好奇地注視了她一會兒，然後才又拿起刷子磨擦著壁爐。她在想，這張平凡的小臉，不再像那天早上初次見面時那麼臭臉了。瑪莉此刻的表情，有點像小蘇珊安很想要某樣東西時的樣子。

　　瑪莎說：「我會問媽媽，她一向都可以想出好法子。今天是我的休假日，我待會兒就要回家了。啊！我好高興。梅德洛太太很尊敬我媽媽，也許可以請媽媽和她談談看。」

　　「我喜歡妳媽媽。」瑪莉說。

　　「妳應該會喜歡她的。」瑪莎說道，一邊擦拭著壁爐。

　　「但是我還沒有看過她。」瑪莉說。

　　「妳是沒看過。」瑪莎回答。她又打直身子坐在腳跟上，用手背磨擦鼻尖，有點感到困惑的樣子，不過接著又很肯定地繼續說：「她很明理，做事勤快，脾氣很好，喜歡乾淨，不管有沒有見過她，任誰都會喜歡她。每當我休假要回去看她，在走過高沼地時都會雀躍地蹦蹦跳跳。」

「我喜歡迪肯，但是我也沒有看過他。」瑪莉又說。

「嗯，」瑪莎語氣堅定地說：「我告訴過汝，小鳥、兔子、野山羊、小野馬還有狐狸都喜歡他。我在想，」瑪莎若有所思地盯著瑪莉看，「迪肯會怎麼看妳這個人呢？」。

「他不會喜歡我的，」瑪莉用她一貫僵硬而冷漠的方式說：「沒有人喜歡我。」

瑪莎又露出若有所思的神情。

「那汝喜歡汝自己嗎？」她問，好像真的很想知道答案。

瑪莉猶豫了片刻，仔細思索了一會兒。

「一點也不喜歡，真的，」她回答：「不過我以前沒想過這個問題。」

瑪莎微微咧起嘴角，像是想起了家裡的事情。她說：「媽媽這麼問過我一次，她那時候在洗衣服，我的心情不是很好，一直在講別人的壞話，她就轉身對我說：『汝這隻小母老虎！汝站在那邊說汝不喜歡這個、不喜歡那個，那汝喜歡汝自己嗎？』我立刻笑了起來，一下子就冷靜了下來。」

瑪莎把瑪莉的早餐送過來之後，興高采烈地離開了。她要穿越五哩長的高沼地回去農舍，然後幫母親打掃家裡，烤一個星期分量的麵包，好好享受這一天。

瑪莉知道瑪莎已經不在屋子裡了，她感到很孤單。她飛快地跑到花園裡，繞著有噴泉的花園跑了十圈。她仔細地數著自己跑了幾圈，跑完之後覺得心情好了許多。

陽光讓這整個地方看起來煥然一新。蔚藍的穹蒼橫在密朔兌莊園和高沼地的上方，她抬起頭來仰望蒼空，想像自己如果躺在白色的小雲朵上四處飄盪，會是什麼樣的感覺。

她走進最前面的菜園，看到班和另外兩個園丁正在忙著幹活。天氣轉好，班也跟著變好了，他主動和瑪莉攀談：「春天到了，汝有沒有聞到啊？」

瑪莉聞了一下，覺得好像聞到了春天的氣息。

「我聞到很香、很清新也很潮溼的味道。」她說。

「那是肥沃土壤的味道。」班挖著土，回答道：「泥土的心情不錯，準備讓植物生長出來。播種的季節到了，它就會很愉快。冬天一到，它就覺得沒勁，無事可做。現在，那邊花園裡就有東西在黑土裡鑽動，太陽給它們溫暖。不久之後，汝就可以看到綠色的小穗從黑土裡冒出來了。」

「它們會長成什麼？」瑪莉問道。

「番紅花、雪花蓮，還有黃水仙。汝沒看過這種花？」

「沒有。在印度，下完雨之後，到處都又熱又溼，一片綠色。」瑪莉說：「我還以為花草都是一個晚上就長出來的。」

班說：「花草不會一個晚上就長出來，汝得再等上一陣子。它們會這裡探一點頭出來，那裡再冒一點出來，葉子也會一天一天慢慢地展開。汝等著看吧！」

「我會的。」瑪莉回答。

不一會兒，瑪莉聽到小鳥拍打翅膀飛行所發出的輕柔窸窣聲，她馬上意識到知更鳥來了。這隻鳥很活潑、很有生氣，在瑪莉的腳邊蹦蹦跳跳的。牠側著頭，害羞地看著瑪莉。瑪莉便問了班一個問題。

「你想牠還記得我嗎？」她說。

班生氣地說：「不要說是記得汝！牠連花園裡的每一根甘藍菜莖都認得，更甭說人了。牠以前沒在這兒見過小姑娘，所以想要知道汝的一切，汝什麼事情都不必對牠隱藏。」

「在牠住的那個花園裡面，黑土下面也有東西在動嗎？」瑪莉問道。

「什麼花園？」班咕噥道，又變得沒好氣的。

「長著老玫瑰樹的花園啊！」瑪莉實在是太好奇了，忍不住問了出來：「那邊的花都死了嗎？是不是有些還會在夏天開花？那邊還有玫瑰花嗎？」

「汝問牠，」班朝著知更鳥聳聳肩：「只有牠才知道，十年來沒有人進去過裡面。」

十年是很漫長的一段時間，瑪莉這麼想。她也是在十年前出生的。

她慢慢琢磨著離開。她開始喜歡上那個花園，就像她已經開始喜歡上知更鳥、迪肯和瑪莎的母親一樣。她還開始喜歡上瑪莎了。她並不習慣喜歡別人，但現在似乎有很多人可以讓她喜歡。瑪莉也把知更鳥當作是人。她走到爬滿常春藤的長牆步道上，在那裡可以看到樹梢。當她第二次在那裡來來回回走著的時候，最有趣、最令人興奮的事情發生了，這都多虧了班的知更鳥。

瑪莉聽到一聲啁啾和鳴囀，她看向左邊光禿禿的花壇，知更鳥正在那裡蹦蹦跳，假裝在土裡啄東西，想讓瑪莉以為牠並沒有跟蹤她。不過瑪莉知道知更鳥一直尾隨著自己，她驚喜得都快顫抖了起來。

她叫道：「你真的記得我！你真的記得我！你是全世界最可愛的小鳥了！」

她啁啾叫、說著話，耐心地誘哄知更鳥，知更鳥蹦蹦跳跳地擺動著尾巴，鳴囀著，像是在說話一樣。牠就像穿了紅色的絲綢背心，牠鼓起自己小小的胸部，精緻、高貴又漂亮，彷彿在向瑪莉展示知更鳥可以多麼神氣、多麼像個人類。牠讓瑪莉慢慢靠近牠，瑪莉這時都忘了自己是很拗的，她彎下身去和知更鳥說話，發出知更鳥的聲音。

哦！牠居然讓瑪莉這麼靠近牠！牠知道瑪莉不會對牠伸出手，稍微驚動牠都不會。牠知道這一點，牠是個不折不扣的人類，而且勝於世間的人。瑪莉開心得都快吸不過氣來。

花壇並非全然光禿禿，是因為園丁把多年生的植物做了修剪好過冬休息，所以才沒有長花的，不過在花床後面還長著高矮不一的灌木。知更鳥在灌木叢下蹦蹦跳跳，瑪莉看到牠跳過一個剛被翻起來的小土堆，停在那裡找蟲吃。這堆土是因為有隻狗想要把鼴鼠挖出來，所以挖了一個很深的洞。

瑪莉看著洞，不是很明白為什麼會有個洞。她看著看著，忽然看到被翻上來的土裡面好像埋了什麼東西，看起來像是生繡的鐵環或是黃銅環。知更鳥飛到附近的樹上時，瑪莉伸手將那個環狀物撿了起來，那不只是個環狀物，而且是一把舊鑰匙，看起來像是埋在土裡了很久。

瑪莉站起身來，看著懸在她手指上的鑰匙，一臉驚嚇。

「這把鑰匙可能已經被埋了十年，說不定這就是花園的鑰匙！」她低聲地說。

第八章

帶路的知更鳥

瑪莉凝視著鑰匙好一會兒，把鑰匙翻來覆去，思索著。前面講過，沒有人教過瑪莉在做什麼事情之前要先問過大人，她只想著這是不是被鎖起來的花園鑰匙，要是找到花園的門，可能就可以將門打開，看看裡面有什麼，也可以看看那些老玫瑰樹變成什麼樣子了。

花園被鎖起來這麼久了，她很想看看裡面的樣子。花園一定很不一樣，這十年來一定有發生過什麼奇奇怪怪的事情。如果她很喜歡那個花園，她可以每天去，把門關上，自己在裡面編故事玩，沒有人會知道她在裡面，大家都以為門被上鎖了，鑰匙被埋在土裡。一想到這裡，她就覺得很有趣。

一個人住在一棟有一百間房間的房子裡，房間神祕兮兮地都上鎖了，什麼好玩的東西也沒有，這樣的生活反而讓瑪莉靜止的大腦活躍了起來，喚醒了她的想像力。毫無疑問地，高沼地上那新鮮、強烈而純淨的空氣起了很大的作用。一如高沼地的空氣讓瑪莉胃口大開，襲來的風也讓她的血液活絡起來，她的心智也一樣受到了刺激。

在印度時，總是覺得很熱，懶洋洋的，什麼都不想做。但是在這裡，她開始想要嘗試新的東西。也不知道為什麼，她不再感到那麼彆扭了。

瑪莉把鑰匙放進口袋，在步道上來回踱步。似乎只有她一個人會來這裡，所以她可以慢慢地走，看著牆壁，更正確地說，應該說是看著牆上的常春藤。那些常春藤是讓人困惑的存在，不管她多麼仔細瞧，都只看得到一層厚厚的、油油亮亮的深綠色葉子，她感到很失望。她走來走去，看著牆裡面的樹梢，執拗的脾氣又發作了。她自言自語地說，離花園這麼近卻不能進去，實在是很蠢的事。

　　她將鑰匙放進口袋帶回屋子，決定以後出門時都要隨身攜帶，一旦發現那扇藏起來的門，就可以把門打開了。

　　梅德洛太太允許瑪莎晚上睡在農舍裡，隔天早上瑪莎回來上工時，臉頰格外紅潤，精神奕奕的。

　　「我四點就起床了，」瑪莎說：「啊！高沼地真是美，小鳥都起來了，兔子們蹦蹦跳跳，即將破曉。我不是一路走回來的，有人用馬車順道載了我一程。我在家真開心。」

　　一講到休假日，瑪莎就有說不完的樂事。媽媽看到她回家，非常高興，她們一整天都在烤麵包和打掃家裡。瑪莎還為每個弟弟妹妹做了加上一些些紅糖的蛋糕。

　　「他們從高沼地玩回來時，蛋糕剛出爐。整個農舍聞起來又香又乾淨，還有烤麵包的味道，爐火正旺，他們開心地大叫。迪肯還說我們家的農舍好得可以請國王來住呢！」

　　晚上，大家圍坐在火爐邊，瑪莎和媽媽縫補衣服和襪子上的破洞，瑪莎跟大家說起了印度來的小女孩，小女孩一直由瑪莎稱為「黑人」的僕人伺候，所以她連襪子都不會穿。

　　「嗯！他們很喜歡聽我講妳的事情，」瑪莎說：「黑人的什麼事他們都想知道，還有妳搭船來這裡的那艘船長得什麼樣子。不過我所知有限，能奉告的不多。」

　　瑪莉沉思了一下子，說道：「妳下次休假的時候，我再跟你說更多事情，這樣妳就可以跟他們說了。我敢說他們一定很想知道騎大象還有騎駱駝是怎麼一回事，還有軍官去獵老虎的事。」

　　瑪莎高興地叫道：「天啊！這會讓他們樂瘋的，汝真的會告訴我嗎，小姐？我們聽說過約克市的野獸秀，應該就像那個樣子吧。」

　　「印度跟約克郡很不一樣。」瑪莉想了想，慢慢地說道：「這我沒想過。迪肯和妳媽媽喜歡聽妳講我的事嗎？」

　　「當然囉！迪肯聽得目瞪口呆，眼珠子都快掉下來了。」瑪莎回答：「不過媽媽得知妳只有自己一個人，就很替妳擔心。她說：『柯萊文先生沒有替她請個家庭教師或保母嗎？』我說：『沒有，梅德洛太太說，如果他有想到的話，就會請了。她還說，柯萊文先生可能要等到兩、三年之後才會想到這件事。』」

　　「我不想要家庭教師。」瑪莉突然說。

　　「媽媽說，妳是時候該開始學讀書了，而且要有個婦女來照顧妳，她說：『瑪莎，妳想想看，要是換了妳住在那麼大的地方，只有自己一個人晃來晃去，沒有媽媽，妳會是什麼樣的感覺呢？妳要盡量讓她開心啊！』她這麼對我說，我就說好。」

　　瑪莉緊緊地盯了瑪莎好一會兒，說道：「妳讓我開心很多，我喜歡聽妳講話。」

　　瑪莎走出房間，回來時，在圍裙下的手裡拿了樣東西。

　　「我帶了個禮物來送汝喔！」她開心地笑了起來：「汝覺得怎麼樣啊！」

「禮物！」瑪莉驚叫道。一個住了十四個飢餓的人的農舍，怎麼可能會有禮物送人呢！

瑪莎解釋道：「有個小販在高沼地沿路叫賣，他將馬車停在我家門口，賣一些鍋盤還有些小東西，不過媽媽沒有錢光顧。就在他要離開的時候，我家的伊莉莎白・愛倫喊了起來：『媽媽，他有賣跳繩，把手是紅色和藍色的。』媽媽就突然大聲叫道：『先生，等一下！跳繩怎麼賣？』他說：『兩辨士。』媽媽就往口袋裡摸錢，她跟我說：『瑪莎，汝是個乖女孩，都把薪水帶回家，這些錢該怎麼花，我都算得好好的，不過現在我要從這裡面拿出兩辨士，來替那個囡兒買條跳繩。』所以她就買了這條跳繩。」

瑪莎將圍裙下的跳繩拿出來，驕傲地展示著。這是一條堅固的細長跳繩，兩端有著紅藍條紋的把手。瑪莉沒看過跳繩，一臉迷惑地盯著它瞧。

「這是做什麼用的？」她好奇地問。

「做什麼用的？」瑪莎大叫起來：「難道印度有大象、老虎和駱駝，卻連跳繩都沒有嗎？這也難怪啦，他們大部分都是黑人。跳繩是這麼玩的，我跳給妳看。」

瑪莎跑到房間中央，雙手各持把手的一端，開始跳了起來。她一直跳、一直跳，瑪莉坐在椅子上看著，那些舊畫像裡的怪臉似乎也在盯著瑪莎看，疑惑著這個農舍的平凡小女子居然敢當著他們的面這樣肆無忌憚，不過瑪莎看都不看他們一眼。瑪莉的臉上露出興致與好奇，這讓瑪莎很滿意。瑪莎邊跳邊數，跳了一百下才停下來。

「我還可以跳更多下。」她停下來後說：「我十二歲的時候可以跳五百下，我那時候比較瘦，而且常常跳。」

　　瑪莉從椅子上站起來，躍躍欲試。

　　「這個看起來很好玩，妳媽媽真好。妳覺得我也可以跳嗎？」她說。

　　「妳就試試看，」瑪莎將跳繩遞給她，催促道：「妳不可能一開始就跳到一百下，不過只要練習，就會愈跳愈多下，這是媽媽說的。她說：『跳繩對她最有幫助了，這是最理想的小孩玩具。讓她到外面的新鮮空氣中去跳繩，這樣可以讓她伸展四肢，變得更有力。』」

　　瑪莉剛開始跳的時候，胳膊和兩腿顯然都不是太有力氣，動作也不是很靈活，不過她喜歡跳繩，不想停下來。

　　「汝把衣服穿上，到外面去跑步和跳繩。」瑪莎說：「媽媽交待我一定要跟妳說，要盡量多待在戶外，就算下一點點雨的時候也去，只要穿暖和些就可以。」

　　瑪莉穿上外套，戴上帽子，將跳繩掛在手臂上。她打開門正要出去時，忽然想到了什麼，又慢慢折返回來。

　　她說：「瑪莎，這是用妳的薪水買的，是妳的兩辨士。謝謝妳。」瑪莉說這話的時候，態度很不自然，因為她不習慣向別人道謝，也不曾去注意到人家為她做了什麼。「謝謝妳。」說完，就把手伸出來，因為她不知道還能做什麼。

　　瑪莎笨拙地握了握她的手，好像也不習慣做這種事一樣，然後笑了起來，說道：「啊！汝真像個奇怪的老太婆，要是我家的伊莉莎白・愛倫的話，她就會親我一下。」

　　瑪莉看起來更不自然了。「妳想要我親妳嗎？」

　　瑪莎又笑了起來，回答道：「不了，那不一樣，要自己想才去做。到外面跑一跑，去跳繩吧！」

　　瑪莉走出房間，心裡覺得有點困窘，約克郡人好像很奇怪，瑪莎就常讓她感到困惑。她一開始很不喜歡她，但現在不會了。

跳繩真好玩。瑪莉邊數邊跳、邊跳邊數，直到臉紅通通的，這可是打她從出生以來，感覺最有趣的事了。陽光普照，微風輕拂，不是狂暴的風，而是令人愉悅的微風，隨風飄來了新翻泥土的新鮮氣味。

瑪莉繞著噴泉花園跳繩，從一個步道跳過去，又從另一個步道跳回來。最後她跳進菜園，看到班邊掘土邊在和知更鳥說話，知更鳥在班的身邊蹦蹦跳跳。瑪莉朝班跳過去，班抬起頭看著瑪莉，一臉好奇。瑪莉想知道班是否注意到了她，她真希望班有看到自己在跳繩。

班嚷道：「啊！真是教人不敢相信！汝畢竟是個囡兒，汝的血管裡流的到底是血液，不是發酵的乳酪。汝跳得臉紅通通的，這是千真萬確的。真不敢相信汝居然做到了。」

「我以前沒有跳過繩，才剛開始學而已。」瑪莉說：「我一次只能跳二十下。」

班說：「汝就繼續跳，對一個跟異教徒住在一起的囡兒來說，汝的身體狀況算是夠好的了。看，牠也在看汝呢！」班將頭偏向知更鳥的方向。「牠昨天一直跟著汝，今天還會一樣，牠一定很想

知道跳繩是啥玩意兒，牠也沒見過！」他對著知更鳥搖了搖頭，「汝要是不當心點，總有一天汝的好奇心可會要了汝的命嘞！」

瑪莉繞著所有的花園和果園跳繩，每隔幾分鐘就停下來休息一會兒。最後，她走到她的專屬步道上，想試試看能否跳完全程。她這次跳得很久，剛開始的時候她慢慢地跳，跳到步道的一半時，身體很熱，喘不過氣來，所以只好停下來。雖然無法繼續跳下去，但是瑪莉不是很在意，因為她已經跳到三十下了。

她停下來，開心地微微笑了笑，然後一看，就在那裡，知更鳥正在常春藤的長枝上搖晃著。牠一路跟隨著瑪莉，現在發出一聲啁啾向她打招呼。瑪莉跳過去，每跳一下，就感覺到口袋裡有個沉甸甸的東西撞她一下。當她看到知更鳥時，她又笑了笑。

「昨天你指了鑰匙給我看，今天你也應該要把門指給我看，但是我想你不知道門在哪裡！」她說。

知更鳥從搖晃的常春藤小枝飛到牆頂上，接著張開鳥喙，發出響亮美妙的鳴囀，純粹是為了炫耀。世界上沒有什麼會比炫耀的知更鳥更迷人可愛的了，而且牠們簡直是時時刻刻都在炫耀。

印度保母跟瑪莉講過很多魔法故事，而這一刻所發生的事情，對她來說就是魔法。

一陣和風往走道這邊吹來，這陣風比較強，樹枝搖曳了起來，從牆上垂下來的那些沒有修剪的小常春藤枝葉，也搖動了起來。瑪莉走近知更鳥，一陣風將一些垂下的常春藤吹了起來，瑪莉突然跳向常春藤，用手抓住常春藤，因為她看到常春藤下面有個球形的把手，被垂下來的常春藤給蓋住了。那是一個門把。

瑪莉將手伸到葉子裡面然後撥開，垂下來的常春藤很茂密，就像膨膨的、搖曳著的簾幕，也有些常春藤是攀爬在木頭和鐵的上面。

瑪莉一陣興奮，心怦怦跳，雙手微微顫抖。知更鳥繼續唱著歌，歪著頭，好像一樣興奮似的。她摸到的那個鐵做的方形物是什麼？她還在上面摸到了一個洞。

那是門鎖，這就是被鎖上了十年的門，瑪莉將手伸進口袋取出鑰匙，發現鑰匙吻合門鎖。她把鑰匙插進去，她得用雙手才能轉動鑰匙，但鑰匙真的轉開了。

她長長地吸了一口氣，看看身後的長走道是否有人走來。一個人影都沒有，就好像沒有人來過這裡似的。瑪莉不由自主地又深深吸了一口氣，將搖晃的常春藤簾幕拉住，緩緩地推開門。

瑪莉輕輕地穿過門，再把門關上，她背對著門，環顧四周。她呼吸急促，振奮不已，又驚又喜。

她此時此刻就站在祕密花園裡。

第九章

世界上最奇怪的屋子

這是所能想像最美麗、最神祕的地方了。花園四周的高牆上攀滿了光禿禿的玫瑰藤蔓，濃密地交纏一起。瑪莉知道這是玫瑰樹，在印度很常見。地上覆滿枯黃的草，長著幾叢灌木，如果樹叢還活著，那一定是玫瑰樹叢。有幾棵莖幹挺直的玫瑰尚未完全伸展開來，看起來像小樹。

園內還有其他樹木，但這些四處蔓生的玫瑰藤，讓這個地方顯得特別奇異而美麗。長長的玫瑰蔓藤垂下，宛如隨風輕輕搖曳的布幕，藤互相糾纏，有的纏住較遠的樹枝，從一棵樹攀到一棵樹，形成一道道可愛的橋。

這些玫瑰藤沒長出葉子和花朵，瑪莉不知道它們是不是還活著。灰色或棕色的細樹枝垂下蔓延到地面上，彷彿一層霧濛濛的幔子，把一切都覆蓋住，牆壁、樹木，甚至是枯草地。就是這些在樹木間糾纏成一團團的東西，讓花園看起來這麼神祕。瑪莉原本是想，花園荒廢這麼久，一定會很不一樣，的確，這個花園別的地方都不一樣。

「這裡好安靜！真是安靜呀！」她低聲地說。

她稍微佇足，聆聽這一片寂靜。飛到樹梢上的知更鳥也和四周一樣沉靜，牠甚至沒有擺動翅膀，一動不動地棲息著，看著瑪莉。

「難怪這麼安靜，」她又低聲地說：「十年來，我是第一個在這裡說話的人。」

瑪莉離開門邊，腳步輕巧，生怕吵醒了誰似的。還好腳底下有草，走起路來靜悄悄的。她來到樹木間那童話般的拱形藤蔓下面，抬頭看著小藤枝和卷鬚。

「不知道它們是不是真的死了，這個花園裡的東西都死了嗎？但願不是。」她說。

如果她是班，只要看看那些樹枝就知道是不是還活著，但是她在灰色或棕色的大小樹枝上看不到任何線索，連一點小葉芽也沒有。

她已經走進這座神奇的花園，隨時都可以穿過常春藤下的門進來，她感覺好像找到了一個完全屬於自己的世界。

太陽照射著牆裡的世界，在密朔兌莊園這特別的地方，高高的藍色穹蒼似乎比高沼地的天空還要明亮柔和。知更鳥從樹梢上飛下來，跟在瑪莉身後，或跳或飛地穿梭在灌木叢間。牠啁啾叫，露出忙碌神情，好像在指什麼東西給瑪莉看。

這裡的一切都既奇怪而安靜，瑪莉好像和人們隔了幾百哩遠，卻沒有一絲孤單感。她只想知道這些玫瑰是不是都死了，有些可能還活著，等天氣暖和了，就會長出葉子和花苞。她不希望花園植物都死光了，這如果是個生機勃勃的花園，那就太完美了，四處都會長出玫瑰花，幾千朵都有！

瑪莉走進花園時，把跳繩掛在手臂上，走了一會兒，她想繞著花園跳繩，可以停停走走地到處看看。四處好像都有草坪步道，有一、兩個角落還有常綠樹形成的小亭子，裡頭有石椅或覆蓋著苔蘚的花甕。

瑪莉來到第二個小亭子時，停下了跳繩。亭中有個花壇，好像有什麼東西從黑土冒出來，那是一些淡綠色的小尖點。她想起班說的話，便跪下去看了看。

「沒錯，這些小東西正在長大，有可能是番紅花、雪花蓮或是水仙花。」瑪莉低聲地說。

她彎下腰靠近這些小綠點，聞著潮濕泥土的新鮮氣味。她很喜歡這個味道。

「別的地方可能也有什麼東西長出來，我要逛遍整個花園看一看。」她說。

瑪莉沒有跳繩，而用走的，走得很慢，眼睛一直盯著地面。她看著那些狹長的舊花床和草地，生怕錯過任何東西，就這樣繞完整個花園。一路上，她發現了更多的小綠點，讓她好不興奮。她低聲對自己叫道：「這不是一個完全死掉的花園，雖然玫瑰花死了，還有其他植物活著。」

瑪莉對園藝一竅不通，不過她覺得有些地方的草好像長得太茂密了，綠色點點得用擠的才能長出來，可能是沒有足夠空間生長。她四周看了看，找到了一根尖尖的木頭。她彎下身去掘土，拔掉雜草，在綠色小點的四周清出一小塊地方。

「現在它們看起來可以呼吸了。」瑪莉除完了第一批草，「我還要清除更多地方的草。只要有看到，就把它清除掉。今天要是做不完，明天再過來。」

瑪莉四處掘土除草，樂在其中。從一個花床到另一個花床，接著是樹下的草地。一番活動後，她覺得很暖和，她先脫掉外套，又脫去帽子，不知道自己一直在對著草地和綠色點點微笑。

知更鳥非常忙碌，牠很高興看到有人在牠的地盤上除草。牠以前就經常對班感到驚奇，因為在翻土除草時，被翻起來的泥土裡有各種美食可以吃。眼前這個新來的人，身高還不及班的一半，一進到牠的花園，就知道要翻土除草。

　　瑪莉小姐在花園一直工作到午餐時間，事實上當她想到該吃飯時已經很晚了。她穿上外套、戴上帽子，拿起跳繩，無法相信自己已工作了兩、三個小時，這期間她都感到很快樂，清理過的地方冒出更多的淡綠色小點，比起被雜草覆蓋時的樣子，它們看起來快活多了。

　　瑪莉環顧著她的新王國，對著樹木和玫瑰叢說：「我今天下午再來。」彷彿它們都聽懂了似的。

　　她輕輕地跑過草地，打開那扇移動緩慢的舊門，悄悄穿過常春藤。

　　她兩頰紅潤，眼睛明亮，胃口極好，瑪莎感到很高興。

　　瑪莎說：「兩塊肉，還有兩個米布丁！嗯！我要是告訴媽媽，跳繩把汝變成了這樣，她一定會很高興。」

　　瑪莉剛才在花園裡用尖頭棒子挖土時，挖到了一個長得很像洋蔥的白色根莖。她將它放回去，把洞上的泥土小心拍平。她想瑪莎可能會知道那是什麼。

　　她問：「瑪莎，那些長得像洋蔥的根莖是什麼？」

　　「那是球莖。」瑪莎回答：「春天時很多球莖都會開花。小小的球莖是雪花蓮和番紅花，大一點的是水仙花、丁香水仙和黃水仙，最大的是百合花和紫菖蒲，這些花都很美。迪肯在我們家的花園裡種了很多這樣的花。」

　　瑪莉問：「這些花，迪肯都認得嗎？」她想到了個點子。

　　「迪肯可以讓花從磚牆裡長出來。媽媽說，迪肯只要對地面小聲說說話，植物就會從裡面冒出來。」

　　「球莖可以活很久嗎？沒有人照顧的話，可以活很多年嗎？」瑪莉焦急地問。

　　瑪莎說：「這些植物不需要人照顧，所以窮人也種得起。你不照顧，它們還是會在地下活一輩子，還會蔓延開來，長出新的小芽。這裡有個森林公園長了上千朵的雪花蓮，春天時，那可是約克郡最美的景致了，但沒人知道它們是什麼時候種下去的。」

「真希望現在就是春天，我想看看在英國生長的所有植物。」瑪莉說。

吃完午餐，瑪莉坐在火爐前毯子她最喜歡的位子上。

「我想要——我想要一把小鏟子。」她說。

「汝要鏟子做啥？」瑪莎笑著問：「汝難道要開始挖土了嗎？我一定也要告訴媽媽這件事。」

瑪莉看著爐火沉思了一會兒，要想保住她的祕密王國，她就得小心一點。她並沒有做什麼壞事，可是柯萊文先生要是發現門被打開了，一定會大發雷霆，然後換上新鑰匙，將門徹底鎖起來。瑪莉無法忍受這樣的事情發生。

「這個地方好大，很孤單，」她慢慢地說，心裡琢磨著，「房子很孤單，公園很孤單，花園也很孤單，而且很多地方都被鎖了起來。我在印度雖然沒有很多事情可以做，但是可以看到比較多的人，有當地人，有行軍經過的阿兵哥，有時還有樂隊演奏，印度保母也會說故事給我聽。可是在這裡，就只有妳和班可以和我說話，但是妳要工作，班又常常不想和我說話。我想，我要是有個小鏟子，就可以找個地方像班那樣挖土，班如果肯給我一些種子，我還可以種個小花園！」

瑪莎面露喜色。

「對啊！」她驚呼道：「媽媽也是這麼說。她說：『那個地方那麼大，為什麼他們不給她一小塊地方，好讓她種些香菜蘿蔔什麼的？她可以在那裡挖挖耙耙的，會很快樂的。』媽媽就是這麼說的。」

「真的嗎？她知道很多事情，對不對？」瑪莉說。

　　瑪莎說：「是啊！就像她說的：『一個拉拔十二個囝兒長大的女人，不只會學到基本常識，也會學到其他的東西。囝兒就跟算數一樣，可以讓我們學到一些東西。』」

　　「一把鏟子要多少錢？小把的就行了。」瑪莉問道。

　　「嗯，」瑪莎沉思後回答：「在兌特村有一家小店，我看到他們有在賣成套的園藝工具，鏟子、耙子、叉子綁在一起賣兩先令，很堅固，夠妳用的了。」

　　瑪莉說：「我口袋裡的錢超過兩先令，摩理森太太給我五先令，柯萊文先生也會叫梅德洛太太拿一些錢給我。」

　　「他還記得要給汝錢？」瑪莎驚呼道。

　　「梅德洛太太說，我每個星期都有一先令的零用錢，她每個星期六會給我一先令，不過我不知道要把錢花在哪裡。」

　　瑪莎說：「天啊！這是一大筆錢！汝想買啥就可以買啥。我家農舍的房租只要一先令三辨士，可是這好像要把我們剝掉一層皮似的。我剛剛想到一件事。」瑪莎叉著腰說。

　　「什麼事？」瑪莉急切地問。

　　「兌特村那家店也賣整包的花種，每包賣一辨士，我們家的迪肯知道哪些種子開出來的花最漂亮，他也還知道要怎麼種那些花。他經常會去兌特村，純粹是去玩玩。汝會寫印刷體字嗎？」她突然問道。

　　「我會寫字。」瑪莉回答。

　　瑪莎搖搖頭。

　　「我們家的迪肯只看得懂印刷體。如果汝會寫印刷體字，我們就可以寫信叫他去買園藝工具和種子。」

　　瑪莉叫道：「哦！妳這個好姑娘！妳真是好心，我不知道妳原來這麼好。我會用印刷體寫信看看，我們去跟梅德洛太太要紙筆和墨水。」

瑪莎說：「這些我有，我自己買的，因為我常在星期天寫信給媽媽。我現在就去拿。」

　　瑪莎跑出房間，瑪莉站在火爐邊，興奮地搓著細瘦的小手。她低聲地說：「我要是有鏟子，我就可以讓泥土變得又鬆又軟，把雜草挖起來。如果還有種子，花就會長出來，花園就不會再死氣沉沉，會甦醒過來。」

　　那天下午瑪莉並沒有出門。瑪莎拿來紙筆墨水後，還得清理桌面，把碗盤端下樓。她去廚房時，梅德洛太太也在那裡，並交待她去辦個事情，所以瑪莉等了很久，瑪莎才回來。

　　接下來，寫信給迪肯是個大工程。瑪莉會寫的字很少，因為以前的家庭教師很不喜歡她，沒多久就走了。她的拼寫不是很好，不過她發現自己還是可以盡量用印刷體寫字。她按照瑪莎所唸的，寫了這封信：

> 　　我親愛的迪肯：
>
> 　　希望你一切都好。瑪莉小姐有很多錢，你可以到兌特村去幫她買一些花的種子和一套園藝工具，好讓她做花床嗎？你挑最漂亮、最容易種的花，因為她沒有種過花，而且她以前住的印度跟這裡不一樣。代我向媽媽和其他的弟弟妹妹問好。瑪莉小姐還會告訴我更多的事情，下次我休假回去，你們就可以聽到大象和駱駝的事，還有紳士們去獵獅子和老虎的事。
>
> 　　你的好姐姐
> 　　瑪莎・菲碧・索爾比

「我們把錢放在信封裡，我會拜託肉販的兒子順路用馬車把信帶過去，他是迪肯的好朋友。」瑪莎說。

「迪肯買到東西以後，我要怎麼去拿？」瑪莉問道。

「他會自己把東西帶過來，他喜歡到處走走。」

「哦！」瑪莉驚呼道：「那我就可以看到他了！我從沒想過會看到迪肯。」

「汝想看到他嗎？」瑪莎突然問道，一臉開心的樣子。

「想啊，我沒見過連狐狸和烏鴉都會喜歡的男生。我很想見到他。」

瑪莎微微變了臉色，好像突然想到了什麼，說道：「我想到一件事差點給忘了，本來早上就想告訴妳的。我問過媽媽了，她說她會自己去問梅德洛太太。」

「妳是說——」瑪莉開口說。

「就是我星期二說的那件事。我們想請梅德洛太太找一天讓人載妳到我們的農舍去，去嚐嚐看媽媽做的熱燕麥餅，還有奶油和牛奶。」

彷彿所有好玩的事情都在這一天發生了。想想看，就要在白天、在天空還是藍色時穿越高沼地！想想看，就要走進一間住著十二個小孩的農舍！

「妳媽媽覺得梅德洛太太會讓我去嗎？」瑪莉焦急地問。

「會啊，她說梅德洛太太應該會同意。她知道媽媽很愛乾淨，把農舍整理得一塵不染。」

「我要是去你們的農舍，那我就可以看到妳媽媽和迪肯了，」瑪莉想了想，很喜歡這個主意，「妳媽媽跟印度的媽媽好像不一樣。」

花園裡的工作和下午的興奮情緒，讓瑪莉感到很平靜，心裡有很多想法。瑪莎一直陪她到喝下午茶的時間，不過她們只是舒適安靜地坐著，沒有多說話。瑪莎準備下樓去拿茶盤時，瑪莉問了一個問題。

　　她說：「瑪莎，幫忙洗碗盤的女僕，今天還會牙痛嗎？」

　　瑪莎稍微嚇了一跳。「汝為什麼問這個？」她說。

　　「我在等妳的時候，打開門去走廊看妳回來了沒有，結果我又聽到遠遠的地方有哭聲，就像我們前幾天聽到的一樣。今天沒有風，所以妳看，那不應該是風聲。」

　　「啊！」瑪莎坐立不安地說：「汝不應該在走廊裡亂走亂聽的，柯萊文先生知道了會很生氣，到時候不知道他會做出什麼事來。」

　　瑪莉說：「我沒有亂聽，我只是在等妳，然後就聽到了那個聲音。這是第三次聽到了。」

　　「天啊！梅德洛太太的鈴響了。」瑪莎說著跑出了房間。

　　「這真是最奇怪的屋子了。」瑪莉昏昏欲睡地說，她把頭靠在身邊扶手椅的座墊上。新鮮的空氣、挖土和跳繩，讓她累得酣睡過去。

第十章

迪肯

這一整個星期，祕密花園裡幾乎都陽光普照。瑪莉一想到這個花園，就稱它為「祕密花園」。她喜歡這個名字，更喜歡花園那道漂亮的舊牆把她關起來的感覺，沒有人知道她在哪裡，那裡就像是世外仙境一般。

少數幾本瑪莉讀過也喜歡的書都是童話書，她在一些故事裡讀過祕密花園。有些人會在祕密花園裡睡上一百年，瑪莉覺得這些人真笨，她才不想睡覺呢，在密朔兌莊園這個地方，她反而一天比一天清醒。她開始喜歡到戶外去，本來討厭風，現在變得很喜歡。她跑得愈來愈快，愈來愈久，跳繩也能跳到一百下了。

祕密花園裡的球莖一定很驚訝，因為周圍的空間變大了，有足夠的地方可以呼吸。此外，還有一件瑪莉不知道的事，那就是球莖正在黑色泥土下振作，努力生長。陽光照拂帶來溫暖，雨水一來就能立即滋潤它們，讓它們變得生氣勃勃。

瑪莉是個意志堅定的奇怪小孩，只要是她有興趣、下定決心要做的事，就會全心全意去做。她孜孜不倦地工作、挖土、除草，隨著時間過去，她不但不感到厭倦，反而愈來愈樂在其中，這對她來說就像是很好玩的遊戲。

她發現了更多正在萌芽的淡綠色小點，比她原本期望的還要多，好像突然從各處冒了出來。她每天都會發現新的小綠點，有一些小到剛剛破土而出。這麼多的綠色小點，讓瑪莉想到瑪莎說的「上千朵的雪花蓮」，還有那些蔓生、長出新芽的球莖。這些植物被冷落了十年，搞不好它們也會像雪花蓮那樣蔓生出上千朵來。瑪莉不知道多久以後才會開花，有時候她會停下挖土的工作，看看花園，想像裡面開滿上千朵美麗花朵的景象。

在陽光普照的這個星期裡，瑪莉和班變得更親密了一些。她好幾次嚇到班，她就像從土裡跳出來似的，忽然在班的身邊冒出來。事實上，瑪莉擔心班看到她就會拿起工具掉頭就走，所以她都盡量悄悄地走近班。

不過班不像一開始那麼排斥瑪莉了。瑪莉顯然想和他這位長輩做朋友，這大概讓他覺得受寵若驚，而且瑪莉也變得有禮貌多了。班不知道瑪莉剛開始對他說話的態度，就是她對印度人說話的方式。瑪莉當時並不知道，這位剛強暴躁的約克郡老人並沒有向主人行額手禮的習慣，他頂多是按照主人的吩咐去做事罷了。

「汝和知更鳥一個樣。」這天早上，當班抬起頭發現瑪莉站在身邊時，說道：「我不知道汝什麼時候會出現，也不知道汝會從哪裡冒出來。」

「知更鳥現在是我的朋友了！」瑪莉說。

「這很像牠的作風，」班厲聲說：「很虛榮、很輕浮，會去討好女人，只要是能擺動尾巴上的羽毛來炫耀一番，牠啥事都做得出來。牠自負到極點了。」

班很少這麼多話，有時他甚至只是哼的一聲來回答瑪莉的問題，不過這天早上他比以往都來得健談。他站了起來端詳瑪莉，一邊將釘了平頭釘的靴子踩在鏟子上。

「汝到這裡多久啦？」他脫口說出。

「大概一個月了吧。」瑪莉回答道。

他說：「汝開始替密朔兌莊園增光了，汝比剛來的時候胖了點，也不那麼黃了。汝第一次走進這個花園時，像個羽毛被拔光的小烏鴉。我心想，真沒見過比妳更醜、臉色更難看的囡兒了。」

瑪莉不是個自負的小孩，也不太在意自己的長相，所以班說的話並不讓她覺得難過。

她說：「我知道我胖了，長襪子變緊了，以前都是鬆垮垮的。班，知更鳥來了。」

的確，知更鳥就在那裡，瑪莉覺得牠今天看起來特別漂亮。牠的紅色西裝外套像絲綢般富有光澤，牠擺動著翅膀和尾巴，側著頭活潑優雅地蹦蹦跳，好像下定決心要讓班欣賞牠。不過班卻挖苦起牠來。

「哈，這就是汝的花招！」他說：「汝沒有別人作伴，就來找我勉強湊合湊合。這兩個星期以來，汝的西裝外套變得愈來愈紅，還不停在整理羽毛。我知道汝在做什麼。汝正在向一位大膽的年輕女士求愛，謊稱自己是兌特高沼地上最出色的雄知更鳥，準備好要打敗其他的雄鳥。」

「哦！你看牠！」瑪莉驚呼。

知更鳥顯然意氣正高昂，跳得愈來愈近，用一副可人的模樣看著班。牠飛到離他們最近的紅醋栗樹上，將頭側向一邊，對著班唱起小曲。

「汝以為這樣就可以騙過我嗎？」班皺起臉來，瑪莉知道他在佯裝生氣，「汝以為沒有人可以抗拒汝，對不對？」

知更鳥展開雙翼，直接飛到班的鏟子把手上面。瑪莉簡直不敢相信自己的眼睛。老人的臉又慢慢皺成另一個表情，他一動也不動，好像不敢呼吸一樣，生怕驚嚇到他的知更鳥。

他輕聲說：「好吧，我認輸了！」班說這話時語氣輕柔，好像在說什麼別的事情。「汝真是知道怎樣收買人心，真是的！汝真是美得太不尋常了。汝什麼都知道。」

班接著又一動也不動，幾乎不敢吸氣，一直持續到知更鳥拍了拍翅膀飛走。班凝視著鏟子的把手，好似那上頭有魔法一般，才繼續挖土。有好幾分鐘的時間，他都沒有再開口說話。

不過由於他現在隔一會兒就慢慢露出微笑，瑪莉不再害怕和他說話。

「你有自己的花園嗎？」她問。

「沒有。我是個單身漢，跟馬丁住在門房裡。」

「如果你有自己的花園，你會種什麼？」瑪莉說。

「甘藍菜、馬鈴薯和洋蔥。」

「如果要種花，」瑪莉繼續追問：「你會種什麼？」

「球莖和一些很香的植物，不過大半還是會種玫瑰。」

瑪莉面露喜色。

「你喜歡玫瑰嗎？」

　　班拔起了一株雜草，扔到旁邊回答：「喜歡啊，我喜歡玫瑰。我是在一位年輕夫人家當園丁時才發現自己喜歡玫瑰的。夫人在自己喜歡的地方種了很多玫瑰花，她愛這些玫瑰花就像是愛小孩或是知更鳥一樣。我看過她彎下腰去親吻玫瑰。」班又拔出一株雜草，對著它皺了皺眉：「這些雜草跟十年前一樣多。」

　　「她現在在哪裡？」瑪莉感興趣地問。

　　班回答，「在天堂，別人是這麼說的。」將鏟子深深地插進土裡。

　　「那些玫瑰花呢？」瑪莉更感興趣地繼續問。

　　「只能自生自滅了。」

　　瑪莉變得很興奮。「它們都死光了嗎？沒有人照顧的玫瑰花是不是會死光呢？」瑪莉大膽地問。

　　「嗯，我很喜歡那些玫瑰花，也很喜歡夫人，夫人很喜歡那些玫瑰花。」班勉強地承認：「我每年會去整理它們一、兩次，修剪樹枝，鬆鬆根部的土。它們到處蔓延，不過那裡的土壤很肥沃，有一些花還是活著的。」

　　「如果它們沒有葉子，看起來灰灰暗暗、乾枯枯的，要怎麼知道它們是死了還是活的？」瑪莉問道。

　　「等春天一到，陽光照在雨上，雨落在陽光上，汝就會明白了。」

　　「那要怎麼做呢？要怎麼做呢？」瑪莉大叫，她忘了要小心行事。

　　「汝只要看看樹枝，如果有很多褐色的小塊凸起來了，下過溫暖的雨之後，汝再看看那些小塊變成什麼樣子。」班忽然停住不說，好奇地看著瑪莉熱切的面孔，問道：「汝怎麼突然對玫瑰花這麼有興趣啦？」

瑪莉感到臉紅，不太敢回答。「我——我想要——想要假裝自己有個花園，」她結結巴巴地說：「我——我在這裡沒有事情做，我什麼都沒有——一個朋友都沒有。」

班看著她慢慢地說：「嗯，這倒是真的，汝沒有朋友。」

他說這話時怪怪的，瑪莉不知道班是不是在同情她。瑪莉倒是不曾為自己感到難過，她只會覺得很不耐煩，什麼都覺得討厭。不過世界好像正在改變，變得越來越好。只要祕密花園不被發現，她就可以一直過得很快樂。

瑪莉在班的身邊又待了十到十五分鐘，大膽地問了許多問題。班用他奇怪的發牢騷方式回答了每一個問題，他看起來並不是真的臭臉，而且鏟子也沒拿就走掉。

瑪莉正要離開時，班談到了玫瑰花，瑪莉想到了班說他以前喜歡的那些玫瑰花。

「你現在還會去看那些玫瑰花嗎？」她問。

「今年我沒去。我的風濕症發作，關節都硬掉了。」班用一貫發牢騷的嗓音說，突然間好像生了瑪莉的氣，瑪莉不知道他幹嘛生氣。

「咳！」他嚴厲地說：「不要再問這麼多問題了，汝是我見過最愛問的丫頭。去別的地方玩，我今天說得夠多了。」

他說這些話時是那麼沒好氣，瑪莉知道多留無益。她到外面的步道上慢慢地跳繩，一邊想著班，一邊對自己說，雖然這樣很奇怪，不過她喜歡班這個人，儘管他脾氣很暴躁。她喜歡老班。是的，她的確是喜歡他。她一直想讓班跟自己說話，還開始相信班對什麼花都瞭若指掌。

有一個月桂籬笆步道環繞著祕密花園，步道盡頭有一扇門開向庭園裡的樹林。瑪莉想要繞著這個步道跳繩，然後去看看樹林裡有沒有兔子跳來跳去。她很喜歡跳繩，來到那扇小門時，她打開門走了進去，因為她聽到一聲低沉而特別的口哨聲，她想查個究竟。

　　眼前的確發生了一件怪事。瑪莉屏住呼吸，停下來望過去。樹下有個男孩背靠著樹幹，正吹著一塊粗糙木頭做成的笛子。這個長相有趣的男孩約莫十二歲，看起來乾乾淨淨的，鼻子朝天，臉頰跟嬰粟花一樣紅。瑪莉沒見過哪個男孩的臉上有這麼圓、這麼藍的眼睛。

　　在男孩靠著的樹幹上，有隻棕色的松鼠緊靠著他，兩眼盯著他看。後面不遠的灌木叢中，有隻雄雉雞優雅地伸長了脖子張望，旁邊有兩隻兔子坐得直直的，抖著鼻子四處嗅著。動物們似乎都圍著男孩靠近過來，牠們望著男孩，聽著笛子發出低沉微弱的奇怪聲音。

　　男孩看到瑪莉，便舉起手，用和笛聲一樣低沉的聲音跟她說：「別動，牠們會跑走的。」

　　瑪莉一動不動地站著。男孩停止吹笛子，從地上爬了起來。他移動得很緩慢，看起來就像根本沒在動一樣。等他最後站直了，松鼠才逃回樹上，雉雞將頭縮回去，兔子們也四腳著地跳走了，但是牠們看起來並沒有受到驚嚇。

　　「我是迪肯，我知道汝是瑪莉小姐。」男孩說。

　　瑪莉發現，不知道怎麼地，她一開始就知道他是迪肯，要不然還有誰能夠這樣迷倒兔子和雉雞，就像印度的弄蛇人一樣呢？男孩的臉上堆滿笑容，彎彎的嘴唇又大又紅。

　　他解釋道：「我剛剛站起來的動作很慢，如果動作太快，就會嚇到牠們。有野生動物在附近的時候，我們的動作

就要輕一點，說話的聲音也要很小聲。」

　　他跟瑪莉說話的樣子，好像他倆本來就很熟，一點也不像陌生人。瑪莉不熟悉男孩子，覺得很害羞，跟迪肯講話時有點僵硬。

　　「你收到瑪莎的信了？」她問。

　　男孩點了點頭，他有一頭紅褐色的鬢髮。「所以我才來的。」

　　男孩彎下腰，從地上拿起一樣東西。他剛剛在吹笛子時，那東西就放在一旁了。「我買來了園藝工具，這裡有小鏟子、耙子、叉子和鋤頭，都是好東西！這裡還有一把移植用的小鏟子。我去買種子時，店裡的夫人送給我一包白色的嬰粟，還有一包藍色的飛燕草。」

「你可以給我看看那些種子嗎？」瑪莉說。

她希望自己可以像迪肯那樣講話。迪肯說話的樣子又快又從容，他似乎很喜歡瑪莉，而且一點也不擔心瑪莉不喜歡他，儘管他是一個生長在高沼地的平凡男孩，穿著有補丁的衣服，長著一張滑稽的臉，還有一頭紅褐色的粗頭髮。

當瑪莉走近迪肯，發現他身上有一股帶石楠混合著草地和樹葉的清新氣味，彷彿他就是由這些植物所做成似的。瑪莉很喜歡這種味道。當她注視著迪肯那張有著紅臉頰和藍色圓眼睛的滑稽臉蛋時，她不再感到害羞。

「我們坐在圓木上來看看種子吧。」瑪莉說。

兩人坐了下來，迪肯從外套口袋掏出一包棕色小紙袋。他解開繩子，裡面一小包一小包的，很整齊，每一小包上面都有花的圖片。

他說：「這裡有很多，有木犀草和嬰粟，木犀草聞起來最香了，不管種在哪裡都長得起來，嬰粟也是一樣，妳只要對著它們吹口哨，它們就會長大開花，是最可愛的花了。」

迪肯停了下來，快速轉過頭去，深紅色的臉蛋露出喜色。「那隻正在叫我們的知更鳥在哪裡？」他說。

長著深紅色漿果的茂密冬青樹裡傳出了啁啾聲，瑪莉知道是哪隻鳥在啁啾叫。

「牠真的是在叫我們嗎？」她問道。

「是啊！」迪肯說，彷彿這是再自然不過的事了，「牠在呼喚朋友，好像是在說：『我來了，看看我，我要串一下門子。』牠就在樹叢裡。牠是誰的鳥？」

「牠是班的鳥，不過我想牠也稍微認識我。」瑪莉回答。

「是啊，牠認識汝。」迪肯用低沉的聲音說：「牠喜歡汝，牠已經接受妳了。牠待會就會跟我說汝的所有事情。」

迪肯像先前那樣慢慢地走到灌木叢邊，然後發出像知更鳥的鳴囀一般的聲音。知更鳥注意聽了一會兒後，像是回答問題似地做出回應。

「沒錯，牠把妳當朋友。」迪肯低聲輕笑道。

「真的嗎？」瑪莉熱切地叫起來，她實在很想知道這是不是真的，「你覺得牠真的喜歡我嗎？」

迪肯回答：「牠要是不喜歡汝，就不會靠近汝，小鳥可是很挑剔的，知更鳥比人類還更瞧不起別人呢。汝看，牠正在討好汝呢。牠在說：『汝不想聊天嗎？』」

事實好像真是如此。知更鳥在灌木叢裡蹦蹦跳，一會兒橫著走，一會兒啁啾，一會兒鳴囀。

「小鳥說的每句話你都聽得懂嗎？」瑪莉說。

迪肯咧嘴微笑，他一笑起來，整個嘴唇就變得又大又紅又彎。他抓了抓自己的粗頭髮說：「應該懂吧，牠們也覺得我聽得懂，我跟牠們一起在高沼地生活很久了。我看著牠們破殼而出、長羽毛、學會飛、開始唱歌，我都覺得自己也是牠們的一分子。有時候我會想，搞不好我是鳥、是狐狸、是兔子、是松鼠，甚至是甲蟲，可是我自己卻不知道呢。」

他笑了笑，又回到圓木這邊來，聊起花的種子。他告訴瑪莉這些種子開花時的樣子，跟她說要怎麼種、怎麼照顧、怎麼施肥、怎麼澆水。

「嘿，」他突然轉過頭去看著她，「我來幫汝種，汝的花園在哪裡？」

瑪莉握緊放在腿上的小手，不知道該如何回答，只好默不作聲。她沒有預料到這件事，感到不知手措，覺得自己的臉好像一陣紅一陣白。

「汝應該有一小塊花園吧，沒有嗎？」迪肯說。

瑪莉的臉色確實一陣紅一陣白，迪肯也注意到了。瑪莉還是沒有應聲，他開始覺得有些困惑。

「他們不願意給汝一小塊地方種花嗎？汝還沒有自己的花園嗎？」他問。

瑪莉將手握得更緊，將視線轉到他的身上，慢慢地說：「不知道男生會不會幫忙守密，我要是跟你講一個祕密，你可以保密嗎？這是個天大的祕密，被發現的話就不得了了，我可能會死掉！」瑪莉激動地說出最後這句話。

迪肯看起來更困惑了，他用手搔搔粗頭髮，愉快地回答：「我一直都在幫動物保守祕密，如果我將狐狸的幼兒、鳥巢、野生動物的洞穴，透露給其他的囝兒知道，高沼地就不再安全了。所以啊，我是守得住祕密的。」他說。

瑪莉並不想伸手去抓迪肯的袖子，不過她卻這麼做了。她急促地說：「我偷了一個花園，那不是我的花園，但也不是誰的花園。沒有人要那個花園，沒有人關心它，也沒有人會進去，裡面的植物可能都死了，我也不清楚。」

瑪莉開始感到前所未有的激動與彆扭，「我不管，我不管！沒有人有權力從我身邊把花園搶走，因為除了我，沒有人在乎它。他們只是把花園關起來，任它自生自滅。」瑪莉激動地把話說完，然後突然用手摀住臉，哭了起來，可憐的小瑪莉。

迪肯好奇的藍眼睛變得愈來愈圓。「啊，啊！」他慢慢地拉長驚嘆聲，意謂著他感到既驚訝又同情。

瑪莉說：「我沒有事情可以做，也沒有什麼東西是屬於我的。我自己找到這個花園以後就進去了，我就像是那隻知更鳥，沒有人會將花園從知更鳥身邊搶走的。」

「花園在哪裡？」迪肯壓低聲音問道。

瑪莉立刻從圓木上站起來。她知道自己又開始變得彆扭又頑固了，不過她一點也不在乎。她拿出以前在印度時的那種蠻橫態度，覺得又興奮又難過。

「跟我來，我指給你看。」她說。

她帶著迪肯繞著兩旁種有月桂樹的小徑走，接著來到攀滿常春藤的步道上。迪肯帶著憐憫的奇怪表情跟著瑪莉走，覺得自己好像被領著要去看什麼奇怪的鳥巢，所以走路的腳步要很輕。

當瑪莉走到牆邊，掀起垂吊的常春藤時，迪肯嚇了一跳，那裡有一扇門。瑪莉慢慢地推開門，兩人一道走了進去。等瑪莉站定之後，她傲慢地揮著手。

「就是這裡，這是一個祕密花園，我是世界上唯一希望它活過來的人。」她說。

迪肯環顧著花園，一遍又一遍。

「啊！」他幾乎是耳語般地說：「這個地方又奇怪又漂亮，感覺好像在夢裡一樣。」

第十一章

兌特的鳥巢

迪肯站在那裡環顧四周好一會兒，瑪莉在一旁看著他。接著，迪肯開始四處看了看，腳步比瑪莉第一次走進花園時還要輕。他的視線似乎不放過任何東西，他看到有灰色爬藤從樹枝上垂下來的灰色樹木，看到牆上和草叢間纏繞在一起的藤蔓，還看到常綠樹形成的小亭子，裡面有石椅和高高的花甕。

「沒想到我親眼目睹了這個地方。」迪肯終於低聲說。

「你以前就知道這個花園了嗎？」瑪莉問道。

她講得很大聲，迪肯對她做了手勢，「我們說話得小聲一點，不然會被人聽到，覺得花園裡面有人。」他說。

「哦！我忘了！」瑪莉嚇得馬上用手摀住嘴巴。「你以前就知道這個花園了，是不是？」她鎮定下來，又問了一次。

迪肯點點頭，回答說：「瑪莎有跟我說過，這個花園沒有人進來過，我們一直都很想知道裡面是什麼樣子的。」

他停下腳步，看著四周糾纏在一起的美麗藤蔓，圓圓的眼睛一副又驚又喜的樣子。

「啊！等春天到了，這裡應該會有很多鳥巢。在英國，在這裡築巢是最安全的了，沒有人會靠近，這裡還有糾纏的樹木和玫瑰可以築巢。我在想，是不是高沼地的小鳥都是飛來這裡築巢的呢。」迪肯說。

瑪莉又將手放在迪肯的手臂上，雖然她自己沒有意識到。

「你看得出來這裡有玫瑰花嗎？我想它們大概都死了。」她低聲地說。

「啊！才沒有呢！它們沒有死，至少沒有全部死光！」迪肯回答道。「汝看這裡！」

他走到最近的一棵樹前面，這是棵很老的樹，樹皮上都是灰色青苔，不過也長出了一團糾結的樹枝。迪肯從口袋裡掏出一把厚厚的刀，打開其中一個刀片。

他說：「這裡有很多已經死掉的樹枝，要割掉。還有一些老樹枝，去年長了新枝，這個就是新長的。」他摸到一根嫩枝，看起來不是硬硬乾乾的灰色，而是略帶褐色的綠色。

瑪莉也熱切恭敬地摸著嫩枝，說道：「這一根嗎？這一根還活著嗎？活得好好的？」

迪肯的大嘴一彎，微笑了起來，說：「它跟我們兩個一樣淘氣呢。」瑪莉想起瑪莎曾告訴過她，「淘氣」就是「活潑」或「有生氣」的意思。

「真高興它很淘氣。」她低聲叫出來：「希望它們全部都很淘氣，我們繞著花園走，數數看有幾棵淘氣的樹吧。」

瑪莉急切得都有些喘氣，迪肯也一樣。兩人穿梭在樹木與灌木叢中，迪肯手上拿著刀子，指著一些東西給瑪莉看，她看了都覺得太奇妙了。

迪肯說：「它們到處生長，強壯的樹長得很茂盛，虛弱的都死光了，沒死的還一直在生長，到處伸展，真是奇觀。看這兒！」說著，他拉下一根灰色乾枯的粗樹枝，「別人可能會以為這根樹枝已經死了，但我想沒有，除非下面的根都死了。我割割看下面的地方。」

迪肯跪下去，用刀切開離地不遠、看起來沒有生命的樹枝。

他得意洋洋地說：「瞧！我告訴過汝的，樹枝裡面還有綠色的東西呢，汝瞧！」

他還沒開口，瑪莉就已經跪在地上，全神貫注地看著。

「看起來帶點綠色，就是還有水分，表示還很淘氣。」迪肯解釋道：「如果木頭裡面很乾，一折就斷，就像我現在砍下來的這一塊，那就表示已經完蛋了。這些生機勃勃的樹枝從大樹根長出來，如果把老樹枝砍掉，鬆鬆附近的土，好好加以照顧，那麼，」他停下來，仰頭看著四周攀緣懸垂的小樹枝，「今年夏天，這裡就會長出很多玫瑰花了。」

他們繼續穿梭在樹木與灌木叢中。迪肯用刀時的力氣很大，動作也很靈活，他知道如何砍掉乾枯的死木頭，也能看得出來哪些樹枝似死猶生。

半個小時後，瑪莉覺得自己也可以判斷樹木是不是還活著。每當迪肯割開看起來沒有生命的樹枝時，瑪莉只要瞥見一丁點潮濕的綠色東西，便會高興地低呼。

鏟子、鋤頭和叉子都很好用。迪肯用鏟子挖動根部的土，然後攪動泥土讓空氣進入，也順便教瑪莉如何使用叉子。他們在一棵最高挺的玫瑰附近辛勤工作，就在這時，迪肯瞥見某樣東西，驚喜地叫了出來。

「哇！」他叫著，指向幾步外的草地。「這是誰弄的？」

那是瑪莉在淡綠色點點附近清理出來的一小塊地方。

「是我。」瑪莉說。

「啊！我還以為汝一點都不懂園藝呢！」迪肯驚呼。

她回答：「我是不懂，不過它們那麼小，雜草那麼密，它們都快沒有地方呼吸了，所以我就幫它們清出一塊地方，但我連它們是什麼都不知道呢。」

迪肯滿臉笑容地蹲到綠色點點的旁邊，說道：「汝做對了，就連園丁也會告訴汝要這麼做的，它們現在會長得像傑克的豆莖那麼快哦。這些是番紅花和雪花蓮，這個是水仙，」他又轉身到另一小塊地上，說道：「這些是黃水仙，它們會長得很壯觀。」

迪肯在這些清出來的地上四處來回走。

「對汝這麼一個小姑娘來說，這可是大工程呢。」他注視著瑪莉說。

瑪莉說：「我長胖了，也變得比以前強壯了。我以前一直覺得很累，可是我挖土時一點也不覺得累，我喜歡聞泥土被翻鬆的味道。」

「這對汝好極了，」迪肯說著，點了點頭，「除了雨水落在剛長出來的新鮮植物上的味道以外，沒有什麼比乾淨肥沃的泥土還好聞的了。我常常在下雨天跑去高沼地，躺在灌木叢下面，聽著雨滴落在帚石楠上發出的輕柔沙沙聲，一直聞啊聞。媽媽說，我的鼻子跟兔子的鼻子一樣在振動呢。」

「你都不會感冒嗎？」瑪莉詫異地注視著迪肯。她沒見過這麼好玩的男生，或者說這麼討人喜歡的男生。

迪肯咧嘴笑著說：「不會啊，打從出生我就沒有感冒過。我不怕冷，不管天氣怎麼樣，我都會在高沼地像兔子一樣跑。媽媽說十二年來我吸進了太多新鮮的空氣，所以不會感冒鼻塞。我跟山楂的節一樣強壯呢。」

他邊說話邊工作，瑪莉拿著叉子或小鏟子在一旁幫忙。

「這裡有好多工作要做！」迪肯興奮地看著四周說道。

「你還會再來幫我嗎？」瑪莉懇求他，「我能幫上忙，我可以挖土除草，你叫我做什麼，我就做什麼。哦！你一定要來哦，迪肯！」

「如果汝要我每天來，我就每天來，不管天氣是好是壞。」迪肯堅定地回答：「這是我做過最有趣的事了，把自己關在這裡工作，讓花園甦醒過來。」

瑪莉說：「如果你肯來，幫忙讓花園活過來，我就──我都不知道該怎麼謝謝你了。」瑪莉無助地把話說完。這樣的一個男孩，我們可以做什麼來回報他呢？

「我告訴汝該做什麼，」迪肯咧著嘴快樂地笑著說，「汝要長胖，然後汝就會跟小狐狸一樣肚子餓。汝可以跟我一樣學著和知更鳥說話，我們會玩得很開心。」

迪肯開始四處走動，若有所思地望著那些樹、牆壁和灌木叢。

「我不希望這個花園變得和園丁的花園一樣，到處修剪得整整齊齊的，汝覺得呢？現在這個樣子比較好，植物到處蔓生搖曳，互相纏繞。」他說。

瑪莉焦急地說：「我們不要把花園弄得太整齊，太整齊的話就不像是祕密花園了。」

迪肯站在那裡，表情困惑地搔了搔紅褐色頭髮，說：「這是個祕密花園沒錯，不過十年來，除了知更鳥，好像還有其他人來過這個花園。」

「可是花園的門一直是關著的，而且鑰匙也被埋起來了，沒有人進得來。」瑪莉說。

「這倒是真的，這個地方很奇怪，我覺得這十年當中，好像有人來這裡稍微修剪過枝葉。」迪肯回答道。

「可是，是誰做的呢？」瑪莉說。

迪肯檢查了一棵莖幹挺直的玫瑰樹枝，搖了搖頭。「對啊！是誰呢？」他喃喃地說：「門被鎖起來，鑰匙也被埋起來了。」

　　她的花園開始生長的那個早晨，令瑪莉感覺終生難忘。的確，就是在這天早晨，花園開始生長了。當迪肯開始清理地方播種，瑪莉記起了巴佐用來嘲弄她的那首歌。

　　「有沒有花長得像鈴鐺？」她問道。

　　「鈴蘭就是了。」迪肯用小鏟子挖土，說道：「還有風鈴草和風輪草也是。」

　　「那我們就來種一些這種花。」瑪莉說。

　　「這裡已經有鈴蘭了，我有看到。它們長得太密了，得把它們分開來種，不過它們實在是太多了。其他的要種兩年才會開花，不過我可以從我們家農舍裡的花園給汝帶一點來。汝為什麼想要種這些花呢？」

　　瑪莉跟迪肯說了巴佐還有他在印度的兄弟姐妹的事，說她很討厭他們，他們還叫她「執拗的瑪莉小姐」。

　　「他們喜歡圍著我一邊跳舞，一邊唱歌：

　　　執拗的瑪莉小姐喲，
　　　你的花園長得如何？
　　　銀色的鈴鐺海扇殼，
　　　金盞花長成一直排。

所以我就想到，是不是真的有花長得像銀色鈴鐺。」

　　說完，瑪莉眉頭微皺，很生氣地將小鏟子插到土裡去。「我才不像他們說的那麼拗呢！」

　　迪肯笑了起來。

　　「是啊！」他說著，一面將肥沃的黑土壓扁，瑪莉看到他在聞泥土的味道，「身邊有這麼多花朵的時候，好像誰都沒有必要拗了，而且還有那麼多友善的野生動物，它們到處忙著築巢、唱歌、吹口哨，不是嗎？」

瑪莉跪在一旁，手裡握著種子，看著迪肯，不再皺眉。

她說：「迪肯，你真的就像瑪莎所說的那麼好。我喜歡你，你是我第五個喜歡的人，沒想到我會喜歡上五個人。」

迪肯坐直在腳跟上，就跟瑪莎擦壁爐時一樣。瑪莉覺得他的藍色圓眼睛、紅色臉頰，還有快樂的朝天鼻，讓他看起來的確有趣又討喜。

「汝只喜歡五個人嗎？那其他四個是誰？」他說。

「你媽媽和瑪莎，」瑪莉用手指數著，「還有知更鳥和班。」

迪肯大笑了起來，不得不將手放在嘴巴上，將聲音壓住。他說：「我知道汝會覺得我是個奇怪的小伙子，不過我倒覺得，汝是我所見過最奇怪的女生了。」

瑪莉接著做了一件很奇怪的事，她傾身向前，問了迪肯一個她從來不敢問別人的問題，她用約克郡的口音問他，因為那是迪肯的語言。在印度，如果你會講當地人的語言，他們會很高興。

「汝喜歡我嗎？」瑪莉說。

「喜歡啊！」迪肯誠懇地回答：「我很喜歡汝，我確定知更鳥也一定很喜歡汝！」

「這樣就有兩個人了，這樣就算有兩個人喜歡我了。」瑪莉說。

接下來，他們又更賣力、更愉快地繼續工作。當瑪莉聽到院子裡的大鐘敲響，提醒她吃午餐的時候到了，她一怔，覺得很可惜。

「我得走了，」她難過地說：「你也該走了吧？」

迪肯咧嘴微笑，說道：「我把午餐帶在身上，媽媽都會在我的口袋裡放點東西。」

迪肯從草地上拾起外套，從口袋裡掏出一小包凹凸不平的東西，東西用藍白相間、質料粗糙而乾淨的手帕包著。裡面是兩塊厚厚的麵包，麵包中間還夾著一片東西。

他說：「平常就只有麵包而已，可是今天麵包裡還夾了一塊燻肉呢。」

瑪莉覺得迪肯的午餐看起來很奇怪，不過他好像已經準備好要享用了。

他說：「汝趕快回去吃飯吧，我要先吃我的了。回家前，我還要再幹些活。」

迪肯背靠著樹幹坐了下來。

他說：「我想叫知更鳥來，把燻肉的皮給牠，牠們很喜歡吃肥肉。」

瑪莉實在不想離開迪肯，她突然覺得迪肯好像是森林裡的小仙子，等她再回到花園時就會消失無蹤。他是那麼的好，好得不像凡人。瑪莉慢慢朝圍牆的門走去，然後停下腳步，又繞回來。

「不管發生什麼事，你──你都不會把這個祕密說出去吧？」她說。

迪肯深紅色的臉頰，被剛吃下的一大口麵包和燻肉脹得鼓鼓的，不過他仍然露出鼓舞人心的微笑。

「如果汝是一隻椋鷯，汝把巢指給我看，汝覺得我會告訴別人嗎？我才不會呢。」他說：「汝跟椋鷯一樣安全。」

瑪莉聽了後，十分確信自己安全無虞。

第十二章

「我可以有一小塊地嗎？」

瑪莉飛快地奔跑，回到房間時都快喘不過氣來了。她額上的頭髮亂蓬蓬的，雙頰泛著明艷的粉紅色。午餐已經擺上桌，瑪莎在桌旁等待著。

她說：「汝回來晚了，汝去哪裡了？」

「我看到迪肯了！我看到迪肯了！」瑪莉說。

「我就知道他會來，」瑪莎興奮地說：「汝喜歡他嗎？」

「我覺得——我覺得他很帥！」瑪莉語氣堅定地說。

瑪莎看起來很驚訝，不過也很高興。

「嗯，他是全世界最棒的囝兒了，不過我們從來就不覺得他帥，他的鼻子太翹了。」她說。

「我喜歡他的翹鼻子。」瑪莉說。

「可是他的眼睛太圓了，雖然顏色很好看。」瑪莎有點猶豫地說。

「我喜歡他的圓眼睛，而且他眼睛的顏色就跟高沼地的天空一樣呢。」瑪莉說。

瑪莎滿意地綻開笑容。「媽媽說，迪肯的眼睛之所以是那個顏色，是因為他喜歡抬頭看小鳥和雲彩。不過他的嘴巴很大，你說是不是？」

「我喜歡他的大嘴巴，我希望我的嘴巴跟他一樣大。」
瑪莉固執地說。

瑪莎愉悅地低聲輕笑。「這樣的話，汝的小臉蛋會看起來很奇怪的。不過我早就知道汝看到他會有這種反應。汝喜歡他買來的種子和園藝工具嗎？」她說。

「妳怎麼知道他把東西帶來了？」瑪莉問道。

「他要是沒帶來，那才奇怪呢。東西只要是在約克郡，他就一定會帶來，迪肯是個可以信任的小伙子。」

瑪莉擔心瑪莎會開始問一些讓她難以回答的問題，不過她沒有問，她對種子和園藝工具很感興趣。瑪莉只有在瑪莎問到花要種在哪裡時被嚇了一跳。

「汝去問誰了？」她問道。

「我誰都還沒問。」瑪莉猶豫地說。

「嗯，我是不會去問園丁領班的。他的職位太高了，這個羅區先生。」

瑪莉說：「我沒看過他，我只看過他手下的園丁，還有班。」

瑪莎建議道：「如果我是妳，我會去問班。雖然班的脾氣比較壞，但是他人沒那麼壞。他想做什麼，柯萊文先生都會任隨他。柯萊文夫人還在世時，班就待在這裡了。他常會逗柯萊文夫人開心，柯萊文夫人很喜歡他。也許他可以找個不礙事的角落讓你去種花。」

「如果那個地方不會妨礙到別人，而且本來就沒有人管，那就不會有人在意我去使用它，對不對？」瑪莉緊張地說。

「他們沒有理由反對的，妳又不會破壞什麼東西。」瑪莎回答。

　　瑪莉火速地吃完午餐。她從桌子邊站起來，正要跑到房間去戴帽子時，瑪莎攔住了她。

　　「我有件事要告訴妳，想說等妳吃完飯再跟妳說。柯萊文先生今天早上回來了，我猜他想見見妳。」她說。

　　瑪莉的臉色一下子刷白。

　　她說：「哦！為什麼？為什麼？我剛來的時候，他並不想見我啊！我聽皮丘先生這麼說的。」

　　「嗯，」瑪莎解釋道：「梅德洛太太說，這是因為我媽媽的緣故。我媽媽在兌特村碰到柯萊文先生。她以前沒跟他說過話，不過柯萊文夫人到過我們農舍兩、三次。這件事柯萊文先生忘記了，可媽媽沒忘，她大膽地將柯萊文先生攔了下來。我不知道她跟他說了什麼跟妳有關的事，不過柯萊文先生聽了之後，決定明天在離開之前見妳一面。」

　　「哦！他明天又要走了嗎？我真高興！」瑪莉叫道。

　　「他會離開很久，秋天或是冬天之前大概不會回來。他要去外地旅行，他常常這樣。」

　　「哦！我好高興，好高興哦！」瑪莉欣喜地說。

　　如果他冬天才會回來，就算秋天就回來，他們還是有足夠的時間讓祕密花園活起來。到時候要是被柯萊文先生發現了，要將花園拿回去，瑪莉也心甘情願了。

　　「妳覺得他會在什麼時候見我——」

　　瑪莉話還沒說完，門就被打開了，梅德洛太太走了進來。她穿戴著她最好的黑色洋裝和軟帽，衣領上別著偌大的胸針，上面有一張男人的相片。那是梅德洛先生的彩色照片，他幾年前去世了，梅德洛太太盛裝打扮時就會別著這個胸針。梅德洛太太看起來既緊張又興奮。

她急促地說：「妳的頭髮真亂，趕快去梳一梳。瑪莎，快幫她穿上最好的衣服，柯萊文先生要我帶她去書房見他。」

瑪莉臉上的粉紅色消失了。她的心怦怦跳，覺得自己又變回那個僵硬、相貌普通又沉默的小孩。她甚至沒有回答梅德洛太太，便轉身走進臥房，瑪莎尾隨在後。

梳妝打扮時，瑪莉一語不發。接著，她便穿著整齊地跟著梅德洛太太沿著走廊默默走去。待會該說些什麼呢？她被迫去見柯萊文先生，他不會喜歡她的，她也不會喜歡柯萊文先生。她知道柯萊文先生會怎麼看她。

瑪莉被帶到屋內一處她沒進去過的地方。梅德洛太太敲了門，裡面應聲道：「進來。」她們便一起進了房間。

一個男人坐在火爐前的扶椅上，梅德洛太太開口對他說話。

「先生，瑪莉小姐來了。」她說。

「把她留下來，妳可以走了。等我按鈴了，妳再來帶她走。」柯萊文先生說。

梅德洛太太走出房間，將門帶上，瑪莉只能站在一旁等待著，這個平凡的小人兒搓揉著自己的小手。她看到椅子上的人，背駝得並不厲害，他的肩膀高聳彎曲，黑髮中挾雜著幾絲白髮。他將頭轉過高聳的肩膀，對瑪莉說話。

「過來這裡！」他說。

瑪莉向他走去。

他長得並不難看，如果不是一臉憂傷的話，應該是很英俊的。一看到瑪莉，他顯得苦惱，不知該拿她如何是好。

「妳好嗎？」他問。

「我很好。」瑪莉回答。

「他們有沒有好好照顧妳？」

「有。」

他端詳著瑪莉，苦惱地抓著額頭。

「妳很瘦。」他說。

「我已經變胖了。」瑪莉用僵硬的語氣回答。

柯萊文先生真是一臉憂愁呀！他的黑眼睛似乎沒有在看瑪莉，像是在看別的東西，心思很難放在她身上。

「我忘記妳來到這裡了，我怎麼記得住呢？我本來想替妳找個家庭教師或保母之類的，可是我忘記了。」他說。

「請你，」瑪莉開口說：「請你——」她話卡在喉嚨裡出不來。

「妳想說什麼？」柯萊文先生問。

瑪莉說：「我——我已經夠大了，不需要保母，而且請你——請你還不要幫我找家庭教師。」

柯萊文先生又抓了抓額頭，注視著瑪莉。

「那位索爾比太太也是這麼說。」他心不在焉地喃喃說道。

瑪莉鼓起了勇氣。

「她是——是瑪莎的媽媽嗎？」她結巴地說。

「應該是吧。」柯萊文先生回答。

「她很瞭解小孩子，她自己就有十二個小孩，所以她知道。」瑪莉說。

柯萊文先生似乎回過神來了。

「妳想要怎麼樣？」

「我想要到屋子外面玩。」她希望自己回答的聲音沒有發抖。「在印度時，我不喜歡去外面玩。可是來到這裡之後，

去外面玩會讓我覺得肚子餓，我已經在長胖了。」

柯萊文先生看著瑪莉。

「索爾比太太說，這樣會對妳比較好，或許吧，」他說：「她覺得等妳變強壯了，再請家庭教師也不遲。」

「當風吹過高沼地，我在外面玩的時候，覺得自己變強壯了。」瑪莉說道。

「妳都在哪裡玩？」柯萊文先生接著問。

「到處玩，瑪莎的媽媽送了跳繩給我。我一邊跳、一邊跑，到處看看是不是有東西從土裡長出來了。我沒有破壞什麼東西。」瑪莉喘著氣說。

「別這麼害怕，」柯萊文先生憂心地說，「像妳這樣的小孩，是不會破壞什麼的！妳想做什麼，就去做什麼吧。」

瑪莉將手放在喉嚨上，她不想讓柯萊文先生看出自己已經興奮得說不出話來。她向柯萊文先生走近一步。

「真的嗎？」她顫抖地說。

瑪莉焦慮的小臉蛋似乎讓柯萊文先生更擔憂了。

「別這麼害怕，」他大叫道：「當然是真的，我是妳的監護人，雖然我對小孩不是很在行。我沒有辦法花時間照顧妳，我很難相處，討人厭，又沒耐心，不過我希望妳可以過得快樂舒適。我不瞭解小孩子，不過梅德洛太太會負責讓妳什麼都不缺。我今天會叫妳來，是因為索爾比太太說我應該見妳一面。她女兒提起過妳，她覺得妳需要新鮮空氣和自由，讓妳可以四處跑跑。」

「她很瞭解小孩子。」瑪莉不由自主地又說了一次。

「應該是，」柯萊文先生說：「她在高沼地把我攔下來時，我覺得她很冒昧，不過她說柯萊文夫人一向對她很好。」

柯萊文先生似乎很難將亡妻的名字說出口，「她是個令人尊敬的婦人，現在看到妳，我覺得她說的話很有道理。妳高興在外面玩，就去外面玩。這地方很大，妳想去哪裡玩，就去哪裡玩。妳有沒有想要什麼東西？」他忽然想到：「妳要不要玩具、書或是洋娃娃？」

「我可不可以……」瑪莉用抖顫的聲音問：「我可不可以要一小塊土地？」

瑪莉因為很急切，所以沒有意識到自己的用字很奇怪，她用錯字了。柯萊文先生一臉吃驚的樣子。

「土地！」他重複道：「妳說的是什麼意思？」

「我想在上面種花，讓東西長出來，我想看它們活過來。」瑪莉結結巴巴地說。

柯萊文先生注視了她一會兒，然後很快將手摀在眼睛上面。

「妳——妳那麼關心花園嗎？」他慢慢說道。

「在印度時，沒接觸過花園，我一直在生病，總覺得很疲倦，那裡太熱了。我有時候會在沙子上做小小的花床，在上面插上花。不過這裡跟印度不一樣。」瑪莉說。

柯萊文先生站了起來，開始在房間裡慢慢地踱步。

「一小塊土地。」他自言自語地說。瑪莉覺得柯萊文先生一定是想起了某件事。當他停下來和瑪莉說話時，他黑色的眼睛看起來既溫柔又和善。

他說：「妳要多少土地都可以，妳讓我想到另一個同樣喜歡泥土和植物的人。妳要是看到想要的土地，它就是妳的了，孩子，讓它長出植物來吧。」他看似微笑地說。

「不管哪裡都可以嗎？如果是沒人要的地方呢？」

「哪裡都可以，」他回答道：「好了！妳該走了，我累了。」說著，柯萊文先生按鈴叫梅德洛太太進來，「再見了，我整個夏天都不會待在這裡。」

梅德洛太太不一會兒就到了，瑪莉想她一定早就在走廊上等著。

柯萊文先生對她說：「梅德洛太太，見過這個小孩之後，我可以瞭解索爾比太太的意思了。等她身體強壯一點，再讓她開始上課。給她吃簡單、健康的食物，讓她去花園裡四處跑跑，不要太照顧她，她需要自由活動和新鮮的空氣，也需要到處去活蹦亂跳。索爾比太太有空會來看她，她也可以偶爾到他們的農舍去。」

梅德洛太太看起來很高興，一聽到不需要太「照顧」瑪莉，她鬆了口氣。她覺得瑪莉是個累人的負擔，能不見她就不見她。此外，她也很喜歡瑪莎的母親。

她說：「謝謝您，先生，蘇珊·索爾比是我以前的同學，她是個少見的婦女，心腸好又有智慧。我自己沒有小孩，而她生了十二個。她家的小孩比誰家的都還健康乖巧，瑪莉小姐跟他們在一起是不會有問題的。只要是講到小孩，我都會聽蘇珊·索爾比的建議。她可以稱得上是個心智健全的人，但願您明白我的意思。」

「我明白，現在將瑪莉小姐帶走，叫皮丘先生來。」柯萊文先生回答。

梅德洛太太把瑪莉帶回到房間的走廊底時，瑪莉飛也似地跑回房間。她看到瑪莎正在等她，事實上瑪莎收走餐具後，就匆忙趕回房間了。

瑪莉叫道：「我可以有自己的花園了！我可以挑我喜歡

的地方！我很長時間都不會有家庭教師！妳媽媽會來看我，我也可以去你們家的農舍。他說像我這樣的小女孩，是不會破壞什麼東西的，我可以做我想做的事，在哪裡都可以！」

「啊！他真好，對不對？」瑪莎高興地說。

瑪莉一本正經地說：「瑪莎，他真是個好人，只是他的臉看起來好悲傷，他的額頭都縐在一起了。」

瑪莉飛快地跑到花園裡，她離開花園的時間比自己預期的要久。她知道迪肯得早早離開，走五哩路回家。當她悄悄穿過常春藤後面的門時，沒有看到迪肯在他們剛剛工作的地方，園藝工具都被放在一棵樹下。瑪莉跑過去，看看四周，都沒有看到迪肯。他已經走了，祕密花園裡空蕩蕩的——除了知更鳥，牠剛剛跳過牆來，棲息在一叢直挺挺的玫瑰樹上，看著瑪莉。

「他走了，」瑪莉傷心地說：「哦！難道——難道——難道他真的是森林裡的仙子嗎？」

就在這時候，她注意到有個白色的東西綁在那個直挺挺的玫瑰叢中。那是一張紙條，是從她和瑪莎寫給迪肯的那封信上撕下來的。紙條被一根長長的刺釘在灌木上，她立刻明白那是迪肯留下的。

信上有一些用印刷體寫成的潦草字跡，還畫了個圖。瑪莉一開時沒看明白，後來才看出來那是個鳥巢，上面坐了一隻鳥。圖的下面用印刷體寫著：

「我會回來的。」

第十三章

「我是柯林」

瑪莉回到屋裡吃晚餐時,也把圖帶回來給瑪莎看。「啊!我不知道迪肯那麼聰明呢。這上面畫的是一隻欄鶇棲息在巢裡,畫得跟真的一樣大,而且比真的還更自然呢。」瑪莎驕傲地說。

瑪莉這時才懂迪肯畫這個圖的用意,他的意思是說,他一定會堅守祕密。瑪莉的花園就是她的巢,而瑪莉就是欄鶇。哦!她是多麼喜歡這個奇怪又平凡的男孩啊!

瑪莉真希望迪肯隔天就會來,期待著早晨的到來,在期待中入睡。

不過,約克郡的天氣變化無常,尤其是春天。夜裡,瑪莉被打在窗子上的重重雨滴聲吵醒。大雨傾盆而下,狂風在大古宅的各個角落和各個煙囪裡「呼嘯」著。瑪莉坐在床上,覺得又討厭又生氣。

她說:「這個雨跟以前的我一樣拗,我不想要它來,它偏偏就來。」

她躺回枕頭上,將臉埋了起來。她並沒有哭,只是躺著。

她討厭雨滴重擊的聲音，也討厭風發出的「呼嘯」聲。她再也睡不著。呼嘯的淒厲聲音讓她睡不著，她覺得自己也很悽慘。如果她心情還可以，或許雨聲還能哄她睡覺。大風「呼嘯」得很厲害，暴雨傾盆而下，敲擊著窗戶的玻璃！

「聽起來像是有人在高沼地迷了路，邊走邊哭。」她說。

瑪莉躺在床上翻來覆去，一個小時後，她突然坐起身來，把頭轉向門邊仔細聆聽。

「現在不是風聲，」她大聲地說：「這不是風聲。這個聲音不一樣，這是我之前聽到的哭聲。」

瑪莉的房門半掩著，聲音來自走廊的另一端，是遙遠而模糊的煩躁哭聲。她聽了好一會兒，愈聽愈確定那是哭聲。她覺得自己一定要查個清楚，這比祕密花園、比被埋起來的鑰匙都還要更奇怪。可能也是因為她現在心情不好，所以人就大膽了起來吧，她將腳伸出床外，站在了地板上。

「我要去查個明白，大家都在睡覺，而且我才不管梅德洛太太，不管她！」瑪莉說。

瑪莉拿起床邊的蠟燭，悄聲地走出房門。走廊看起來又深又暗，不過她興奮得沒去留意。她覺得自己記得要拐過哪些轉角，就可以走到那一小段走廊，那裡有個門用織錦畫覆蓋著。她迷路那天，梅德洛太太就是從那個門走出來的。聲音是從那個走道裡面傳出來的。

瑪莉拿著微弱的燭光繼續前進，她幾乎是摸著路在走，心跳得很厲害，她都可以聽到自己的心跳聲。那個遙遠而模糊的哭聲仍持續著，引導她前進。有時哭聲稍停一會兒，然後又開始哭。應該在這裡轉彎嗎？她停下來想了想。對，沒錯，走到走廊底，向左轉，爬上兩個寬廣的階梯，再向右轉。

沒錯，被織錦畫蓋住的門就在這裡。

　　瑪莉輕輕地推開門，再把身後的門關上。她現在就站在走道上，哭聲並不大，但是可以很清楚地聽到。聲音來自左邊牆面的另一邊，再過去幾呎的地方有一扇門。瑪莉可以看到門的下緣露出微光。有人在那個房間裡哭，而且是個小孩。

　　瑪莉走到門前，將門推開，進到了房間裡！

　　這個房間很大，擺設著古色古香的氣派家具。壁爐裡有低低的爐火發出微光，一張有著四根帷柱的床邊垂掛著織錦畫，床邊點著夜明燈，床上躺著一個哭哭啼啼的煩躁男孩。

　　瑪莉搞不清楚眼前這一幕是真是幻，還是自己又睡著了，只是在做夢而已。

　　男孩的臉蛋很纖細，臉色跟象牙一樣蒼白，眼睛大得不成比例。濃密的頭髮雜亂地披在額頭上，散成好幾綹，讓細瘦的臉顯得更小。他看起來好像生病了，但是哭聲聽起來像是不耐煩，而不是因為病痛的緣故。

　　瑪莉拿著蠟燭，站在門邊屏息不動，然後才躡手躡腳地穿過房間。當她走近男孩時，火光吸引了他的注意力，躺在枕頭上的頭轉了過來，盯著瑪莉看，灰色的眼睛睜得斗大。

　　「妳是誰？」他終於害怕地低聲問：「妳是鬼嗎？」

　　「我不是，」瑪莉也很驚怕地低聲回答：「你是嗎？」

　　男孩一直盯著她看。瑪莉沒法不注意到他長了一雙多麼奇怪的眼睛。眼睛是瑪瑙的灰色，被黑色的睫毛圍繞。相對於他的臉來說，他的眼睛實在是太大了。

　　「不是。」他愣了半晌後回答：「我是柯林。」

　　「柯林是誰？」她結巴地問。

　　「我是柯林·柯萊文。妳是誰？」

「我是瑪莉‧雷諾克斯，柯萊文先生是我姑丈。」

「他是我爸爸。」男孩說。

「你爸爸！」瑪莉喘著氣說：「沒人跟我說過他有小孩！他們為什麼不告訴我？」

「過來這裡。」男孩說著，繼續用他那雙奇怪的眼睛緊緊地盯著瑪莉。

瑪莉走近床邊，柯林伸出手去觸摸她。

「妳是真的人，沒錯吧？我常常會做很真實的夢，搞不好我正在做夢。」他說。

瑪莉離開房間前，套了件寬鬆的羊毛便袍，她把便袍的一角放到柯林的手裡。

「摸摸看，它又厚又溫暖。我也可以捏捏你，這樣你就可以確定我真的是人。我剛剛也以為自己在做夢呢。」瑪莉說。

「妳是從哪裡來的？」柯林問。

「從我的房間來的。風吹得好大聲，我睡不著，後來我聽到有人在哭，我很好奇，想知道是誰在哭。你在哭什麼？」

「因為我也睡不著，而且我的頭好痛。再跟我說一次，妳叫什麼名字？」

「瑪莉‧雷諾克斯。沒有人告訴你，我來這裡住了嗎？」

柯林一直用手指摸著瑪莉便袍上的縐摺，不過他已經開始相信瑪莉是個真實的人了。

「沒有，他們不敢跟我講。」他回答。

「為什麼？」瑪莉問道。

「因為他們要是跟我講，我就會害怕被妳看到。我不讓別人看到我或是談論我。」

　　瑪莉繼續問道：「為什麼？」她更迷惑了。

　　「因為我老是像現在這樣生病，需要躺在床上。我爸爸不讓人家討論我，佣人們也不可以講我的事。如果我活下來，也可能會是個駝子，不過我活不了的。我爸爸討厭看到我變得跟他一樣。」

　　「哦！這個屋子真是奇怪啊！」瑪莉說：「真是個奇怪的屋子！什麼都像是祕密。房間被鎖起來，花園也被鎖起來──還有你！他們也把你鎖起來了嗎？」

「沒有。我待在房間裡，是因為我不想出去，出去會讓我覺得很累。」

「你爸爸會來看你嗎？」瑪莉大膽地問。

「偶爾，通常是在我睡著的時候，因為他不想看到我。」

「為什麼？」瑪莉壓抑不住地繼續問。

男孩的臉上閃過憤怒的陰影。

「我媽媽生下我之後就死了，所以爸爸討厭看到我。他以為我不知道，可是我有聽到人家這麼說。他可以說是討厭我的。」

「他討厭那個花園，因為你媽媽死了。」瑪莉喃喃自語。

「哪個花園？」男孩問道。

「哦！那只是——只是一個你媽媽很喜歡的花園。」瑪莉結結巴巴地說，「你一直都在這裡嗎？」

「差不多。有時候他們會帶我去海邊，不過我在那裡待不久，因為大家都會盯著我看。我以前戴著一個鐵做的東西，要讓我的背變直，不過一個從倫敦來的名醫看過我以後，說這樣做很愚蠢。他叫他們把那個東西拿掉，帶我出去呼吸新鮮的空氣。可是我討厭新鮮的空氣，不想出去。」

「我剛來的時候也不喜歡，」瑪莉說：「你為什麼一直這樣看著我？」

「因為有些夢就像真的一樣，有時候我睜開眼睛，都不相信自己是醒著的。」柯林煩躁地回答。

瑪莉說：「我們兩個都是醒著的。」她環顧房間，房間的天花板很高，有一些角落很陰暗，火光也很暗淡。「看起來很像個夢，現在是半夜，屋子裡的人都在睡覺，除了我們。我們清醒得很。」

「我希望這不是夢。」男孩不安地說。

瑪莉立刻靈機一動。

「既然你不想讓別人看到你，那你要我走開嗎？」她問。

柯林一直握著瑪莉便袍上的縐摺，他聽到瑪莉這麼說，輕輕地拉了袍子一下。

他說：「不要，妳要是走掉，那我就確定自己是在做夢了。妳如果是真人，就坐在那個大腳凳上和我講話。我想要聽聽妳的事。」

瑪莉將蠟燭放在床邊的桌上，坐在那個有座墊的凳子上。她一點也不想離開，她想待在這個被藏起來的神祕房間裡，和這個神祕的男孩說話。

「你想要聽什麼？」她說。

柯林想要知道瑪莉來密朔兌莊園多久了，她的房間在哪個走廊上，她平常都做些什麼，她是不是跟他一樣討厭高沼地，還有她來約克郡之前住在哪裡。

瑪莉一一回答了這些問題，還跟他說了更多的事情，柯林就躺在枕頭上聽著。他要瑪莉跟他多說一點印度的事，還有她搭船渡海來到這裡的經過。瑪莉發現，柯林因為體弱多病，孩子們會學到的東西他都沒學到。柯林很小的時候，有保母教他看書，所以他大部分時間都在看書，或是看書本裡的圖片。

雖然爸爸很少在他醒著的時候來看他，但是他什麼好玩的東西都有。然而，他似乎一點也不快樂。他想要什麼就有什麼，也沒有人會強迫他做不喜歡做的事。

「每個人都得讓我開心，」柯林冷冷淡淡地說：「我一生氣就會生病。沒有人覺得我可以活到長大。」

他說得好像他已經習慣這個想法了，所以無所謂了。他很喜歡聽瑪莉的聲音，在她在講話時，他雖然想睡，但聽得津津有味。有一、兩次，瑪莉懷疑他是不是打起瞌睡來了，不過他又問了一個問題，繼續展開新的話題。

「妳幾歲？」他問道。

瑪莉忘形地回答：「我十歲，你也是。」

「妳怎麼知道？」柯林驚訝地問。

「因為你出生的時候，花園的門被鎖起來，鑰匙也被埋了起來，而花園已經鎖了十年了。」

柯林用手肘支撐著身體，稍微坐了起來，轉向瑪莉。

「哪個花園的門被鎖起來了？是誰鎖的？鑰匙被埋在哪裡？」他突然大叫起來，很感興趣似的。

「那是——那是柯萊文先生討厭的花園，他把門鎖起來了。沒有人——沒有人知道他把鑰匙埋在哪裡。」瑪莉緊張地說。

「那是什麼樣的花園？」柯林熱切地追問。

「十年來，沒有人可以進去那個花園。」瑪莉小心翼翼地回答。

不過已經來不及，柯林跟瑪莉太像了，而且他也一樣無所事事，所以祕密花園吸引了他，就像瑪莉當初被吸引那樣。他問了一連串的問題，花園在哪裡？她有沒有去找過花園的門？她有沒有問過園丁？

瑪莉說：「他們不會說的，一定有人囑咐過他們不可以透露。」

「我要讓他們說。」柯林說。

「你辦得到嗎？」瑪莉開始感到害怕而結巴起來，如果柯林強迫他們說出真相，誰知道會發生什麼事！

　　他說：「每個人都得讓我開心。我告訴過妳的，如果我活下來的話，這個地方有一天就會是我的，他們都知道這一點。我會叫他們說出花園在哪裡的。」

　　瑪莉並不覺得自己被寵壞，不過她很清楚地看出來這個神祕的男孩被寵壞了，以為全世界都是他的。他真是個奇怪的人，當他說自己活不久時，是那麼冷靜。

　　「你覺得自己不會活下來嗎？」瑪莉這麼問，一方面出於好奇，一方面是想讓他忘掉花園這件事。

　　「我想我活不下去。」他的語氣和先前一樣不在乎，「從我有記憶以來，我就聽到別人說我活不久了。起初他們以為我太小，不知道他們在說什麼，現在他們則是以為我聽不到，但我聽得到。我的醫生是我爸爸的堂弟，他很窮，如果我死了，將來等爸爸死了，整個密朔兌莊園就是他的了。我想他不會希望我活下來。」

　　「你想活下來嗎？」瑪莉問道。

　　「不想，」柯林焦躁又疲倦地回答：「但是我也不想死。我生病時就躺在這裡想著死亡，然後一直哭、一直哭。」

　　「你的哭聲我聽過三次，那個時候我還不知道是誰在哭。你是因為想到自己會死掉才哭的嗎？」瑪莉這麼問是希望柯林忘掉花園的事。

　　「大概吧，我們來說點別的。」柯林回答：「我們來聊聊那個花園吧，妳不想看看那個花園嗎？」

　　「想啊！」瑪莉壓低聲音回答。

　　「我也想，」柯林繼續說道：「在這之前，我沒有什麼真的想看的東西，不過我現在很想去看那個花園。我想把鑰匙挖出來，把門鎖打開，要他們將我連同椅子推進花園裡，這樣我就可以呼吸到新鮮空氣了。我要叫他們把花園的門打開。」

柯林變得很興奮，怪異的雙眼像星星一樣發光，眼睛看起來更大了。

「他們得讓我開心，我會叫他們帶我去花園，我也會讓妳去的。」他說。

瑪莉握緊雙手，一切都要完蛋了，徹底完蛋了，迪肯不會再回來，她也再不會像檞鶇那樣有個安全隱密的鳥巢了。

「哦！不要——不要——不要——不要那麼做！」她高聲呼叫。

柯林凝視著瑪莉，覺得瑪莉好像快瘋掉了一樣！

「為什麼？」他驚呼道：「妳說妳想看那個花園的。」

「我是想看，可是如果你叫他們把門打開讓你進去，那它就永遠不再是個祕密花園了。」瑪莉用帶點嗚咽的聲音回答。

柯林的身體又更向前傾。

「祕密，什麼意思？告訴我。」他說。

瑪莉幾乎是口齒不清地說著接下來的話。

「你想想看——你想想看，」她喘著氣說：「假如只有我們知道這件事——假如常春藤下面藏著一扇門——假如有門的話——而我們找到了門，假如我們一起偷偷地穿過門，然後把門關上，那就沒有人知道我們在裡面了。我們把說它是我們的花園，然後假裝——假裝我們是檞鶇，花園是我們的巢，我們就可以每天在裡面玩，可以挖土播種，讓花園活過來——」

「花園死了嗎？」柯林中斷瑪莉的話。

瑪莉繼續說：「如果沒有人照顧，它很快就會死了，球莖會活下來，可是玫瑰花——」

柯林又中斷瑪莉的話，變得跟瑪莉一樣興奮。

「球莖是什麼？」他很快地插嘴問。

「它們會長成水仙、百合和雪花蓮。它們現在正在土裡忙碌著，把淡綠色的點點給推出來，因為春天就要來了。」

「春天要來了嗎？春天是什麼樣子？像我這種待在房間裡的病人，是看不到春天的。」柯林說。

「春天時，陽光會照射在雨水上，雨水會落在陽光上，植物會長出來，在泥土下面忙碌著，」瑪莉說：「如果花園是個祕密，我們就可以進去看那些每天都會長大的植物，看看還有多少玫瑰花是活著的。你不明白嗎？你看不出來如果花園是個祕密的話，該有多好嗎？」

柯林又躺回枕頭上，表情古怪。

「我從來就沒有祕密，除了活不到長大這個祕密之外。他們不知道我知道這件事，所以這也算是個祕密。不過我更喜歡花園這種祕密。」他說。

瑪莉繼續找藉口說：「如果你不叫他們帶你去那個花園，搞不好有一天我可以找到路進到花園裡。然後，如果醫生要你坐在椅子上出去戶外，如果你想怎樣就可以怎樣，那我們也許可以找到個男孩來幫你推椅子，那我們就可以自己進去花園，花園就可以永遠是祕密花園了。」

「我想我會——喜歡——這麼做的。」柯林緩慢地說，他的眼睛看起來像在做夢，「我會守住祕密的，我不會介意祕密花園裡的新鮮空氣的。」

瑪莉的呼吸開始恢復正常，覺得自己比較安全了，因為柯林似乎很喜歡這個保密的想法。她差不多可以確定，如果再繼續說下去，讓柯林像她之前那樣去想像花園，他就會很喜歡這個花園，無法忍受別人隨意進到花園裡。

　　「我要告訴你我想像中的花園是什麼樣子，」瑪莉說：「花園被鎖起來太久了，裡面的植物可能都糾纏在一起。」

　　柯林一動不動地躺著聽她說話，瑪莉繼續說著。她說玫瑰花可能會攀上樹木垂下來，有很多鳥會在裡面築巢，因為裡面很安全。接著瑪莉跟他說了知更鳥和班的事情。講到知更鳥，她有太多事情可以講了，可以滔滔不絕地講，而且這個話題很安全，讓她不再膽戰心驚。柯林很喜歡知更鳥，聽得笑瞇瞇，看起來很可愛。瑪莉一開始還覺得，柯林的大眼睛和厚重的髮綹看起來比自己還醜。

　　柯林說：「不知道小鳥是什麼樣子的，待在房間裡不出門，是什麼都看不到的。妳知道的事情可真多，我覺得妳好像進去過那個花園。」

　　瑪莉無言以對，所以沒有應聲。顯然柯林也不期待她回答。不過接下來，他讓瑪莉感到很驚訝。

　　「我要讓妳看一樣東西，」他說：「壁爐架上方的牆那邊，妳有沒有看到那裡吊著玫瑰色的絲綢簾子？」

　　瑪莉之前沒有留意到簾子，不過她現在仰起頭就看到了。這塊柔軟光滑的絲綢簾子好像覆蓋著一張畫像。

　　「有。」她回答道。

　　柯林說：「那上面有一條繩子，妳過去拉它。」

　　瑪莉困惑地站起來，找到那條繩子。她將繩子一拉，簾幕便捲了上去，出現了一幅畫。畫中是一位滿臉笑容的女子，明亮的髮絲上繫著藍色的蝴蝶結，她美麗的灰色眼睛就跟柯林那雙憂鬱的眼睛一模一樣，黑色的睫毛讓瑪瑙灰的眼睛看起來比實際大兩倍。

「那是我媽媽，我不知道她為什麼會死掉。有時候我恨她就這樣死了。」柯林用不滿的語氣說。

「真是奇怪啊！」瑪莉說。

「如果她還活著，我想我就不會這樣一直生病。」他語帶抱怨地說：「我保證我會活下來，而且我爸爸也就不會討厭看到我了，我的背也會很強壯。把簾子再拉上吧。」

瑪莉照著他的話做，又坐回凳子上。

「她比你好看多了，不過她的眼睛跟你一樣，至少形狀和顏色都一樣。為什麼要給她的畫像蓋上簾子？」瑪莉說。

柯林不高興地動了動。

他說：「是我要他們這麼做的，有時候我不喜歡她這樣看著我。我生病難過時會覺得她笑得太燦爛了，而且她是我的，我不想讓別人看到她。」

他們沉默了一陣子，瑪莉接著繼續說。

「如果梅德洛太太發現我在這裡，她會怎麼樣？」她問。

「她會照我說的去做，我會告訴她，我要妳每天來這裡和我說話。我很高興妳來了。」柯林回答。

瑪莉說：「我也是，我會盡量過來，可是，」她猶豫著，「我每天還得去找花園的門。」

柯林說：「對啊，妳還可以告訴我找得怎麼樣了。」

柯林跟先前一樣躺在床上想了一會兒，才又說：「我覺得妳也應該是個祕密，我不會告訴他們的，除非他們自己發現。我可以把護士叫出去，說我想要自己一個人獨處。妳認識瑪莎嗎？」他說。

「認識，我跟她很熟，都是她在照顧我。」瑪莉說。

柯林朝著外面的走廊點頭。

「瑪莎就睡在另外一個房間裡。護士昨天晚上去住她妹妹家了，她不在時就會叫瑪莎來伺候我。瑪莎會告訴妳什麼時候過來這裡。」

瑪莉終於明白為什麼只要她一問到哭聲的事情，瑪莎就會露出不安的神情。

「瑪莎一直都知道你的事嗎？」她說。

「當然，她經常照顧我。護士喜歡離我遠遠的，這時候瑪莎就會過來。」

「我已經來很久了，」瑪莉說：「我是不是該走了？你的眼睛都快閉上了。」

「等我睡著了，妳再離開。」柯林害羞地說。

「閉上眼睛，」瑪莉將凳子拉近，說道：「我要學我的印度保母，我會輕輕拍著你的手，低聲唱歌給你聽。」

「這個我應該會喜歡。」柯林昏昏欲睡地說。

瑪莉為他感到難過，不希望他睡不著覺。她將身體靠在床邊，輕輕拍著他的手，用印度語低聲唱了首小曲。

「真好聽。」柯林更想睡了。瑪莉繼續著唱歌，輕拍他的手。她看到柯林的黑睫毛蓋在臉頰上，閉上了眼睛，沉沉睡去。

瑪莉輕輕地站起來，拿起蠟燭，悄聲離去。

第十四章

年輕的印度小王侯

隔天早上，高沼地隱沒在一片霧茫茫之中，雨水不斷傾盆而下。今天是無法出門了。瑪莎很忙，瑪莉沒有機會和她說話。到了下午，她把瑪莎叫來了兒童室。瑪莎帶著襪子過來，她有空檔時就會織襪子。

「汝怎麼啦？」兩人一坐下，瑪莎便問道：「汝看起來好像有話要說。」

「對，我已經知道那個哭聲是怎麼一回事了。」瑪莉說。

瑪莎手上的織襪掉到了膝蓋上，驚慌地注視著瑪莉。

「不會吧！」她大叫道：「不可以的！」

「我昨天晚上聽到哭聲，就爬起來找聲音的來源，那是柯林在哭，我看到他了。」瑪莉繼續說。

瑪莎嚇得臉都漲紅了。

她喊道：「啊！瑪莉小姐！汝不應該這麼做的——汝不應該這麼做的，汝這樣會給我招來麻煩的。我沒有跟汝說過他的事——汝會給我惹麻煩的，我會丟掉飯碗的，那媽媽要怎麼辦？」

「妳不會丟掉飯碗的，他很高興看到我。我們一直在聊天，他說很高興看到我。」瑪莉說。

「他這麼說嗎？」瑪莎叫道：「汝確定嗎？汝不知道他

生氣起來是什麼樣子。他是個大孩子了，卻還像小嬰兒那樣哭鬧，一不高興就放聲尖叫來嚇唬我們。他知道我們不敢不順從他。」

瑪莉說：「他看到我的時候並沒有生氣，我說我是不是該走了，他還叫我留下來。他問了我很多問題，我就坐在凳子上，跟他講了印度、知更鳥和花園的事。他不讓我走，還給我看他媽媽的畫像。我要走前還唱歌哄他睡覺呢。」

瑪莎驚奇地喘著氣。

「我真不敢相信！」瑪莎表示：「汝就像是進了虎穴一樣，如果是平常時的樣子，他一定會大發脾氣，把整屋子的人都吵醒。他是不讓陌生人看到他的。」

「他讓我看著他。我一直看著他，他也一直看著我，我們大眼瞪小眼！」瑪莉說。

「這該怎麼辦！」瑪莎激動地叫道：「要是被梅德洛太太知道了，她會說我破壞規矩，跟你透露口風，那我就得收拾行李回家了。」

「他不會跟梅德洛太太透露半句話的，這件事還沒有人知道，而且他說大家都得順他的意才可以。」瑪莉語氣堅定地說。

「是啊，這倒是真的，這個傷腦筋的囝兒！」瑪莎嘆口氣，用圍裙擦擦額頭。

「他說梅德洛太太一定要順他的意，他要我每天都去陪他聊天。他要是想找我，就會叫妳來跟我說。」

「我！」瑪莎說：「這樣會讓我丟掉飯碗的，一定會的！」

「妳照辦就不會了，大家都得聽他的。」瑪莉說道。

　　瑪莎睜大眼睛喊道：「汝的意思難道是說，他對汝很好？」

　　「我覺得他應該是很喜歡我。」瑪莉回答。

　　「妳一定是對他施了什麼妖術！」瑪莎下結論似地說，長長地吸了一口氣。

　　「妳是說魔法嗎？」瑪莉問道：「我在印度是聽說過魔法，不過我不會變魔術。我只是走進他的房間，看到他，我很驚訝，就站在那裡盯著他看。他也轉過身來盯著我看，還以為我是鬼，要不然就是在做夢。這我也有同感。我們兩個三更半夜碰在一塊兒，互不相識，這種感覺實在很奇怪，所以我們就開始互相問問題。我問他說，我是不是該走了，他就叫我不要走。」

　　「世界末日要到了！」瑪莎喘著氣說。

　　「他是怎麼了？」瑪莉問。

　　「沒有人知道他到底是怎麼了。他出生時，柯萊文先生的精神狀況出了問題，醫生都想把他送到精神療養院去呢。這是因為柯萊文夫人過世了，這我之前跟你說過了。柯萊文先生不喜歡看到這個囝兒。他一直吼著說，這個孩子也會變成駝子，最好死了算了。」瑪莎說。

　　「柯林是駝子？看起來不像呀。」瑪莉問道。

　　「他還沒變成駝子，不過他一出生就不對勁。」瑪莎說：「媽媽說，這屋子裡發生了太多不幸的事情，所以不論哪個囝兒在這裡出生，都會變得不對勁。他們很擔心柯林的背部會太脆弱，所以小心翼翼地照顧他，都讓他躺著，不讓他走路。有一次還給他戴上夾板，可是這樣讓他變得很煩躁，生了一場大病。後來一個名醫過來看他，叫人把夾板拿掉。

他態度禮貌、直言不諱地對另一個醫生說，我們給他吃太多藥了，而且不該讓他這麼為所欲為。」

「我覺得他被寵壞了。」瑪莉說。

「他是我見過最糟糕的囝兒了！」瑪莎說：「我得說，他老是在生病。有兩、三次，他咳嗽感冒得都快沒命，還有，他也得過急性關節風濕症和傷寒。啊，梅德洛太太都嚇壞了。他那時候很失常，梅德洛太太以為他聽不到，就跟護士說：『他這次是死定了，這樣對他自己、對大家何嘗不是好事。』接著她看了看少爺，少爺正睜大眼睛瞪著她看，意識跟她一樣清楚，然後說道：『給我水喝，閉上你的嘴巴。』」

「妳覺得他會死嗎？」瑪莉問道。

「媽媽說，一個囝兒如果不去呼吸新鮮空氣，啥都不做，就只躺著看圖畫書、吃藥，那是活不下去的。他很虛弱，別人要幫他弄出門，他覺得很討厭、很麻煩，而且他很容易著涼，總是說出門會讓他生病。」

瑪莉坐下來看著爐火。

「我在想，」她緩緩說道：「讓他去花園看看植物的生成，可能會對他有好處，至少這樣對我很好。」

「他發作得最嚴重的一次，是有人把他帶到噴泉邊的玫瑰花叢去，他在報紙上看過有人得了『玫瑰傷風』，他那時打了幾個噴嚏，就說自己也得了這種病。新來的園丁不知道這裡的規矩，就好奇地看了看他，柯林少爺一陣脾氣就上來，說園丁盯著他看是因為他要變成駝子了。那天他就哭得整晚都在發高燒。」

「他要是敢對我發火，我就不理他。」瑪莉說。

「他要找汝去，汝就得去，」瑪莎說：「汝最好一開始就要知道這一點。」

不久，鈴聲響了起來，瑪莎將針織物捲成一團。

「應該是護士要我去陪一下少爺，希望他沒有在鬧情緒。」她說。

瑪莎出去了大概十分鐘，然後一臉困惑地回來。

「好吧，汝讓他著魔了，」瑪莎說：「他現在竟然起床坐在沙發上看圖畫書。我在隔壁房間等著，他要護士六點再過來，護士一走，他就把我叫去，跟我說：『我要瑪莉‧雷諾克斯過來陪我聊天，記住，這件事不可以透露出去。』妳最好趕快去。」

瑪莉很開心地趕過去，因為她也很想看到柯林，雖然她更想看到的人是迪肯。

瑪莉走進柯林的房間，火爐裡燒著熊熊烈火。白天時，這間房間看起來很漂亮，有五顏六色的地毯和壁毯，牆上擺著圖片和書本，房間明亮又舒適，儘管天空灰濛濛的，還下著雨。柯林看起來就像一幅畫像，他裹著天鵝絨晨袍，坐在織錦大座墊上，雙頰紅通通的。

「進來，我整個早上都在想著妳的事情。」他說。

「我也是，」瑪莉回答：「你不知道瑪莎有多害怕，她說梅德洛太太會以為是她跟我透露你的事，她會被趕走的。」

柯林皺起眉頭。

「去叫她過來，她在隔壁的房間裡。」他說。

瑪莉便去把瑪莎找過來，可憐的瑪莎不住地顫抖，柯林還是皺著眉頭。

「妳是不是該做讓我開心的事啊？」他問道。

「是啊，少爺。」瑪莎結結巴巴地說，臉變得通紅。

「梅德洛是不是該做讓我開心的事啊？」

「每個人都是啊，少爺。」瑪莎說。

「這樣的話，如果我要妳把瑪莉小姐帶過來，就算梅德洛發現了，她憑什麼把妳解雇？」

「請不要讓她把我解雇，少爺。」瑪莎懇求道。

「她如果敢，我就先把她解雇。」柯萊文少爺很有威嚴地說：「我敢說她並不想丟掉這份工作。」

「謝謝您，少爺，」瑪莎向他屈膝敬禮，「我會盡我的本分的，少爺。」

「我就是要妳盡本分，」柯林又更嚴肅地說：「事情包在我身上，妳不用擔心。妳現在可以走了。」

當瑪莎把門關上時，柯林發現瑪莉一臉詫異地看著他。

「妳為什麼這樣看我？」他問瑪莉：「妳在想什麼？」

「我在想兩件事。」

「哪兩件事？坐下來告訴我。」

「第一件事就是，」瑪莉在大凳子上坐下，說道：「在印度時，我看過一個全身都是紅寶石、綠寶石和鑽石的小王侯，他跟臣民說話的樣子，就像你剛剛和瑪莎說話一樣。每個人都要立刻奉命行事，我猜要是沒有遵照命令，可能就會小命不保。」

「我很想聽這個王侯的事，」柯林說：「但是妳先告訴我第二件事是什麼。」

「我在想，你跟迪肯可真不一樣啊。」瑪莉說。

「迪肯是誰？他的名字真奇怪！」柯林說。

瑪莉覺得可以跟他講迪肯的事，她可以聊聊迪肯，只要不要提到祕密花園就好。她自己就很喜歡聽瑪莎講迪肯的事，還有，她也很想聊迪肯的事，這樣會讓她覺得自己跟迪肯更親近些。

「他是瑪莎的弟弟，今年十二歲。」瑪莉解釋道：「世上沒有人能像他那樣，他可以迷住狐狸、松鼠和小鳥，就像印度的弄蛇人能把蛇迷住一樣。他會用笛子吹出輕柔的旋律，動物就會圍過來聽。」

柯林身邊的桌子上有幾本大書，他忽然抓起其中一本。

「這裡面有弄蛇人的圖片，你過來看看。」他喊道。

這本書很漂亮，有華麗的彩色插圖，柯林翻到其中的一張插圖。

「這個他會嗎？」柯林急切地問。

「動物會聽他吹笛子，不過他說那不是魔法。」瑪莉解釋道：「只是因為他在高沼地待久了，知道動物的習性。他說他有時候都覺得自己就像小鳥或兔子，他特別喜歡動物。他會問知更鳥問題，他們好像會用啾啾的聲音互相溝通。」

柯林躺回座墊上，眼睛愈睜愈大，臉頰發燙。

「再跟我講他的事。」他說。

「他知道所有鳥蛋和鳥巢的位置，也知道狐狸、獾和水獺住在哪裡。」瑪莉繼續說：「不過他都不會跟人家講，他怕小孩子們會去找牠們的洞穴，嚇到牠們。他對高沼地的動植物都瞭如指掌。」

「他喜歡高沼地？」柯林問：「他怎麼會喜歡那種地方？光禿禿的，很枯燥的一大片地方。」

「高沼地是世上最漂亮的地方了，」瑪莉抗議道：「那裡長著很多可愛的花草，還有很多小動物在那裡忙著築巢，地上地下到處挖洞，互相啁啾、唱歌或是吱吱叫。大夥在地底下或是帚石楠間忙得不亦樂乎，那是牠們的世界。」

「妳怎麼會知道這些？」柯林用手肘撐著身子，轉身看著瑪莉。

「我沒有真的去過那裡。」瑪莉說，她突然回想起來，「我只有晚上坐車經過那裡一次，那時候我覺得很可怕。後來瑪莎跟我講到高沼地，迪肯也跟我提到那裡。聽迪肯講高沼地，會覺得自己好像身歷其境地看到了、聽到了，彷彿自己就站在陽光下的帚石楠間，荊豆聞起來有蜂蜜的味道，周圍滿是蜜蜂和蝴蝶在飛舞。」

「生病的人什麼也看不到。」柯林煩躁地說。他看起來像是聽到遠方傳來陌生的聲音，摸不透那是什麼聲音。

「你待在房間裡就什麼也看不到了。」瑪莉說。

「我不能去高沼地。」柯林用憤恨的語氣說。

瑪莉沉默了一會兒，然後放膽地開口。

「搞不好有一天你可以去。」

柯林吃驚地動了一下。

「去高沼地！怎麼可能？我會死掉的。」

「你怎麼知道？」瑪莉不喜歡聽柯林談到死，她並不同情他，她甚至覺得柯林是在拿死這件事來誇耀。

「哦，從我有記憶以來，就聽別人這麼說。」他生氣地回答：「他們老是低聲在談論這件事，以為我沒有聽到。他們也希望我死掉。」

瑪莉小姐一個拗勁起來，抿緊雙唇。

「他們如果希望我死掉，我就偏偏不要死。誰希望你死掉？」她說。

「那些傭人，當然還有柯萊文醫生，因為這麼一來他就可以繼承莊園，從窮人變成有錢人。他是不敢這麼說，但是只要我的身體狀況變差了，他的精神就特別好。我得傷寒時，他的臉就長胖了。還有，我想我爸爸也希望我死掉。」

「我才不相信。」瑪莉固執地說。

柯林又轉過身看著她。

「妳不相信？」他說。

接著他又躺回座墊上，動也不動，若有所思的樣子。兩人沉默了好一陣子，大概都在想一些小孩子通常不會去想的事情。

「我喜歡那個倫敦來的名醫，因為他叫人把那個鐵做的東西拿掉。」瑪莉終於開口說：「他有說你會死掉嗎？」

「沒有。」

「他說了什麼？」

「他沒有刻意放低聲量說話，」柯林回答：「他大概知道我討厭人家說悄悄話。我聽到他很大聲地說：『這個孩子自己想活下來，就可以活下來，盡量讓他開心吧。』他的口氣聽起來不是很好。」

「我跟你說，有一個人可能可以讓你開心。」瑪莉靈機一動地說道，她想實現醫生的囑咐。「我想迪肯可以讓你開心，他講的都是活生生的東西，不會滿口又是死又是病。他總是抬頭看天上的飛鳥，或是低頭看地上生長的植物。他的眼睛又圓又藍，常常睜得大大地四處瞧。他寬寬的嘴巴總是掛著笑容，臉頰紅紅的，像櫻桃一樣。」

瑪莉將凳子拉近沙發，一想到那張彎彎寬寬的嘴巴和那雙睜得大大的眼睛，她的表情就變得不一樣。

她說：「這樣吧，我們不要再講死的事了，我不喜歡。

我們來聊聊活著的東西。我們可以講講迪肯的事，然後再來看你的圖畫。」

這是瑪莉生平所說過最好的話了。聊迪肯的事，也就等於是聊高沼地的事，還有聊那個住著十四個人的農舍，他們每星期靠著十六個先令過活，家裡的孩子就像小野馬一樣，是被高沼地的草餵肥的。還有迪肯的媽媽、跳繩、陽光普照的高沼地，還有從黑土裡冒出來的淡綠色點點。

一切都顯得生氣盎然，瑪莉還是頭一次開口說了這麼多的話，柯林也是第一次這樣和別人聊天。兩人開始沒來由地笑，像孩子一樣嬉鬧。他們喧嘩大笑，像兩個正常健康的十歲小孩，而不是一個殘酷無情的小女孩，和一個覺得自己病得快死掉的男孩。

他們玩得太開心了，都忘了看圖畫，也忘了時間。班和知更鳥的事情讓他們開懷大笑，柯林坐了起來，忘了自己脆弱的背部。這時，他忽然想起一件事。

「妳知道嗎？我們都沒想到一件事，」他說：「我們是表兄妹呢。」

這可怪了，他們聊了那麼久，卻沒有想到這麼簡單的事，這讓他們笑得更大聲了，現在他們見了什麼都能笑。就在一片歡樂聲中，門被打開了，柯萊文醫生和梅德洛太太走了進來。

柯萊文醫生驚恐地跳了起來，梅德洛太太差點往後跌倒，因為柯萊文醫生不小心撞到了她。

「天啊！」可憐的梅德洛太太驚呼起來，眼珠子都快掉了出來，「這是怎麼回事？」

柯萊文醫生走向前說：「怎麼會這樣？是怎麼了？」

　　這時瑪莉又想起了那個印度小王侯。柯林不把醫生的驚慌和梅德洛太太的恐懼當一回事，他不為所動，彷彿走進來的是一隻老狗和老貓。

　　他說：「這是我的表妹，瑪莉·雷諾克斯，我叫她來和我聊天。我喜歡她。不管什麼時候，只要我叫她來，她就得來。」

　　柯萊文醫生帶著責備的神情轉向梅德洛太太。

　　她喘著氣說：「哦，先生，我不知道這是怎麼一回事。這裡沒有哪個僕人敢說出去，都交待他們要緊守口風的。」

　　「沒有人跟她講，是她自己聽到我在哭，就找到了我。我很高興她來找我。別搞錯了，梅德洛。」柯林說。

　　瑪莉看到柯萊文醫生的臉色不是很好看，不過顯然他不敢違抗他的病人。他坐在柯林的旁邊，幫他量了量脈搏。

　　「我擔心你會太亢奮了，那對你不好，孩子。」他說。

　　柯林回答：「她如果離開，我會更激動。」他的眼睛露出了威脅的光芒，「我已經好多了，都多虧了她。以後護士端茶過來時，瑪莉的茶也一起端過來，我們要一起用茶。」

　　柯萊文醫生和梅德洛太太不安地看著對方，不知所措。

　　「他看起來的確是比較好了，先生。」梅德洛太太壯著膽子說：「可是，再仔細想想，今天早上瑪莉小姐還沒有過來之前，他的氣色更好。」

　　柯林說：「她昨天晚上就來過這裡，陪了我很久，還唱了印度歌哄我睡覺。早上醒來的時候，我就覺得好多了，還想吃早餐。我現在想喝茶。梅德洛，去叫護士準備。」

　　柯萊文醫生沒有待太久。護士進來時，柯萊文醫生和她說了幾分鐘的話，又告誡了柯林一番，要他不可以說太多話，

不可以忘記自己是個病人，不可以忘記自己很容易疲倦。瑪莉覺得柯林似乎得記住許多討厭的事情。

柯林看起來很煩躁，他用長著黑睫毛的怪眼睛盯著柯萊文醫生看。

「我想忘了這些，」柯林終於開口：「瑪莉讓我都忘了這些事，所以我才要她過來。」

柯萊文醫生走出房間時，臉色不是很好看，他困惑地瞥了一下坐在大凳子上的小女孩。柯萊文醫生剛剛進房間時，瑪莉又變成拘謹沉默的小孩，他看不出來她哪裡吸引人了。然而，柯林現在看起來的確開朗了許多。柯萊文醫生來到走廊，重重地嘆了一口氣。

「他們一天到晚要我吃東西，我又不想吃。」柯林說。護士把茶送了上來，擱在沙發旁的桌子上。「現在，只要妳吃，我就吃，那些鬆餅看起來又熱又好吃。再跟我講講印度小王侯的事吧。」

第十五章

築巢

又下了一個星期的雨之後，藍色的穹蒼又高掛天空，灑下火辣的陽光。這段期間，瑪莉雖然無法去祕密花園找迪肯，但還是過得很充實。這星期並不漫長，她每天都去柯林的房間消磨好幾個小時，聊聊印度王侯、花園、迪肯、高沼地的農舍。

他們一起看了精彩的書本和圖片，有時候還會讀故事給彼此聽。當柯林顯得興味十足的時候，瑪莉覺得他根本不像個病人，只是臉色比較蒼白，而且老是坐在沙發上。

「妳真是調皮，隨便聽到什麼聲音，就從床上爬起來亂闖，」梅德洛太太有一回這麼說：「不過這也不是什麼壞事。他沒有大哭大鬧，你們倒成了好朋友。護士原本是受夠了他，都想辭職了，現在她倒是改口說，只要值班時有你在，她就不介意留下來。」梅德洛太太笑了笑。

瑪莉在跟柯林說話時，會特別小心避免提到祕密花園。她想跟柯林探聽，不過她覺得不要單刀直入地問比較好。首先，她已經開始喜歡和柯林在一起了，她想知道柯林是不是那種可以守住祕密的男孩。柯林和迪肯很不一樣，不過他顯然會對一座無人知曉的花園感興趣。瑪莉覺得應該可以信得過柯林，不過他們剛認識不久，還不能確定。

　　她想知道的第二件事是：如果柯林真的能信得過，那她能偷偷帶他去花園而不被發現嗎？那位名醫說，柯林需要呼吸新鮮空氣，柯林也說他不介意去祕密花園呼吸新鮮空氣。說不定他只要呼吸新鮮空氣，認識迪肯和知更鳥，看看生物的成長，就不會滿腦子想著死亡。

　　最近，瑪莉有時候會看看鏡子裡的自己，覺得和剛從印度過來的樣子很不一樣。她現在看起來可愛多了，連瑪莎也覺得她不一樣了。

　　「高沼地的空氣帶給了汝好處，」瑪莎這麼說過：「汝看起來不會那麼又黃又瘦了，連頭髮也沒麼塌了，比較蓬鬆，也比較多。」

　　瑪莉說：「我的頭髮就跟我一樣，愈來愈健壯了，我確定我的頭髮變多了。」

　　「的確是這樣啊。」瑪莎撩了一下瑪莉臉上的頭髮，「汝沒那麼醜了，臉色也變紅潤了。」

　　花園和新鮮的空氣要是對瑪莉有好處，那應該也會對柯林有幫助。可是如果柯林討厭被別人盯著看，那他可能不會想見到迪肯。

　　「為什麼人家看到你，你會生氣？」有一天瑪莉問他。

　　柯林回答：「我一直都很討厭人家看我，從小就這樣。以前他們會帶我去海邊，我通常躺在輪椅裡，大家就會盯著我看。女士們會停下來和我的護士聊天，然後竊竊私語，我知道她們在說我活不久了。有些女士還會拍拍我的臉頰說：『可憐的孩子！』有一回，有位女士要拍我，我大聲尖叫，還咬了她的手，她嚇得跑掉了。」

　　「她大概覺得你像條瘋狗。」瑪莉一點也不欣賞地說。

「我才不在乎她怎麼想！」柯林皺著眉頭說。

「那我進來你的房間，你怎麼沒有大叫然後咬我？」瑪莉說，緩緩露出笑容。

柯林說：「我以為妳是鬼，要不然就是我在做夢，鬼或是夢裡的東西又不能咬，而且就算我大叫，也嚇不跑。」

「你會討厭被其他的男孩看到嗎？」瑪莉不確定地問。

柯林躺回座墊上，停下來思索著。

「只有一個男孩，」他說得很慢，彷彿在仔細斟酌每一個字，「只有一個男孩，我應該不會介意讓他看到我，就是那個知道狐狸住在哪裡的男孩迪肯。」

「你一定不會介意讓他看到你的。」瑪莉說。

「小鳥和其他的動物都不介意讓迪肯看，」柯林說道，繼續思索著：「所以我應該也不會介意吧，他是個動物術士，而我就是隻小動物。」

說著他就笑了出來，瑪莉也跟著笑。兩人最後想到男孩動物躲在自己的洞穴裡，那種感覺真有趣，便笑得樂不可支。

瑪莉覺得以後就不用再擔心迪肯的事了。

隔天早晨，天空也是一片蔚藍，瑪莉早早就起床。傾斜的陽光從百葉窗外灑進來，令人心曠神怡，瑪莉從床上跳下來，跑到窗邊拉起百葉窗，打開窗子，一陣新鮮的芳香向她襲來。高沼地是藍色的，像被施了魔法般。四處都有輕柔的鳴叫聲，鳥兒們彷彿在為音樂會做排演。瑪莉把手伸出窗外，攤在陽光下。

她說：「好暖和，暖烘烘的！這樣那些綠色的點點就會往上冒，一直往上生長。球莖和根莖也會掙扎著要從地底下探出來。」

　　瑪莉跪下來，將身子盡量往外面伸，大口呼吸，嗅著空氣，然後笑了出來，因為她想到迪肯的媽媽說，迪肯的鼻子像兔鼻子一樣顫動。

　　她說：「現在一定還很早，小小的雲朵都是粉紅色的，沒見過這樣的天空。大家都還沒起床，連馬童的聲音也沒有聽到。」這時瑪莉突然想到什麼，立刻站了起來。

　　「等不及了！我要去看花園！」

　　瑪莉已經學會自己穿衣服，五分鐘後她就換好了衣服。有一扇小邊門的門栓她拉得動，她就從那裡出去，穿著襪子飛奔下樓，來到大廳才穿上鞋子。

　　她解開鎖鏈，拉開門閂，開門後跳下台階，來到草坪上。草地一片綠色，陽光灑在她身上，溫暖芬芳的風輕拂著她，所有的灌木和樹叢都傳出了鳴囀的歌聲。

　　瑪莉興奮地握緊雙手，望著天空，天空交織著藍色、粉紅色、淺藍灰色、白色，春光明媚。瑪莉忍不住想大聲吹口哨唱歌，她知道畫眉、知更鳥和雲雀都會情不自禁地吹口哨唱歌。接著她跑過灌木叢和小徑直奔祕密花園。

　　她說：「這裡變得都不一樣了，草比較綠了，到處都有東西冒出來，葉子伸展開來，綠芽也冒了出來。今天下午迪肯一定會過來的。」

　　這場溫暖的雨下了很久，為矮牆旁走道邊的花壇帶來了神奇的變化。樹叢的根部有東西在發芽，番紅花的莖四處可見紫紅色和黃色的斑點。半年前，瑪莉還不知道世界甦醒是什麼樣子的，現在這一刻她什麼也沒錯過。

瑪莉來到被常春藤掩蓋住的門前，一個奇怪的聲響嚇了她一跳。那是烏鴉在叫，聲音從牆頂上那頭傳過來，她往上看，那裡棲息著一隻羽毛光滑的深藍色大烏鴉，正機警地俯視著她。瑪莉沒這麼近地看過烏鴉，有點緊張，不過下一秒烏鴉就展開翅膀，穿過花園飛走了。

　　瑪莉希望烏鴉不會停在花園裡，她把門打開，看看牠是否在裡面。等她走進花園，發現烏鴉停在一棵矮小的蘋果樹上，好像有意待下來。樹下躺著另一隻紅色的小動物，尾巴毛茸茸的，牠們都盯著一頭紅褐色頭髮的迪肯。迪肯正彎著身子，跪在草地上認真地工作。

　　瑪莉朝迪肯飛奔過去。

　　「哦，迪肯！迪肯！」瑪莉大叫道：「你怎麼這麼早就來了！你怎麼做到的！太陽才剛起床啊！」

　　迪肯站起身來，容光煥發地笑著，他的頭髮蓬亂，湛藍的眼睛像是一小片天空。

　　他說：「啊！我比太陽還貪早，在床上待不住！全世界一早就又活過來了，所有的生物都在忙碌著，嗡嗡叫、又搔又抓、吹口哨、築巢、吐露芬芳，在床上是躺不住的。太陽一升起來，整個高沼地都樂瘋了，我站在帚石楠叢上，瘋了一樣地跑，又是叫喊、又是唱歌，然後就直接到這裡來了。我非來不可，花園在等著我呢！」

　　瑪莉將手放在胸前喘著氣，就像自己也是剛奔跑過一樣。

　　「哦，迪肯！迪肯！我太高興了，都快喘不過氣來了！」她說。

　　那隻尾巴毛茸茸的小動物看到迪肯跟陌生人講話，便從樹下起身走向迪肯，而剛才那隻嘎嘎叫的白嘴鴉，也從枝頭上飛下來，悄悄地停在迪肯的肩膀上。

「這是隻小狐狸，牠叫隊長。」迪肯說著，撓了撓這隻紅色小動物的頭，「這隻叫煤灰，煤灰剛剛跟著我一起穿越高沼地。隊長跑起來就像有獵狗在追趕似那麼快。牠們和我心有靈犀。」

這兩隻動物看起來一起也不害怕瑪莉，迪肯四處走動時，煤灰就停在他肩膀上，隊長也亦步亦趨地跟在旁邊。

迪肯說：「嘿！妳看這些東西都長出來了，還有這裡和這裡。啊！妳看這些！」

迪肯跪了下去，瑪莉也跪在一旁，他們發現了一整叢開滿紫色、橙色和金色的番紅花。瑪莉將臉湊過去，不斷地親吻著花朵。

「我們就不會這樣親吻人類了。」瑪莉抬起頭來說：「花跟人很不一樣。」

迪肯困惑地微笑著。

他說：「有時候我在高沼地玩了一整天，回家時看到陽光下的媽媽心滿意足地站在門口，我就會這樣親媽媽。」

他們在花園四處來來回回，找到了很多驚奇的東西，不得不刻意壓低聲說話。迪肯指著玫瑰樹枝上開出的葉苞給瑪莉看，那些樹枝原本看似已經枯死了。

迪肯又指著無數個從地上冒出來的新綠色點點給瑪莉看，他們熱切地將小鼻子貼近地面，嗅著泥土散發出的春天溫暖氣息。他們邊挖土、邊除草，雀躍地低聲笑著。瑪莉的頭髮變得和迪肯的頭髮一樣亂，臉頰也一樣紅。

這天早晨，祕密花園裡的每一吋土地都洋溢著歡樂的氣氛，而且還發生了一件更令人開心的事情。有個東西飛快地越過牆，穿過樹林，來到枝葉茂密的角落。那是一隻飛行的紅胸小鳥，形成了一道小閃光，鳥喙上還銜著東西。迪肯靜止不動，把手搭在瑪莉的肩膀上，就好像他們突然發現自己在教堂裡失聲大笑一樣。

迪肯用約克郡方言低聲說：「我們不要動，要屏住呼吸。我上次看到牠正在求偶。那是班的知更鳥，牠現在正在築巢，只要不要嚇到牠，牠就會留在這裡。」

他們輕輕地坐在草地上，一動也不動。

迪肯說：「不要讓牠覺得我們太靠近，牠要是覺得我們妨礙到牠，就會一走了之。等牠築完巢，就會變得不一樣了。牠現在正在整理自己的家，比較害羞，警戒心比較重，也沒有時間找朋友串門子。我們要安靜一點，看能不能裝成小草、樹木或是灌木，等牠習慣看到我們，我會吹個口哨，讓牠知道我們不會妨礙到牠。」

瑪莉不知道自己是否能像迪肯那樣，把自己變成小草、樹木或是灌木。不過迪肯說話的樣子，好是這是再普通、再自然不過的事了。瑪莉想，這對迪肯來說一定很簡單，而且她仔細觀察了迪肯好一會兒，看他的身體會不會真的變成綠色，長出枝葉來。不過迪肯只是文風不動地坐著，而且說話的聲音小聲到好像聽不到，但是瑪莉聽得一清二楚。

「築巢是春天的事，」他說：「我敢保證，從開天闢地以來，每年都是這樣子。動物有牠們想事情和做事情的方式，我們不應該插手去管。如果妳太好奇了，尤其是在春天，你會更容易失去動物朋友。」

「我們聊牠的事，我就會忍不住想看牠。」瑪莉盡量輕聲說話：「我們來聊別的，我有事情要跟你說。」

「牠會比較喜歡我們聊點別的，」迪肯說：「汝要跟我說什麼呢？」

「嗯，你知道柯林嗎？」瑪莉低聲地說。

迪肯轉過頭看著瑪莉。

「汝知道他的什麼事嗎？」他問道。

「我看到他了。這個星期我每天都去跟他聊天，是他要我去找他的。他說我讓他忘記了自己有病、快要死了。」瑪莉說。

迪肯鬆了口氣，圓臉上沒有了驚訝的表情。

他大叫道：「真高興聽到這個，太好了，我放心多了。他們叫我不要講，可是我不喜歡隱瞞。」

「你也不喜歡隱瞞花園的事嗎？」瑪莉說。

「我永遠也不會把這個祕密說出去，我跟媽媽說：『媽媽，我要守個祕密，那不是壞事，汝知道的。那個祕密跟把鳥巢藏起來差不多，汝應該不會介意吧？』」迪肯回答。

瑪莉很喜歡聽迪肯媽媽的事。

「她怎麼說？」瑪莉問道，一點也不擔心。

迪肯溫和地咧嘴笑。

「她的回答就跟她的人一樣，她摸了摸我的頭，笑著說：『囝兒，汝高興藏什麼祕密都可以，我已經認識汝十二年了。』」迪肯回答道。

「你是怎麼知道柯林的？」瑪莉問道。

「大家都知道柯萊文主人的小孩長大以後可能會變成殘廢，也都知道他不喜歡別人講少爺的事。大家都替柯萊文主人感到難過，柯萊文夫人生前又年輕又漂亮，大家都很喜歡她。梅德洛太太每次去兌特村都會順道來我家找媽媽聊天，她不在意有囝兒在場，因為她知道我們家的囝兒都可以信任。汝又是怎麼發現柯林少爺的？瑪莎上次回家時很煩惱，她說汝聽到了柯林少爺的哭聲，就跟她打聽，讓她都結巴了。」

瑪莉跟迪肯講了那晚的經過，說她半夜如何被呼嘯的風聲吵醒，接著聽到遠處隱約傳來發牢騷的聲音，她便拿著蠟燭沿著黑暗的走廊走，最後打開那間燈光暗淡的房間門，看到角落有張四柱的雕刻床。瑪莉描述了那張象牙白的小臉，還有那雙長著黑睫毛的奇特眼睛，迪肯這時搖了搖頭。

「那跟他媽媽的眼睛很像，只是他媽媽的眼睛總是在笑。」迪肯說：「他們說，柯林少爺醒著的時候，柯萊文先生沒法忍受看到他的眼睛，因為跟他媽媽太像了，可是在他的臉上看起來卻顯得很悲哀。」

「你覺得他不想活嗎？」瑪莉低聲問。

「我不覺得，他只是但願沒有被生下來吧。媽媽說，對囝兒來說，這是最悲哀的事了，沒人要的囝兒是長不好的。柯萊文主人可以花錢買任何東西給可憐的柯林少爺，卻想忘掉柯林的存在，因為他害怕哪天會看到柯林少爺也變成駝子。」

瑪莉說：「柯林也很怕自己會駝背，所以都不肯坐起來，他說他一直在想，哪天他的背上要是發現腫塊了，他一定會發狂大叫到死。」

「啊！他不應該躺在那裡想著這些事情。小孩子一天到晚想這種事，是長不好的。」迪肯說。

狐狸躺在迪肯旁邊的草地上，不時仰頭望望迪肯，要迪肯輕輕拍拍牠。迪肯彎下身，溫柔地撫弄狐狸的頸部。他沉思了一會，然後抬起頭來環顧花園。

他說：「我們第一次進來這裡的時候，看起來灰灰的一片。汝現在看看四周，是不是變得不一樣了。」

瑪莉看看四周，微微屏住了呼吸。

「怎麼會這樣！」她叫道：「灰色的牆變得不一樣了，好像籠罩了綠色的霧氣，就像綠色的薄紗。」

迪肯說：「是啊，而且會愈來愈綠，到最後灰色會都不見了。汝猜得出來我在想什麼嗎？」

「我猜一定是很好的事，」瑪莉熱切地說：「而且跟柯林有關。」

「我在想，他要是能到這裡來，就不會在那裡等著看背上長出腫塊來了。他會看著玫瑰叢的花苞迸出來，這樣可能會讓他變得健康些。」迪肯解釋道：「不知道我們能不能讓他願意坐上輪椅到這裡來。」

「我也這麼想過，每次跟他說話時都會想到這件事。」瑪莉說：「只是不知道他能不能守住祕密。不知道我們能不能偷偷把他帶到這裡來，不讓人發現，也許你可以幫忙推椅子。醫生說他要呼吸新鮮的空氣，如果柯林想要我們帶他出來，沒有人敢違背他。他不會為了別人出門，可是如果他願意跟我們出來，可能也是大家所樂見的。他可以命令園丁都離開，這樣就不會發現了。」

迪肯一邊撓隊長的背，一邊仔細地思索著。

「我敢保證這樣對他一定有好處的，」他說：「我們不用去想他是不是希望自己沒有被生出來。我們只是兩個看著花園生長的囝兒，現在再多加他一個。兩個男生、一個女孩，一起觀察著春天的花花草草，保證這比醫生的治療還有效。」

「他老是在房間裡躺著，擔心自己會駝背，所以變得很奇怪。」瑪莉說：「他從書本裡面學到很多東西，對書本以外的事情就一無所知。他說他病得很重，所以對什麼都漠不關心，而且他討厭到戶外去，也討厭花園和園丁。不過他很喜歡聽我講這個花園，因為它是個祕密。我不敢跟他講太多，但他說他想看這個花園。」

「我們一定要找一天把他帶到這裡來，我可以幫他推椅子。」迪肯說：「汝有沒有注意到，我們坐在這裡的時候，知更鳥跟牠的伴侶都在很認真地在忙碌著？汝看牠停在那根樹枝上，正在思考著要把嘴裡的小樹枝放在哪裡。」

迪肯低聲吹起口哨，知更鳥轉過頭來，好奇地看著他，嘴裡還銜著小樹枝。迪肯像班那樣和知更鳥說話，但是用著友善的忠告語氣。

「汝把樹枝放哪兒都可以，汝還沒從殼裡出來之前就知道怎麼築巢了。繼續工作吧，小伙子，時間寶貴哦。」他說。

「哦！我真喜歡聽你跟牠說話！」瑪莉說，一邊愉快地笑著，「班會罵牠、會嘲笑牠，但是牠還是在班的面前跳來跳去，好像每個字都聽得懂似的，牠樂在其中。班說牠很自負，寧可被人家丟石頭，也好過被冷落。」

迪肯也笑了起來，繼續說。

「汝知道我們不會打擾汝的，」他對知更鳥說：「我們自己也像是野生動物，我們也在築巢，願上帝保佑汝。汝要幫我們保守祕密喔。」

知更鳥的嘴裡銜著東西，沒有回答，不過當牠銜著小樹枝飛到花園裡屬於牠的角落時，瑪莉知道，知更鳥黑露水般明亮的眼睛正在說，牠決不會把他們的祕密洩漏出去。

第十六章

「我不要！」瑪莉說

那天早上，他們找到很多事情做，瑪莉回到屋子已經有點晚了，然後又匆匆忙忙想趕回花園裡工作，到最後一刻才想到了柯林。

「跟柯林說，我還不能過去找他，」瑪莉對瑪莎說：「花園裡很忙。」

瑪莎的神情顯得很害怕。

「啊！瑪莉小姐，」她說：「我要是這麼跟他說，他一定會耍脾氣的。」

但是瑪莉並不像其他人那樣怕柯林，而且她可不是個會自我犧牲的人。

她回答：「我不能再待下去了，迪肯在等我。」說完便跑掉。

那天下午比早上還來得愉快、忙碌。花園裡的雜草差不多都清理好了8，大部分的玫瑰和樹木也都修剪好或鬆過土了。迪肯帶來了自己的鏟子，還教瑪莉如何使用她的工具。這個可愛而荒蕪的地方雖然不太可能變成「園丁的花園」，但在春末之前這裡會長出很多植物。

「這上面會長出蘋果花和櫻花，牆邊的桃樹和李樹會開

461

花，草地上也會開滿花。」迪肯說道，一邊專心地忙著。

小狐狸和白嘴鴉跟他們一樣開心忙碌，知更鳥和伴侶飛來飛去，像一道道小小的電光。有時白嘴鴉會拍拍黑色翅膀，飛到庭園樹梢上，每次又會飛回來停在迪肯身邊叫個幾聲，好像在跟迪肯講自己的冒險故事，迪肯也會像跟知更鳥講話一樣地和牠說話。有一次迪肯忙得沒能馬上回答牠，煤灰就飛到他肩上用大嘴巴輕輕拉他耳朵。

當瑪莉想稍微休息一下時，迪肯就跟她一起坐在樹下。有一次他從口袋裡拿出笛子，吹起輕柔奇怪的小曲，就有兩隻松鼠出現在牆上看，聽他吹笛子。

「汝變得比以前更強壯了，」迪肯看著瑪莉掘土，說道：「和以前不一樣了，真的。」

瑪莉因為運動較多，心情愉快，看起來特別容光煥發。

她興奮地說：「我一天天長胖了，梅德洛太太說要幫我買大一點的衣服了。瑪莎說我的頭髮變多了，不像以前那樣又塌又稀疏。」

他們離開花園時，太陽已經快下山，樹下灑著金色的斜暉。

「明天會是好天氣，太陽一出來，我就會開始工作。」迪肯說。

「我也是。」瑪莉說。

瑪莉用最快的速度跑回屋內，迫不及待地想跟柯林說迪肯的小狐狸和白嘴鴉，還有春天所帶來的變化，柯林會喜歡聽這些的。可是當她一打開門，就看到瑪莎一臉愁容地站在那裡等她，氣氛不是很好。

她問道：「怎麼了？妳跟柯林說我不能去看他，他怎麼說？」

瑪莎說：「哎！但願汝有去看他，他又大發脾氣了，我們整個下午都在忙著安撫他。他就一直盯著時鐘看。」

瑪莉緊抿雙唇。她和柯林一樣，一向不會為別人著想，她不明白這個壞脾氣的男生憑什麼干涉她做自己喜歡做的事。她無法體諒那些生病又神經質的人的可憐之處，也不同情那些不知道自己其實可以控制脾氣、以免讓別人心神不寧的人。以前在印度，她頭痛的時候，就想辦法也要別人跟著頭痛或是哪裡也不舒服了，她覺得這是很合情合理的。當然，現在她就會覺得柯林這樣是很不對的。

瑪莉走進柯林的房間，柯林並沒有坐在沙發上。他平躺在床上，沒有轉過頭來看她。這是很不妙的開場，瑪莉侷促地朝著柯林走過去。

「你為什麼不起來？」瑪莉問道。

「我今天早上有起來，我以為妳會來。」柯林回答時並沒有看瑪莉，「我下午叫他們把我抬回床上。我的背在痛，頭也在痛，覺得很累。妳為什麼沒有來？」

「我跟迪肯在花園裡忙。」瑪莉說。

柯林皺起眉頭，放下了架子，看著瑪莉。

「如果妳不來跟我聊天，而是跟那個男生在一起的話，我就不要讓他到這裡來。」他說。

瑪莉聽了一陣脾氣上來。她不動聲色地生著悶氣，她已經不管三七二十一了，天塌下來了也沒關係。

「你要是把迪肯趕走，我就再也不會進到這個房間來。」瑪莉回嘴道。

「我要妳來，妳就得來。」柯林說。

「休想！」瑪莉說。

「妳一定得來，他們會把妳拖進來的。」柯林說。

「那就讓他們拖吧，小王侯先生！」瑪莉兇暴地說：「是可以把我拖進來，但是沒有辦法叫我開口說話。我會坐在這裡把嘴巴閉得緊緊的，什麼也不告訴你。我甚至不會看你，只盯著地板看！」

他們互相瞪著對方的樣子真是可愛。如果他們是在街上遊蕩的小混混，料想早就撲向對方扭打成一團了。但現在的情況是，他們跳過扭打，直接進入扭打後互相叫罵的階段。

「妳這個自私鬼！」柯林叫道。

「那你呢？」瑪莉說：「自私的人都會說別人自私，自私的人不讓別人去做他想做的事。你比我還自私，你是我見過最自私的男生。」

「才不是呢！」柯林憤怒地說：「我哪像妳的好迪肯那麼自私！他明知道我只有自己一個人，卻把妳留在那邊玩泥土。他這樣就是很自私！」

瑪莉的眼裡閃爍著火光。

她說：「他比全世界的任何男生都要好！他——他就像是天使！」這句話聽起來有點蠢，不過瑪莉不在乎。

「一個好天使！」柯林殘酷地譏笑說：「他只不過是高沼地農舍裡的一個平凡男孩！」

瑪莉反駁道：「他好過一個平庸的印度王侯！好上一千倍！」

瑪莉因為比較強壯，所以已經開始占上風。事實上，柯林還沒有遇過勢均力敵的對手，總體來說這對他是有好處的，雖然他們倆都沒有意識到這一點。

　　他將頭轉向枕頭，閉上眼睛，眼裡擠出一大顆淚珠，順著臉頰滑下來。他開始為自己感到傷心難過，不是為了別人。

　　「我才不像妳那麼自私，我是個病人，而且我確定我的背上已經開始長出腫塊了，我快要死了。」他說。

　　「你才不會死！」瑪莉一點也不同情地回答。

　　柯林憤怒地睜大眼睛，因為沒有人這樣說過他，他感到很生氣，卻又有一絲絲的高興。

　　他叫道：「我不會死？我會死的，妳明知道我會死的！大家都這麼說。」

　　「我才不信！」瑪莉酸言酸語地說：「你這樣說只是為了

讓別人覺得對不起你，你根本是覺得自己這樣很了不起，但我才不信！如果你是個好小孩，可能還真的是怎樣了，但是你太討人厭了！」

柯林顧不得虛弱的背部，氣得在床上坐直了起來。

「出去！」他大叫起來，抓起枕頭扔向瑪莉。他不夠強壯，所以枕頭丟得不夠遠，只落在她的腳邊，可瑪莉的臉像胡桃鉗一樣皺得緊緊的。

「我要走了，我以後再也不過來了！」她說。

瑪莉向門口走去，快到門口時又轉過頭來。

她說：「我本來想告訴你很多好玩的事，迪肯把他的狐狸還有白嘴鴉帶來了，我本來想跟你講這些的。以後我什麼也不跟你說了！」

她走出房間，將身後的門關上，這時她嚇了一跳，因為她看到護士好像站在那裡偷聽，而且居然還在笑。

這個年輕漂亮的護士長得很高，她不配當個合格的護士，因為她受不了自己的病人，老找藉口把柯林丟給瑪莎或是其他人去應付。瑪莉一點也不喜歡她，所以只是站在門前看著護士用手帕捂著嘴巴吃吃地笑。

「妳在笑什麼？」她問護士。

護士說：「我在笑你們兩個小傢伙啊，對於一個體弱多病、嬌生慣養的小子，碰到了跟他一樣被寵壞的對手，真是再好不過的事了。」說完，她又用手帕捂著嘴巴笑，「他要是有個潑辣的姊妹來跟他打架，那他就有救了。」

「他會死掉嗎？」

「我不知道，這我不管，」護士說：「他會生病，有一半的原因是因為歇斯底里和壞脾氣。」

「什麼是歇斯底里？」瑪莉問道。

「像他這樣發完脾氣以後，妳就會見識到了。總之，妳已經給他歇斯底里的理由了，我可真高興。」

瑪莉回到房間，完全沒有從花園回來時的好心情了，她既煩躁又失望，但一點也不為柯林感到難過。她本來想告訴他很多事情，還準備下決心看看要不要跟他講那個大祕密。她本來覺得可以說的，不過她現在徹底改變主意了。她永遠也不要告訴柯林這個祕密，他可以一直待在房間裡，不要出去呼吸新鮮空氣，就這樣死掉算了，他想怎樣就怎樣！算他活該！

瑪莉覺得太討厭、太生氣了，甚至都快忘了迪肯，忘了牆上攀爬的綠色薄紗，忘了高沼地吹來的輕柔的風。

瑪莎正在等瑪莉，瑪莎的憂愁神情暫時變得好奇起來了。桌上放著一個蓋子打開的木盒子，裡面放滿了整齊的包裹。

瑪莎說：「這是柯萊文先生寄給妳，裡面好像是圖畫書。」

瑪莉想起那天去柯萊文先生的房間時，他問她想要什麼，「妳有沒有想要什麼東西，洋娃娃、玩具或書？」瑪莉打開包裹，心想柯萊文先生會不會是送她洋娃娃，如果是洋娃娃，那她要洋娃娃做什麼呢？不過，柯萊文先生不是送她洋娃娃。

包裹裡有幾本漂亮的書籍，就像柯林的書一樣，其中有兩本是在講花園的，裡面都是圖片。另外還有兩、三個遊戲組合，和一個漂亮的小文具盒，上面印著金色的花押字，盒內有一支金色的鋼筆和一個墨水瓶。

每樣東西都很精美，喜悅逐漸擠走了她心中的怒氣。她完全沒有想到柯萊文先生會記得她，她那顆冷酷的小小心靈被溫暖了起來。

她說：「我的字可以寫得比印刷體好看，我要用這隻鋼筆先寫信給柯萊文先生，告訴他我很感激他。」

　　她跟柯林如果是好朋友的話，她會立刻跑去把禮物拿給他看。兩人可以一起看圖片、閱讀園藝書，應該還會一起玩遊戲。柯林會玩得很開心，就不會再想著自己快死了，也不會把手放在脊椎上，看是不是有腫塊長出來了。柯林這個動作實在讓瑪莉很受不了，她會覺得既不舒服又害怕，因為柯林總是一副怕得要死的樣子。他說要是哪天摸到了小腫塊，他就知道自己要開始變成駝子了。

　　他聽過梅德洛太太跟護士說的悄悄話，讓他有了這樣的想法。他一直偷偷想著這事，這樣的想法就在他心裡根深柢固了。梅德洛太太說，柯萊文先生的背部就是在小時候開始彎曲的。柯林只跟瑪莉一人透露過，說自己之所以發脾氣，是源自於深藏的歇斯底里的恐懼感。聽到柯林這麼說，瑪莉很替他感到難過。

　　「他只要覺得焦躁或疲倦，就會開始這麼想，」瑪莉自言自語地說：「他今天脾氣很不好，搞不好是他整個下午都在想這件事。」

　　瑪莉靜靜地站著，看著地毯沉思著。

　　「我說過我再也不會回去找他了，」她皺起眉頭猶豫著，「不過，說不定，我明天早上會去看他，如果他想的話。搞不好他還會拿枕頭丟我，但是我想──我還是會去的。」

第十七章

大發脾氣

今天一大早就起床，在花園裡忙著工作，瑪莉覺得又累又睏。瑪莎把晚餐送上來，她一下子就吃光了，高興地上床睡覺了。她躺在枕頭上喃喃自語：

「明天吃早餐之前，我會去和迪肯一起做事，之後——我想——我會去看他。」

半夜，瑪莉被一個可怕的聲音吵醒，她立刻從床上跳下來，那是什麼——是什麼聲音？下一刻她就明白了。好幾個房間的門被打開又關上，走廊裡傳來匆忙的腳步聲，有人又哭又叫，聲音很恐怖。

她說：「是柯林，他又發作了，就是護士所說的歇斯底里。聽起來好恐怖！」

瑪莉聽著嗚咽的叫聲，終於瞭解為什麼大家會那麼害怕，他們寧可讓柯林為所欲為，也不願聽到這個聲音。瑪莉用手摀住耳朵，覺得很難受，不停地顫抖。

「我不知道該怎麼辦，我不知道該怎麼辦，」瑪莉不斷地說：「我受不了了。」

瑪莉想，如果她敢去找柯林，他會不會就不哭了，不過她又回想起柯林把她趕出房間的樣子。她想，柯林要是看到她，說不定會發作得更厲害。

她用手緊緊摀住耳朵，可是還是會聽到那可怕的聲音。她太討厭那聲音了，覺得自己快要發脾氣了，她也想嚇嚇柯林，就像他現在嚇她那樣。除了她自己，她才不忍受別人的壞脾氣。她把雙手從耳朵上放下來，跳著跺腳。

「他應該停下來了！應該有人去叫他停下來！應該有人去打他！」她大叫起來。

她聽到走廊上有人跑動的聲音，她的房門被打開，護士走了進來。她現在已經笑不出來了，臉色看起來很蒼白。

「他又變得歇斯底里了，」護士匆促地說：「他會傷害自己的。沒有人拿他有辦法，妳可以去試試看，好孩子，他很喜歡妳的。」

「今天早上是他把我趕出房間的。」瑪莉激動地跺著腳。

護士看到瑪莉跺腳還頗為高興，她還擔心瑪莉會把頭埋在被單裡哭。

「這就對了，妳現在正好可以這樣去罵罵他，讓他想點別的。快去吧，孩子，越快越好。」她說。

瑪莉事後回想起來，才覺得這件事雖然可怕，但也很好笑，大人們都嚇壞了，才會跑來求助一個小女孩，而他們之所以來求助她，是因為覺得瑪莉的脾氣和柯林一樣壞。

瑪莉飛奔過走廊，愈接近哭叫聲，她的脾氣就變得愈暴躁。她來到柯林的房門時，脾氣已經發整發作了。她啪地一聲將門打開，穿過房間，一直跑到四柱床的前面。

「你給我安靜！」瑪莉幾乎是用吼的叫喊著：「你給我安靜下來！我討厭你！大家都討厭你！我希望大家都跑出去，讓你自己一個人在這裡哭到死掉！待會你就會哭到死翹翹了，我希望你會真的哭到死掉！」

　　一個心地善良、富有同情心的小孩，是不可能想到或說出這樣的話的。然而對這個歇斯底里的男孩而言，這些話正中下懷，以前都沒有人敢管他、反駁他。

　　柯林原本臉朝下，用手打著枕頭，他一聽到憤怒的小聲音，很快翻過身來。他的臉看起來很可怕，一陣紅一陣白的，還腫腫的。他喘著氣，一邊哽咽著，不過野蠻的小瑪莉才不在乎。

　　她說：「你再叫看看，我也要叫了，而且我會叫得比你大聲，我會讓你害怕，嚇死你！」

　　柯林真的停下不叫了，他確實被瑪莉嚇到了。他被原本要叫出來的尖叫聲噎到了，淚水從臉上流下來，全身顫抖。

　　「我停不下來！」他喘著氣，抽噎地說：「我停不下來！我停不下來！」

　　「你可以的！」瑪莉大叫道：「你會生病，有一半都是因為歇斯底里和暴躁的壞脾氣──就是歇斯底里、歇斯底里、歇斯底里！」瑪莉每說一聲「歇斯底里」，就踩一下腳。

　　「我感覺到腫塊了，我感覺得到，」柯林哽咽地說：「我知道會這樣的，我知道我會變成駝背，然後就會死掉。」他又扭動身子將臉撇過去，嗚咽哭泣，不過並沒有尖叫。

　　「你沒有腫塊！」瑪莉兇狠地反駁說：「你要是覺得有腫塊，那也是歇斯底里的腫塊。歇斯底里會讓腫塊長出來，那跟你可惡的背一點關係也沒有──都是歇斯底里引起的！你轉過去，我看看。」

　　瑪莉很喜歡「歇斯底里」這個詞，而且看來這個詞也對柯林產生了作用。可能柯林也喜歡這個詞，他第一次聽到。

　　瑪莉命令道：「護士，過來，我現在馬上要看他的背！」

護士、梅德洛太太和瑪莎三人在門邊擠成一團，目瞪口呆地看著瑪莉，嚇得抽了好幾口氣。護士有點驚恐地往前走去，柯林正用力地抽咽著。

　　「他可能——不會讓我動手的。」護士猶豫地低聲說。

　　柯林聽到她說的話，趁著抽咽的空際間喘著氣說：「讓她看！這樣她就知道我真的有腫塊了！」

　　柯林裸露的背看起來瘦得可憐，每一根肋骨和脊椎骨上的關節都歷歷可數，但瑪莉並沒有去數。她彎下身去檢查，兇兇的小臉很嚴肅，看起來刻薄又老派。護士把頭別到一邊去，免得別人看出她在偷笑。

　　他們沉默了一分鐘，瑪莉上上下下地打量他的脊椎骨，柯林屏住了呼吸。瑪莉的神情專注，彷彿她就是那位從倫敦來的名醫似的。

　　「一個腫塊也沒有！」最後她終於開口：「沒有一個腫塊比大頭針大——除了脊椎骨上的腫塊，那是因為你太瘦了，所以才摸得到。我的脊椎骨上面也有腫塊，以前也跟你一樣凸出來，等我開始變胖了以後就好多了，不過我還不夠胖，還不能把它們完全藏起來。你的背上沒有一個腫塊比大頭針大，你要是繼續說有的話，我就會取笑你！」

　　只有柯林自己知道這些氣呼呼的童言，對自己產生了什麼樣的影響。柯林要是有人可以傾訴自己內心的恐懼，要是他敢把自己的問題講出來，要是有別的孩子當他的玩伴，而不是整天躺在封閉的大屋子裡，籠罩著大家對他退避三舍的低氣壓，多數人對他忽略又厭倦。如果不是這樣的話，柯林可能就會發現，恐懼和病痛大多是自己製造出來的。

　　然而他卻只是躺在那裡，每個鐘頭、每一天、每個月，年復一年地想著自己、想著病痛和虛弱。可如今這個沒有同情心的憤怒小女孩，卻堅決說他沒有自己想的那麼嚴重，他覺得搞不好她說的才是事實。

護士鼓起勇氣說：「原來他自以為脊椎上面有腫塊。他的背部沒有力，可那是因為他不肯坐起來。早知道他是這麼想的話，我就會跟他說他背上並沒有長腫塊。」

柯林將頭稍微轉過去看著護士，吸了一口氣。

「真的嗎？」他可憐兮兮地說。

「是的，少爺。」

「你看吧！」瑪莉也有些哽咽。

柯林又將臉轉向枕頭，不過這一次是為了深吸一口氣來止住激烈的啜泣。他靜靜地躺了一會兒，大顆的淚珠還是順著臉龐滑了下來，滴落在枕頭上。這些眼淚意謂著他大大地鬆了一口氣。現在他又將臉轉過去看著護士，奇怪的是，這次他跟護士說話的態度一點也不像印度小王侯。

「妳覺得——我可以——活到長大嗎？」他說。

護士不機靈，也不是個心軟的人，不過她倒是能重複那位倫敦醫生說過的話。

「很有可能，不過你得照醫生說的去做，不要隨便發脾氣，多去呼吸新鮮空氣。」

柯林的怒氣已經消了，他哭得很累很虛，人也溫和了下來。他將手微微伸向瑪莉，瑪莉的火氣也消了，人也柔軟了下來，她也將手伸了出去，兩個人算是握手言和了。

「我會——我會跟妳一起出去的，瑪莉。」他說：「我不會討厭新鮮空氣，要是我們可以找到——」他突然想到了那是祕密，就沒有接著說出「要是我們可以找到祕密花園的話」，而是改口說：「如果妳和迪肯可以幫我推椅子，我就跟你們一起出去。我很想看看迪肯，還有他的狐狸和烏鴉。」

護士整理了弄亂的床舖，把枕頭搖一搖拍平，接著給柯林和瑪莉一人一杯牛肉湯。瑪莉很高興可以在這麼激動地鬧了一場之後喝到牛肉湯。梅德洛太太和瑪莎欣慰地悄悄走掉了。等一切恢復秩序後，護士很想溜走，這個健康的年輕女子討厭別人剝奪她的睡眠時間，她看著瑪莉，嘴巴張得大大地打著哈欠，瑪莉將大腳凳推近四柱床，握著柯林的手。

「妳得回去睡覺了，他一會兒就會睡著了，只要他沒有太煩躁。我會睡在隔壁房間的。」護士說。

「我唱那首印度保母教我的歌給你聽，好不好？」瑪莉低聲對柯林說。

柯林的手輕輕拉著瑪莉，疲倦的雙眼懇求似地看著她。

「哦，好啊！那首歌聽起來好輕柔，我很快就會睡著。」柯林回答。

「我會哄他睡覺的。」瑪莉對正在打哈欠的護士說：「妳可以先走。」

「好吧，」護士有點勉強地說：「他半個小時內如果沒有睡著，妳一定要來叫我。」

「好的。」瑪莉回答。

護士很快走出房間。她一走，柯林就又拉住瑪莉的手。

「我差點脫口而出，」他說：「幸好及時打住了。現在不聊天，我要睡覺了，不過妳說妳有很多有趣的事要告訴我。妳是不是──已經找到進去祕密花園的路了？」

看著柯林疲倦可憐的小臉、腫脹的眼睛，瑪莉心軟了。

「是啊，我想我應該已經找到了。你乖乖睡覺，我明天

就告訴你。」她回答。

柯林的手顫抖得很厲害。

「哦，瑪莉！」他說：「哦，瑪莉，我如果可以進去那個花園，我想我就可以活下來了！妳可不可以不要唱印度保母的歌，就像第一天那樣，輕聲跟我說妳想像中的花園景象？我聽這個一定可以睡著的。」

「好啊，把眼睛閉起來。」瑪莉回答。

柯林閉上眼睛靜靜地躺著，瑪莉握著他的手，低聲地慢慢說話。

「我覺得花園已經很久沒有人照顧了，所以裡面的植物都糾纏在一塊，看起來很漂亮。玫瑰花爬得到處都是，從樹枝和牆上垂下來，在地上到處攀爬，就好像把一切都蒙上了一層奇怪的灰色薄霧。有些玫瑰花已經枯死了，不過大部分都還活著。等夏天玫瑰花盛開，看起來就像簾幕和噴泉。還有水仙花、雪花蓮、百合花和鳶尾花也會用盡全力從地下冒出來，長得滿地都是。現在春天已經來了，也許，也許——」

瑪莉低沉輕柔的聲音，讓柯林變得愈來愈安靜，看到他這個樣子，瑪莉繼續說了下去。

「也許它們會從草地裡長出來——也許現在就已經長出好幾叢紫色和金色的番紅花了。也許葉子都已經開始冒出來了——也許——灰色薄霧已經變成綠色了，四處攀爬，一直爬，爬過所有的東西。還有，小鳥也會飛來看看，因為那裡很安全又很安靜。」瑪莉的聲音又輕柔又緩慢，「也許——也許——也許知更鳥已經找到了伴侶——正在築巢呢。」

柯林已經酣然入睡了。

第十八章

「別再浪費時間了」

隔天早上瑪莉當然沒能早起。她太累了，所以起得很晚。瑪莎把早餐送上來，跟她說柯林是安靜了下來，但是生病發燒了。他只要大哭，就會把自己弄得疲累不堪。瑪莉一邊聽瑪莎說話，一邊慢慢地吃早餐。

「他說希望汝可以快點過去看他，」瑪莎說：「沒想到他居然會喜歡汝。汝昨天可真是把他狠狠地痛罵了一頓——難道不是嗎？再沒有別人敢這麼做了。啊！可憐的団兒！他實在是被寵壞了。媽媽說団兒最怕兩件事，一件是不能做自己想做的事，另一件是永遠都可以為所欲為。她不知道哪種情況會比較嚴重。昨天汝大發雷霆，可是剛剛我去他房間時，他對我說：『請妳去問問瑪莉小姐能不能過來和我聊天？』他居然會說『請』這個字！妳會過去嗎，小姐？」

「我想先去找迪肯，」瑪莉突然靈機一動，「不，我先去看柯林好了，然後告訴他——我知道我要跟他說什麼。」

她戴著帽子出現在柯林的房間，柯林瞬間變得有些失望。他躺在床上，臉色蒼白得可憐，眼睛四周還有黑眼圈。

「我很高興妳來了，」他說：「我頭痛，全身都痛，我太累了。妳是不是要出去？」

瑪莉走過去，靠在柯林的床邊。

　　「我不會去很久的，我要去找迪肯，但是我會回來的。柯林，那——那跟祕密花園有關。」她說。

　　柯林的整個臉為之一亮，臉色也微微紅潤起來。

　　「哦！是嗎？」他大叫起來：「我整個晚上都夢到這個花園。我聽到妳說灰色的東西變成綠色，我就夢見自己站在一個四周都有小綠葉顫動的地方——那裡到處都有小鳥停在鳥巢上，小鳥看起來溫柔又安靜。我會躺在這裡繼續想著，等妳回來。」

　　五分鐘後，瑪莉已經來到花園和迪肯在一起了。狐狸和烏鴉還是陪在迪肯的身旁，他這次還帶了兩隻溫馴的松鼠來。

　　「我今天早上騎了小野馬過來，」他說：「牠真是個不賴的小伙子！牠叫『跳躍』！我也把這兩隻放在口袋裡帶來了，這隻叫做『豆子』，另一隻叫做『果殼』。」

　　迪肯叫豆子時，其中一隻松鼠跳到了他的右肩上。叫果殼時，另一隻也跳上了他的左肩。

　　他們坐在草地上，隊長蜷曲在他們的腳邊，煤灰在樹上一臉嚴肅地聽著他們說話，豆子和果殼在他們身邊聞來嗅去的。瑪莉實在沒法離開這些討人喜歡的小可愛們。不過，當她開始跟迪肯講昨晚發生的事情時，不知道為什麼，迪肯臉上的表情變化，逐漸改變了她的想法。瑪莉看得出來，迪肯比她更為柯林感到難過。迪肯抬頭看向天空和周遭圍繞的一切。

　　「汝聽小鳥的叫聲，整個世界好像充滿了牠們的口哨聲和叫聲，」他說：「汝看牠們到處快速飛翔，再注意聽牠們的互相呼喚！春天一到，全世界好像都在呼喚著彼此。葉子都伸展開來了，還有，天啊，到處聞起來都好香！」迪肯用他快樂的朝天鼻嗅著，「那個可憐的傢伙卻關在房間裡躺著，看不到任何東西，所以才會胡思亂想到大叫起來。唉呀！我們要帶他來這裡——帶來這裡來看一看、聽一聽、聞一聞空氣，讓他曬一曬太陽。要快點行動，別再浪費時間了。」

迪肯講到自己特別感興趣的事情時，就會說起約克郡方言，但是平時會盡量改自己的口音，好讓瑪莉聽得懂他在說什麼。其實瑪莉很喜歡他的約克郡口音，也想學著說看看，所以她現在也會說一點約克郡方言。

「是啊，我們莫要浪費時間了，」她說著：「我知道第一步該做啥。」迪肯咧嘴笑了起來，這個小姑娘舌頭打結說著約克郡方言的模樣真有趣。

「他喜歡上汝了，他想要看看汝，還想看煤灰和隊長。我待會回去就去問他，看汝能不能明天早上去看他，順便帶上汝的小動物們一起去。還有，等不久葉子再長多一點，再冒出一、兩個花苞時，我們就可以領他出來，汝可以推他的椅子，我們把他帶到這裡來，給他瞧瞧這裡的一切。」

瑪莉說完後覺得特別自豪，她第一次用約克郡方言講了這麼多話，而且該注意的地方她都注意到了。

「汝跟柯萊文少爺說話時，一定要帶點約克郡方言。」迪肯咯咯地輕笑著，「他聽了一定會笑，對生病的人來說，能笑是再好不過的了。媽媽說，得斑疹傷寒的人，每天早上笑上半個鐘頭，病就會好了。」

「我今天就用約克郡方言跟他說話。」瑪莉也咯咯地笑。

這時節的花園彷彿早晚都有魔術師來過似的，將美麗的植物從土裡拉出來，再用魔杖變出樹枝來。要離開這美好的一切，對瑪莉來說實在太難了，尤其是豆子現在已經爬到她的裙子上來了，而果殼剛從蘋果樹幹上爬下來，正好奇地盯著瑪莉，但她還是回到了屋子裡。當她坐在柯林的床邊時，柯林開始像迪肯一樣地嗅著，雖然動作不是很熟練。

「妳的身上有花香，還有其他新鮮的味道。」他高興地叫道：「那是什麼味道？聞起來很清爽，暖暖香香的。」

「那是高沼地的風，」瑪莉說：「我和迪肯、隊長、煤灰、豆子還有果殼一起坐在樹下的草地上。春天到了，外面的陽光聞起來特別香。」

瑪莉用很重的方言說著，你得親耳聽到，才會知道約克郡的口音有多重。柯林開始笑了起來。

「妳在幹什麼？沒聽過妳這樣說話，太好笑了。」他說。

「我在用約克郡方言跟汝說話。」瑪莉得意洋洋地回答：「我的口音沒有迪肯和瑪莎的那麼重，可是汝看，我還是有進步的。汝難道聽不懂約克郡方言嗎？汝可是個土生土長的約克郡囝兒啊！真是羞羞臉！」

瑪莉也笑了起來，兩人停不住地笑，房間裡充滿了笑聲。梅德洛太太開門進來又退了出去，站在走廊上詫異地聽著。

「我的媽啊！」她也說著約克郡方言，反正沒人會聽到，她感到很驚訝。「真是讓人跌破眼鏡！誰想得到事情會變成這樣呢！」

他們之間有說不完的話。柯林似乎永遠也聽不膩迪肯、隊長、煤灰、豆子、果殼，還有那隻叫做跳躍小野馬的故事。

瑪莉跟著迪肯跑進樹林裡去看過跳躍，那是高沼地的一隻粗毛小野馬，眼睛上方垂著幾綹濃密的毛，有張漂亮的臉，天鵝絨般的鼻子到處嗅來嗅去。牠吃高沼地的草，體型很瘦，不過滿結實強壯的，小腿的肌肉就像是鋼板彈簧做成的一樣。

牠看到迪肯就抬起頭來
發出輕柔的嘶鳴，朝著
迪肯小跑步過去，將頭
擱在他的肩膀上。迪肯
在牠耳邊說話，跳躍就
用奇怪的小聲嘶鳴、喘
氣聲和噴鼻聲回答他。
迪肯要跳躍向瑪莉伸出
小前蹄，用絨絲般的鼻
子親吻瑪莉的臉頰。

　　「牠真的聽得懂迪
肯所說的每一句話嗎？」柯林問道。

　　「看起來好像是聽得懂，」瑪莉回答：「迪肯說，我們
只要跟牠們變成朋友，就可以互相瞭解了，可是一定要先跟
牠們做朋友才行。」

　　柯林靜靜地躺了一會兒，奇異的灰色眼睛像是盯著牆壁
看，瑪莉知道他在想事情。

　　「但願我也有動物朋友，」最後他說：「可是我沒有任
何朋友，況且我也受不了別人。」

　　「你能忍受得了我嗎？」瑪莉問。

　　柯林回答：「當然，我還很喜歡妳呢，雖然聽起來有點
好笑。」

　　瑪莉說：「班說我跟他很像，他敢保證我的脾氣跟他的
一樣壞。我想你跟他也很像，我們三個都很像，你、我還有班。
他說我跟他都長得不好看，脾氣也和長相一樣壞。可是我認
識迪肯和知更鳥以後，覺得自己的脾氣沒有那麼壞了。」

「妳以前會討厭別人嗎？」

「會啊，我如果是在認識迪肯和知更鳥之前就先認識到你，那我一定會討厭你的。」瑪莉坦率地說。

柯林伸出細瘦的手碰了碰瑪莉。

他說：「瑪莉，我真希望沒有說過要把迪肯趕走的話。當妳說他像天使時，我好討厭妳，還嘲笑妳，可是——可是他可能真的是個天使吧。」

「其實我那樣說也是有一點好笑，」瑪莉坦白地說：「迪肯有一個朝天鼻和大嘴巴，衣服上都是補丁，約克郡的口音很重，但是——如果約克郡的高沼地真的住了天使——如果約克郡真的有天使的話——我想他一定會很瞭解綠色植物，知道怎麼讓它們長出來。他應該會像迪肯那樣知道怎麼跟野生動物講話，動物們會把他當成朋友。」

「我應該不介意讓迪肯看到我的，」柯林說：「我想要見他。」

「真高興你這麼說，」瑪莉回答：「因為——因為——」

就在這一刻，瑪莉突然下定決心告訴他實情。

柯林知道就要發生新鮮事了。

「因為什麼？」柯林熱切地叫道。

瑪莉緊張地從凳子上站起來，走向柯林，抓住他的雙手。

「我可以相信你嗎？我相信迪肯，因為小鳥也相信他。可是我可以完完全全相信你嗎？」瑪莉用懇求的語氣問道。

瑪莉的表情很嚴肅，柯林幾乎是用耳語般的低聲回答。

「可以，可以的！」

「那好，明天早上迪肯會來看你，他會把他的動物也帶來。」

「哇！哇！」柯林高興地大叫。

「我話還沒說完，」瑪莉繼續說，她的臉色由於嚴肅和激動而變得蒼白，「接下來的更精彩。有扇門可以進到花園裡，我已經找到那扇門了，它被牆上的常春藤遮蓋住了。」

如果柯林是個健康強壯的孩子，他大概會大叫「萬歲！萬歲！萬歲！」不過他又虛弱又歇斯底里，所以只是把眼睛愈睜愈大，不停地喘著氣。

「哦！瑪莉！」他幾乎快要哭出來，「我可以看到花園嗎？我可以進去裡面嗎？我可以活著進去裡面嗎？」他抓緊瑪莉的雙手，將她拉向自己。

「你當然看得到花園！你當然可以活著進去！別說傻話了！」瑪莉憤怒地說。

瑪莉並沒有歇斯底里，她的神情很自然，帶著孩子氣，很快就讓柯林冷靜下來了。柯林開始嘲笑自己，幾分鐘後瑪莉又坐回凳子上。不過這一次她跟柯林講的不是想像中的祕密花園，而是花園真正的樣子。柯林忘記了病痛和疲倦，出神地聽著。

他最後說：「它就跟妳原本想像的一樣，彷彿妳早就看過那個花園似的，我是指妳第一次跟我講的花園的樣子。」

瑪莉猶豫了兩分鐘，才大膽地說出實話。

「我那時候就已經看過花園了，而且也進去過了。」她說：「好幾個星期之前，我找到了鑰匙，進到了花園裡。可是我不敢跟你講，因為我擔心你靠不住！」

第十九章

「它來了！」

柯　林發過脾氣後的隔天早上，柯萊文醫生照慣例會被請過來。他每次過來，都會看到一個臉色蒼白、不住顫抖的男孩躺在床上，臉色陰沉、歇斯底里，隨時都可能再度啜泣起來。事實上，這樣的探視讓柯萊文醫生既害怕又討厭，有一回還下午才來到密朔兌莊園。

「他的情況怎麼樣了？」他到達後煩躁地問梅德洛太太，「總有一天，他的血管會在發脾氣的時候爆掉。這個孩子太過歇斯底里和任性，已經快瘋掉了。」

梅德洛太太回答道：「先生，等您看到他，您會無法相信自己的眼睛。那個平凡普通的苦瓜臉小女孩，脾氣跟柯林少爺一樣壞，可她卻讓柯林少爺著了魔。沒人知道她是怎麼辦到的，天知道她長得那麼平庸，很少聽到她講話，但是她卻做了我們不敢做的事。昨天晚上，她就像隻小貓一樣撲向柯林少爺，一邊跺腳，一邊命令少爺不要再叫了，柯林少爺被她嚇得就不叫了。到了今天下午——好吧，先生您來看看吧，實在難以置信。」

柯萊文醫生走進病人房間，眼前的景象著實讓他吃了一驚。梅德洛太太把房門打開時，他聽到了笑聲和說話聲。柯林穿著晨袍，直挺挺地坐在沙發上，看著園藝書的圖片，還和那個不起眼的小女孩說著話。小女孩現在已經不能說是不起眼了，她的臉龐因為開心而容光煥發。

「我們也要種很多這種藍色的長細葉植物，它們叫翠雀花。」柯林宣布道。

瑪莉叫道：「迪肯說這是又大又高的飛燕草，那邊已經有好幾叢了。」

他們一看到柯萊文醫生走進來便住嘴不說。瑪莉一動也不動，柯林看起來很焦躁。

「聽說你昨晚病了，我很難過，孩子。」柯萊文醫生有點緊張地說。他其實是個容易緊張的人。

「我現在已經好多了，」柯林像個印度王侯般地回答：「等天氣比較好了，我要坐在椅子上出去一、兩次，呼吸一點新鮮空氣。」

柯萊文醫生坐在柯林身邊，量他的脈搏，一臉好奇地看著柯林。

「一定要等天氣很好的時候才可以出去，而且一定要小心不可以累著了。」他說。

「新鮮空氣不會讓我覺得累的。」小王侯說道。

這位小紳士曾用憤怒的尖叫聲嚷道，新鮮的空氣會讓自己染上風寒，甚至會要了自己的命，所以也難怪柯萊文醫生這時候一臉驚訝。

「我還以為你不喜歡新鮮空氣。」他說。

王侯回答：「我自己一個人的時候就不喜歡，可是我表妹會跟我一起出去。」

「護士當然也會跟你們去吧？」柯萊文醫生提議道。

「不要，我不要護士跟我們去。」柯林的態度非常嚴肅，瑪莉不由地想起那位年輕的印度王子，手上戴滿了鑽石、藍寶石和珍珠，揮舞著戴了斗大紅寶石的黝黑小手，要僕人過來行額手禮，接受他的指令。

「我表妹知道要怎麼照顧我，有她陪我，我身體愈來愈好了，昨天晚上就是她讓我覺得好多了。還有一個我認識的強壯男生會來幫我推椅子。」

柯萊文醫生聽了一陣慌，這討人厭的歇斯底里男孩要是好轉了，他就沒有機會繼承密朔兌莊園。不過他也不算是個無恥之徒，不會故意讓柯林身陷危險之中。

他說：「那個男生要很強壯、很穩健才可以，我還要知道一點他的背景，他是誰？叫什麼名字？」

「他叫迪肯。」瑪莉突然壯起膽子說了出來。

不知道為什麼，她覺得只要是知道高沼地的人，就一定會知道迪肯。她這麼想是對的，因為她看到柯萊文醫生嚴肅的臉一下子就放鬆地笑起來。

他說：「哦！原來是迪肯，你跟他在一起應該會很安全，他跟高沼地的小野馬一樣強壯，這個迪肯。」

「而且他很可靠，他是約克郡最可靠的团兒了。」瑪莉剛剛用約克郡方言和柯林說話，現在她也忘形地說著方言。

「這是迪肯教妳的嗎？」柯萊文醫生問，不客氣地笑了起來。

「我當成是在學法文。」瑪莉冷冷地說：「就好比夠聰明的人才會學印度方言一樣。我很喜歡約克郡方言，柯林也是。」

柯萊文醫生說：「好吧，開心就好，反正沒什麼壞處。柯林，你昨天晚上有沒有吃鎮定劑？」

「沒有，剛開始我不想吃，後來瑪莉低聲跟我說話，哄我睡覺，我就變安靜了。她跟我講了春天是怎麼悄悄地爬進花園裡的。」柯林回答。

「聽起來很能安慰人。」柯萊文醫生更感到迷惑不解了，他瞥了一眼瑪莉，她就安靜地坐在凳子上，低頭看著地毯。「你看起來有明顯的好轉，可是你一定要記住──」

「我什麼都不想記住，」小王侯柯林再次出現，中斷了他的話：「我自己一個人躺在床上想著那些該記住的事情，就會全身痛。想到一些討厭的事情，我就開始尖叫。如果有哪個醫生可以讓我忘掉我在生病，而不是一直提醒我是個病人，那就把他請過來。」他揮揮細瘦的手，手上像是真的戴滿了由紅寶石做成的皇家紋章戒指似的，「表妹讓我忘了我在生病，她會讓我好轉。」

柯萊文醫生第一次在柯林發過脾氣後只停留這麼短時間，他通常都要待很久，有許多事情要處理。這天下午，他沒有開藥物，也沒有新的醫囑，也不用去看什麼煩人的場景。他若有所思地走下樓，梅德洛太太在書房跟他說話時，看到他一臉疑惑。

「先生，您相信這一切嗎？」她大膽地說。

醫生說：「狀況的確是有了新的變化，毫無疑問，他現在的情況要比以前好。」

「我想蘇珊·索爾比說得沒有錯，」梅德洛太太說：「昨天我去兌特村，順道經過她家的農舍和她聊了一下。她跟我說：『瑪莉小姐或許不是個乖孩子，不是個漂亮的孩子，可畢竟是個小孩，小孩就需要有小孩作伴。』蘇珊‧索爾比是我以前的同學。」

「我知道她是最會照顧病人的護士了，」柯萊文醫生說：「有她在，我就知道我的病人有救了。」

梅德洛太太露出微笑，她很喜歡蘇珊‧索爾比。

她滔滔不絕地繼續說：「蘇珊很有一套，我整個早上都在想著她昨天說的一件事。她說：『有一次我家的囝兒打完架後，我跟他們上了一堂課。我告訴他們，我以前在學校的地理課學到的，地球就像顆橘子。我不到十歲就發現這整顆橘子不屬於任何人的，每個人都有應該拿到的份量，有時候會覺得自己拿到的那一份好像不夠，但是你們每一個人都不可以以為整顆橘子都是自己的，汝們以後就會發現這種想法是錯誤的。不付出慘痛的代價，汝們是不會瞭解到這一點的。小孩子能夠互相學習。』她還說：『囝兒們就會瞭解到，搶奪整顆橘子是沒有意義的，這樣可能連苦到不能吃的籽都拿不到。』」

「她是個聰慧的婦女。」柯萊文醫生穿上外套一邊說著。

「是啊，她講話很有一套，有時候我會跟她說：『蘇珊啊，如果妳是別人，而且口音沒有那麼重，有時候我都想說妳很精明呢。』」梅德洛太太開心地說。

那天，柯林一覺睡到天亮。等他睜開眼，已經是早上了。他靜靜地躺著，不自覺地笑了起來，覺得很舒暢。醒來的感覺真好，他翻過身，舒服地伸展手腳。他覺得以前緊緊束縛他的繩子都鬆開了。柯萊文醫生要是看到他這個樣子，就會說那是因為神經放鬆、得到休息了。

柯林不再像往常一樣躺在床上盯著牆壁看，暗自希望自己沒有醒來，相反地，他的腦海裡縈繞著昨天和瑪莉一起說好的計畫、花園的景象，還有迪肯和他的動物們。有這麼多東西可以佔據思緒，是件好事。

　　他醒來還不到十分鐘，就聽到走廊傳來腳步聲，接著瑪莉就出現在門口了。她跑到柯林的床邊，身上還散發著早晨新鮮空氣的芬芳。

　　「妳出去過了！妳出去過了！妳的身上有葉子的香味！」柯林叫道。

　　瑪莉是跑著過來的，頭髮被風吹得蓬亂，外面的空氣讓她容光煥發、臉色紅潤，不過柯林沒有注意到這些。

　　「花園好漂亮！」因為跑太快，她有點喘不過氣來，「你一定沒看過這麼漂亮的景象！它來了！我以為它前幾天的早上就來了，不過它是現在才來的，它已經來了！春天已經來了！這是迪肯說的！」

　　柯林叫道：「它來了嗎？」他雖然對春天一無所知，不過還是可以感覺自己的心在怦怦跳。他從床上坐了起來。

　　「快把窗戶打開！」他笑著說道，這笑容一半是因為喜悅興奮的情緒，一半是因為自己腦海中的想像，「也許我們可以聽到金色喇叭的聲音呢！」

　　瑪莉立刻跑到窗邊，不一會兒便將窗戶敞開，清新的氣息、柔和的空氣、芬芳的氣味和小鳥的歌聲，一湧而入。

　　「這就是新鮮空氣，你躺著深呼吸。」她說：「迪肯躺在高沼地時就是這樣做的。他說他可以感覺到新鮮空氣流進血管裡，讓他變得強壯，他覺得自己好像可以長生不老。你就一直吸、一直吸。」

瑪莉只是重複著迪肯告訴她的話，柯林聽了很著迷。

「『長生不老！』，他真的這麼覺得嗎？」說著，柯林便照瑪莉說的一直深呼吸，感到前所未有的清新和愉快。

瑪莉又走到他的床邊。

「泥土裡長出很多東西來，」她滔滔不絕地說：「花都開了，到處都有花苞，灰色的東西差不多都被綠色的薄紗蓋住了。小鳥急著築巢，擔心會來不及，所以在祕密花園裡搶位子，有些小鳥還因此打了起來。玫瑰叢淘氣極了，小徑和樹林裡有很多報春花，我們種下去的種子也長了出來。迪肯帶來了他的狐狸、烏鴉、松鼠，還有一隻剛出生的小羊。」

說到這裡，瑪莉停下來喘口氣。三天前，迪肯在高沼地的荊豆叢裡找到了這隻剛出生的小羊，躺在死去的媽媽身邊。迪肯並不是第一次撿到像牠這樣變成孤兒的小羊，所以他知道該如何處理。他將小羊用外套包起來帶回農舍，讓牠躺在火爐邊，用溫牛奶餵牠。小羊全身軟綿綿的，可愛的小臉蛋帶著傻氣，四隻腳很長。

迪肯將小羊抱在懷裡穿越高沼地，口袋裡除了松鼠，還有小羊的奶瓶。瑪莉坐在樹下，腿上躺著蜷縮成一團、柔軟溫暖的小羊，她感到一種很不一樣的喜悅，幾乎說不出話來。小羊，小羊！一隻活生生的小羊像嬰孩般躺在她的大腿上！

瑪莉欣喜萬分地向柯林描述這一切，他一面聽，一面深呼吸。就在這時護士走了進來，看到窗子被打開，她有點驚訝。天氣暖和時，她常覺得柯林的房間快悶得透不過氣來，因為柯林覺得把窗戶打開會著涼。

「柯林少爺，您確定不會冷嗎？」護士問道。

柯林回答道：「不會，我在呼吸新鮮空氣，這樣會讓我變得強壯。我要坐到沙發上吃早餐，瑪莉也要跟我一起吃。」

護士忍住笑意離開，她吩咐佣人送兩份早餐過來。她覺得僕人室比病房還有趣，大家都想聽聽樓上的最新消息。他們很喜歡開那個小隱士的玩笑，廚師說：「他終於碰到一個比他厲害的角色了，算他走運。」僕人們都受夠了柯林的壞脾氣。有家室的男管家不只一次表示過，應該把那個病人給「好好修理一頓」。

兩人的早餐送上來時，柯林坐在沙發上用最具威嚴的口氣向護士宣布：「今天早上會有一個小男生帶著一隻狐狸、一隻烏鴉、兩隻松鼠，還有一隻剛出生的小羊來看我。他們一到，就立刻帶他們上來。你們不可以把這些動物留在僕人室玩，要把牠們帶上來。我要牠們待在這裡。」

護士輕聲驚叫了一聲，企圖用咳嗽來掩飾。

「是的，少爺。」她回答道。

「我會告訴妳該做些什麼，」柯林揮著手補充道：「妳可以叫瑪莎把他們帶過來。那個男生是瑪莎的弟弟，叫做迪肯，他可以把動物迷住。」

「我希望那些動物不會咬人，柯林少爺。」護士說。

「我告訴過妳，他可以迷住動物，他的動物從不咬人。」柯林嚴厲地說。

瑪莉說：「印度有弄蛇人，他們可以把蛇的頭放到自己的嘴巴裡。」

「天啊！」護士毛骨悚然地說。

他們在清晨空氣的吹拂下吃著早餐。柯林的早餐很豐盛，瑪莉很感興趣地看著他。

「你會跟我一樣開始變胖，」她說：「在印度，我都不想吃早餐，可是現在會想吃了。」

柯林說：「今天早上我也想吃早餐了，可能是新鮮的空氣讓我想吃東西吧。妳想迪肯什麼時候會來呢？」

迪肯就快到了。大概十分鐘之後，瑪莉舉起手來。

「你聽！你有沒有聽到烏鴉在呱呱叫？」她說。

柯林聽到了，在屋內聽到粗嘎的烏鴉叫，真是再奇怪不過了。

「有啊。」他回答道。

「那是煤灰，」瑪莉說：「你再聽！有沒有聽到小羊在咩咩叫，很小聲？」

「哦，我聽到了。」柯林興奮地叫道。

「是那隻剛出生的小羊，迪肯來了。」瑪莉說。

迪肯那雙專門在高沼地穿的靴子又厚又重，當他走過長廊時，雖然小心不要發出聲音，但靴子還是發出了笨重的腳步聲。瑪莉和柯林聽著他腳步聲走著、走著，直到走過覆蓋著織錦畫的門，來到柯林門前柔軟的地毯上。

「少爺，如果可以的話，」瑪莎打開門說，「少爺，如果可以的話，我想向您介紹迪肯和他的動物們。」

迪肯帶著一臉燦爛的微笑走進來，懷裡抱著新生的小羊，紅毛小狐狸亦步亦趨地跟著，豆子和煤灰分別坐在他的左右肩膀上，果殼的頭和腳掌從迪肯外套的口袋裡探出來。

柯林慢慢地坐起來，一直盯著他們看，就像他第一次見到瑪莉時那樣，不過，他這次是充滿了好奇地開心凝視著。儘管柯林之前聽了很多迪肯的事，但是他根本無從知道這個男孩會是什麼樣子的。狐狸、烏鴉、松鼠和小羊都緊緊地挨著好心的迪肯，彷彿就是他身上的一部分。柯林還沒有跟別的男孩說過話，他沉浸在開心和新奇感中，都忘了要開口說話。

　　迪肯一點也沒有害羞或膽怯的樣子，他並不覺得尷尬，他第一次遇到那隻烏鴉時，也沒有因為烏鴉不懂他的語言，一直沉默地盯著他看，就感到困窘。動物在沒有完全熟識你之前，都是那個樣子的。迪肯走到柯林的沙發前，靜靜地將剛出生的小羊放在柯林的大腿上。這隻小動物很快就靠向柯林溫暖的天鵝絨晨袍，開始用鼻子輕觸晨袍的縐摺，接著有點急躁地用滿是捲毛的頭抵在柯林的側腹，當然，這種時候每個男孩都會開口問。

　　「牠在幹什麼？牠想做什麼？」柯林叫道。

　　「牠想找媽媽。」迪肯說道，越笑越開。「我還沒有餵牠就把牠帶來了，我想汝會想看我餵牠吧。」

　　說著，迪肯便跪在沙發旁，從口袋取出奶瓶。

　　「來吧，小東西。」他用曬黑的手輕輕地將小羊毛茸茸的白色小頭轉過來。「汝要找的東西在這裡，汝在天鵝絨的絲綢外套裡是吸不出奶的。汝看！」說著，他把奶瓶的橡皮奶嘴塞進小羊的嘴巴裡，小羊便開始貪婪、忘我地吸吮起來。

　　這之後他們當然就聊起了小羊的事。小羊睡著了，柯林劈哩啪啦問了一堆問題，迪肯都一一回答了。他告訴他們，三天前他是如何在天亮時發現這隻小羊的，當時正他站在高沼地聽雲雀唱歌，看著雲雀慢慢高飛到藍天裡，直到變成高空裡的一個小點。

　　「要不是因為有聽到雲雀的歌聲，都不知道牠飛到哪裡去了，好像一下子飛出了世界之外，可是我們還是可以聽到牠的歌聲。就在這時，我聽到遠遠的荊豆叢傳來另一個聲音，是很微弱的羊咩聲，我知道是剛出生的小羊在叫肚子餓了。我還知道，如果有媽媽在身邊，牠就不會這麼叫了，所以我立即去找。啊！我找了好久，在荊豆叢中跑進跑出，在附近找啊找，好像每次都轉錯地方。後來，我在高沼地頂端的一塊岩石邊看到一小團白白的東西，一爬上去就看到這隻又冷又餓的小羊奄奄一息。」

　　迪肯說話時，煤灰一本正經地從打開的窗戶飛進飛出，絮聒地對這兒的風景下評論。豆子和果殼跑到外面的大樹上爬上爬下，探勘著每根樹枝。迪肯坐在火爐前的地毯上，隊長蜷著身子依偎在旁。

　　他們看著園藝書的圖片，迪肯知道所有花的俗名，也很清楚有哪些花已經在祕密花園裡長出來了。

　　他指著底下寫著耬斗菜（Aquilegia）的植物說：「我不知道那叫什麼名字，我們是叫它夢幻草（columbine），那邊那個是金魚草，這兩種都可以長成籬笆。但這個是種在花園裡的，比較大、比較高。花園裡有許多大叢的夢幻草，開花就像藍色和白色的蝴蝶在飛舞一樣。」

　　柯林叫道：「我要去看，我要去看！」

　　「對，汝一定要去，」瑪莉認真地說：「而且汝應該馬上就去。」

第二十章

「我會永遠活下去──
永遠、永遠！」

不過他們還得再多等一個星期，因為接下來幾天風很大，而且柯林受到了風寒。這兩件事接連發生，原本以為柯林會很生氣，不過幸好他們還得先仔細規畫好祕密計畫，而且迪肯差不多每天都會來，哪怕只是來幾分鐘而已。他會跟他們說高沼地、小徑、籬笆、河邊發生的事情。

迪肯說的那些水獺、獾、河鼠窩的事，聽了就叫人興奮得發抖，更不用說還有鳥巢、田鼠和田鼠的地下洞穴了。當我們從這個動物術士的口中得知那些詳盡的細節時，就能知道地底動物正多麼熱切緊張地忙碌著。

迪肯說：「牠們就跟我們人類一樣，只是牠們每年都要蓋房子，所以忙得團團轉，一直要忙到房子蓋好為止。」

他們最全神貫注的事，是偷偷把柯林帶到花園的準備工作。他們要繞過灌木叢角落，去到常春藤牆壁那邊的走道上，絕對不可以讓人看到他們和柯林的輪椅。

隨著時間過去，柯林愈覺得籠罩著花園的那股神祕氣氛，讓花園特別吸引人，所以一定不可以讓這種感覺被破壞，千萬不可以讓任何人啟疑竇。要讓大家覺得，柯林是因為喜歡瑪莉和迪肯，所以才要和他們出去，不反對兩人看著他。

他們開心地花了不少時間討論路線，從這條步道走過去，從另一條往下走，再穿越另一條步道，然後沿著噴泉邊的花床走，假裝是在欣賞園丁工頭羅區先生花圃裡的植物。這樣聽起來很合理，沒有人會懷疑他們有什麼祕密。接著他們就轉進灌木叢裡的走道，假裝迷路，最後來到長牆邊。他們精心設計了這條路線，簡直就像戰爭時大將軍規畫出來的行軍路線一樣。

柯林房裡發生的新鮮事，已經從僕人廳裡傳到了馬房，又傳進了園丁的耳中。儘管如此，羅區先生這天接獲柯林少爺的命令時還是很驚訝，少爺要找他談話，要他來房間報到，他的房間還沒有外人進去過。

「好的，好的。」羅區先生很快穿上外套，自言自語說：「唔，會是什麼事呢？少爺殿下一向不喜歡被別人看到，現在卻要見這個他看不上眼的人。」

羅區先生也是有好奇心的，他沒見過這男孩，但耳聞過柯林的誇張事蹟，包括柯林怪異的外表舉止和瘋狂的壞脾氣。他最常聽到的傳言是柯林隨時會死去，有些人還會把他的駝背、無力的四肢講得很誇張，但他們根本就沒看過柯林。

「這房子裡面開始有所改變了，羅區先生。」梅德洛太太說著，一邊領著羅區先生爬上後面的樓梯，來到通向神祕房間的走廊。

「但願是在往好的方向改變啊，梅德洛太太。」羅區先生回答。

「情況不會再糟了。」梅德洛太太繼續說：「很奇怪，大家都覺得工作變得輕鬆很多。羅區先生，您待會可不要驚訝，您會發現自己站在一群動物和蘇珊·索爾比的兒子迪肯的中間，他比我們都還適應這個地方呢！」

就像瑪莉相信的那樣，迪肯的身上的確有種魔法，羅區先生一聽到迪肯的名字也露出了慈祥的微笑。

　　「不管他是在皇宮還是在礦坑深處，都很能適應，我這可不是說他魯莽喔，他是個乖囝兒。」他說。

　　幸好羅區先生事先有心理準備，不然可能真的會被嚇到。臥室的門一打開，有隻大烏鴉悠然地棲息在雕刻椅的高椅背上大聲地嘎嘎叫，宣告著訪客的到來。儘管梅德洛太太事先向羅區先生提醒過，他還是差點失禮地往後跳了起來。

　　小王侯沒有在床上或沙發上，而是坐在扶椅上。一隻小羊站在他身邊做出吃奶的姿勢，迪肯跪在地上用奶瓶餵小羊奶。一隻松鼠坐在迪肯彎下去的背上專心地嚼著豆子。印度來的小女孩則坐在大凳子上眼觀著這一切。

　　「柯林少爺，羅區先生來了。」梅德洛太太說。

　　小王侯轉過身端詳著僕人，至少園丁工頭是這樣覺得。

　　「哦，你就是羅區嗎？我叫你來，是因為我有很重要的事情要吩咐你去做。」他說。

　　「少爺，請吩咐。」羅區答道，心裡想著小主人會不會命令他砍掉公園所有的橡樹，或將果園變成水上植物花園。

　　柯林說：「今天下午我要坐在椅子上出去，如果我能適應新鮮空氣，以後可能就會每天都出去。我出去的時候，所有的園丁都不可以出現在花園牆邊的『長道』上，大家都不准到那邊去。我大概會在兩點左右出去，所有人都要走開，等我叫你們回去工作，你們才可以回去。」

　　「是的，少爺。」羅區回答。當他聽到橡樹不用被砍掉，果園也安然無恙，鬆了一口氣。

　　「瑪莉，」柯林轉向她：「在印度，把事情交待完畢，要怎麼叫人離開？」

「我們會說：『我允許你退下。』」瑪莉回答道。

王侯揮揮手，說：「我允許你退下，羅區。要記得，這件事很重要。」

「嘎嘎！」烏鴉粗嘎卻不失禮地叫了叫。

「是的，少爺。謝謝，少爺。」羅區說完，梅德洛太太便把他帶到了門外。

房外走廊上，好脾氣的羅區差點要笑了出來。

他說：「天啊！他還真有君主架勢呢！簡直集整個皇族的威嚴於一身啊！」

梅德洛太太抗議：「唉，從他一出生，我們就都被他踩在腳底下，他以為別人就應該這麼被踩躪。」

「他要是活下來，長大後或許就不會這樣了。」羅區先生說。

「好吧，有一件事我很確定，」梅德洛太太說：「如果他真的活下來了，那個印度來的小女孩也一直留在這兒的話，我保證她一定會讓柯林少爺知道，整顆橘子不是屬於他一個人的，就像蘇珊‧索爾比說的那樣，他就會了解自己擁有的那份到底有多少。」

房裡的柯林又躺回了座墊上。

「現在一切都安全了，今天下午我就可以看到花園了，今天下午我就可以進去花園了！」他說。

迪肯帶著動物先去了花園，瑪莉留下來陪柯林。她覺得柯林看起來並不累，可是午餐前他都不太講話，吃午餐時也是，瑪莉問他是怎麼一回事。

她說：「柯林，你的眼睛真大啊，你想事情時眼睛會變得跟茶碟一樣大。你現在到底在想什麼？」

「我一直在想它究竟是什麼樣子的。」柯林回答道。

「花園嗎？」瑪莉問道。

「春天。」他說：「我在想，我以前沒有真正看過春天，我很少出去，就算出去也不會去看看春天，連想都不想。」

「我在印度也沒看過春天，印度沒有春天。」瑪莉說。

柯林足不出戶的臥病生活，讓他變得比瑪莉更有想像力，最起碼他花了很多時間閱讀有趣的書籍和圖畫。

「那天早上妳跑進來說：『它來了！它來了！』我覺得很奇怪，聽起來像是來了個大陣仗的遊行隊伍，有響亮喝采聲和陣陣音樂聲。我的書裡面有一張像這樣的圖片，一群可愛的大人和小孩，戴著花環，拿著開花的樹枝，大家邊笑邊跳舞，擠來擠去，吹著笛子。所以我那時候才會說：『搞不好我們會聽到金色喇叭的聲音。』才叫妳去把窗子推開。」

瑪莉說：「這還真有趣！春天的感覺真的就像這樣。所有的花朵、樹葉、綠色植物、小鳥、野生動物，要是都跳起舞來，那可真的是一大群呢！我敢說它們一定會唱歌、跳舞、吹笛子，讓空氣中充滿音樂聲。」

兩人都笑了出來，不是因為這樣的想法很好笑，而是他們都很喜歡這樣的景象。

不久，護士幫柯林打點妥當。她注意到柯林不再像以前那樣木頭似的動也不動地躺著讓別人幫他穿衣服，而是坐直起來，會配合移動手腳，還一直和瑪莉有說有笑。

「他這幾天的狀況很好，先生。」柯萊文醫生順道來檢查柯林時，護士這麼對他說：「心情好，身體就健康多了。」

柯萊文醫生說：「下午等他回來，我再過來，看看他是不是真的適合出去。」他低聲說：「希望他肯讓妳陪著去。」

「先生，我寧可現在就辭職，也不會在這裡聽您的這種建議。」護士態度忽然堅定了起來。

醫生有點緊張地說道：「是不一定要這樣要求啦，就先這樣試看看。就算是把新生兒丟給迪肯照顧，也沒問題的。」

府邸最強壯的僕人將柯林背下樓，放在輪椅上，迪肯在屋外等候著。男僕將柯林的毯子和墊子整理好，小王侯便對僕人還有護士揮了揮手。

他說：「我允許你們退下。」男僕和護士很快就消失，等他們安全回到屋裡，還不住地吃吃笑。

迪肯穩穩地慢慢推著椅子，瑪莉走在一旁，柯林把身子往後傾，仰頭望向天空。穹蒼高掛著，小小的白色雲朵宛如白色小鳥，展開雙翼地飄浮在水晶般的藍天下。一陣微風從高沼地吹來，送來奇異、野性的清新芳香。柯林鼓起細瘦的胸膛，吸著空氣，大大的眼睛看起來彷彿是在傾聽。對，是眼睛在傾聽，不是耳朵。

他說：「我聽到好多歌聲、嗡嗡聲、叫聲，那陣風吹來的是什麼的味道？」

「那是高沼地的荊豆開花了，」迪肯回答：「啊！蜜蜂今天可開心了。」

他們經過步道時沒有看到任何人影，事實上，園丁或園丁的小孩都不在。不過，他們還是在灌木叢裡繞進繞出的，沿著噴泉邊的花壇走，遵循著精心策畫好的路線，這樣才神祕有趣。當他們轉進常春藤牆邊的長走道時，驚險刺激的感覺讓他們開始不禁低聲說話。

「就是這裡了，我以前常會在這裡蹓躂，覺得很好奇。」

瑪莉低聲說。

　　柯林叫道：「就是這裡嗎？」他的眼睛熱切好奇地查看著常春藤。「可我什麼都沒看到，這裡沒有門！」他低聲說。

　　「我原本也是這麼以為。」瑪莉說。

　　接著一陣美好的靜默，迪肯繼續推著輪椅前進。

　　「那是班工作的花園。」瑪莉說道。

　　「是嗎？」柯林說。

　　走了幾步路後，瑪莉又低聲說話。

　　「這裡就是知更鳥飛過牆的地方。」她說。

　　「是嗎？哦！真希望牠再飛過來！」柯林叫道。

　　「牠就是停在那邊的小土堆上，指出鑰匙給我看的。」瑪莉開心而慎重地指著一大叢紫丁香的下方。

　　柯林坐起身來。

　　他喊道：「在哪裡？在哪裡？那裡嗎？」眼睛就跟小紅帽裡那隻大野狼的眼睛一樣大，讓小紅帽看了很吃驚。

　　迪肯動不動地站著，輪椅也停了下來。

　　「還有這裡，」瑪莉說著，走向常春藤的花圃，「這是知更鳥在牆上對著我啁啾叫時，我站的地方。這裡是被風吹開的常春藤。」說著，便拉起垂下來的綠色簾幕。

　　「哦！就是這個嗎？」柯林喘著氣說。

　　「這裡有個把手，門在這裡。迪肯推他進去──快推他進去！」

　　迪肯用力而靈巧地將柯林推了進去。

　　柯林往後倒在靠墊上，興奮地喘著氣，用手摀住眼睛，

直到他們像變魔法般進到花園裡，輪椅停住，門也關上了。

　　這時柯林才將手拿開，不斷地環顧著四周，一遍又一遍，就像迪肯和瑪莉當初那樣。柔嫩小葉子形成的綠色薄紗，爬過牆壁、泥土、樹木和搖曳的小樹枝。樹下草地和小亭子裡的灰色甕中，都是金色、紫色和白色的點點。柯林的頭頂上綻放著粉紅和雪白的花朵。還有鳥羽拍動的聲音，隱約傳來悅耳的鳥鳴聲和嗡嗡聲，散發著濃郁的香氣。

　　溫暖的陽光照拂他臉上，像隻手溫柔地撫摸著他。瑪莉和迪肯好奇地凝視著柯林，他看起來很不尋常，一陣粉色的光芒將他籠罩住──籠罩住他象牙般的白色臉龐、脖子、雙手和全身。

　　「我會好起來的！我會好起來的！瑪莉！迪肯！我會好起來的！我會永遠、永遠地活下去！」他喊道。

第二十一章

班

活在世間，最奇妙的事是我們有時會覺得自己將永遠活下去。有時在柔和神聖的清晨醒來，走到戶外，仰頭看著暗淡的天空慢慢變成薔薇色，神奇地變化著，東方的天空令人驚嘆。億萬年來，太陽日復一日地升起，那奇異永恆的莊嚴令人屏息。就這瞬間，感受到自己能夠永遠活下去。

有時是在日落時分，在樹林獨處時意識到了這一點。神祕寂靜的金黃色斜暉穿過樹枝，照射在樹枝下，像是在緩緩地重複訴說著什麼，但人總無法聽明白。

有時是在無限靜謐的深藍色夜晚，無數星星在那裡靜觀著，讓我們覺得自己會永遠地活下去。還有時是遠方傳來的樂聲，有時是人們的一個眼神，就是會帶來這種感覺。

對柯林來說，感覺自己會永遠活下去的時刻，是他在這個被四道高牆圍住的祕密花園裡，第一次看到、聽到、感覺到春天的時候。

那天下午，整個世界彷彿在努力讓自己變得更美好，散發出美麗光彩，要善待這個男孩。或許是上天大發慈悲，春天才會到來，讓這地方一片多采多姿。迪肯不止一次佇足，靜靜地站著，眼裡充滿了驚訝，輕輕搖了搖頭。

「啊！真是太棒了，」他說：「我就要十三歲了，在這十三年裡有過許許多多的下午，就今天下午最棒了。」

「對啊，真是太棒了！」瑪莉高興地嘆氣說：「我敢說這會兒這裡是全世界最棒的下午了。」

「汝覺得這一切都是為了我，才會這樣的嗎？」柯林呢喃似地小心翼翼說道。

瑪莉讚賞地叫道：「天啊！汝的約克郡腔真不賴，汝學得真快啊，真的耶！」

他們洋溢著歡欣。他們將輪椅拉到開滿雪白花朵的李樹下，蜜蜂嗡嗡地奏出樂章，宛如仙境國王寶座的華蓋。旁邊的櫻桃花盛開，粉紅、白色的蘋果花苞四處恣意地綻放著。在繁花盛開的樹枝花頂間，藍天像奇妙的眼睛俯視著。

柯林看著瑪莉和迪肯四處忙著。他們會拿東西來給柯林看，有綻放的花苞、含苞待放的花蕊、剛長出嫩葉的小樹枝、啄木鳥飄落草地上的羽毛、最早一批孵出來的小鳥所留下的空殼等等。

迪肯慢慢推著輪椅漫步花園，不時佇足下來，好讓柯林欣賞從土裡冒出來或是從樹上垂下來的神奇事物。柯林像是被帶入了魔法國王和皇后的王國中，向他展示著王國裡所有的神祕寶物。

「不知道我們會不會看到那隻知更鳥？」柯林說。

迪肯說：「汝之後就會常常看到牠了，等小鳥孵出來，牠會忙得團團轉。汝會看到牠咬著跟自己差不多大的蟲子飛來飛去，飛回鬧哄哄的鳥巢時一陣慌亂，不知道要把蟲子先放到哪隻雛鳥的大嘴巴裡才好。到處都是張大的鳥嘴，還有嘎嘎的叫聲。媽媽說，她只要看到知更鳥在餵雛鳥，就會覺得自己是個無所事事的貴婦。她說，雖然人看不到，可是知更鳥一定是忙得滿頭大汗。」

　　聽到這裡，大夥開心地吃吃笑了起來，笑到不得不用手遮住嘴巴，因為他們記得不能讓別人聽到聲音。幾天前，瑪莉和迪肯就跟柯林講過，在這裡要低聲細語。柯林很喜歡這種神祕感，他盡量小聲說話，可是當他一興奮雀躍起來，實在很難不笑出聲音來。

　　這天下午的每时時光都充滿了各種新奇事物，金黃色陽光愈加燦爛。輪椅又被推回華蓋下，迪肯坐在草地上拿出笛子。這時，柯林才有空檔注意到一樣事物。

　　「那邊那棵樹很老了吧？」他說。

　　迪肯的目光橫越草地看到了那棵樹，瑪莉也看著，片刻沉靜。

　　「是啊。」迪肯低聲回答，聲音很輕柔。

　　瑪莉凝視著那棵樹沉思。

　　「樹枝是灰色的，沒有葉子，」柯林又說：「它應該是死的吧？」

　　「是啊，」迪肯同意，「不過樹上爬滿了玫瑰花，等那裡長滿了葉子和花朵，就會把死掉的樹枝蓋住了，到時候看起來就不會是死的，而會是這裡最漂亮的了。」

　　瑪莉依舊凝視著樹沉思。

　　「看起來好像有一根大樹枝斷掉了，」柯林說道：「我想知道它為什麼會斷掉的。」

　　「那是好幾年前斷掉的。」迪肯回答，「啊！」他忽然鬆了口氣，把手搭在柯林的身上：「汝看那隻知更鳥！就是牠！牠正在幫伴侶覓食呢。」

　　柯林太慢了，只稍微瞥見紅色的胸脯一閃而過，嘴裡啣著東西。知更鳥快速飛過綠葉叢，進入枝葉茂密的角落消失不見。柯林又躺回座墊上輕輕笑了起來。

「牠在給女朋友送茶，現在大概是五點吧，我也想喝點茶了。」

瑪莉和迪肯總算逃過一劫。

「是魔法把知更鳥送來的。」瑪莉後來悄悄地跟迪肯說：「我知道那是魔法。」

她和迪肯早就擔心柯林會問起十年前斷掉的那根樹枝，他們一起討論過這件事，迪肯苦惱地抓著頭。

「我們要假裝這棵樹跟別的樹沒什麼兩樣，不可以跟這個可憐的囝兒說樹枝是怎麼斷的。他要是問起來，我們就要假裝很開心的樣子。」迪肯說。

「對，我們一定要這樣。」瑪莉回答道。

不過當她盯著那棵樹時，她知道自己看起來並沒有多高興。她一直在想迪肯所說的另一件事是不是真的。

迪肯還在困惑地搔著自己紅褐色的頭髮，不過藍眼睛裡已經浮現出安心的神情。「柯萊文夫人是個迷人的年輕女士。」迪肯吞吞吐吐地說：「媽媽說，或許她回來過密朔兌莊園很多次，想照顧柯林，就像所有過世的媽媽一樣，都會回來。也許她就在花園裡，也許就是她讓我們開始整理花園，要我們把柯林帶過來的。」

瑪莉覺得迪肯說的就是魔法，她是魔法的虔誠信徒。私底下她深信迪肯對身邊事物都施展了魔法，當然啦，都是好的魔法。這就是為什麼大家那麼喜歡他，連動物也要跟他做朋友。

瑪莉想，柯林問起那個危險的問題時，搞不好就是迪肯的魔法把知更鳥及時召喚過來的。瑪莉覺得迪肯整個下午都在施展魔法，讓柯林看起來像完全變了一個人。現在的柯林看起來一點也不像那個搥打枕頭尖叫的瘋小孩。甚至他象牙般蒼白的臉色也起了變化。他剛進到花園時，在臉上、頸部和手上所出現的光彩，都還沒有完全褪去。他現在看起來像有血有肉的人，不再像象牙或是蠟那麼蒼白了。

他們看到知更鳥送了兩、三趟食物給女伴，這讓柯林想起了下午茶，他覺得大家也該喝點下午茶了。

他說：「叫個男僕用籃子帶些茶到杜鵑花道上，妳再跟迪肯把茶帶到這裡來。」

這是個好主意，而且容易實行。他們將白色的餐巾鋪在草地上，愉快地享用熱茶、奶油土司和鬆脆圓餅。好幾隻正忙著築巢的小鳥都停下來看看他們在做什麼，又忙不迭地來撿麵包屑吃。

豆子和果殼咬著餅乾又消失在樹上，煤灰咬走了一片塗了奶油的圓餅，跑到角落去啄著餅乾檢查，將餅乾轉來轉去，粗嘎地發表意見，最後決定高興地一口吞下。

慢慢地來到了向晚時分，金色陽光顏色漸深，蜜蜂都回家了，天上飛鳥稀落。迪肯和瑪莉坐在草地上，將裝茶的籃子收拾好，準備帶回屋子裡。柯林躺在靠墊上，將額前濃密的髮絡撥到兩邊去，臉色看起來很自然。

「但願今天下午不會就樣就結束了。」他說：「我明天還要再來，後天、大後天、大大後天都會來。」

「這樣你就可以呼吸到很多新鮮空氣了，對不對？」瑪莉說。

柯林回答：「我不求什麼了，我看了春天，還要看夏天，

要看這裡生長的一切，也要自己在這裡種東西。」

「沒問題，我們會幫助汝學走路，不久汝就可以像其他孩子一樣挖土了。」迪肯說。

柯林的臉上泛起大片的紅光。

「走路！挖土！我真的能做到嗎？」他說。

迪肯小心翼翼地看著柯林，他和瑪莉都沒問過柯林的腿究竟有什麼問題。

「汝一定可以的，汝自己有腿，就跟其他人一樣！」迪肯語氣堅決地說。

瑪莉原本很擔心，但是聽到柯林的回答後就放心了。

他說：「我的腿其實不會痛，只是太瘦弱了，還會發抖，所以我不敢站起來。」

迪肯和瑪莉都鬆了口氣。

「等汝不再害怕，汝就可以站得起來了，」迪肯開心地說：「過不了多久，汝就不會害怕了。」

柯林說道：「真的嗎？」他靜靜地躺著，若有所思。

他們沉默半晌，太陽漸漸低垂，此刻萬籟俱寂。他們三人都度過了忙碌興奮的下午。柯林休息著，一副很舒服的樣子。動物們不再四處亂跑，而是聚攏他們的身邊。煤灰棲息在一根低低樹枝上，縮起一隻腳，昏昏欲睡地垂下灰色的眼翳，瑪莉覺得牠都快打鼾了。

在這片寂靜中，柯林突然抬起頭來，驚慌地低聲說：「那是誰？」

迪肯和瑪莉連忙站起身來。

「有人嗎？」他們兩個低聲叫出來。

柯林指著高牆。

「你們看！你們看！」他激動地輕聲說。

瑪莉和迪肯轉過身去，班正站在梯子的頂端，從牆的另一邊氣呼呼地瞪著他們，還對瑪莉揮舞著拳頭。

「如果我不是王老五，而汝是我的囡兒的話，我一定痛打汝一頓！」他叫道。

班又面帶威脅地再往上踩了一級階梯，好像精力充沛地想要跳下去和瑪莉對決，不過等她主動走近他，他又改變了心意，決定站在梯子最上面一級，往下對著瑪莉揮舞拳頭。

班滔滔不絕地說著：「我從不把汝放在眼裡！我第一眼看到汝就對汝沒好感，汝這個面無血色、瘦巴巴的小掃帚，老是問個沒完，還到處去不該去的地方打探。我真不知道怎麼汝可以變得跟我這麼親近，要不是因為知更鳥的話，真是見鬼——」

「班。」瑪莉終於回過神來，她站在班的下方，喘著氣向他叫著：「班，是知更鳥指路給我的！」

聽到這句話，班差點跌到牆的這一邊來，他實在是太生氣了。

「汝這個壞囡兒！」他對瑪莉說：「汝還把壞事推到知更鳥身上，雖說牠平常是很不謹慎，但牠指路給汝看！牠！哎呀！汝這個囡兒。」瑪莉知道班接下來會說什麼，因為他實在是太好奇了，「汝究竟是怎麼進去的？」

「的確是知更鳥指路給我看的！」瑪莉又說道：「牠不是有意這麼做的，可就是牠指的路。如果你這樣一直對我揮拳頭，我就沒辦法告訴你事情是怎麼發生的。」

班突然停住揮舞的拳頭，嘴巴張得大大的，因為他看到有什麼正從草地上過來。

　　聽到班破口大罵，柯林很驚訝，像被符鎮住一樣，只是坐直身子聽著。他冷靜下來，很有威嚴地向迪肯招了招手。

　　「推我到那邊去！」他命令道：「把我推近一點，就停在他的面前！」

　　就是這幅景象，讓班驚嚇得下巴掉了下來。朝著他推來的輪椅上裝飾著豪華的座墊和長袍，看起來就像王室的馬車。椅子上躺坐著一位小王侯，大大的黑眼睛露出皇帝般的威嚴，細瘦蒼白的手高傲地伸向班。輪椅馬車停在班的面前，難怪他的嘴巴會張得那麼大。

　　「你知道我是誰嗎？」小王侯問道。

　　班看得目瞪口呆，一雙紅色的蒼老眼睛，像見到鬼似地盯著前方，直盯盯地注視著，嚥下一大口的口水，一句話都說不出來。

　　「你知道我是誰嗎？」柯林又問了一次，語氣更加高傲，「回答我！」

　　班舉起自己粗糙的手，揉揉眼睛，又摸摸額頭，才用怪異顫抖的聲音回答。

　　「汝是誰？」他說：「我知道汝是誰——在汝的臉上，汝媽的眼睛在看著我。天知道汝是怎麼進來的，汝就是那個可憐的殘廢吧。」

　　柯林頓時滿臉通紅地坐直起來。

　　「我沒有殘廢！沒有殘廢！」他憤怒地大叫道。

　　「他才沒有殘廢！」瑪莉氣沖沖地對著牆大吼：「他背上的腫塊還沒有大頭針那麼大！我看過了，他背上一個腫塊也沒有！」

　　班又摸摸額頭，盯著他們看，似乎怎麼也看不夠。他的手、嘴巴和聲音都在顫抖。班是個無知笨拙的老人，他只記得他聽來的事情。

「汝——汝不是駝子嗎？」班用粗嘎的聲音說。

「不是！」柯林大吼。

「汝——汝的腿也不彎嗎？」班用更粗嘎的聲音顫抖地問。

這實在是太過分了，柯林平常發脾氣的那股力量以新的方式在奔流著。從來也沒有人說過他的腳畸形，就算有人竊竊私語也沒有這樣說過。小王侯無法容忍從班的口中聽到這樣的事，怒氣和自尊心讓他忘掉一切，他感受到身上充滿了一種前所未有、簡直像是超自然的力量。

「過來這裡！」他對迪肯吼道，然後將覆蓋在腿上的毯子掀開，「過來這裡！過來這裡！快點！」

迪肯立刻跑到柯林身邊，瑪莉屏息以待，覺得自己的臉色都刷白了。

「他做得到！他做得到！他做得到！他可以的！」她急促含糊地低聲自言自語。

柯林把毯子粗暴地抓起來丟到地上，迪肯扶著柯林的手臂，柯林細瘦的腿露了出來，細瘦的腳掌站到了草地上。柯林站得很直、很直，像箭那麼直，而且看起來異常的高。他把頭高高抬起，奇異的眼裡閃耀著光芒。

「你看我！你看我——就是你！你看著我！」他朝著班昂起頭來。

「他站得跟我一樣直，跟約克郡所有的囝兒都一樣直！」迪肯叫道。

班的反應讓瑪莉覺得很奇怪，他一邊哽咽，一邊抑制著自己的感情，眼淚倏地就從飽經風霜的臉龐流了下來，蒼老的手緊緊握在一起。

他突然開口：「啊！他們都是胡說八道！汝雖然瘦巴巴的，白得跟鬼一樣，可是汝身上一個腫塊也沒有，汝會長成男子漢的。上帝保佑汝！」

迪肯強而有力地扶著柯林的手臂，柯林穩如泰山，站得更挺直了，正面直視著班。

柯林說：「我爸爸不在時，我就是你的主人，你得聽我的話。這是我的花園，你最好不要說出去！你現在從梯子上爬下來，走到長走道上，瑪莉小姐會在那裡和你碰面，把你帶到這裡來，我有話要跟你說。我們本來不希望被你看到的，現在既然你發現了，我們就把祕密告訴你。快一點！」

剛才那一陣眼淚，讓班那張滿腹牢騷的老臉還是濕濕的，他的視線簡直無法從站得挺直、頭抬得高高的柯林身上挪開。

「啊！囝兒，」他幾乎是耳語道：「啊！我的囝兒。」接著他意識到自己的失態，突然摸了摸他的園丁帽，說：「是的，少爺！是的，少爺！」他遵命地從梯子上爬下來，消失在圍牆上。

第二十二章

當太陽下山時

班爬下梯子，柯林轉過身對瑪莉說：「妳去帶他進來。」瑪莉便飛奔過草地，跑到常春藤下的門邊。

迪肯目光敏銳地看著柯林，柯林的臉頰有紅色斑點，看起來很不可思議，也沒有要跌倒的樣子。

「我站得起來。」他說著，頭抬得高高的，講話的樣子很有威嚴。

「我告訴過汝，只要汝不再害怕，馬上就能站起來，汝現在已經不怕了。」迪肯回答道。

「對，我已經不怕了。」柯林說。

這時他忽然想到瑪莉跟他說過的一件事。

「你在施魔法嗎？」柯林突然問。

迪肯嘴角一彎，開心地笑了起來。

「是汝自己在施法，就跟讓花草從土裡長出來的魔法一樣。」說著，就用厚厚的靴子碰了碰草地上的一叢番紅花。

柯林低頭看著花。

「是啊，」他慢慢地說：「不可能有比這更神奇的魔法了——不可能有了。」

他又站得更加挺直。

「我要走到那棵樹那裡。」他指著幾呎外的一棵樹，

「等班進來，我要站著。我想休息時可以靠著樹休息，想坐時也可以坐下，不過我要先站著等班來。從椅子上拿條毯子給我。」

柯林走向那棵樹，雖然迪肯扶著他的胳膊，但他自己也走得很穩健。他靠著樹幹站立，但看不太出來有利用樹幹來支撐身體。他還是站得很挺直，看起來很高。

班穿越牆門進來，看到柯林正站在那裡，這時他聽到瑪莉低聲地喃喃自語。

他焦躁地問：「汝在嘀咕個啥？」他可不想分心，想把全副精神都放在那個神情驕傲、高瘦挺直的男孩身上。

瑪莉沒有回答，其實她是在說：「你做得到！你做得到！我說過你做得到的！你做得到！你做得到的！你可以的！」

她這番話是對柯林說的，她想施展魔法讓柯林能一直那樣站著。柯林如果在班進來之前就放棄，她會受不了的。不過柯林並沒有放棄。瑪莉忽然發覺柯林雖然骨瘦如柴，卻長得很俊俏。他用著有趣的高傲神情看著班。

「你看著我！」他命令道：「你好好看清楚！我是個駝子嗎？我的腿是彎的嗎？」

班的情緒還沒有完全平復下來，但已經稍微冷靜了些，他用慣有的語氣回答柯林。

他說：「沒有，一點也沒有。汝為什麼要把自己藏起來，讓大夥兒以為汝是個殘廢、傻瓜？」

「傻瓜！誰說我是傻瓜？」柯林生氣地說。

「很多笨蛋都這麼說，」班回答：「世界上到處都是只會胡說八道的傻瓜。汝為什麼把自己關起來？」

「大家都以為我會死掉，」柯林馬上說：「我不會！」

　　柯林說這話時意志堅定，班從頭到腳不住地打量他。

　　「汝會死？」班帶著乾巴巴的喜悅說，「沒這回事，汝太勇敢了。我看到汝那麼急地把腳放在地上，我就知道汝不會有問題的。少爺，汝先坐在毯子上，有啥事儘管吩咐吧！」

　　班的態度奇特地混合了暴躁的溫柔和敏銳的體諒。剛剛瑪莉和班在長走道行走時，瑪莉急著告知他要記住一件事，那就是柯林的身體正在好轉，是這個花園讓他變好的，大家都不可以讓他再想到駝背和死亡的事。

　　小王侯不擺架子地坐在樹下的毯子上。

「班，你在花園裡都在忙些什麼？」柯林問道。

「人家叫我做啥，我就做啥，」老班回答：「我是蒙受別人的恩惠才能留在這裡的——因為她喜歡我。」

「她？」柯林說。

「就是汝媽媽。」班回答。

「我媽媽？」柯林說著，安靜地看了看四周，「這是她以前的花園，是不是？」

「是啊！」班也看看周圍說，「她很喜歡這個花園。」

「現在這裡變成我的花園了，我很喜歡這個花園，我每天都要來這裡，」柯林宣布道：「但這是祕密，我的命令就是不准讓任何人知道我們來到這裡。迪肯和瑪莉很努力地讓花園重新活了過來。以後我會偶爾叫你過來幫忙——可是你來的時候不能讓人家看到。」

班的臉擠成一團，露出乾癟蒼老的微笑。

「我以前也會偷偷進來這裡，不讓任何人看到。」他說。

「什麼！什麼時候？」柯林叫道。

「我上次來的時候，」班抓抓下巴，四處看看，「大概是兩年前的事了。」

「可是這裡已經有十年『沒有人』進來過了！沒有門可以進來！」柯林叫道。

老班冷淡地說：「我就是那個『沒有人』，再說我也不是從門進來的，我是爬牆過來的。這兩年我風濕痛得厲害，就沒再進來了。」

「汝進來修剪植物，對不對？難怪我一直想不通，為什麼樹木看起來好像有修剪過的樣子。」迪肯叫道。

「她以前很喜歡這個花園，真的！」班慢慢地說：「她是那麼的年輕漂亮，有一次她笑著跟我說：『班，如果我生病或是不在了，你一定要來幫我照顧玫瑰花。』她過世後，主人命令不准任何人進來這裡，但我還是照來不誤。」班暴躁而固執地說：「我爬牆進來，一直到風濕發作了，才沒再進來。我每年會來整理花園一次，是她先吩咐我這麼做的！」

「我想，汝如果沒有來照顧花園，花園現在看起來就不會這麼有生氣。」迪肯說道。

柯林說：「班，我很高興你這麼做了。你知道該怎麼保密吧。」

「是啊，我知道的，少爺。」班回答：「對患風濕的人來說，直接從門走進來是容易多啦。」

樹旁的草地上擺著瑪莉的小鏟子，柯林伸手把鏟子撿起來，臉上露出很不一樣的神情，開始在地上挖土。柯林的手細瘦無力，但他們現在看到柯林將小鏟子插進土裡，攪動泥土。瑪莉屏息地看著他的動作。

「你做得到的！你做得到的！」瑪莉自言自語地說：「我告訴你，你做得到的！」

迪肯的圓眼睛裡充滿了好奇，可他什麼也沒說。班也是興致盎然地看著。

柯林繼續挖，挖了幾鏟子土後，他得意洋洋地用道地的約克郡方言跟迪肯說話。

「汝說會讓我跟其他人一樣在這裡走路，還說會讓我挖土，我以為汝只是在哄我。今天是我第一次進到花園，我已經會走路了，現在我還在挖土呢！」

班聽到這話，嘴巴張得大大的，低聲地咯咯笑。

他說：「啊！看來汝很聰明，汝是個百分之百的約克郡団兒。汝還會挖土。汝有沒有想要種啥呀？我可以給汝帶盆玫瑰花來。」

「去拿！快點！快點！」柯林說道，興奮地挖著土。

班速度飛快地去拿玫瑰花拿，似乎忘了自己的風濕痛。迪肯拿起鏟子，將柯林用細瘦的手所挖出的洞，再挖得更深、更寬些。瑪莉悄悄地跑出去拿了灑水壺回來。迪肯挖著洞，柯林把柔軟的土翻鬆。柯林望著天空，這個奇妙的新運動雖然強度很低，卻讓他容光煥發。

「我想在太陽下山前把玫瑰花種下去。」他說。

瑪莉覺得今天的太陽好像故意晚了幾分鐘才下山。班從溫室把玫瑰花裝在盆子裡帶來，蹣跚的步伐奮力快步地走過草坪。班也開始變得很興奮。跪在洞旁，將花盆打破。

「拿去吧，団兒，」他將花遞給柯林，「汝自己把花種到土裡面，國王每到一個新的地方都會這麼做。」

柯林細瘦蒼白的手微微顫抖著，他把玫瑰花放到土裡面，臉色愈來愈紅潤。柯林握著花，老班把泥土壓實，在洞裡填滿泥土，牢牢壓平。瑪莉把身子向前傾，撐在手和膝蓋上。煤灰飛下來看看他們在做什麼。豆子和果殼在櫻桃樹上，喋喋不休地討論這件事。

「花種好了！」柯林說道：「太陽現在才落下。迪肯，扶我一下，我想要站著看太陽下山，這也是魔法的一部分。」

迪肯把柯林扶起來，而魔法——不管它究竟是什麼——賦予了柯林極大的力量。等到太陽終於落下，這個美妙愉快的下午也落幕了。柯林真的用自己的雙腳站起來了，而且滿臉笑容的。

第二十三章

魔法

等他們回到屋子裡的時候，柯萊文醫生已經等候一陣子了，甚至想是否該派人去花園步道找他們。等柯林返回房間，這可憐的男人仔細地檢查了他一番。

他說：「你不應該在外面待這麼久的，不要累壞了自己啊。」

柯林說：「我一點都不累，我覺得去戶外好多了，明天早上和下午我還要出去。」

「我不知道能不能答應，」柯萊文醫生回答：「我擔心這樣不太明智。」

「想阻止我出去才是不明智，」柯林嚴肅地說：「我就是要出去。」

就連瑪莉也發現了柯林的這個特點，當他在指使別人時，像個蠻橫的小暴君，但他不自知。柯林就像個活在荒島上的國王，他想怎樣就怎樣，沒有人能夠壓得住他。

瑪莉原本跟柯林很像，但來到密朔兒莊園以後，她慢慢發現自己的這種態度並不正常，也不受人歡迎。發現這一點之後，瑪莉覺得把這個心得告訴柯林應該會有幫助。等柯萊文醫生離開後，瑪莉坐在一旁，好奇地看了柯林幾分鐘，想讓柯林問她在看什麼。當然，她成功辦到了。

「妳為什麼這樣看著我？」柯林問。

「我真替柯萊文醫生感到難過。」

「我也是，」柯林露出些許滿意的神情，平靜地說：「現在我已經不會死了，他不會得到密朔兌莊園的。」

「當然，會替他難過也是有這個原因，」瑪莉說：「可是我剛剛在想，要對著一個粗魯的小孩這樣畢恭畢敬十年，一定是件很可怕的事。要是我就做不到。」

「我很粗魯嗎？」柯林不為所動地問道。

瑪莉說：「如果你是他的小孩，而他又會打人的話，他一定會打你耳光的。」

「他不敢。」柯林說。

「他是不敢，」瑪莉不帶偏見地思考著，「沒有人敢做你不喜歡的事，這是因為大家都以為你會死掉呀什麼的，你以前可真是個可憐蟲。」

柯林倔強地宣布：「但是我不要再當可憐蟲了。我不要別人把我當成可憐蟲看，今天下午我已經可以站起來了。」

「你就是為所欲為，才會讓你變得很奇怪。」瑪莉說著自己的想法。

柯林皺起眉頭，將臉轉過來。

「我很奇怪嗎？」他問。

瑪莉回答：「是啊，很奇怪。不過，你用不著生氣。」她公平地補充道：「因為我也很奇怪，班也很奇怪。不過我現在不像以前那麼奇怪了，我開始喜歡別人，而且還發現了祕密花園。」

柯林說，「我不想當怪人，我以後不要當怪人。」他又意志堅定地皺起眉頭。

柯林是個自尊心很強的孩子。他躺著沉思了一會兒，瑪莉看到他露出美麗的笑容，整個臉看起來都不一樣了。

　　「如果我每天都去花園，就不會奇怪了。那裡有魔法，而且是好的魔法，瑪莉，我確定那裡有魔法。」他說。

　　「我也這麼覺得。」瑪莉說。

　　柯林說：「就算沒有真的魔法，我們也可以假裝有，那裡一定有什麼東西存在著，真的！」

　　瑪莉說：「那是魔法，但不是什麼黑魔法，而且和白雪一樣純潔。」

　　他們就這樣一直稱它是魔法，在接下來的幾個月，他們真的度過了奇妙燦爛、不可思議的日子。哦，花園裡發生了一連串神奇的事！如果你從未有過花園，你就無法瞭解。你要是有花園，你就會明白那得要一整本書才能描述花園裡所發生的一切。

　　先是綠色植物不斷從土裡冒出來，草坪、花床甚至牆壁縫隙中也是，接著開始發芽，花苞綻放出五顏六色的花朵，有深淺不一的藍色和紫色，還有濃淡不一的深紅色。花兒們快樂地從每個小洞和角落裡冒出來。

　　班目睹這些事情一一發生，他刮下牆上磚塊間的砂漿，做成袋袋的營養土，用來培育漂亮的藤蔓。鳶尾花、白色百合花紛紛從草地裡冒出來，綠色小亭裡長滿了一大片花瓣細長、藍白相間的高大飛燕草、夢幻草和風鈴草，令人驚嘆。

　　班說：「她很喜歡這些花，她總說她喜歡朝向藍天的植物。她並不是瞧不

起泥土，反而是很喜歡，只是她說，藍天看起來讓人歡欣鼓舞。」

迪肯和瑪莉播下的種子，彷彿有小仙子照料過似地生長出來。絲緞般的各色嬰粟花成群地在風中搖曳舞動，使得那些在花園裡生長多年的植物感到好奇，這麼多陌生的花朵是如何來到這裡的。

還有玫瑰——那些玫瑰花！它們從草地裡冒出來，繞滿日晷儀，捲繞著樹幹，垂下樹枝又蔓延到牆上，形成長長的花圈，宛如瀑布般垂下來，一天天、一分一秒地活了過來。

到處都長滿了漂亮的新葉和花苞，原本小小的花苞漸漸膨脹，像是被施展了魔法，最後綻放成裝滿芬芳香氣的杯子，香氣溢出杯緣，瀰漫整個花園。

柯林目睹了這一切變化的發生。每天早上他都會被帶到外面去，只要不下雨，就在花園裡度過一整天，即使是陰天也很開心。

他說他會躺在草地上，「看東西長出來」。他還說，如果看久一點的話，就會看到花苞綻放開來，還可以認識一些忙碌的怪蟲子，雖然不知道牠們在忙什麼，但顯然牠們是在辦重要的差事。有時是搬運一些小根稻草、羽毛或是食物，有時像是爬樹般地爬上葉刃，在那上頭可以瞭望整個地區。

一隻鼴鼠在地洞的盡頭，用長著長指甲的腳掌，將土堆成小丘，挖出地道，牠的腳掌看起來就像小精靈的手。這隻鼴鼠吸引了柯林一整個早上的注意力。

迪肯跟柯林介紹了螞蟻的習性、甲蟲的習性、蜜蜂的習性、青蛙的習性、小鳥的習性、植物的習性，這成為了柯林探索的新世界。迪肯還說了狐狸的習性、水獺的習性、白鼬的習性、松鼠的習性、鱒魚的習性、河鼠的習性和獾的習性，有源源不絕的話題可以聊、可以想。

這還不到魔法的一半呢，事實上柯林能夠站起來之後，有了許許多多的想法。當瑪莉說自己所施展的魔咒時，柯林感到很興奮，也很認同，不斷地談論著魔法。

「世界上一定存在著許多魔法。」有一次他用博學的語氣說：「只是人們不知道魔法是什麼樣子，也不知道該怎麼變魔法。或許只要開始說會有好事發生，好事情就有可能真的會發生。我要來試一試，做做實驗。」

第二天早上，他們一進到祕密花園，柯林馬上把班叫了過來。班很快趕來，看到小王侯正站在樹下，氣度恢宏，臉上帶著迷人的微笑。

「早安，班，」柯林說：「我希望你、迪肯和瑪莉站成一排聽我說話，因為我有很重要的事情要跟你們說。」

「是的，是的，少爺！」班將手放在額邊敬禮回道。班有一個向來不為人所知的魅力，他年少時曾在海上航行好一段時間，所以會用水手的方式應答。

小王侯解釋道：「我要做個科學實驗，等我長大以後，我要做很多偉大的科學發明，現在就從這個實驗開始吧。」

「是的，是的，少爺！」班很快回答，雖然這是他第一次聽到什麼「偉大的科學發明」。

這也是瑪莉第一次聽到這個詞，不過她現在開始意識到柯林雖然很奇怪，卻讀過很多稀奇古怪的東西，而且是個具有說服力的男孩。當他把頭抬得高高，用奇異的眼神緊盯著你看，你似乎會不由自主地相信柯林所說的話，即使他才快要十一歲而已。在這一刻，他更是深具說服力，忽然可以像個大人一樣地演講了，連他自己都覺得很著迷。

「我現在要做的偉大科學發明，」他繼續說：「和魔法有關。魔法是很了不起的東西，可是除了古書裡的一些人，幾乎沒有人知道魔法。瑪莉知道一點點魔法，因為她是在印度出生的，那邊有苦行者。我相信迪肯也懂一點魔法，但是他大概不知道自己懂魔法，他可以迷住動物和人類。如果不是因為他是個動物術士，我是不會叫他來見我的。他還可以迷住小男孩，因為男孩也是動物。我確定所有東西裡面都有魔法，只是我們沒有足夠的能力去掌控魔法——讓魔法為我們服務，就像電力、馬匹還有蒸汽為我們服務一樣。」

這一切聽起來是那麼了不起，班激動得再也無法保持冷靜。

「是的，是的，少爺！」班答道，身體站得挺直。

「當瑪莉剛發現這個花園時，這裡一片死氣沉沉，」演說家繼續說：「然後有某種東西開始把植物從土裡推出來，讓一切無中生有。這些東西原本不在那裡，突然間它們就出現。以前我從來沒有仔細看過什麼東西，現在這一切讓我很好奇。科學家都是富有好奇心的，我也會成為科學家。我一直在心裡問：『這是什麼？那是什麼？』一定有一股力量存在，不可能沒有東西！我不知道它叫什麼，姑且就稱它是魔法。」

「我沒有看過日出，可是瑪莉和迪肯看過，根據他們的描述，我確定那也是魔法。有什麼東西把太陽往上推，拉著它走。自從我進入這個花園，有時我會從樹叢中望向天空，很奇怪，我會覺得很快樂，就好像我的胸中有什麼東西在推拉，讓我的呼吸加快。魔法總是在推拉，讓一切無中生有。

所有的東西都是由魔法變出來的，綠葉和樹木、花朵、小鳥、獾、狐狸、松鼠、人類。魔法一定環繞在我們的周遭，在這花園裡，在所有地方。是這個花園裡的魔法讓我站起來的，也讓我知道我會一直活著，一直長成大人。」

「我要做的科學實驗就是去獲得魔法，將魔法放在我身上，讓它推著我、拉著我，讓我變得強壯。我不知道該怎麼做，可是我想如果我一直想著它、呼喚它，或許它就會來了。也許這就是獲得魔法的第一步。當我第一次試著站起來時，瑪莉一直自言自語說：『你做得到的！你做得到的！』我就真的做到了。當時我自己當然也有努力，不過是她的魔法幫了我，迪肯的魔法也同樣幫了我。以後的每天早上和晚上，只要我記得，我就要說：『我身上有魔法！魔法讓我的身體變好了！我會跟迪肯一樣強壯，我要和他一樣強壯！』你也要這麼做，班。這是我的實驗，你會幫我嗎？」

「會的，會的，少爺！是的，是的！」班回答。

「如果每天像士兵操練一樣規律地做，我們可以看看會發生什麼，看看這個實驗會不會成功。就像我們學東西的時候要一直唸它們的名字，不停地想，它們就會永遠留在腦海裡，我想魔法也是這樣的。如果你一直召喚它來幫助你，它就會變成你的一部分，留下來幫你做事。」

「在印度，我聽過一個軍官跟我媽媽說，那些苦行者會一直唸著某些字，唸上好幾千遍。」瑪莉說。

「我聽過傑姆·費多沃斯的太太一直重複說，『傑姆是個酒鬼』，說了好幾千遍，」班冷淡地說：「傑姆就把他老婆痛打一頓，然後到『藍獅』去喝得醉醺醺。」

柯林皺起眉頭，沉思了幾分鐘。不一會兒，他又高興了起來。

「你看，魔法真的有用，她就是用了不正確的魔法才會挨打。如果她使用了正確的魔法，講些好聽的話，她老公就不會喝得爛醉如泥了，甚至還可能買頂新帽子給她呢！」

班低聲地咯咯笑了起來，蒼老的小眼睛露出敏銳的讚賞之情。

「柯林少爺，汝是個聰明的囝兒，就像汝站得直直的腿一樣。」他說：「下次我要是再看到貝絲‧費多沃斯，我會稍微給她一些暗示，告訴她魔法能幫上什麼忙。如果汝的科學實驗成功了，那她一定會很高興，傑姆也會很高興的。」

迪肯站著聽了柯林的這一席話，圓圓的眼睛閃耀著好奇與喜悅的光芒。豆子和果殼停在他肩上，懷裡抱著一隻長耳的白兔，迪肯不時輕柔地撫摸著，兔子把耳朵伏貼在背上，玩得很高興。

「你覺得我的實驗會成功嗎？」柯林問迪肯，他很想知道迪肯的想法。每當迪肯帶著快樂的微笑看著他或是他的動物時，柯林總是很好奇迪肯在想什麼。

迪肯現在笑了，笑得比以往更加燦爛。

「是啊，」他回答：「我想實驗會成功的，就像太陽照在種子上，種子會發生變化一樣。實驗一定會成功的，我們要不要現在就開始？」

柯林和瑪莉都很高興，插圖裡的苦行者刺激了柯林的想像力，他提議大家兩腿交叉、盤坐在那棵樹的罩篷下。

「這樣我們就像是坐在寺廟裡一樣。」柯林說：「我很累，我想要坐下來。」

迪肯說：「啊！汝不可以一開始就說累，這樣會破壞魔法的。」

柯林轉過身去看著迪肯無邪的圓眼睛。

「你說得對，」他慢慢地說：「我只可以一心一意想著魔法。」

他們圍成一圈坐下來，一切看起來莊嚴而神祕。班覺得自己好像被帶進了祈禱會裡，通常他對祈禱會裡的人很有成見，可是現在涉及到小王侯的事，所以他並不討厭，甚至還很感激可以被叫來參加。瑪莉感到了神聖的喜悅，迪肯懷裡抱著兔子，或許是他暗中給了動物們什麼特殊信號，當他跟著其他人盤腿坐下時，烏鴉、狐狸、松鼠還有小羊也慢慢地靠攏加入圓圈，各自找地方安頓下來。

「動物們也來了，」柯林嚴肅地說：「牠們也想來幫忙。」

瑪莉覺得柯林看起來很英俊，他把頭抬得高高的，像個祭司一樣，奇異的雙眼流露出奇妙的眼神看著他們。太陽光穿過罩篷般的樹枝，照射在他身上。

「我們現在要開始了，」他說：「瑪莉，我們是不是應該像伊斯蘭教的苦行僧一樣，身體前後搖擺？」

「我的身子沒辦法前後搖來搖去，」班說：「我有風濕。」

「魔法會帶走你的風濕，」柯林用大祭司的語氣說：「那我們就等你風濕好了再來做這個，我們現在先來吟唱。」

「我不會唱歌，」班有點暴躁地說：「我以前試過一次，但是被唱詩班拒絕了。」

大家聽了都沒有笑，態度很認真。柯林一點也沒有流露出不耐煩的樣子，他心裡只想著魔法。

「那我來唱。」說著便像個奇怪的精靈開始唱起歌來：「陽光普照、陽光普照，那就是魔法。花兒盛開，樹根在動，那就是魔法。活著就是魔法，身體強壯就是魔法。魔法在我的體內，魔法在我的體內，它在我的體內，它在我的體內，它在每個人的體內。它在班的背上。魔法！魔法！來幫助我們吧！」

柯林重覆了很多次，雖然還不到一千次，不過確實重覆了很多遍。瑪莉聽得有點精神恍惚，覺得這些話聽起來奇怪又美妙，她希望柯林能一直唱下去。班開始感受到一種令人愉悅的夢境感。

花叢中的蜜蜂嗡嗡聲和柯林的唱誦聲交雜一起，讓人昏昏欲睡。迪肯盤坐地上，一隻手抱著睡著的兔子，另一隻手放在小羊的背上。煤灰將一隻松鼠推開，在迪肯的肩膀上縮成一團，灰色的眼瞼蓋住了眼睛。柯林最後終於停住不唱了。

「現在我要繞著花園走。」他宣布道。

剛才低著頭的班，突然猛地抬起頭來。

「你睡著了。」柯林說。

「才沒有呢，」班喃喃地說：「汝的講道很好，但我要趁還沒開始募捐趕快出去。」

班還沒有完全醒來。

「你現在不是在教堂裡。」柯林說。

班說著伸直了身子：「我當然不是在教堂裡，誰說我在教堂裡？我清清楚楚聽到汝說的每一句話，汝說魔法在我的背上，可是醫生管它叫風濕病呢。」

小王侯揮了揮他的手。

「那是錯誤的魔法，」他說：「你會好起來的。你現在可以回去工作了，但是明天記得還要再過來。」

「可是我想看汝繞著花園走。」班咕噥地說。

這咕噥並非是不友善，可終究還是咕噥。其實這個頑固的老頭，對魔法半信半疑，他已經打定主意，要是被遣走，他就要爬上梯子，從牆外偷偷看他們。這樣一來，柯林少爺要是跌倒了，他還可以蹣跚地趕過來幫忙。

小王侯並不反對班留下來，因此遊行隊伍就這麼形成了，看起來真是有模有樣。柯林站在隊伍的最前端，迪肯和瑪莉站在柯林兩旁。班走在後面，動物們尾隨在後。小羊還有小狐狸緊跟在迪肯身邊，小白兔向前蹦跳或停下來咬咬東西，煤灰也莊嚴地跟隨著隊伍，感覺像是隊伍的負責人。

隊伍前進得很緩慢，可是很莊嚴。他們每走幾步路，就停下來休息一會，柯林會靠在迪肯的手臂上，班會偷偷地留意他。不過柯林有時會把手放開，自己走幾步路。他的頭總是抬得高高的，看起來甚具威嚴。

他不斷說：「魔法在我的體內！魔法讓我變強壯了！我感覺到了魔法！我感覺到了！」

似乎真的有什麼力量在支撐著柯林。他在小亭的椅子上坐下，也在草地上坐了一、兩次，還有好幾次在步道上停下來靠著迪肯，但是他就是要繞完整個花園才肯罷休。當他走回那棵罩篷般的樹下時，臉色容光煥發，帶著勝利的神色。

他叫道：「我做到了！魔法生效了！這是我的第一個科學發明。」

「柯萊文醫生不知道會怎麼說？」瑪莉突然說道。

「他什麼都不會說的，」柯林答：「因為他什麼也不會知道，這是最高機密。等我變得更強壯，可以跟別的男孩一樣走路、跑步了，才能讓其他人知道這件事。我要每天坐著輪椅來這裡，再坐輪椅回去。我不要讓人竊竊私語或是問東問西的，我也不要讓爸爸知道這件事。要等實驗徹底成功才能讓大家知道。等爸爸回到密朔兌莊園，我要走到他的書房，告訴他：『你看，我跟別的小孩一樣，我的身體很好，我會長大成人的。這是科學實驗的結果。』」

「他會以為自己在做夢，」瑪莉叫道：「他會不敢相信自己的眼睛。」

柯林得意得紅了臉，他相信自己一定會好轉的。如果他有察覺到，就會發現自己已經掌握成功的要領了。最讓他感到鼓舞的是，他想像著當父親看到他跟其他小孩一樣挺直強壯時，會是什麼樣的表情。在過去生病的日子裡，最深沉的痛苦就是，他痛恨自己是個身體虛弱、背部有問題的小孩，連自己的爸爸都害怕見到他。

「他會不得不相信的。」他說：「在魔法成功後，在開始做科學發明之前，我想做一名運動員。」

班說：「我們大概一個星期以後就可以送汝去參加拳擊比賽了，汝一定會打贏比賽，成為英國的冠軍職業拳擊手。」

柯林嚴肅地盯著班看。

他說：「班，你這麼說很無禮，你應該要保守祕密，不可以自作主張。不管魔法的效力如何，我都不會成為職業拳擊手的，我要當科學發明家。」

「啊，失禮了，對不起，少爺，我早該知道不能拿這事來開玩笑的。」班摸著額頭敬禮回答。不過他的眼睛卻閃耀著光芒，暗自感到非常欣慰，不在乎被斥責了，因為這代表著這孩子的身心正在積攢力量。

第二十四章

「讓他們笑」

迪肯並不只有在花園工作，高沼地的農舍有塊地，四周圍著粗石矮牆。在清晨、黃昏，或是在沒有去找瑪莉和柯林的時候，迪肯大多在這塊地播種或照料馬鈴薯、甘藍、鬱金香、胡蘿蔔和香草，幫媽媽分擔工作。

在動物們的陪伴下，迪肯在這塊土地上創造奇蹟，像是永遠不會累一樣。挖土或除草時，他都會吹口哨或唱著約克郡的高沼地民謠，要不然就是和煤灰、隊長或是弟弟妹妹說話，教他們如何插手幫忙。

索爾比太太說：「要不是有迪肯來照顧菜園，我們不會過得這麼愜意。他種什麼就會長什麼，馬鈴薯和甘藍比別人家的大兩倍，味道也特別好。」

索爾比太太一有空就喜歡到外頭和迪肯聊天。吃過晚飯、天色還很亮的時候，屬於她的休憩時間。她會坐在矮牆上看著迪肯，聽他說這天發生的趣事，她很喜愛這段時光。

菜園裡不只有蔬菜，迪肯有時也會買些花的種子，將鮮艷芬芳的花種在醋栗甚至是甘藍菜當中。他還種了好幾個花

Gooseberries

床的木犀草、石竹、三色紫羅蘭，他可以將這些植物種子保存好幾年，每年春天都會開花，蔓生成美麗的花叢。

這道矮牆是約克郡最美麗的景致，因為迪肯在每個縫隙都塞滿了高沼地毛地黃、羊齒植物、筷子芥菜和灌木樹籬，生長繁茂，幾乎掩蓋住了牆上石頭。

迪肯會這麼說：「媽媽，要讓它們長得茂盛的方法，就是一定要跟它們作朋友。它們就像是動物，要是渴了，就給水喝；要是餓了，就給一點東西吃，它們跟我們一樣想要活著。如果它們死掉了，我會覺得自己是個壞囝兒，沒有用心照料它們。」

就在這樣的薄暮時分，索爾比太太聽到了密朔兌莊園裡所發生的一切。起初她只聽說柯林少爺特別喜歡跟瑪莉小姐去庭園，身體因此起色了不少。但不久前，這兩個小孩同意讓迪肯的媽媽也知道他們的祕密。不知道為什麼，他們覺得迪肯的媽媽很可靠。

所以在一個美麗寂靜的黃昏，迪肯跟媽媽說了整個來龍去脈，包括一些驚險的細節，像是被埋起來的鑰匙、知更鳥、看起來死氣沉沉的灰霧，和瑪莉小姐打算永遠不要洩露出去的祕密，然後迪肯出現，瑪莉是怎麼跟迪肯講這個祕密的，還有瑪莉對柯林少爺的疑慮，最後他被帶到祕密花園時的戲劇場景。此外，還有班在牆上怒氣沖沖出現的意外事件，以及柯林少爺在憤怒中忽然力氣大增等等。聽到這些，索爾比太太和善臉龐上的表情變了又變。

「天啊！」她說：「那個小姑娘來到莊園可真是件好事。不只是自己得到了成長，也救了柯林少爺。他居然可以站起來！我們都以為他是個可憐的傻瓜，身上沒有一塊骨頭是直的。」

她問了許多的問題，藍色的眼裡一直在沉思著。

「他變得這麼健康快樂、不再抱怨，莊園裡的人有什麼反應呢？」她問道。

「他們也不知道是什麼造成的，」迪肯回答：「他的臉每天看起來都不一樣，臉也愈長愈胖，不再那麼消瘦，連蒼白的臉色也不見了。不過他還是會偶爾得發一下牢騷才可以。」迪肯打趣地咧嘴笑了起來。

「天啊！為什麼呢？」索爾比太太問道。

迪肯咯咯地笑著。

「他是故意這麼做的，以免讓大家猜到有什麼事。要是醫生發現他可以自己站起來，可能就會寫信給柯萊文主人，但是柯林少爺想要自己告訴他這個祕密。他要每天在腳上練習魔法，一直等到爸爸回來，到時候他就可以自己走進爸爸的房間，向他展示自己也可以像別的囝兒一樣站得那麼直。他和瑪莉小姐都覺得最好偶爾發一下牢騷，才不會讓人起疑心。」

迪肯還沒有說完，索爾比太太感到安慰地低聲笑了起來。

她說：「啊！我敢說他倆一定玩得很開心，可以在這當中演戲，囝兒們最愛演戲了。跟我說他們都演些什麼，迪肯。」

迪肯停下除草的工作，坐下來說給索爾比太太聽，眼裡閃耀著快樂的光芒。

他解釋：「柯林少爺每次要出去時，都會有人把他背到樓下的輪椅上。他會故意激怒男僕約翰，說他背的時候不夠小心。他盡量假裝成很無助的樣子，等我們走到都看不見房子時，他才抬頭抬起來。在被抱進輪椅之前，他也會來一陣牢騷。這樣的事他和瑪莉小姐樂在其中，他一抱怨，瑪莉小姐就會說：『可憐的柯林！你痛得那麼厲害嗎？你真的那麼虛弱嗎？可憐的柯林！』麻煩的是，有時候他們會忍不住笑出聲來。等我們安全抵達花園，他們就會笑到喘不過氣來，還得把臉塞進柯林少爺的墊子裡，不讓附近的園丁聽到。」

「他們笑得愈開心，對他們愈好！」索爾比太太說著，自己也笑了起來。「健康乖囝兒的笑聲，比任何藥片都管用。這兩個囝兒一定會長得圓圓胖胖的。」

「他們已經開始變胖了，」迪肯說：「他們簡直是餓瘋了，不知道怎樣才可以填飽肚子而不讓人起疑心。柯林少爺說，如果他一直要人送食物來，他們一定不會相信他是個病人。瑪莉小姐說，她可以把自己的食物分給他吃，可是柯林少爺說，瑪莉小姐要是挨餓，就會變瘦。他們兩個要快點一起長胖。」

索爾·比太太聽到他們的難題之後很開心，笑得藍色斗篷裡的身子前後搖動，迪肯也跟著一起笑。

索爾比太太終於止住笑聲，說道：「我跟你說，囝兒，我想到一個法子可以幫他們。早上汝去找他們的時候，帶一桶新鮮牛奶過去，我會替他們烤一條香脆的麵包，或是一些夾葡萄乾的小圓麵包，就是汝們喜歡吃的那種。沒有什麼比得上新鮮的牛奶和麵包，這樣他們在花園裡就有東西可以充饑了，等他們回到屋內再吃點精緻的食物就會飽了。」

「啊！媽媽！」迪肯讚賞地說：「汝真是了不起！汝都可以想出好主意。昨天他們鬧哄哄的，覺得很餓卻又不知道怎麼辦。」

索爾比太太說，「這兩個囝兒正在發育，他們會變得很健康，這樣的囝兒看見食物就像小狼見到血肉一樣。」她笑了笑，對正彎著嘴笑的迪肯說：「啊！他們一定玩得很開心。」

這位總讓人感覺很舒服的神奇媽媽說得很對。她說「演戲」會讓人很開心，說得真是對極了。柯林和瑪莉覺得這是最刺激的娛樂。他們小心不讓別人起疑心，因為困惑的護士和柯萊文醫生所說的話讓他們不得不小心。

有一天護士這麼說：「您的胃口好了很多，柯林少爺，以前您什麼都不吃，很多東西都不合您的口味。」

「現在沒有東西不合我的口味了。」柯林回答。當他看到護士好奇地看著他時，才忽然想起他不應該表現出身體很好的樣子，「至少，很多東西不像以前那樣讓我感到不適了，這是新鮮空氣帶來的好處。」

護士說，「大概吧，可是我得跟柯萊文醫生談一談。」仍用迷惑的眼神看著他。

「她很注意地看著你，好像覺得事有蹊蹺。」等護士走開，瑪莉如此說道。

柯林說：「我不會讓她發現任何事的，誰都不能發現一點蛛絲馬跡。」

那天早上柯萊文醫生過來看柯林，一臉困惑地問了許多的問題，讓他很生氣。

「你現在很常待在外面的花園裡，都去什麼地方了？」他問。

　　柯林擺出那副他最喜歡的冷漠高傲的神情。

　　「我不會讓任何人知道我去哪裡的，」他回答：「我去了我喜歡的地方。我命令大家都不可以在那裡出現，我不要人家盯著我看，這個你是知道的！」

　　「你好像每天都在外面，但我不覺得這對你有什麼壞處──應該是沒有壞處的。護士說你現在吃得比以前都多。」

　　「這大概是，」柯林靈機一動說：「大概是不正常的胃口吧！」

　　柯萊文醫生說：「應該不是，你的食物似乎很適合你，你在很短的時間內長胖了，氣色也變好了。」

　　「大概──大概是因為我發燒虛胖吧，」柯林說，裝出令人洩氣的憂鬱模樣，「快要死的人通常都──和別人不一樣。」

　　柯萊文醫生搖搖頭，握住柯林的手腕，把袖子拉高，摸摸他的手臂。

　　「你沒有發燒，」他若有所思地說：「而且你這樣長肉是很健康的。繼續保持下去的話，孩子，我們就不用再談死呀什麼的了。你爸爸要是知道你有這樣的進展，一定會很高興。」

　　「我不會讓他知道！」柯林激動地說：「如果我要是再惡化了，他反而會更失望。我今天晚上就有可能惡化，可能會發高燒，我覺得我好像要發高燒了。你不可以寫信給我爸爸，不可以，不可以！你把我惹火了，你知道這樣對我的身體不好。我覺得渾身發熱了，我討厭人家寫信談論我，就像我討厭別人盯著我看一樣！」

　　柯萊文醫生安慰他：「安靜一點！孩子，如果你不同意，沒人會寫信的。你太敏感了，你都已經變好了，可不能再走回頭路。」

　　他不再提要寫信給柯萊文先生的事，他看到護士時，也私底下提醒她不要向病人提到這件事。

　　「這孩子很有起色，進展得有點不太正常了。以前我們沒有辦法叫他做的事情，現在他都自願去做了。只是他還很容易激動，我們不要說話刺激他。」他說。

　　瑪莉和柯林很驚慌，焦慮地討論這件事，「演戲」計畫也是從這個時候開始的。

　　「我大概得發一頓脾氣了，」柯林遺憾地說：「我不想發脾氣，而且現在也沒有可憐到想大發雷霆，也許我根本就沒有辦法發脾氣。我現在不會覺得難過了，心裡想的都是快樂的事，而不是討厭的事。不過假如他們要寫信給我爸爸，我一定要採取行動制止。」

　　他決定少吃一點東西，不幸的是這高明的主意根本無法實行。因為柯林每天早上醒來時胃口都很好，而沙發邊的桌子上擺滿了自製的麵包、新鮮的奶油、雪白的雞蛋、覆盆子果醬和濃縮奶油。瑪莉都會和他一起吃早餐，當他們坐在桌前，尤其是當僕人送來熱騰騰的美味火腿片，熱熱的銀色蓋子下冒出令人垂涎的香味，兩人就會絕望地互相對看。

　　「瑪莉，我想今天早上我們就把這些全部吃掉，午餐我們不要全吃光，晚餐我們只要吃一點點就好。」柯林最後終於這樣說。

　　可是他們總是吃到一點也不剩，那些吃得一乾二淨的盤子被送回食品室時，大家都會議論紛紛。

　　「真希望火腿片可以再厚一點，而且一個人只有一塊鬆餅，根本就不夠。」柯林會這麼說。

　　瑪莉第一次聽到柯林這麼說，說：「對一個快死的人來說是夠的，可是對一個要活下去的人來說是不夠的。當高沼地的帚石楠和荊豆清新的芳香從打開的窗子湧進來時，我有時覺得自己好像可以吃上三塊火腿片。」

　　那天早上，他們在花園裡待了大約兩個小時之後，迪肯提了兩個錫桶出現在一大叢玫瑰後面。一桶是新鮮牛奶，上面還浮著一層奶油，另一桶是農舍烘焙的葡萄乾小圓餅，外面用藍白相間的乾淨餐巾包著，包得很仔細，還熱烘烘的。瑪莉和柯林興奮得騷動不已，索爾比太太的主意真是妙啊！她一定是個友善又聰明的婦人！小圓餅真好吃！新鮮的牛奶也很美味！

　　柯林說：「她身上有魔法，就像迪肯身上也有魔法一樣，所以都想得出好主意。她是個有魔法的人，迪肯，你要告訴她，我們很感謝，真的是感激不盡。」

　　柯林偶爾會用大人的口氣說話，他很喜歡大家，想把話說得更好。

　　「告訴她，她是個非常慷慨的人，我們實在是萬分感激。」

　　接著他就忘掉了自己的威嚴，開始往嘴裡猛塞小圓餅，大口地喝著牛奶，他這個樣子就像個呼吸著高沼地新鮮空氣的小男孩，在做了大量的運動後飢腸轆轆了，儘管兩個多小時前才吃過早餐。

　　許多令人愉快的巧合都是這樣開始的。他們後來突然想到一件事，索爾比太太已經得應付十四個人的食物，可能沒錢再每天多準備兩個人的食物，所以他們便請索爾比太太讓他們付錢買食物。

迪肯發現了一件令人興奮的事情，花園外面的庭園樹林裡，也就是瑪莉第一次看到他對著野生動物吹笛子的地方，有一個很深的小洞。他們可以在那裡用石頭堆成小爐子，用來烤馬鈴薯和雞蛋。以前他們並不知道烤雞蛋是這麼奢華，再加上在熱騰騰的馬鈴薯裡面灑上鹽巴和新鮮奶油，這對森林裡的國王來說，真是美味又令人飽足。他們可以買馬鈴薯和雞蛋，高興吃多少就吃多少，而不會覺得自己是從十四個人的嘴裡搶了食物過來。

每個美麗早晨，他們會在李子短暫開花凋謝後、濃密綠葉形成的罩篷下，圍成一個神祕的圓圈來施展魔法。儀式過後，柯林會練習走路，偶爾也會做新的練習。他日益強壯，步伐愈形穩健，也能走得更遠了。他對魔法的信念與日俱增，身體愈來愈強壯，他開始嘗試另一個的新實驗，那些是迪肯教給他的絕佳技術。

有一回，迪肯昨天沒有去花園，隔天早晨他說：「昨天我替媽媽跑了一趟兌特村，在藍牛客棧附近碰到了鮑伯·哈沃斯，他是高沼地最強壯的小伙子。他是摔角冠軍，跳得比其他囝兒都高，鐵鎚也丟得比人家遠。有幾年他跑到蘇格蘭去參加運動比賽。在我很小的時候，他就認識我了，他很友善，我就問了他許多問題。大家都叫他運動員，我就想到了汝。我問他：『鮑伯，汝是怎麼把肌肉練得這麼結實的？汝是不是有什麼祕訣讓自己變得這麼強壯？』他就說：『有啊，小伙子。從前有個大力士來兌特村表演，他教我怎樣鍛鍊四肢和身上的每塊肌肉。』我就說：『鮑伯，身體虛弱的囝兒做這些練習也會變強壯嗎？』他笑了笑說：『那個身體虛弱的囝兒是汝嗎？』我說：『不是，可是我認識一位年輕的先生，他病了很久，正在慢慢康復當中，我想知道一些鍛鍊身體的祕訣，好去告訴他。』我沒說是誰，他也沒問，我說過他人很好。他就站起來很親切地做給我看，我模仿他的動作跟著做，把動作都背下來了。」

柯林興奮地聽著。

「你可以做給我看嗎？可以嗎？」他叫道。

「沒問題，」迪肯站起來說：「他說剛開始的時候要輕輕地做，小心不要讓自己累到。中間要休息，然後做深呼吸，不要做過頭了。」

「我會小心的，」柯林說：「做給我看！做給我看！迪肯，你是全世界最有魔力的男生了！」

迪肯站在草地上，小心地慢慢做了一系列簡單的肌肉練習。柯林看著他，眼睛睜得大大的。當他坐在地上時，也能做一些動作。過了一會兒，他可以站得穩穩地做練習了。瑪莉也開始跟著一起做。煤灰看著他們表演，漸漸變得騷動不安，飛離樹枝，很不安寧地四處亂跳，因為牠沒辦法跟著一起做。

從這天開始，這些練習就跟魔法一樣成為他們每天的功課。柯林和瑪莉每次都可以做得更多，兩人的胃口也就愈來愈好。要不是迪肯每天早上都會帶來一籃食物放在灌木叢後面，他們準會餓慌了。不過，那個洞裡小爐子烤出來的東西，還有索爾比太太慷慨替他們準備的食物，讓他們感到無比滿足。因此梅德洛太太、護士還有柯萊文醫生又開始困惑了起來，因為你的肚子裡面如果塞滿了烤馬鈴薯、烤雞蛋、新鮮營養的泡沫牛奶、燕麥餅、小圓麵包、帶石楠蜂蜜和凝脂奶油，你也會對屋子裡的食物不屑一顧的。

護士說：「他們沒吃什麼東西，如果我們不勸他們吃點東西，他們會餓死的，可是看他們的氣色又不像沒吃東西。」

「氣色！」梅德洛太太憤怒地叫道：「啊！我簡直被他們給弄糊塗了，他們真是一對魔鬼。今天可以吃飯吃到肚子撐，明天卻看也不看一眼廚子準備的美味食物。昨天他們一口也沒吃那隻美味的小雞和果醬麵包，可憐的廚子還特地為他們做了一種新布丁，結果被送了回來。她差點就叫出來了。她很擔心要是這兩個小孩餓死了，人家會把責任怪到她身上。」

柯萊文醫生來仔細地端詳了柯林好一會兒，護士來跟他說話，還特地留下沒怎麼被動過的早餐給他看，他臉上露出憂心的神色，等到他坐在柯林沙發旁檢查身體時，表情又更加焦慮了。

先前他有事去了倫敦，已將近兩個星期沒看到柯林。小孩開始變壯後總是進展神速，柯林的臉色不再那麼蒼白，甚至還帶些溫暖紅潤的氣色，漂亮的眼睛看起來很清澈，原本在眼睛下方、臉頰和太陽穴的凹陷，現在也豐滿起來了。原先厚重的黑色髮絡，現在也在額頭上健康地飛揚著，看起來很柔軟、充滿溫暖的生命力。他的嘴唇變得豐滿，色澤也變得很正常。事實上，他現在這個樣子要假裝成病弱的男孩，實在有點可恥。柯萊文醫生用手托著下巴沉思著。

他說：「我聽說你又不吃東西了，我很難過，這樣是不行的。你好不容易增加的體重會掉下來的，你已經胖了不少。不久前你的飲食還很正常。」

「我說過，那種食欲是不正常的。」柯林回答。

　　瑪莉坐在旁邊的凳子上，忽然發出很奇怪的聲音，她想要強行把聲音壓住，結果差點哽到了。

　　「怎麼啦？」柯萊文醫生轉過頭看著她問。

　　瑪莉的態度變得很嚴肅。

　　「我剛剛不知道是想打噴嚏還是咳嗽，結果噎到了。」她責備著自己。

　　瑪莉後來對柯林說：「我那時候實在是忍不住了，因為我滿腦子裡都是你最後吃下去的那塊大馬鈴薯，還有你朝著夾了火腿和凝脂奶油的美味厚麵包片張大嘴巴的樣子。」

　　「這些孩子們有沒有什麼辦法可以偷偷弄到食物？」柯萊文醫生問梅德洛太太。

　　梅德洛太太回答道：「除非他們挖地上或是採樹上的東西吃，不然是不可能的。他們一整天都待在外面的庭園裡，而且就只有他們兩個。他們要是真的想換口味，只需要跟我們說就可以了。」

　　柯萊文醫生說：「好吧，他們要是沒有什麼問題，我們也不用太操心。柯林現在變得很不一樣了。」

　　梅德洛太太說：「瑪莉小姐也是，自從她開始變胖，小臉蛋看起來不再那麼醜醜的、讓人討厭了，可說是變得很漂亮了，頭髮變得濃密，看起來很健康，臉色也很紅潤。以前她是個悶悶不樂、脾氣很壞的小孩，現在她跟柯林少爺兩個人會像瘋了一樣地笑成一團，這可能就是他們變胖的原因吧。」

　　「或許吧，」柯萊文醫生說：「讓他們笑吧。」

第二十五章

簾幕

祕密花園的繁花盛開又盛開，每天早晨都會出現新的奇蹟。知更鳥的巢裡現在有了蛋，牠的伴侶坐在上面孵蛋，用毛茸茸的小胸口和翅膀小心翼翼地為蛋保暖。

一開始牠很緊張，知更鳥也時刻保持警戒。在這種時刻，即使是迪肯也不敢走近鳥巢的角落。他悄悄地在那對小鳥身上施展神奇的魔咒，讓知更鳥知道花園裡的一切都跟牠們一樣，都能夠領會即將發生在牠們身上的奇蹟——都明白那窩蛋的美麗與莊嚴所蘊含的無限性，既溫柔又令人敬畏、也令人心碎。

花園裡只要有一人不發自內心地深刻瞭解這件事情，要是有一顆蛋被拿走或被碰傷了，世界就會開始旋轉而坍塌結束。要是有人感受不到這一點，不依此行事，那麼即使處在金黃色的春日氣息中，也不會有一絲的幸福存在。幸好所有的生物都知道、都能感受到這一點，知更鳥和伴侶也知道大家都明白這一點。

起初，知更鳥緊張地防備著瑪莉和柯林，神奇的是，牠知道自己並不用留心迪肯。牠那露珠般明亮的黑眼睛第一次看到迪肯時，就知道他不是外人，而是一隻沒有鳥喙和羽毛的知更鳥。他會說知更鳥的語言（這是個能輕易分辨的語言，

不可能會被誤認為其他語言）。對知更鳥說知更鳥話，就像
是對法國人說法語一樣。

　　迪肯總是會對知更鳥說知更鳥話，而他跟人類說的那些
嘰哩咕嚕的話，對知更鳥來說一點也無關緊要。知更鳥認為
迪肯之所以會和人類講那些嘰哩咕嚕的話，是因為那些人不
夠聰明到能聽懂鳥兒的語言。迪肯的舉止也跟知更鳥一樣，
他從不妄動驚嚇到鳥兒，讓鳥兒覺得身陷危險或威脅。任何
知更鳥都能瞭解迪肯，因此迪肯的現身並不會引來騷動。

　　但一開始似乎有必要防備著另外兩個小孩，那男孩起初
並不是用雙腳走進花園的，而是坐在裝著輪子的東西上讓人
推著走，身上還披著野獸的皮，令人起疑。而當他開始站起
來走動時，動作也很奇怪，似乎得依靠別人幫助。

　　知更鳥常藏在灌木叢裡不安地看著，頭斜向一邊，一會
又斜向另一邊。牠覺得這男孩緩慢的動作也許表示他正準備
要展開猛撲，就像貓那樣。當貓在地上緩慢地匍匐前行，就
表示牠準備要猛撲。這幾天，知更鳥跟伴侶反覆談論這件事，
不過後來牠決定住口不談，因為另一半嚇壞了，牠擔心這樣
會傷害到蛋。

　　那男孩可以開始自己走路，甚至越走越快，牠們總算大
大地鬆了一口氣。可是牠們已經因為男孩而緊張了很久（至
少對知更鳥而言是很長的時間）。他的一舉一動都與旁人不
同，他似乎很喜愛走路，可是會坐下或躺一會兒，又會起身
搖晃跌撞地繼續走。

　　有一天，知更鳥想起當年父母教牠飛行時也是這樣子
的，牠先飛短短幾碼就要停下來休息，所以牠馬上想到這男
孩其實正在學飛行，或者說是在學走路。

牠告訴伴侶，等牠們的蛋長出羽毛後，也許也會像這樣學飛行。另一半聽了安心不少，甚至會很感興趣地在鳥巢邊觀察男孩，覺得樂趣無窮。不過牠總在想牠們的小孩會比男孩聰明多了，學得更快。牠用充滿溺愛的口吻說，人類總是比鳥笨拙遲鈍，絕大部分的人類好像永遠都學不會飛行，牠們就沒有在空中或樹梢上遇過人類。

　　過了一段時間，男孩開始跟其他人一樣四處走動，可是這三個小孩偶爾會一起做些不尋常的事情。他們會站在樹下運動手腳和頭部，那個樣子既不像走路、跑步，也不像坐著。他們每天就會做這些動作，知更鳥都不知道該怎麼向伴侶解釋這些人類到底在幹什麼。牠只能說，牠很確定孩子們絕不會像他們那樣拍打翅膀。不過，既然那個說著流利知更鳥話的男孩也跟他們一起做動作，小鳥們便可以十分確定這些動作不會帶來威脅。

　　知更鳥和牠的伴侶當然從沒聽說過摔角冠軍鮑伯·哈沃斯，也不知道哈沃斯那套訓練可以讓肌肉變得突出結實。知更鳥跟人類不一樣，牠們的肌肉從一出生就不斷地鍛鍊，牠們用很自然的方式在發展肌肉。牠們要靠飛行尋找每一餐，所以肌肉不會萎縮（萎縮的意思是由於缺乏使用而衰弱）。

　　當男孩可以和其他人一樣走路、到處跑、挖土除草了，角落裡的鳥巢也籠罩在祥和知足的氣氛裡。知更鳥的恐懼已經煙消雲散，牠們知道自己的蛋就像是被鎖在銀行的保險箱裡一樣安全，看著這麼多奇怪的事情發生，真是很有意思。有時候碰到下雨天，孩子們沒有進到花園裡來，母鳥甚至覺得有點無聊。

　　可是即使在下雨天，瑪莉和柯林也不會覺得無聊。一天早上，大雨傾盆而下，柯林開始感到有點煩躁，因為他只能坐在沙發上，如果站起來四處走動，就有可能會被人撞見。這時候，瑪莉突然靈機一動。

「現在，我是個真正的男生了，」柯林說道：「我的雙腳、雙手、全身上下都充滿了魔法，我沒辦法叫它們不動，它們無時無刻不想做點什麼。瑪莉，妳知道嗎？我很早就醒來了，小鳥在外頭吱吱叫，所有的一切好像都在大聲歡呼，就連樹木還有那些我們聽不到的東西也一樣在叫喊著。我就很想跳下床和它們一起大聲呼喊。我要是真的這麼做了，妳猜會發生什麼事？」

瑪莉大聲地咯咯笑了起來。

「護士和梅德洛太太會馬上跑過來，她們一定會認為你瘋了，然後把醫生找來。」她說。

柯林自己也咯咯笑了起來。他可以想像他們的神情，如果他們看到柯林這麼大叫的話，該有多驚慌，倘若他們看到他站得直挺挺的，又會如何的吃驚。

「真希望爸爸趕快回家，」他說：「我想自己跟他說我能站了，我一直在想這件事。我們不能在這樣瞎耗下去，我不能一直躺在床上裝病，而且我現在看起來已經很不一樣了。真希望今天沒有下雨。」

就是在這時候，瑪莉的靈感來了。

「柯林，你知道這個屋子裡面有幾間房間嗎？」她神祕兮兮地說。

「我猜大概有一千間吧。」柯林回答道。

「大約有一百個房間沒有人進去過，」瑪莉說：「有一次下雨的時候，我進到很多房間裡面蹓躂。沒有人知道這件事，雖然差一點被梅德洛太太給發現了。我要回自己的房間時迷路了，正好停在了你房間前的走廊底。那是我第二次聽到你哭聲。」

柯林從沙發上跳起來。

他說：「一百間沒有人進去過的房間，聽起來就像是祕密花園，我們何不去看看？妳可以幫我推輪椅，沒有人會知道我們去哪裡的。」

「我就是這麼想的，」瑪莉說：「沒人敢跟蹤我們的。那邊有很多走廊可以讓你跑來跑去，我們可以在那裡做運動。還有一個印度式的小房間，裡面有個櫃子滿滿都是象牙做的大象，各式各樣的房間都有！」

「搖一下鈴。」柯林說。

護士一來，他便下達命令。

「把我的輪椅推過來，」他說：「瑪莉小姐和我想去逛逛屋子裡沒人使用的地方，叫約翰把我推到畫像陳列的走廊那裡，那邊有樓梯。然後他就走開，留我們在那裡，直到我叫他來才可以來。」

那天早上雖然下了雨，他們卻不再感到厭煩。男僕順從地把輪椅推到畫像陳列走廊，把兩個小孩留在那裡，柯林和瑪莉高興地對看著。等瑪莉確定約翰已經走下樓回到僕人廳了，柯林便從椅子裡跳了出來。

「我要從走廊的這一邊跑到另一邊去，」他說：「我還要跳一跳，接下來我們可以做鮑伯·哈沃斯的練習。」

除此之外，他們還做了許多其他的事情。他們看了牆上掛著的畫像，找到了那個穿著綠色織錦洋裝、手指上停了隻鸚鵡、相貌平凡的小女孩。

柯林說：「這些人應該都是我的親戚，他們是很久以前的人。手上有鸚鵡的那個，應該是我的曾曾曾姑婆。瑪莉，她看起來跟妳長得很像，但不是像妳現在的樣子，而是像妳剛來的那個樣子。現在的妳比較胖，比較好看了。」

「你也是。」瑪莉說著，兩人都笑了起來。

他們來到了那間印度風格的房間，開心地玩著象牙製的大象。他們也找到了那間有著玫瑰色錦緞的閨房，還有老鼠在墊子上咬的洞，可是那些小老鼠長大後都跑走了，現在洞裡面是空的。他們又參觀了別的房間，發現了許多瑪莉第一次遊逛時沒有發現的東西。他們發現了新的走廊、轉角、樓梯和一些他們喜歡的舊畫像，還有一些用途不明的奇怪古物。

這天早上特別新奇有趣，他們和其他人待在同一個房子裡，在這裡遊蕩著，可是又覺得那些人離他們很遠，這種矛盾的感覺讓他們很著迷。

柯林說：「我很高興我們來這裡，我不知道自己原來住在這麼大、這麼奇怪的老房子裡。我很喜歡這裡，以後遇到下雨了，我們就來這裡逛。我們應該還可以發現更多的新地方和新東西。」

這個上午他們發現了很多東西，胃口也出奇的好。他們回到柯林的房間之後，根本沒辦法叫人把午餐原封不動地送回去。

護士把盤子收到樓下去時，啪的一聲把盤子放在餐具櫥上，廚子盧米斯太太看到碗盤的東西被吃得一乾二淨。

「看看！」她說：「這個房子很神祕，其中最神祕的又屬這兩個小孩。」

「他們要是這樣繼續下去，」強壯的年輕僕人約翰說：

「也難怪他今天的體重比一個月前增加了一倍。我得趕緊辭職才行，不然我擔心我的肌肉會受傷。」

　　那天下午，瑪莉注意到柯林的房間裡發生了一件新鮮事。其實她前一天就注意到了，她想可能只是偶然發生的事，所以就沒多問。她今天也一樣沒說什麼，但是她坐下來盯著壁爐架上的畫像看，因為簾幕拉開了，可以看得到畫像。這就是她所注意到的變化。

　　「我知道妳想要我跟妳說原因。」瑪莉凝視了一會兒後，柯林說道：「妳想知道什麼，我都能看得出來。我知道妳很好奇為什麼簾幕拉開了。我以後都要把簾幕拉開。」

　　「為什麼？」瑪莉問道。

　　「因為現在我看到她的時候，已經不會生氣了。兩天前我半夜醒來，月光很明亮，我覺得屋子裡好像充滿了魔法，讓一切看起來都很奇妙。我在床上躺不住，就爬起來看看窗外。房間裡很亮，簾幕上灑了一小道月光，不知怎地，我就走過去拉下繩子。她俯看著我，好像在對我笑，很高興看到我站在那裡。這讓我也變得很喜歡看她，我希望一直看到她那樣子笑著。我在想她應該也是個有魔法的人。」

　　「你現在太像她了，」瑪莉說：「有時候我在想，搞不好你就是她投胎變成的小男孩。」

　　這樣的想法烙印在柯林的心裡。他沉思片刻後，慢慢地回答瑪莉。

　　「如果我是她的化身，爸爸應該會喜歡我的。」他說。

　　「你希望他喜歡你嗎？」瑪莉問道。

　　「我以前很恨他為什麼不喜歡我。如果以後他逐漸喜歡上我，我想我會跟他說魔法的事，這樣可能會讓他開心些。」

第二十六章

「是媽媽！」

他們對於魔法的信念十分堅定，有時候早上念過咒語之後，柯林會對他們發表一些魔法的演說。

「我很喜歡演講，」他解釋道：「等我長大了，完成了很多偉大的科學發明之後，我也就得做演講，所以我現在要開始練習。我現在只能講很短的內容，因為我還小，而且要是我講得太久的話，班會以為是在教堂裡聽佈道，會聽到睡著了。」

「演講最棒的地方，」班說：「就是某個傢伙可以站起來講他任何想說的話，其他人都沒辦法答話。有時候我自己也想來點演講。」

然而，當柯林在樹下發表演說時，老班會目不轉睛地看著他。班感興趣的並不是柯林演講的內容，而是他那雙愈來愈直、愈來愈強壯的腿。柯林把頭抬得高高的，從前瘦削的下巴，還有凹陷的雙頰，已經開始變得豐腴起來，眼睛也散發出跟另一雙眼睛同樣的光芒。

柯林有時候能夠感覺得到班那誠摯懇切的眼神，他很好奇班究竟在想什麼。有一次，在班看得兩眼出神的時候，柯林問了出來。

「你在想什麼，班？」他問。

「我在想，」班回答道：「汝這個星期一定又胖了三、四磅。我在看汝的小腿和肩膀，真想秤秤看汝有多重了。」

「這都要歸功於魔法，還有索爾比太太的小圓麵包、牛奶那些的。你看，我的科學實驗成功了。」柯林說。

那天早上，當迪肯到來的時候，柯林的演講已經結束。迪肯一路跑著過來，臉紅通通的，那張有趣的臉比以往更加容光煥發。

由於下過雨，他們有許多除草的工作要做，尤其在溫暖的大雨過後會有更多事情要忙。水分有助於花朵的生長，但也會助長了雜草，這些雜草會長出小小的草葉，一定要在它們的根牢固之前拔除。柯林跟其他人一樣很會拔草，還可以邊拔草邊演講。

「當你幹活的時候，魔法的效果最好，」這天早上他說：「你可以感覺到魔法就在你的骨頭和肌肉裡面。我要讀一些介紹骨頭和肌肉的書，還要寫一本和魔法有關的書。我現在已經在著手準備了，我一直都有新的發現。」

說完這話不久，他放下小鏟子站起來，沉默了好幾分鐘。大家都看得出來他正在思考接下來要演講的內容，他經常這個樣子。瑪莉和迪肯看到柯林放下小鏟子站起來，就知道他一定是忽然有了什麼強烈的念頭。

柯林將身子往上挺直，興奮地將手臂甩出去，他的臉上泛著紅光，那雙奇異的眼睛高興地睜得大大的，突然頓悟到了什麼。

他叫道：「瑪莉！迪肯！你們看看我！」

瑪莉和迪肯停下除草的動作，望向柯林。

　　「你們還記得第一次帶我到花園裡來的那個早晨嗎？」
他問道。

　　迪肯仔細地端詳著他。身為動物術士，迪肯可以看到人
們看不到的東西，但是他大都不會透露看到了什麼東西。現
在他就在柯林的身上看到了一些別人看不到的東西。

　　「是啊，我們記得。」迪肯回答道。

　　瑪莉也仔細地看著柯林，不過什麼話也沒說。

　　「就在此刻，」柯林說：「我突然想到一件事──當我
看到自己用小鏟子在除草──我站起來看看這是不是真的。
結果我發現這是真的！我的病好了！──我的病好了！」

　　「是啊！」迪肯說。

　　「我的病好了！我的病好了！」柯林重複地說道，一下
子變得滿臉通紅。

　　柯林之前便隱約感覺到自己的病好了，自己一直期待
著、感覺著，一直在想著。就在剛剛，有什麼衝擊著他整個
人，那像是信仰成真的狂喜感覺，強烈到柯林無法控制自己
不叫出來。

　　「我會一直、一直活下去」！他莊嚴地宣告：「我會發
現很多、很多東西，會學到人類、動物、所有生物的一切東
西，就像迪肯一樣，我永遠都不會停止施行魔法。我好了！
我好了！我覺得──我感覺我好想喊出一些話───一些感
激、快樂的話。」

　　在玫瑰叢附近忙著的班向著他看了看。

　　「汝可以唱《榮耀頌》。」他不帶感情地咕噥提議道。
他對《榮耀頌》沒什麼感覺，所以提出這個建議時也不帶有
尊敬之情。

柯林雖然對《榮耀頌》一無所知，卻很有探索的精神。

「《榮耀頌》是什麼？」他問道。

「我敢說迪肯一定知道怎麼唱。」班回答道。

迪肯一面回答，一面露出動物術士無所不知的微笑。

「他們在教堂裡會唱這個。」他說：「媽媽說，她相信雲雀早上起床的時候也會唱《榮耀頌》。」

「如果她這麼說的話，那就表示這一定是首好歌，」柯林回答：「我都在生病，沒去過教堂。迪肯，唱給我聽，我想要聽。」

迪肯樸實而純真，他比柯林更懂得柯林的感受。他天生就有這樣的直覺，不知道這就是所謂的感同身受。他脫下帽子，微笑地環顧四周。

「汝得把帽子脫下來，」他對柯林說：「而且汝要——汝要站起來。」

柯林脫掉帽子，溫暖的陽光照著他濃密的頭髮，他專注地看著迪肯。班也趕緊站起來把帽子脫掉，蒼老的臉上露出困惑而微慍的神情，似乎不是很清楚為什麼要做出這樣不尋常的舉動。

迪肯從樹木與玫瑰叢中站出來，用簡單的方式吟唱，聲音悅耳有力：

「讚美上帝賜福，地上子民都讚美祂。
讚美天上的主人，讚美聖父、聖子與聖靈。阿門。」

迪肯唱完後，班一動也不動地站著，他的嘴唇固執地繃緊著，表情困惑地盯著柯林，柯林的臉上帶著沉思與讚賞的神情。

「這首歌很好聽，我喜歡。歌詞的意思，跟我想大聲喊出對魔法的感激之情大概是一樣的。」柯林停了下來，困惑地思考著：「也許它們是相同的東西，我們不可能知道每樣東西的確切名稱。迪肯，再唱一遍。瑪莉，我們來試試看，我也想要唱，這是我的歌。開始是怎麼唱？『讚美上帝賜福』是嗎？」

他們又唱了一次《榮耀頌》，瑪莉和柯林盡最大的努力唱得悅耳，迪肯的聲音既響亮又動聽。唱到第二行時，班刺耳地清了清喉嚨，等唱到第三行時，班也加了進來，他的聲音很有力，簡直可以說是粗暴了。當他們唱完阿門的時候，瑪莉注意到班的反應，那就跟他當初發現柯林不是殘廢時一樣，下巴抽動著，一邊凝視著柯林，一邊眨眼，飽經風霜的蒼老臉頰已經淚濕了。

班用粗啞的聲音說：「我以前都不覺得《榮耀頌》有啥意義，現在我改變想法了。柯林少爺，汝這個星期應該又重了五磅吧，五磅呢！」

這時，柯林望向花園的另一邊，有個東西吸引了他的注意力，他露出驚訝的表情。

「誰來這裡了？那是誰？」他急促地說著。

常春藤下的門輕輕地被打開了，一個婦女走了進來。她在《榮耀頌》剛好唱到最後一行就進來了，她看著他們，靜靜聽他們唱歌。她站在常春藤前，陽光穿透樹枝，在她藍色的長披風上形成許多斑點。她佇立在綠色植物之間，清新美好的臉龐帶著笑容，看起來就像是柯林的書本裡面一張色彩柔和的插圖。她一雙非常慈愛的眼睛，彷彿將一切都看在眼裡，包括在場的所有人，甚至包括班和那些動物們，還有一切盛開的花朵。雖然她出人意料地出現，卻沒有人覺得她是個入侵者。迪肯的眼睛像燈火般明亮。

「是媽媽，那是媽媽！」他叫著跑過草地。

柯林也開始朝她走過去，瑪莉跟隨在後，他們倆都覺得心跳加速。

「是媽媽！」大夥迎向前去，迪肯又重複說了一遍：「我知道汝們想看媽媽，所以就跟她說門藏在哪裡了。」

柯林紅著臉，禮貌又害羞地把手伸出去，眼睛一直注視著她的臉。

「我生病的時候也很想見妳，」他說：「我想看妳、看迪肯、看祕密花園，可我以前什麼人、什麼東西都不想看。」

看到柯林的頭抬得高高的，媽媽的表情也瞬間改變了。她的臉紅了起來，嘴角抽動著，眼裡泛著淚光。

她忽然用顫抖的聲音說：「啊！親愛的囝兒。啊！親愛的囝兒！」她彷彿是不知不覺說出這句話的。她並沒有叫他「柯林少爺」，而是突然叫他「親愛的囝兒」。當她在迪肯的臉上看到讓她感動的東西時，她也會這麼叫迪肯。柯林很喜歡聽她這樣叫他。

「妳是不是很驚訝我的身體現在變得這麼好？」他問。

媽媽將手放在柯林的肩膀上微笑著，不再淚眼模糊。

她說：「是啊！汝長得真像汝媽媽，所以我的心猛然地跳了一下。」

「妳覺得，」柯林有點畏縮地問：「我爸爸會因為這樣而喜歡我嗎？」

「當然囉，親愛的囝兒，」她回答道，很快地輕拍了一下柯林的肩膀，「他一定要回來——他一定要回來。」

「蘇珊‧索爾比，」班走近她，說道：「汝有沒有看到囝兒的腿？兩個月前，他的腿還像是穿了襪子的鼓槌，而且我聽人家說他又是膝蓋外彎、又是膝蓋內彎的。汝看看他的腿現在的樣子！」

蘇珊‧索爾比欣慰地笑了起來。

「他的腿不久之後就會變得更強壯，」她說：「讓他在花園裡玩耍種花，吃營養一點，還要讓他喝很多美味的鮮奶，他就會有約克郡裡最健壯的腿，感謝主。」

她將雙手放在瑪莉的肩膀上，像媽媽一樣端詳著瑪莉的小臉。

她說：「啊！汝也是！汝已經長得快跟我家的伊莉莎白‧愛倫一樣壯了。我保證汝長得也很像汝媽媽。瑪莎跟我說，梅德洛太太聽說汝媽媽長得很漂亮。汝長大以後一定會像朵紅玫瑰的，小姑娘，祝福汝。」

她並沒有提到一件事，那就是瑪莎休假回家時，說過這個小女孩的氣色很難看，長得很不起眼。瑪莎說她不相信梅德洛太太聽來的一切消息。「這麼討人厭的囝兒，她的媽媽不可能長得很漂亮的。」瑪莎堅持地說。

瑪莉之前沒有時間去注意自己的長相發生了什麼變化，她只知道自己現在看起來「不一樣」，而且頭髮好像多了很多，也長得很快。可是，她想起來自己以前很喜歡看的美麗「夫人」，很高興自己有一天會長得跟她一樣。

蘇珊‧索爾比跟著大夥逛著花園，跟她說著花園裡的點點滴滴，指出每一棵活過來的灌木和樹給她看。柯林和瑪莉走在媽媽的兩旁，仰望著她那人感到舒心的紅潤臉龐，心裡想著媽媽帶給他們的喜悅感覺，一種被支持的溫暖感覺。

　　媽媽好像很懂他們，就好像迪肯很懂動物一樣。她俯身看著花，談到花時，好像也把花當成孩子一樣。煤灰跟著她，對著她叫了一、兩聲，飛到她的肩膀上，就好像那是迪肯的肩膀一樣。他們跟她說知更鳥的事情，還有雛鳥已經開始會飛行了。她聽了以後，溫柔慈祥地笑了起來。

　　「我猜牠們學飛行，就像囝兒學走路一樣，可是我的囝兒如果長的是翅膀，而不是腿的話，我可能會很煩惱，不知道要怎麼教他們飛呢。」她說。

　　她看起來是一位如此奇妙的高沼地農婦，大家最後決定跟她說魔法的事。

　　「妳相信魔法嗎？」柯林在解釋了何謂印度的苦行僧後問：「希望妳會相信。」

　　「我相信魔法，囝兒，」蘇珊‧索爾比回答道：「只不過我不知道魔法這個名字，但叫什麼名字都無所謂，我相信在法國就會有不一樣的名字，在德國又有另外的名字。同樣的東西可以讓種子膨脹長大，陽光也讓汝變成一個健康的囝兒，那是好東西。我們這些可憐的傻瓜總以為被人提及自己的名字是很重要的事。『大好事情』從來不會停下來杞人憂天，它護佑著汝。它推動著萬千世界，那些世界就像我們的世界一樣。永遠要相信『大好事情』的存在，要知道世界上充滿了『大好事情』，汝高興叫它什麼就叫它什麼。我剛剛走進花園時，汝們正在為它唱歌。」

　　「我剛剛好開心，」柯林睜著漂亮奇怪的眼睛看著迪肯的媽媽，說道：「我忽然覺得自己變得很不一樣，妳知道嗎？我的手臂和腿變得好強壯——我可以挖土，可以站起來，還可以跳起來，我很想對所有聽得到我的東西大叫。」

「汝在唱《榮耀頌》的時候，魔法聽到了。不管汝唱什麼，它都聽得到。最重要的是要開心。啊！团兒啊，团兒，汝自己就是歡樂的泉源。」她又輕輕拍了一下柯林的肩膀。

她帶來了個籃子，裡面照例放著上午的盛宴。大家要是肚子餓了，迪肯就會把籃子從藏匿的地方拿了出來。迪肯的媽媽和他們一起坐在樹下，看著他們狼吞虎嚥，胃口那麼好，心滿意足地笑了起來。媽媽非常風趣，講了許多離奇的事讓大夥都笑了。她用約克郡方言跟他們講故事，還教他們一些新的字。當他們說柯林愈來愈難假裝是個暴躁的病人時，她無法自制地笑了起來。

柯林解釋道：「妳看，我們在一起的時候就會一直想笑，我看起來一點也不像個病人。我們會盡量忍住，可是總會忍不住笑出來，結果反而笑得更厲害。」

「我經常會想到一件事，」瑪莉說：「每次我忽然想到這件事時就會忍不住大笑。我一直在想，要是柯林的臉變得像滿月那麼圓，會是什麼樣子啊。他還沒有變成那個樣子，可是他每天都慢慢地變胖，如果哪天早上，他的臉真的變得跟滿月一樣圓，我們該怎麼辦！」

蘇珊說：「保佑你們呀，看來汝們還得繼續假裝下去，可是汝們不用裝很久了，因為柯萊文主人要回來了。」

「真的嗎？為什麼？」柯林說。

蘇珊輕聲地咯咯笑。

「我在想，如果汝不能親自跟他說汝的身體已經好轉了，汝一定會很難過。我猜汝晚上一定都睡不著覺，在計畫著要怎麼親自告訴他這件事。」她說。

柯林說：「如果我不能親自告訴他這件事，我會受不了的。我每天都在想著各種方法，我現在想到的是用跑的跑到他的房間去。」

　　「那他一定會很驚喜的，我真想看看他的表情呢，真的！他一定得趕快回來，一定要。」蘇珊說。

　　他們也聊到要去拜訪她的農舍。他們把一切都計畫好，打算坐車橫越高沼地，然後在戶外的帚石楠地野餐。他們也要看看她的十二個小孩，還有迪肯的花園，等玩累了再回家。

　　蘇珊‧索爾比最後站起身來，準備回屋裡去見梅德洛太太。他們也到了該把柯林推回去的時候了。在坐回椅子之前，柯林站到蘇珊的身邊，用崇拜的眼神楞楞地注視著她，然後突然抓住蘇珊藍色披風的一角。

　　「妳就是我想要的，我真希望妳也是我媽媽！」他說。

　　蘇珊彎下身去，用溫暖的手臂把柯林拉到懷中，就好像柯林是迪肯的弟弟一般，淚水瞬間模糊了她的雙眼。

　　「啊！親愛的囝兒！」她說：「我相信汝的媽媽一定就在這個花園裡。她不可能離開這個花園的。汝爸爸一定得回來看汝，一定要！」

第二十七章

在花園裡

打從盤古開天闢地以來，每個世紀都有許多美妙的事物被發現。上一個世紀不可思議的發現，比以前任何一個世紀都來得多。而我們所處的這個新紀元，還有更多令人震驚的事物會被發現。剛開始人們會不肯相信奇怪的新事物能夠完成，也不期待它會實現。可是等他們看到事情竟然成功之後，世人又會納悶為什麼它沒有在幾個世紀前就完成。

在上個世紀人們所發現的新事物當中，有一個就是思考——就僅是思考而已——它跟電池一樣有力，它可以像陽光一樣對人體產生幫助，也可以像毒藥一樣有害。讓悲傷或負面的念頭進入人的心靈，就會像猩紅熱的病菌侵入人體一樣危險，如果讓它繼續停留在你的體內，那你一輩子都好不了。

以前瑪莉的心裡充滿了負面的想法，看什麼事、什麼人不順眼了，不打算快樂也不打算去喜歡任何東西，所以成了一個臉色蠟黃、病懨懨、無聊、令人討厭的小孩。不過她的機緣很好，雖然她自己並沒有發現到這一點。

機緣將她推向好的地方，她的心靈逐漸充滿了知更鳥、高沼地擠滿小孩的農舍、古怪暴躁的老園丁、平凡的約克郡小女僕、春天和生機愈發盎然的祕密花園，此外，還有一個高沼地的男孩和他的動物們。她的心裡面再也容納不下那些對她的肝臟與消化有著不良影響的想法了，這讓她的氣色看起來好多了，也不再那麼容易累了。

　　以前柯林把自己關在房間裡，只想著自己的恐懼與脆弱，他憎恨那些盯著他看的人，不停地想著駝背還有自己可能早夭之類的事。那時候的他是個歇斯底里、幾近瘋狂的憂鬱症病患。他不知道陽光和春天是什麼樣子，也不知道只要自己願意去嘗試，身體就可以好轉，自己可以站得起來。

　　當美好的新念頭將那些可憎的舊念頭推開，他重新獲得了生機，血液在他的血管裡健康地流動，力氣像洪流般湧進體內。他的科學實驗實用又簡單，而且一點也不奇怪。如果在不愉快或是令人沮喪的念頭產生時，能夠立即想到把它們拋開，用激勵人心的愉快念頭來取而代之，任何人的身上都會發生令人驚喜的事情，因為這兩種念頭不會同時並存。

　　　「孩子，在你照料玫瑰花的地方，
　　　不會長出刺薊。」

　　在祕密花園恢復生氣之際，兩個孩子也日漸充滿活力，這時遠方有個男人正在美麗的挪威峽灣和瑞士的山間溪谷漫遊。十年來，這個男人的心裡充滿了黑暗而傷心的念頭。他並不勇敢，沒嘗試過用其他的念頭來取代灰暗的想法。

　　他在藍色的湖畔漫遊，想著那些傷心事。他躺在山坡上，身邊開滿了一大片深藍色盛開的龍膽，空氣中充滿了花香，然而他卻還是想著那些傷心事。他曾經那麼快樂，但是一件可怕的傷心事降臨到他的身上，他的靈魂從此充滿了黑暗，固執地拒絕讓任何一絲光亮穿透這片黑暗。他把自己的家園和自己責任都丟卻，置之不理。

　　他四處旅行，身上卻籠罩著一層濃厚的黑暗，這對遇見他的人來說並不公平，因為他的憂鬱彷彿也毒害了四周的空氣。許多外地人認為他不是有點瘋，就是在靈魂深處隱藏了一些不可告人的罪孽。他身材高大，臉部因痛苦而扭曲，肩膀歪斜。住進旅館時，他登記的姓名和地址都是「阿契勃・柯萊文，英國約克郡，密朔兌莊園」。

　　他在書房見過瑪莉，說她可以擁有一小塊土地之後，便到處旅行。他到過歐洲許多美麗的地方，但都落腳不久。他都選擇最安靜、最偏僻的地點，爬上那些深入雲霄、俯視群山的山頂，日出時陽光照射山峰，世界彷彿剛剛誕生一樣。

　　然而光明似乎從未觸及到他，直到有一天，他感覺到發生了一件奇怪的事情，十年來第一次有這樣的感覺。當時，他正在奧地利提洛爾的一個美麗山谷裡，他沿著這片美景散步，如此美麗的風光似乎能夠掃除心靈的陰霾。他走了很長的一段路，心頭的陰影卻總是揮之不去。後來他感到疲憊了，便在溪邊的一片苔蘚上休息。

　　這條清澈的小溪，雀躍地沿著狹窄的河道流動，河道兩旁是芬芳潮溼的綠地。有時，河水在石頭四周激起泡沫，發出低低的笑聲。他看到小鳥飛過來，將頭探進溪裡去喝水，然後拍拍翅膀飛走。小溪彷彿有生命一般，溪水的聲音微弱，卻讓四周顯得更為寂靜。整個山谷闃然無聲。

　　阿契勃・柯萊文坐下來，凝視著流動的清澈溪水，身心逐漸感到平靜，就像寧謐的山谷一般。他感覺好像要睡著了，但他沒有睡著。

　　他坐在那裡看著沐浴在陽光下的溪水，開始注意到溪邊的植物。溪邊長著一大片美麗的藍色勿忘我，草葉都被溪水濺濕了，他猛然憶起幾年前，自己也看過這樣的風景。他現在覺得這些植物很美，綻放著幾百朵小花，一片藍色的奇觀。他並不知道自己的心裡逐漸被這個簡單的念頭所填滿，然後將其他的念頭輕輕推開。就像是在一潭死水中，一股芬芳乾淨的泉源不斷湧出，最終將那些骯髒的水沖走。

　　他自己當然並沒有意識到這些，他只知道當他坐著凝視鮮艷柔和的藍色花朵時，山谷似乎愈來愈安靜。他不知道自己坐了多久，也不知道在自己身上發生了什麼。最後，他好像甦醒過來似的開始動了起來，他慢慢站起身來，站在苔蘚地上深深吸了一口氣，對自己感到詫異。他體內似乎有什麼東西慢慢地被鬆開，釋放了出來。

　　「這是怎麼回事？我覺得自己好像重新活了過來！」他輕聲地說，摸了摸額頭。

　　對於一些尚未被發掘出的奇妙事物，我沒有足夠的認識，所以我不能解釋在他身上怎麼會發生這樣的事，沒有人可以解釋這個現象。他完全不知道這是怎麼一回事，可是幾個月之後，當他回到密朔兌莊園，他仍然記得這個奇異的時刻。後來他才意外地發現，就在這同一天，柯林走進祕密花園，大聲地喊出：

　　「我會永遠一直、一直活下去！」

　　那天晚上，這份特殊的寧靜一直占據著他的心靈，他前所未有地睡得很安穩，不過睡眠並沒有持續很久。他不知道這樣的感覺是否可以繼續維持下去。

　　隔天晚上，他又給那些灰色的想法打開了大門，它們成群地湧了回來。他離開了山谷，繼續到別的地方漫遊。然而奇怪的是，儘管他自己不知道是怎麼回事，有時有幾分鐘，有時甚至長達半小時，那些灰暗的負荷似乎又消失了，每每在這個時候，他會發現自己是個活人而不是死人。慢慢地——他想不出是什麼原因——他和花園一起「活了過來」。

當金色的夏日轉為深黃色的秋天，他來到了義大利北部的科木湖，在那裡發現了夢境一般的美景。他在水晶般的藍色湖邊停留了好幾天，有時他會走回山丘，在輕柔濃密的綠色草木之間徒步行走，直到累了為止，這樣晚上就可以安然入睡。這時他已經可以睡得比較沉了，他自己也知道這一點，他的夢不再那麼可怕了。

「也許，我的身體變得比較強壯了。」他想。

他的身體的確是在變強壯，舊念頭改變時，他感受到罕有的平靜，靈魂也慢慢地變得堅強。他開始想到密朔兌莊園，想到自己是不是應該回家了。有時他會有些好奇兒子現在怎麼樣了，他不知道自己回去以後，站在四柱雕刻的床邊時會有什麼感覺。他會趁小孩睡著時低下頭去看他，那孩子瘦削蒼白的臉，和閉攏的眼睛四周的黑睫毛，讓他畏縮不前。

在一個美好的日子裡，他走到了很遠的地方，當他回來時，天上已經高掛著滿月，大地是一片銀白的月光和紫色的影子。寂靜的湖面、湖岸和樹林是如此美好，他沒有回去別墅，而是走到湖邊一個有涼亭的小台地，坐在椅子上呼吸著夜晚絕妙的芳香。他感到那股奇怪的平靜又悄悄來到他的身上，他感到愈來愈寧靜，直到睡著了。

他不知道自己睡著了，也不知道自己在做夢。夢境是如此真實，他不知道是在作夢。一直到後來，他都還記得當時他以為自己很清醒、很警覺。他坐在湖邊，聞著夜晚綻放的玫瑰芳香，聽著腳邊波浪輕輕的拍打聲，就在這時他聽到一個聲音在呼喚。聲音甜美而清脆、愉悅而遙遠，似乎來自很遠的地方，但他聽得一清二楚，彷彿聲音就在他的身邊。

「阿契！阿契！阿契！」聲音如此喚道，接著又更甜美、更清晰地喊著：「阿契！阿契！」

他忽然跳了起來，但不是因為被嚇到。這個聲音是如此真實，而他聽到這個聲音似乎是再自然不過的事。

「莉莉拉絲！莉莉拉絲！莉莉拉絲！妳在哪裡？」他說。

「在花園裡，在花園裡！」聲音如金笛聲般動聽。

然後夢境結束了，但是他並沒有醒來。這個美好的夜晚，他睡得又沉又香甜。他醒來時，晨光燦爛，一個侍者正站在一旁盯著他看。那是一個義大利僕人，他跟別墅裡所有的僕人都一樣，已經習慣按照外國主人的囑咐去做事就好，不管事情多麼奇怪，也不能多問。沒有人知道他何時會出去，何時會回來，會在哪裡睡覺，是否會在花園裡遊逛，或是整夜躺在湖裡的船上。

僕人手上拿著金屬圓盤，上面放著幾封信，安靜地等待柯萊文先生把信拿過去。僕人離開後，柯萊文先生把信握在手中，望向湖水，心裡仍然覺得異常平靜。他也覺得很輕盈——好像那件殘酷的事情並沒有如他所想的那樣發生過——似乎有什麼改變了。他想起那個夢——極為真實的夢。

「在花園裡！」他感到不解，「在花園裡！可是門被鎖起來了，鑰匙也被埋得很深！」

幾分鐘後，他瞥向那幾封信，最上面有一封寄自約克郡的英文信。信上的筆跡很明顯是女性的筆跡，但他沒見過。他將信打開，沒去猜想寫信的人是誰，信的開頭幾個字吸引了他的注意力。

親愛的先生：

　　我是曾經冒昧和您在高沼地談話的蘇珊・索爾比。那一次我向您談到了瑪莉小姐，容我再度斗膽和您談一件事情。先生，如果我是您的話，我一定會回家。我想您一定會很高興回到家裡的，而且，恕我冒昧，如果您的夫人還在的話，她也會請您回家的。

　　您忠實的僕人
　　蘇珊・索爾比

柯萊文先生把信讀了兩遍，然後放回信封裡。他一直想著那個夢。

「我要回去密朔兌莊園，沒錯，我要立刻回去。」他說。

他穿過花園走去別墅，吩咐皮丘準備回英國的行李。

幾天後，他回到了約克郡。他坐在火車裡，發現自己十年來第一次想起了兒子。過去這十年，他只希望將兒子忘掉，現在他雖然並沒有刻意要去想柯林，可是對於柯林的記憶一幕幕浮現出來。

他想起在那些晦暗的日子裡，自己像瘋子一樣咆哮，因為孩子活了下來，而孩子的母親卻死了。他一開始不肯看到這個孩子，等他終於看到時，孩子是那麼虛弱可憐，大家都認為他活不了幾天。然而，日子一天天過去了，孩子並沒有死去，那些照料孩子的人很吃驚，他們又覺得小孩一定會變成畸形或是殘廢。

柯萊文先生並不想當個壞父親，但是他壓根兒不覺得自己是個父親。他為孩子提供醫生、護士、奢侈品，卻總是避免去想起他。他將自己埋在過往的悲傷中，孩子出生後，他離開了密朔兌莊園一年。當他返回，看到那個小可憐蟲無力冷漠地抬起頭，灰色的大眼睛有著黑色的長睫毛，像極了他以前摯愛的那雙快樂的眼睛，卻又極為不像。他無法忍受看到這雙眼睛，便將頭轉開，臉色一片死白。

從此之後，他就幾乎不在孩子醒著的時候去看他。他只知道他長期臥病，歇斯底里，脾氣很壞，會失控。只好在大小事情上順著他，以免氣出什麼問題。

回想起這些事情，讓人心情低落，可是當火車疾駛過山中的小路和金色平原時，這個「活過來」的男人開始用一種嶄新的方式思考。他想得很遠，而且冷靜又深刻。

「這十年來我可能都錯了，」他自言自語道：「十年這麼長的時間，要做什麼可能都太遲了。我以前是怎麼搞的！」

一開始就說「太遲」，顯然不是正確的魔法，就連柯林也知道不應該這麼想。然而柯萊文先生一點也不瞭解魔法，不管是純正的魔法還是妖術，這一點他可還有的學。他在想，蘇珊‧索爾比這個深具母性的人鼓起勇氣寫信給他，也許是因為她發現柯林的情況惡化了，甚至病危了也說不定。

要不是那股奇異的平靜將他鎮住，或許他會更鬱鬱寡歡，是心裡的平靜給他帶來了勇氣與希望。他不但沒有往壞的方向去想，反而試著去相信一些更好的可能。

「她會不會認為我可能會對柯林有幫助，可以控制住他，所以希望我回來？回去密朔兌莊園時，我要去見見她。」他這麼想。

當他坐馬車橫越高沼地時，他在農舍停了下來，有七、八個小孩在一起玩，看到他來，孩子們聚攏過來，友善又禮貌地行了七、八次鞠躬。他們告訴柯萊文先生，媽媽一早就到高沼地的另一頭去幫婦女接生。他們又接著說，「哥哥迪肯」在莊園的花園裡工作，每個星期都會過去好幾次。

柯萊文先生看著他們健壯的小身體和紅潤的圓臉，每個孩子都對他露出了獨一無二的笑容，發覺他們健康又可愛。看到孩子們友善地對著自己露出笑容，他也以微笑回敬，然後從口袋裡掏出一磅金幣，交給年紀最大的伊莉莎白‧愛倫。

「你們把金幣分成八等分，每個人就有兩塊半先令了。」他說。

在孩子咧嘴的咯咯笑聲與鞠躬中，柯萊文先生駛離了農舍。這群興奮的孩子在他身後互相用手肘推來推去，高興地活蹦亂跳。

他坐車橫越高沼地，美景撫慰了他的心情。他很奇怪自己有一種回家的感覺，他原本以為再也不會有這樣的感覺了。當他駛近這棟具有六百年歷史的家族古宅，看著美麗的土地、天空和遠方紫色的花朵，一種溫馨的感覺襲上心頭。

他上一次離開這棟房子時，全身發抖地想著那些被關起來的房間，還有兒子房間裡那張四柱床和織錦畫。柯林是否有可能稍微好轉一些呢？他可以不再迴避與自己的兒子見面嗎？那個夢是多麼真實啊，那個呼喚他的聲音又是多麼清晰美妙啊！「在花園裡，在花園裡！」

他說：「我要想辦法把鑰匙找出來，然後把門打開。我一定要這麼做，雖然我不知道為什麼要這麼做。」

當他抵達莊園時，僕人們按照一貫的儀式迎接他，他們發現主人的氣色比以前好了很多，而且沒有馬上和皮丘一塊走到偏遠角落的臥房。他直接走進書房，要梅德洛太太過來。梅德洛太太去見他時，一副有些興奮、好奇又激動的樣子。

「柯林少爺現在怎麼樣，梅德洛？」柯萊文先生問道。

「先生，他現在可以說變得不一樣了。」梅德洛太太回答。

「更不好了嗎？」他說道。

梅德洛太太滿臉通紅。

「先生，是這樣的，」她解釋說：「不管是柯萊文醫生、護士或是我自己，都不瞭解他到底怎麼了。」

「怎麼說？」

「先生，老實跟您說，柯林少爺有可能變得比較好，也有可能是惡化了。他的胃口讓人猜不透，而他的舉止——」

「他是不是變得更——更奇怪了？」柯萊文先生焦慮地皺起眉頭。

「是啊，先生。跟以前比起來，他的確是變得更奇怪了。以前他什麼都不吃，可是現在他會突然吃很多的東西，接著又突然什麼都不吃，把食物都送回來，就跟以前一樣。先生，您或許不知道，以前他不讓人家帶他到外面去，要把他放在輪椅上推出去是很可怕的事情，他會大發脾氣，就連柯萊文醫生也說他不敢強迫柯林少爺。可是在毫無預兆的情況下，有一次柯林少爺在發過一頓脾氣之後，忽然要求瑪莉小姐和蘇珊·索爾比的兒子迪肯每天帶他出去，要迪肯幫他推輪椅。他忽然喜歡上了瑪莉小姐和迪肯，迪肯會帶著他那些溫馴的動物過來。而且，先生，不知道您相不相信，柯林少爺從早到晚都待在外面。」

「他看起來怎麼樣？」柯萊文先生接著問。

「如果他正常吃飯，您可能會覺得他變胖了些，但我們擔心他可能只是虛胖。有時他和瑪莉小姐單獨在一起時，會笑得很奇怪。他以前從來都不笑的，如果您允許的話，柯萊文醫生很快就會來見您，他一輩子都沒有這麼煩惱過。」

「柯林少爺現在在哪裡？」柯萊文先生問道。

「在花園裡。他整天都待在花園裡，誰都不可以靠近，因為他不要讓人家看到。」

柯萊文先生幾乎沒有聽到最後這幾句話。

「在花園裡！」他說道。他打發梅德洛太太離開，然後站在那裡不斷重複著這句話。

「在花園裡！」

他花了好大的力氣才把心思收回來，回到現實，然後轉身走出房間。他採取瑪莉走過的路線，穿越灌木叢和月桂樹中的門，來到噴泉邊的花壇。噴泉現在會噴水了，四周環繞著鮮艷的秋季花卉的花床。他越過草坪，來到覆蓋著常春藤那道牆旁邊的長走道上。

他走得很慢，眼睛一直看著步道，覺得自己好像正被拉回長久以來被自己所遺棄的地方，他不知道為什麼會這樣。他愈接近那個地方，腳步便愈緩慢。即使常春藤覆蓋著門，他仍然知道門在哪裡，可是他不知道埋著鑰匙的確切位置。

他停了下來，站在那裡環顧四周，這時候他吃了一驚，專注地聆聽著，問自己是不是正在夢裡。

門上覆蓋著茂密的常春藤，鑰匙被埋在灌木下面，在這孤單的十個年歲月裡，沒有人進出過那扇門，然而花園裡這時卻傳出了聲音，那是有人跑來跑去的聲音，似乎是在樹下互相追逐。那些低沉的聲音聽起來很奇怪，像是刻意壓低的尖叫和歡呼聲，聽起來像是小孩子無法控制的笑聲，他們雖然希望不要被發現，可是當他們變得愈來愈興奮時，卻又忍不住會突然笑出來。

他究竟是夢到了什麼──他究竟是聽到了什麼？他是否正逐漸喪失理智，才會聽到這些肉耳聽不到的聲音？這是否就是那個遙遠而清晰的聲音所要告訴他的東西？

接著那些聲音又無法控制地爆發出來，腳步聲愈來愈快，正逐漸接近花園的門，有孩子急促而強烈的呼吸聲，還有抑制不住的狂野笑聲。牆上的門突然被撞開，常春藤又搖了回去。一個男孩全速衝過那扇門，沒有發現門外站著人，差一點就撞了個滿懷。

柯萊文先生及時把手臂伸出去，男孩才沒有跌倒。當他把男孩拉開，看清楚他的時候，他驚訝得簡直喘不過氣來。

男孩長得又高又英俊，容光煥發，散發著生命力，跑得一張臉紅通通的。他將額頭上濃密的頭髮撥到後面，奇異的灰色眼睛仰望著柯萊文先生，眼裡充滿笑意，周圍的黑睫毛就像流蘇一般。就是這對眼睛讓柯萊文先生喘不過氣來。

「誰，是誰？」他結結巴巴地說。

這並不是柯林期望會發生的事情，不在他的計畫裡面。他沒想到會這樣跟父親碰面，但他這樣衝出來或許更好，他在柯萊文先生面前站得直直的。瑪莉剛剛也和柯林一起跑著衝出門，她覺得此刻的柯林企圖讓自己看起來比平常還高。

他說：「爸爸，我是柯林，你不會相信的。我自己也很難相信，我是柯林。」

柯林的反應和梅德洛太太一樣，不知道柯萊文先生為什麼急促地說著：

「在花園裡！在花園裡！」

柯林趕緊說：「對，這是花園的功勞，還有瑪莉、迪肯和那些動物，還有魔法。沒有人知道這件事，我們一直守著這個祕密，想要等你回來的時候再告訴你。我的身體很好，我可以跑贏瑪莉，我要成為運動員。」

柯林說話的樣子就像個身體健康的男孩，他臉色泛紅，因為過於急切，話說得很急。柯萊文先生難以置信地看著他，靈魂深處因歡躍而顫抖。

柯林將手伸出去，放在父親的手臂上。

他說：「你不高興嗎？爸爸，你不高興嗎？我會一直、一直活下去！」

柯萊文先生將手放在柯林的雙肩，靜靜地抱著他，有好一會兒連一句話也說不出來。

「兒子，帶我到花園裡去，」他終於開口說話：「然後告訴我，這一切究竟是怎麼一回事？」

他們將柯萊文先生帶進了花園裡。

花園裡蔓生著金色和紫色的秋季植物，還有藍紫色和火紅色的植物，到處都是成團的晚開百合花，有白色的，也有紅白相間的。柯萊文先生還記得最早的一批百合種下之後，遲開的百合都會這個時節綻放。晚開的玫瑰花四處攀爬、垂掛、簇生，陽光讓黃色的樹葉顯得更加金燦燦，讓人覺得好像站在被樹木環繞的金色寺廟裡。

花園裡的這位新客人靜靜地站著，就像當初這幾個孩子剛進到花園時一樣，只不過那時候的花園還只是灰灰一片。柯萊文先生不停地環顧四周。

「我還以為花園裡的植物都死了。」他說。

「瑪莉一開始也是這麼想，可是花園活過來了。」柯林說。

接著他們在那棵樹下坐了下來，只有柯林還站著，因為他想要站著說這件事情。

當柯林一股腦倒出整件事情之後，亞契柏·柯萊文覺得這是他所聽過最奇怪的事了，祕密、魔法、野生動物、奇怪的午夜相會、春天的到來，在受辱的自尊心驅動下，小王侯站起來挑戰老班。奇怪的同伴、演戲、不為人知的大祕密。他聽得笑出了眼淚，有時即使不笑，眼眶裡也含著淚水。這名運動員、演說家、科學家，真是一位有趣、可愛、活力充沛的少年。

柯林講完後說道：「從現在起，我們不用再保密了。我敢說，大家看到我的時候，一定會嚇壞的，我以後再也不要坐輪椅了。爸爸，我要跟你一起走回房子裡。」

　　班因為工作的關係很少離開花園，可是這次他藉口說要拿一些蔬菜到廚房去，被梅德洛太太請去了僕人廳喝杯啤酒。當密朔兌莊園最具戲劇性的事件發生時，班也如願以償地在現場。

　　有一扇俯視庭院的窗戶可以稍微瞥見草坪，梅德洛太太剛看到班從花園裡走來，她希望班剛才看到了柯萊文先生，甚至希望他有可能看到柯林少爺。

　　「班，你有沒有看到主人或是少爺？」梅德洛太太問。

　　班將馬克杯從嘴邊移開，用手背擦擦嘴唇。

「有啊！」他意味深長地回答道。

「兩個都看到了嗎？」梅德洛太太問道。

「兩個都看到了，真謝謝汝，太太，我還可以再喝一杯呢！」班回答。

「他們兩個在一起嗎？」梅德洛太太說著，興奮得把啤酒倒得都溢滿了出來。

「他們倆是在一起啊，太太。」說著，班一口灌下半杯的啤酒。

「柯林少爺在哪裡？他看起來怎樣？他們說了什麼？」

「我沒聽到，」班說：「我那時候站在梯子上往牆裡看。不過我可以告訴汝，屋子外面發生了很多事情，汝們在裡面的人啥都不知道。汝不久就會知道發生啥事了。」

離班嚥下一口啤酒還不到兩分鐘，他莊重地朝窗外揮揮馬克杯。透過灌木叢，從這個窗子可以看到草坪的一角。

「看那兒，」他說：「汝要是好奇的話，就看看誰從草地那邊走來了。」

梅德洛太太往外看了一眼，猛然把手舉起來尖叫了一聲，僕人廳裡的男女僕人們聽到叫聲，也都急忙跑到窗邊一瞧究竟，看得眼珠子都快掉了下來。

從草坪那邊走來的是密朔兌莊園的主人，他的神色是許多人從未看過的模樣。在他的身邊，有一個把頭抬得高高的男孩，眼裡充滿了笑意，他的步伐比約克郡任何一個男孩都要穩健。那正是──柯林少爺！

THE SECRET GARDEN

祕密花園
原著雙語彩圖本

作者 _ 法蘭西絲·霍森·伯內特（Frances Hodgson Burnett）

插圖 _ 高嘉玟

譯者 _ 李桂蜜

中文校對 _ 代雲芳

英文校對 _ 吳思薇

編輯 _ 安卡斯

封面設計 _ 林書玉

製程管理 _ 洪巧玲

發行人 _ 周均亮

出版者 _ 寂天文化事業股份有限公司

電話 _ +886-2-2365-9739

傳真 _ +886-2-2365-9835

網址 _ www.icosmos.com.tw

讀者服務 _ onlineservice@icosmos.com.tw

出版日期 _ 2019年6月 初版一刷（250101）

郵撥帳號 _ 1998620-0 寂天文化事業股份有限公司

國家圖書館出版品預行編目資料

祕密花園（原著雙語彩圖本）/ 法蘭西絲·
伯內特（Frances E. H. Burnett）；李桂蜜 譯.
一初版. 一[臺北市]：寂天文化, 2019.6 面；
公分. 中英對照; 譯自 : The Secret Garden

ISBN　978-986-318-783-7 (25K平裝)

873.59　　　　　　　　　　　108002323